Moustache

Man

and the

Deadly
Whiskers

www.moustacheman.co.uk

Moustache Man and the Deadly Whiskers

Rick Senley

Matador
5 Weir Road
Kibworth Beauchamp
Leicester LE8 0LQ, UK
Tel: (+44) 116 279 2299
Fax: 0116 279 2277
Email: books@troubador.co.uk
Web: www.troubador.co.uk/matador

Cover Art courtesy of Tracy Strathdee www.traceystrathdee.co.uk

ISBN 978 1848762 435

British Library Cataloguing in Publication Data.
A catalogue record for this book is available from the British Library.

Typeset in 11pt Sabon MT by Troubador Publishing Ltd, Leicester, UK

Matador is an imprint of Troubador Publishing Ltd

Printed in Great Britain by the MPG Books Group, Bodmin and King's Lynn

To M, B, S, M, R, C and the doctor that accidentally saved my life in an oxygen tent

'Oh bloody hell.' Anonymous

Prologue

June 7, 1857
A Peak Behind The Curtains Of Shame

Ooh that hurts. And that. My eyes weep. Unguent? Surely that would help.

I wish he weren't so boisterous as he pounds me so, his awful sack hanging beneath the furs of my tum-tum. My third man of the day and this the worst. Quite nauseating I suppose, if one pondered for long. I don't though. Not these days.

Things never were so bleak for once I led a life of glamour. It was quite excellent. Damson pie at eleven, beer pots to sup, ladies to touch here and there and certain other places rarely mentioned in literature.

My background was excellent; my luncheons were boisterous and included several courses; my education was first class and my manners were impeccable. The same is no longer true.

I was a younger man than now. Thirty-two years, seven months and nineteen days when everything was changed for all time. I am older now, but slim nonetheless.

Jesus Christ was I dishy, for I sported terrific side-whiskers and an impressive middle part, hair dressed with Macassar oil which set off my scarf pins and pearl buttons so.

It was claimed that a visitor could style his hairs in my front tooth, so shiny were my fangs.

How I loved the gaslight dances of youth, the tippity tap of canes in the Holborn, the gilt mirrors and the strumpets, gaudy curtains and trumpets; the men-only Song and Suppers on the Strand, fat on oysters, tiddly with brandy, rollicking in the night houses of the Haymarket, stuffy and plummy with the fumes of cheap liquor, bloated and squiffy like a horse with gout.

But wait, first must I alert the cumbersome gentleman whose ninnynannynoo hums a tune upon my derriere. Ooh, it is as a porcupine nudging through a railway tunnel a loaf of bread. At great speed.

As I ponder on my elbows, the beast dozes sullenly upon my haunches.

What a fiend is the man, a brute; podgy and sulky too. A hideous bellowing steals from his mouth, rattling his teeth and warming my bare back, like the huff from a spluttering hound. Some may say he has rather overstepped the limits of good taste. I rouse the man with a knee to the chin.

'If you would please, young man, I wish to leave' he splutters.

'I have enjoyed myself something awful but an appointment presses. Nonetheless, there is a villainous pong - quite remarkable. Your anus perhaps?'

He dressed in a hurry, his pantaloons flinging whiffs of cigars across the room as he battled for purchase.

He struggled indecorously, wedging one foot beneath the bed while with the other he performed a bizarre sort of jig.

'By God, you beastly drawers, I shall have you, my word, I swear I will. Never again, *never* again do you hear me? Tits, tits tits. Oh, you bastard shits. Open now you heavens and swoop me from this monstrous hell. By Christ never again will I lower myself to such foul depths, never, *never*....but maybe for a wonk and if so, so beseech me my Lord, nothing more.'

He went on thus, guzzled by rage and down he went, with a meaty crack of his blubbery derriere, a veritable Beelzebub indeed.

The landlady will wonder about the hullabaloo. Poor old Mrs Gough.

I snuff the candle pon my sooted sill, flickering its miserly glow against my curtain, wriggling to get beyond the cheap lace of second-hand lodgings and into the celerity of the Strand, the belching lanes of Piccadilly, the dream of life outside.

Perhaps the flame shall follow its master, nestled in tight breeches and a light rouge into the smudge of omnibuses, the pelter of Hackney Carriages and the awful rumpus of life?

But perhaps not. Perhaps the lick of orange shine, the pansy flutter of the dripping flame is content here to watch this repulsion, its wick to be snuffed out surely as is the joy from my life.

The cackle of harlots floats up from without my window and takes me back to my younger days.

Because, once, not so long ago, I earnt a powerful crust and could have bathed in quail and pâté if I so wished. But I didn't for that would be unhealthy. These days I eff men for cash. My life, in short, is a disgrace.

The killer leaps from the shadows, blackened hair as black as the deed he seeks to do. A nasty blow to the man's windpipe knocks the very stuffing from him and he falls to the ground, a mighty sigh from the lungs breathing on the fetid puddles that stink the alley so. There is a touch of the exotic about the man in black, something strange, small eyes and a bizarre hue. Few round here have seen the likes of it, yet today no one will see him, nor the blade that pierces the dying man's chest, then his throat and eyes, a savage ritual of death dripping with horror. As he pulls the cream-bladed knife from the man's shaking body which has just released a torrent of faeces around his breeches, he garbles a strange tongue then spits on the victim, before dropping onto the corpse an item of underclothing. Women's underclothing.

Time For Luncheon. Can There Be A Grub More Foul Than That Cooked In Piccadilly?

The man had left me a guinea-and-a-half, blackened coins that mirrored my soul. That should deter Mrs Gough and may see me luncheon in a greasy place full of hernias and badman's language, for before all went to hell, when I lived on fun and other men's money, I knew not that such rough caverns did exist.

Now I do.

I strolled through the city, as miserable as a black, down the hustle bustle of the Strand, the stench of sweltering horse plop in the thoroughfare. Too many people, too many people. My, how did burn the heat. I traipsed past Trafalgar Square and the column erected not long past to commemorate some battle of sorts. If only we had lion statues too. But alas, the city's ancient ways were choked with rattling carriages and hansoms, the metallic clomp of hooves and the sunlight picked through the grime of Regent Street's dusted lanterns.

'Pies all 'ot! Beef and mutton pies! Penny pies, all 'ot -all 'ot!' sang the men with pastries on their arms and gravy in a can, the ringing of the muffin-man's bell, boiled puddings and minced meat, oppressive in the sun.

The din, the din, the terrible din. One day, all this shall travel underground.

And so I found myself in a Piccadilly chophouse, the gust of traffic outside, my face unknown in the smeared window, a presence of a phantom perhaps at my shoulder. I turned quickly for I fancied I could feel its breath and the faint spice of something exotic, but there lurked nothing unusual and I twisted my neck in the deed.

I prepared my moustache spoon – a natty invention to save one's whiskers from the hazards of foodstuffs such as soup, or sandwiches – and ordered with haste; potatoes, chop and a pint of hot tea. Life is what you make of it say some. Two sugars for me please.

Beginning

April 13, 1855
How Fate Can Bite With The Sweetest Of Teeth

'Mrs Gough? Please, a tincture of "Unparalleled Curling Fluid," one too of "Tyrian Hair Dye", another yet of "Olden's Eukeirogenion" and some "Sicilian Bloom", for I have exemplary looks to preserve.'

'Sir?'

'Mrs Gough?'

'You are outstanding.'

'Indeed, I am. I thank you for the compliment. I certainly am a regular dish. Some say my finest features be my teeth, forever white as china cups, others, my locks, one physician claimed my nose, an-'

'Sir, I meant your hotpot.'

'Mrs Gough?'

'You is erect and have popped oooot your pantaloons. Cook still has a gammy eye cos of last time.'

'I see. Thank you.'

'Not at all.'

'Mrs Gough?'

'Sir?'

'Hair cream.'

It was a glorious day, truly it was, bursting with the warm bosoms of Easter in Regent Street that my fate proved written, inexorably scrawled on the future by the common teats of a madame.

I had dressed well; glinting leather boots, crisp white stockings, black-as-a-wog breeches, a brocade vest of the deepest green and a glorious beaver fur. One could never rely on the fickle climes of this mollycoddled country. The dark swirls of my hairs were coated with a light sheen of Rowland's Macassar Oil, my whiskers pressed and smoothed like a dog and a handkerchief sat folded in my breast pocket much like the sail of a miniature schooner. Only free of gulls. My watch hung suitably from its chain and I clicked my steps with a gold-headed cane. Ruffians eyed me up, but they gave me no fear because frankly I looked ever so saucy.

A lady approached, thighs swirling, eyelashes batting, teeties drumming too. A tremendous looking creature she was in an emerald shawl and a lovely little bonnet. Her neck snuck from her collar, white the colour of mice. She pleased the eye, her bust proud and firm like a teety mantelpiece and above it swung a golden crucifix and her meaty arms poked from her leg o'mutton sleeves like two fine noses a-peeking through a privy door. She put me in mind of an asparagus slut with knockers. Her name was Sally and I loved her from thence on. Foolish perhaps and hasty too, but then again perhaps not, for who really knows the workings of a mind on fire? She was coy and timid but my Lord was she tasty.

'Evenin' sir, what's a fine gent like you doin' on your own? I dares say you might fancy some company?' she purred, her voice silken and pure, her meaning simple for a sharp looking fellow as me.

I allowed her to put her arm in mine and she took me to her lodgings, bare of furnishings and comfort, yet awash with the treasured perfume of golden nights and sultry days, the lost memories of a ribald Sultan, a minxy whore, the love of my life to be. And a little bit of wee in the pot.

Yet How Did It All Get To This?
How The Chap On All Fours Passed His Early Days

I was by no means a novice with the ladies; indeed, like many swells of my age, had I heard the bleating of low women, mucky women, hairy women and one woman, whose breasts were so beastly, that I ran from the scene in a terrible tizz.

I was known to the temptations of the flesh, and they known to me. For to tell the truth, was I a heated young buck.

Through much graft and more of my inheritance, I learnt who was slender – Sarah-Jane – who was firm and merry – Alice Wilmot – and who bit her guests – Mildred Newman.

Nuneaton Nancy had a fur pouch as sweet as any lamb yet had nasty nip-nops no larger than a bee's father.

I knew too that Jemima Norton made disrobing an art; her aunt, Samantha was the toast of Holborn for her prominent hills, while grandmamma Hatty was famed for her parsley bed.

I carried always a French letter, fashioned for intercourse from the guts of a beast to prevent what the surgeon could not cure.

Over the years and many nights, I had left the oyster houses of Piccadilly, half-tipsy with a randy doodle, and doffed my hat for swift relief in a doorway.

Oh had I whiled away the dark hours of February chills,

rampant hands fondling my balls in my pockets, admiring the nippy streetwalkers in the echoes of Burlington Arcade. I had spotted the signals flittered to men on the prowl in the Haymarket's Hell Corner. And heavens, had I bitten!

I knew that Hannah Betson, who slept in Soho, was a dirty nymph with mediocre teeth.

Polly Tufnell, at seventeen, knew much about the desires of men and proved an agreeable piece for the winter season.

Maggy Troughton howled like a monkey when she came of the heat and as a bed-fellow was excellent.

While Jenny Furnish could drink a glass or two.

Once the bitch fell into a mighty slumber upon my lap, her fangs missing my glans akip in her moooth. I quit the room while she snored as a hyaena from Africa.

In short I knew the ways of the lady and knew little limits.

I had nuzzled well-bred daughters beneath pianofortes, had freckled the toots of school marms left and right, fuddled the snatch of females many years my junior, milk-maids and seamstresses and cooks.

I too had canoodled with madams thrice my years, grey as goblins yet spicy to boot.

Frankly, I had effed left right and centre. Oh life – how things change. What misery awaits the man who lives to see his hairs first turn white.

The Weakness Of A Heart In Turmoil
And The Might Of Titty Puffs

But with this bleeding monkey, was I well and truly snared for red-muffed Sally held me in bliss.

She loved me that afternoon and loved me more that night, as the sun faded from the sky and the gasman lit his lamps with a wick and a wheeze. As we lay together I hoped our hours would never end. My heavens, how I effed. My performance was delightful and I barely stopped. Those hours we spent, I believed, came from God. She charged me though, an ample fee and as I steadied the shillings, I knew then that I was caught in something I could never even hope to know. I left her and tripped home as happy as a pansy bummer. For many nights, I lay awake for hours and the days swept past me locked as I was in my thoughts of love. I saw her face in the West End clubs, her voice trickled from restaurants. I saw her bing-bongs in clouds and her nip-nops in the thumbs of piemen. Her anus I saw with my dreams and her tufty mufty in parsley clumps. I vowed I was to find her again for I was trapped. And why? She had laughed not at Mr Winky.

A Step Back In Time;
Good Dinners And The Nonsense Of Half-Wits

My late father was the proprietor of a successful and highly resented branch of the East India Company. At first he brought tea from China, then opium from India to sell in China to raise cash to buy the tea in China to bring to England. And the opium. And little biscuits with cryptic messages inside. He employed several men; many were bright yellow.

I had, consequently, led a leisurely life, as easy as a strumpet on a quart of gin. As a boy I was well looked after. I asked for nothing and was given everything. I dressed as a prince as soon as hairs did sprout pon my chin. I moved to the clubs; Mondays the Pall Mall, Tuesdays the Carlton, Wednesdays the Garrick, Thursdays the Parthenon, weekends St James – ballot elected members only mind you. Stuffy types but wild for a drink.

Now, though a very outcast of my former existence, I still feel a shudder of glee when I recall the most fabulous club of them all: The Sublime Society of Beef Steak. We called ourselves The Steakers and dedicated our hours to 'Beef and Liberty.'

On Saturdays when five o'clock rang we would supper at the oaked rooms behind the Lyceum Theatre where we gorged on the rarest steaks in London. Sod the peasants plopping in the streets. We ate and chuffed and traded bawdy fictions of tits and fannies; we took wine and puffed on cigars and sometimes punched each others' cocks. A sport, my friend, a simple sport.

We were only four-and-twenty in number and entrance-money was heavy at 25 guineas. I am no longer proud of those societies, nor for that matter, would I be welcome for my appearance was none too flattering. I lived these days a different existence.

Many an allegiance was sworn over bloodied gristle. Many a fork was pointed in admiration. Glasses toasted, buttocks roasted, hands shaken and, possibly, trousers unbuckled when gazes drifted elsewhere. The well-bred patter of sated bellies boomed into the streets, waking the vagrants without.

We experienced no shame in our extravagance, for our society displayed little charity at all. Indeed, we, the leisure class, were a parasite, a suckler on mankind's tats. Unwanted potatoes sat like tubby children on our chinaware, eventually crumbling into the puddles of beefy gravy and blood. Yet how happy would be those urchins outside with our off-casts, those poor souls who made do with the meagre findings the Lord would bestow upon them? Stewed eel in a cracked teacup, a stolen soup, a hand of stinking fruit from a costermonger, meagre thanks for hauling carts and lighting tallows in the icy nights. Yet did we consider giving up our waste? Maybe I speak too harshly about the fellows, but had they spoken such things, I shudder to think of the response.

Yet what were we to do, we who had never known hardships? We were the swells, born of the country's gentry.

Some in our number were men in the House of Commons, a playground with river views and gallons of port. The braver bought commission into the British Army until the winters swept in and back they came to England for the summer season frolics.

And it was there that I first made the acquaintance of Ambrose Tedworth, a hoary figure, as robust in manner as in build. He enjoyed endless whiskers that curled like wisps of smoke, hearty cheeks laced with red and a laugh that was very infectious. When he chortled, the very glassware upon the table rattled. He was perpetually puffing away at an ancient pipe, clouding the salon with fumes. Yet for all his geniality, his views were of a set so firm, not even his belly laughs could seek to dislodge them.

His ideals though, in most, came via the pages of the Newgate Chronicle or the London Times. Often he would jabber his pipe at the facts in black and white.

'Somers Town' he would bellow over our sirloins, 'has a murder rate twice that of Holland Park. Whitechapel at least threefold, Waterloo higher still. Why is that gentlemen, pray, why is that?'

Murmurs would spread, like brisket soup across the linen; assents, consents, dissents and absents.

'Jump upon any growler, tell the driver to point his horse east and you will hear the ting of black in the streets, the bicker of the Jews, the squeal of the Dutchman,' hoofed he and here would he oftentimes pause to relish the bloated audience and rub his hands together, hunched over.

'The streets of Bethnal Green are brim full of Irish like so many damned lice' he spat.

'Call to mind the Rookeries and you are in Dublin.

'Add to this the street walkers and the pest-houses and really gentlemen, is there any surprise at the crimes in these neighbourhoods? Then, too are the funny people, the arse-ban-'

'What about the Angles and the Normans you crook?' squawked one Quintin Macintosh one afternoon, he of the garrulous whiskers propping up his ears. 'What about them and their odd ways, och aye?' he shouted, throwing Mr Tedworth quite off key.

'Ah yes my man, yes indeed. Why should they escape unscathed? They are no better. In fact they are worse by far. They seldom bathe and hundreds are thieves. In fact, in the recent Gazette, I recall an incident involving a girl, sent to work the streets by her parents and instructed to return home only when with cash. A poor urchin, selling her adolescent body, her sweet, and supple and easy to bend body, oooh, her sugary and syrupy young body, smelling of apples and summer roses and with nary a hay in her stack, and her gentle feet and tongue and ooooh, I feel distinct.'

'You've popped' shouted the waiter.

'Ooh, ooh, I've got flu. As I was aherm, saying, these people attract the wrong sorts, one follows another and before you know it .....' but before he could proceed, a passing guest threw back: 'You silly old duffer, we're Angles and Normans ourselves.'

Tedworth, a tad uneasy, cast his beagle eyes around for confirmation, and, coughing into his necktie muttered, a wee bit lower: 'Hhhhhmm. Well, gentlemen, joking aside, which, of course, was what I did, is what I mean by the problem. Get to the bottom of these street walkers and you will see there lurks moral dereliction in all. Look at crime and look at the sign. The two are inevitably linked. Like a string of sausages.'

Tedworth did not stay for his afters. Tedworth I liked not, though others I did.

I fraternised with Lord Hastings, absolutely eccentric, for madness stalked the leisure classes with zest; the Marquis of Waterstones too, a giddy man with deplorable ways. He and his cohorts were in cahoots to seek mischief across the land. Indeed had he not the cash of generations to pay his way and pass his fines, were he a mumbling wreck of a man, ambling the alleys of London town, would truly he be an outcast. But he were not for the cash ran through his pockets like blood in a bully's heartbeat. We fell out over an error and would meet again in strange times to come.

Spray of shits were they, yet I loved them all for I knew no better.

Yet as he traipses home to spend another long night in his long empty bed, he begins to wonder if in fact he does love this life at all. Occasionally he will seek to ask himself that very question, but afeard perhaps of the answer, he discards it in a flash, buries the niggling concerns somewhere in his mind, hides the troubles neath porter and gin and yet another woman, for a man with a restless mind is not a man at all.

The Girl With The Red Snuff. Who She Really Is

I appeared smitten. For more than a week, I bypassed whores, disregarded strumpets left, right and centre, flicked Vs at moving fannies until I was back at the Haymarket and like a moth to a flame and a gay to a bum, she was soon wrapped in my arms, cooing creaturely murmurs into my ear and nuzzling my noodle. Spring grew into summer, a dreadful heat that stoked the worst stinks of the river. Still would we meet, evenings, afternoons, mornings too. I grew to love the poor girl, abandoned by her family. Her mother was taken in child-birth and her tailor father had been blinded in a workshop row. An employee had accused the man of crime, the pair came to blows and the Jew rammed a needle into his eye. The scene, so they say, was sickening. He never worked again.

There was a sister to keep and a simpleton brother, too poorly for the chimney, a little dim for the streets.

So it was that Sally found herself doing the West End, letting men frig her in drink, slap her face when not. She began as a child, unbooby and not a little toothy too. Her body was an easel of scars from brutish men and envious women and I smarted as I learnt the touches of each.

Cursed by abominable luck, did she think she had found

some way to soothe the claws of poverty whilst regaining some dignity too. For partway through nibbling on her nay-nays, one sniffly customer slurped 'are you addicted to pickles or snuff my dear?'

'No' was the reply, muffled by the peaks of her tits. 'You know' he ventured, emboldened by the fleshy tap of her teat, 'these blubbers are exceedingly full and your summits are ample. Indeed I feel you have a good breast of milk. Perhaps you shall become a wet nurse.'

'A wet what?' quizzed my dear-to-be but with a hoot at her udders, before he even poop-noddied her, had her away to a good-looking house to the West of town.

So did Sally live with Mr Melbourne, a wealthy man with some children and less manners. Yet ere long, was she no more than a suckling machine to the entire Melbourne family. His wife Mathilda, his offspring, Bert, Anna, Horace and even their retriever Lawrence. For all had an utter taste for balmy milk fresh from the nip. The complete clan would cradle the creature's magnificent bosom; gnaw, nudge and nuzzle it. She was fed stout throughout, thinking the noxious pot would sweeten the lactate. Yet although she smiled while the household inhaled her chest, sometimes two or three at a time, she dreamed to leave this dungeon of guzzlers.

Time passed slowly, the hours and days dripping like the milk from an unplugged bun until one day, so sickened was she by the persistent suckling of the youths (Horace was fourteen and sported teeth like a hawk, the other two were twins of a year) that she embarked on a fortuitously risky trick.

Whilst Mama snored, Papa whored and Lawrence eyed

Sally's dugs almost sinisterly, dear Sally raided the bathroom pharmacy and prepared a perilously snoozy potion. Mixing laudanum with syrup of poppies, Godfrey's Cordial and a pinch of tea, she watered her sleeping knockers. Post-supping, the bongers lay as peaceful as a lamb's ears and from then on, not a single squeak was heard. Of course the children did wake eventually. Sally is no murderer. They returned from sleep, amply refreshed and a wee bit smaller on Christmas Evening, and rather than face the press hounds whose grubby paws would lap up, rather like a booby suckle an Old Bailey trial, the Melbournes gave my beloved's buds a farewell wash and bid her goodday.

May 29, 1855

Tea And Biscuits. And A Mouse

Sally told me her woes one afternoon in her quarters, the sun playing with the motes of dust that waltzed across her room like debutantes at the Holborn.

We had made love in the smothering half-light of netted curtains and post-jizz, she had invited me to linger over a drink. The intercourse had been commodious.

'I am to brew a pot,' she whispered. 'Would you care to join me?'

'Yes' I poked, 'for although I cannot stay long, a tea would be prime' for I had read that a hot drink was optimum at cooling the body.

Coyly, she twisted towards the grate where she placed a pot over the coals. I watched, enamoured and somewhat enlarged as she scooped a spoonful of leaves into two old cups and we both awaited the waters' bubblings. Soon the gurgles rattled against the pan and the tea was prepared.

'Your room boasts a magnificent view' I began more from discomfort than of appreciation, for in fact the picture was none too cordial. Indeed the stains of the glass gave on to a pitiful prospect of grubby urchins, barely clothed, plaguing conventional men about their business.

I was apprehensive though. Although we effed like bears,

tea was rare. I feared a weighty question, like a brick in a baby's knickers.

She faced me in a chair laced with time and loneliness. All the puff had been swept from it. Her red locks sat loose, caressing the bones of her shoulders just peeking forth from her dress. I gazed around the room. There was little of any worth: some miniature hounds cast from cheap Staffordshire china above the fire, I think they were Spaniels, a grubby washstand by the window, rusty tongs for the coals, a foot bath, a watercolour of a gnu, a bill from the Jerusalem Coffee House in Cornhill. Hhmm. I knew of the place for father would often take coffee and cinnamon biscuits there with traders from the Orient.

She blew softly on her tea, whistling ripples across the murky pond of her cup, a manner picked up no doubt from lowly men and builders. She eyed me modestly over the rim. I was perched on the edge of her bed where we had shared the most intimate of passions. They were costly too. Until now she had not enquired as to my status, my calling, my loves, for indeed she knew of no reason. I paid for her services dearly and promptly, she performed them commendably and deserved her fees. A carriage clock, once a good resemblance of a French design from Versailles, now musty and dull, ticked out the minutes. Time seemed trapped as if in a bottle as we gazed everywhere but at each other.

'Would you care for some toast? I've got me some lovely butter. Butterman came round for a session on Wednesday. I were out of money so I paid in kind likes.'

'Toast, hhm,' I thought, sparing a thought for the tummy treats later with the Beef Steakers. Oysters, venison, fine ceps from Hampshire. Yet there sat I with a whore, toast the carte du jour.

I kept such counsel in check and agreed, for the lass was civil. Besides it would cost not a penny. Once more, she raised herself and drifted towards the range. She gathered two slabs of bread and then set about them with a large knife, its handle fashioned from ivory (imagine the hours saved if loaves came ready carved) and put them over the coals while she sat a square of butter upon the browning hunks.

Whilst her back was turned I hastily scrubbed the cup, for with women like that, disease was at a premium. Then, much as a woodland bird, perhaps a pigeon or a cock, I dipped towards my tea and drank it all off in one gulp. Strange how despite the throes of the corpulent we had recently shared, we now sat apart like two strangers on an omnibus, with nary a word to say, her very vulgarity and ordinariness, once so attractive, now ever so repellent. Doubtlessly the ardour would return.

'Today has been very hot, do you not think?' I invited, keen to break the horrid silence.

'Yes it has. I like it when it is warm, cos it makes your sniff snoff all 'ot. Fancy anuvver 'umpin' m'lord?' and with that she made a fair play towards the furry gentleman that lay a-slumber in my womb.

'Madame, pray, I say, that will not be a necessity for the noooo. Off, off, off.'

Time ticked and time tocked; slowly, ever so slowly. I would discuss current affairs with the thing, break the quiet, break the gloom.

'Are you familiar with the latest compositions of Georges Bizet my child?'

'Beg pardon sir?'

'Perhaps the works of Flaubert, the Bessemer process of mass producing steel? You are aware, are you not, of the world's first potato chip?'

Silence.

'My dearest ninny' began I again. 'It would appear all is not well in The Crimea. Because of Lord Palmerston's fears of Russian encroachment upon India and Afghanistan, the British government has tried to weaken said threat under the pretext of the covert ramification of ancient treaties between France and Russia in relation to the protection of holy places in Palestine which involved the Sultan Abd-ul-Mejid I, several Orthodox monks, Nicholas I, Tsar of Russia and an Anglo-French ultimatum to Russia to withdraw troops from Moldavia and Wallachia....my dear it would appear you are making some curious noises. Madame. Madame. MADAME. You are snoring as an orang-utan.'

'What, who, eeeeeeeee. Sorry. My eyelids. Heavy. Orthodox, orthodox, orthodox, orthodox.'

'Awake! Hhhhmm. Perhaps bonnets or bloomers then?'

It was apparent the girl knew nothing. She was an ignoramus. Her manners were lacking and she was backward.

All twixt us was wrong.

I espied a mouse scuttle across her floor. She feigned not to have seen the little fellow for she launched at once into a tuneless song. It put me in mind of a large African beating a child with a chisel. For a moment I felt drowned beneath a tempestuous wave of sadness, I felt what some would term tragedy in her breast and then, glimpsing a spy down that very chest indeed of hers, all was soon forgot apart from a gentle tremor of my pantaloons. In the front region you see. I needed must go, for my presence only unnerved her the more. She was merely a child, and I had sought her goosy pleasures, making me no better than the pimps who don duffs to fluffs and muffs.

I had already buttoned so I placed down my cup and made to leave.

'Thank you, I have had a lovely time' I said as morose as a ghost, knowing I should bring an end to this nonsense, knowing the words that next I would say. 'Would you mind if we met once more?'

Monkey plops.

I hated her for making me feel so. Once my seed had been spilt I felt nothing towards her, the very moment my passions had simmered, I felt a plain indifference, a contented ambivalence towards the creature, before my surges would once more boil over and for a moment I had images of my throttling the girl to keep her from my mind. Yet such notions evaporated as rapidly as if they had never existed. Weakly, I sought again approval of my returning for more of the same. I wanted out of the room, yet could not suffer that to be the final occasion. The bare hand was offered to kiss, yet this time she slowly stood, smoothing down her skirts, her pale skin deathly white and trod softly forwards, perching forward and pecking me on the lips. My heart melted and I saw the tear in her eye.

During his lower tempers, when ravished by terrible humours and an ulcer, our hero's father would talk to his son of his days in the Orient. He would speak of the heat, the draining sun that distempered him so. His recollections would infect his listeners, even in the fearful winter of England, his deathly nights shattered by the growl of beasts flowing from his whiskers, past his yellowed teeth, his bloated belly, sated with pork, years of port and sherry told over the flicker of the flames warming his listeners, but back then, a life before the murders began, he thought of that heat as a something unknown, imaginable even and would dream of those distant jungles, the bites that would swell a man's arm so, but London now has become most unbearable and it festers all in the ever-growing grime; the rats grow big, plumped by the people's appetites for savouries and everywhere run the rodents, bloated and swollen on grub, their fur dried to skin by the sun.

Still May 29, 1855
Tears And Booze, Together Never Good News

We had lain together some dozen times, yet not once had we kissed, for she would not have it. And to be true, neither would I.

But without warning, she came upon me like an octopus, tendering forward her twittering lips. I hesitated and glanced down at the lass but it was when I saw the tears bulging in her eyes that my heart paused and caught a beat yet again.

'Please sir.' She could not tell my name, for she knew it not.

'Do not go. I needs you here, please' and she made to unfasten her outfit once more, swelling a breast so like a snowball it very nearly flowed from her basque.

Recoiling backwards I implored the girl no: 'Sally, I am more or less sated and will not be able to perform for at least an hour and really I needs must leave. Besides I have paid you all I can for now. I am, in short, out of pocket and, frankly I am as peckish as a snake.'

But I fear she took my words all wrong, for the droplets fell from her eyes, smoothing a stream down her soft little cheeks.

I did think, with a raise of her hand, she meant to strike me. What nonsense, a man of my breeding, most smacked by a prossy, a dolly monger, a naughty dicky-bird. An end was called for, so I grabbed her wrist, feeling the bones click under the skin, the veins almost pop and I glared into her face, until in pure abhorrence and not just a spot of fear, she spat venom at me.

Never had my ears beheld such language from a lady, indeed had not I even supposed the female brain, for want of a better word, would be aware of such filths. Tears dribbled into her mouth, remembering me of the times she had sucked my pepperpot, like a sightseer lapping an ice on a hot day. She too gripped my arm with quite some violence til she fell upon the bed, atop the glistening patch of our love-making that flickered in the grimy close of day.

She thought me different to other fellows and claimed to love me wailed the bastard, but her declarations were none appreciated, for I abandoned the child, sobbing and wheezing and left with my fingers in my ears. Perhaps my feelings were all a-tizz. Perhaps my heart is not made as others'.

I headed for a nice little club I knew of, not far from her rooms. They were selective as regards their customers who were only four-and-twenty in number, stocked an outstanding range of wines and besides, served beef steak ever so well.

At the very end of May 29, 1855. Or perhaps even the
beginning of May 30, 1855. God only knows.

Getting Drunk And Then Back To Sally's. Or The Love Of Death Is A Wicked Joy. Glass Eyes And Curry

I sought to put the nasty experience from my mind so visited
the club, for there was no call for emotions behind the
Lyceum, no need for a man to unburden himself of his true
conscience. I sat with the fellows, with Tedworth and
Waterstones, Crowfork and Hastings and talked dogs and
fruit and war and once by error I mentioned love but blamed
it on the staff and drank much, swigged porter, oozed several
half-quarterns of gin and peppermint, then reeled to a pest-
house hard by Wigmore Street. I did not remain long for
curious images flooded my head of Sally bended before me all
a-flow with tears, and my mind in a fug, the visions true
pained me and each time I shook the picture from my skull,
it returned more intense still. A battle raged within, good and
bad, love and hate, booze and food, for I wanted the girl from
my mind, yet no sooner had she gone than I craved for her
return. And her teeties. Indeed never before had I felt such
roaring emotions for a lady so loose.

Perhaps I needed the beast to make of me a better man,
improve my several failings, and nuzzle the testes of my soul.
My existence required perhaps some enrichment. I was
aimless and goalless and, following a light-hearted incident

beneath one testicle, extremely hairless. Someone once advised that there was more to life than port and sport. Trotters said I, but now I fear I think different. Sally's improvement would be my improvement; her bettering, my bettering. Besides she had heavenly breasts. I hailed a cab to her rooms, stopping several times to piddle from the step.

I was there again, sat on the edge of Sally's bed in her Piccadilly whore's room. She was not so welcoming as before yet she serviced promptly for well she needed the money.

Weeks earlier I would have performed admirably and left, with nary a word, yet that day did something stir within my being, a feeling with no name, for my stomach very lurched at the sight of her downcast eyes and I felt I needed to make amends. Indeed, *wanted* to make amends.

'Sally? About my comportment upon my last visit—'

'Beggin' your pardon sir?'

'My behaviour.'

'What of it? I'm a whore, you're a mister and you pays me well. Ain't no more to be said.'

'But Sally dear, I wa-'

'Beggin' your pardon sir, but I ain't no one's dear' and her eyes fair lit with venom.

'Or course, of course. What I sought to say, was that if in any way I did offend you, or-'

'Sir please, let us speak no more of it. If you want me titties for less, I can't really, cos I needs the money for to pay me rent an-'

'No, please, I beg of you my de-, you Sally, please, my tempers were ill for I was mildly consumptive, and had, well, I think, swallowed a bat an-'

'Sir, really, if you want more fiddly dee, let's get winky out 'is snug, but if not, I've got to 'urry, cos I got a fella comin' over soon. Dr Mansfield. Wears spectacles.'

'Oooh, not sex now, but how about I pay for the time. Bid Dr Mansfield wait a while, for I should very much like to sit with you.'

And so it was that again, the idle tick of the faded clock beat out the most painful seconds London Town has yet known, as all around came the sounds of life and death, the coster calls and the giggle of drink. Try anew I might, and try anew I would.

'Did you read in The Times of the Fejee Mermaid from Calcutta? Real fins and legs?'

'No, I am afraid I did never.'

'What about Madame Babault, the Lobster Claw Lady? She can knit with her crustaceoid hands. The Talking Fish? The Laughing Baboon? A fully-grown simian who chuckles at jokes and rhymes? The Flying Hare? His whiskers are grown so long they are become wings and is to be exhibited in Piccadilly next month. Perhaps you would care to come with me, for I know a fellow who may arrange our admission?'

'I feel sick.'

'And as for that funny little chap with the three, uhhm, (my God, I near spoke of a man's genitals) ears, *ears,* (pleased with the speedy invention, I continued). It is said he can hear through walls and uhhm, metal. In fact he can even pick up voices in France. Yes. France. But uhhm, he cannot say what the people talk of, for he is English and he uhhm, does not speak French. A little may be, but not much, enough to request a baguette and the lavatory, certainly not enough to decipher a conversation. Hhhm?'

'No.'

A dimwit apparent. Too soon in our relationship to perform my chicken impression or a Korean in the bath, I sought to rouse her passions still by reading from my favourite page, the lowest yet finest amusements in the city of London – Deaths and Accidents.

'*Some days ago a rat-catcher in Golden Lane, being disordered in his senses, destroyed himself by taking a dose of the poisonous preparation used to kill the vermin. He had attempted to hang himself some time before from a tree. On Friday the Coroner's jury brought in their verdict; Lunacy.*'

'Like it?'

'Nutter. Lunatic. Quite good I reckons' and I fancied I saw her face lit with the faintest joy.

Her heart was melting, her passions perhaps thawing.

'*On 26 May, a false eye-maker was found dead within his pantry. A post-death examination showed that the wretched man, Edmund Prostrate had in fact eaten several of the bogus orbs for they had been put among his pickled onions. Too had all of the man's silverware been taken. His coachman is still at large. He is presumed guilty for he is an African. Verdict: Murder most foul.*'

'Absolutely funny' roared she slapping my tum-tum. 'Eyes, onions, murder' wept I, a mirth watering my eyes; ocular and Japanese.

She next: 'Bogus, pickles, most.'

'How hootable.'

'How hootable.'

'Perhaps' sighed she, 'no more death today cos although I am beginnin' to find it 'ilarious, I fears my wit be too weak for more.'

'Dear, you may be correct. Are you fond of curry? *I* am, I

do so enjoy the heat of a spicy dish. I relish what it does to my organs. We must visit together the Hindostanee Coffee House in Portman Square. The chef is swarthy yet he prepares a terrific chicken.

November 3, 1855

Oh What Rot!

Tedworth did not appear again until chilly November, when the gusts of autumn were well and truly upon us. The wind whistled a sinister tune through the baring trees, their knobbly branches all a-potty with fear. Windows shook and rattled and leaves flapped into the wheels of carriages. One poor horse got it right in the snout.

That evening, Tedworth brought a guest, a well-mannered one, though not particularly forthcoming - Dr Michael Ryan, who had recently published a pamphlet: Prostitution In London With A Comparative View Of That Of Paris And New York.

He subtitled the work: Proving Moral Depravation To Be The Most Fertile Source Of Crime And Of Personal And Social Misery.

Dr Ryan was unused though, to steak, a trait upon which we did frown as the visitor was brought forth by the surprisingly effervescent Tedworth. No mention was made of his whereabouts for several months, nor why his eyes honed a feverish stare. Between bites of sharp French red, Tedworth made his chatter. Dr Ryan came over most bashful. He met our eyes briefly as each of our names was proffered with the clogged prongs of a fork.

Dr Ryan twitched his waistcoat, checked his pocket

watch (barely eight) and guided a clog of Angus down his gullet, with what looked in the gas light, disgust.

'Gentlemen, allow me to ask of you a question' he opened to the room, deathly quiet save for the gurglings of a dozen tums and the natural bangs and bashes from the streets, someone weeping as though the world was very ended, an explosion in a back room too, the gaff of an old horse, and a right rotten mouthful from an outdoor fucker.

'Which of you has not walked down Haymarket or Regent Street, whether under natural light or gas and not been accosted by street-walkers?'

The nervous rattle of uneasy laughter took to the table, as each looked to one another for reassurance. Or guilt.

'Who amongst you has not had his eyes stung by this dreadful parade - the most *depraved* of' and here he developed a new shade of discomfort 'til his face appeared like some country pudding, '*women.*' That very last was half whispered, half strangled, half spat.

'Why can not we walk these streets with our wives, our mothers, our daughters, our aunts, nannies and nieces without having to cower from them? Or sisters-in-law? Why must we for ever be compelled to look at these unnatural women? Why must we be impelled to gawk down their busts? Look about you and you will see all drunks, thieves, cricketers, foreigners, gangs, beggar men. Ask yourselves for why have they visited?

'They are all, to a man, or child, attracted like bees to pollen, like bears to honey, like a fly to a pie to the crime that goes with such women. As a man sates his basest needs, the pimp waits in the shadows to rob. Intoxicated husbands, prowling for sex, fall drunk under the carriage wheels.

Children beg spare pennies and where there is one laxness more will follow.'

We paused to sup and munch. I unbuttoned my shirt collars.

'The Hidden Scourge eh? We all have seen men limping the streets, pock-marked from the syphilitis.

'Look inside the city's Lock Hospitals to witness the disease that maims not only those whose morals are lost, but think too of the greater picture. Think of the war in Crimea, our soldiers ill with venereal disease. Think too of the innocent women, victims of their husbands' sexual immorality who too become awful clogged with gonorrhoea.

'Why must our avenues be awash with whores, pounding 'neath heavy bosoms under slender silk, blouses soaked by spring rains offering a glimpse of heaven through the buttons, blood red lips and *Jesus* son of God, is that the time?'

The doctor began to wheeze.

'Your fathers' he pointed, 'fought for this country, and many have lost their lives, their limbs, their elbows even and for what eh? For what? FOR *WHAT*? A few minutes of pleasure from a woman who is no more than a beast, copulating in the streets like an ox. Or a bear. A physical pleasure that begins with the rubbing of one's breeches, the unclasping of the member, so heavy and dignified, so big and heaving and my *God*, why this insufferable *warmth*? WAITER!!!Please lower the heating. Brand these women rascals. Sear them upon the forehead.

'Give them the mark of D for devil, of T for trollop or SW for sauce witch. Hang them from their necks. And kick them in the muffs.

'Only then will man be safe to walk the streets' he

concluded to a room, which was utterly quiet, deathly still once more, save for some merry squeaking from some part of the doctor. It appeared he had damaged himself some.

November 4 1855
The Joys Of Food And A Spoon In The Conkers.
Is Life Never Sweet?

On Friday, with a new cravat and a penny shave I took Sally's hand, eyed her tits and kissed her.

'If you promise,' I began, 'that you will cease this whoring, then stay with you I shall.' She wept blue tears of joy.

And thus was a deal of sorts struck. She would turn her back on the streets and I would care for her. At a price, for as she instructed me as to her many costs and outgoings, her incomings and upstandings, her expenses and nutrition, I knew it would not come cheap. I wavered again with ditching her once more, but then again I enjoyed monkeying with the dear and some part of me felt not a little tenderness for the thing.

I vowed to do better for Sally, so I instructed her for starters in the ways of the knife and fork, as she slurped through her courses like a goose. I set forth for her, the instruments of dining; for example, the flesh of walnuts, hazels and the like, were removed with a nut fork.

Sardines were only to be handled with light-fingered tongs; grapes required a scissor; pies – pigeon or game – called for a particular spoon; pickles necessitated the accompaniment, rather like a classical pianist and a viola, of a pickle fork.

Sally was want to use her hands so I had to slap her.

No more mutton cutlets in low-down chop houses. We ate like hogs, and chefs trawled the Thames of all: sole poached in Chablis; grilled smelt with potato Dauphinois, filleting the slithery flesh with the delicate fish blade. My poor dear had known only eel and whitebait, potatoes and sheep head, yet she enjoyed a particular fondness for rice. Bizarre. Our orders were plucked from the skies and gathered from the forests: turkey in aspic; grouse; pheasant stuffed with Continental truffles; sparrow puddings and little lapwings. Yet still her manners were extraordinary. When not spooning high-class creams into her mouth with the crassness of a pig, she would dally with her hair at the table. Also she dined at times with two pieces of finely cut wood. How odd. One such afternoon, whilst awaiting the arrival of a grapefruit sorbet with which to cleanse the organs, did she beat time with her hands. Oh she was like a minstrel.

I made a wee commotion for there were tuts and clanks. I felt my neighbour's eyes eat into me, with a stare as chilled as pudding. The restaurant – The Ship and Turtle in Leadenhall Street – quite tinkled with light. Chandeliers, flamed by gas, and cut like lace, boomed a friendly glow and the linen was excellent. As white as a child's bum. I explained thus to other eaters.

'I am sorry. This is my younger brother. He was born upside down and fell out of my mama's bottom. Thus his brain is wanting and his ears terrible. Carry on. There is nothing worse than a cold trout.'

'Bugger my teeth. If he is your brother, he has the most prime tooties in town' said a diner to a meaty roar of approval.

'I will give you a Brie for a squooze of his biscuits. What say you sir? I am a good man and have never faltered.'

'*Brother* you say? *Tatties* you jape? Oh. I see. This here is my *sister*. My brother left during the terrine. She too once had a pre-nuptial whoopsie and is certainly maladjusted. *Brie* you scoundrel? How dare you.' The man was repulsive. He was as podgy as a pig, with unreasonable hair, as curly as a negro's with the colour of a Bird's Eye custard. His face appeared broiling and was frightfully pink, much like one who has dropped off to sleep next a roaring fire. He smiled at Sally with several teeth's of spinach. Quite from where it sprang I do not know, for the vegetable appeared not on the menu. I leant backwards, and bypassing the pepper and salt, in a hushed custom breathed into his earhole: 'Three Bries, a quart of port and your necktie and they're all yours.'

My *God*! What the chicken legs was I saying?

'Get out' ordered me in quite an outburst. 'You are dirtier than a porpoise and twice as gory. *Out* you gorilla!' and with that I stabbed his testicle with a dessert spoon.

'Garçon! This man is sanguine. He has damaged his own organs with the cutlery and struggles for breath.'

'Quick' I hissed to my table-partner, 'we must depart, effing now' and I grabbed the lady's paw, fancying I could hear a little crack of a bone. I forget how masculine I could be. What's done was done and she had several more beside.

She was a damned nuisance, her deportment was intolerable, and as dim-witted as an ass, but she nibbled the old boy admirably and she would save me a fortune on calling cards.

The rest of 1855
How Many Rooms Holds The Human Heart?

I was *different* she howled. (I had lied; she believed her wares were the first I had tasted for cash.) And for a while I did not use the vaginas of other women, prossies or no. I was delightful and caring and this made me glow outside, but inside I died each time she sang my name, my heart drained of love when she told I was the first man whom she allowed to sleep with my arms wound around her in the dark. I was a liar. My life was a lie and I wanted to tell her, confide in her my wrong-doings, I longed to speak of the child I fucked by error that morning, of how I have never worked, merely fawned and pawned and once by error spawned. I wanted to break to her the low esteem in which I held all her gender, the abhorrence I harboured against the French, my irrational fear of blackmen, my hatred of the Hottentot. One must agree, they can appear rather frightening. But I said nothing. I merely lapped up her simple devotion, treasured the gratitude that she dealt me. For it seemed I was falling in love.

The Beef Steakers saw less of me that year. If the topic of low-houses should come about, I melted into a silence, for as fond as I was of Sally, I knew her name should not be mentioned. True to my deception she was known to none of my number.

Instead, we took in the theatre, matinées in Drury Lane, a world away from the penny gaffs in Waterloo she spoke of. While she learnt the ways of the gentleman and his knife and fork, I too learnt a little of a life without love, fuelled by hunger and want.

She drew for me a world unknown, of raucous halls piped with smoke from child braggarts, a patched hat on the head, a swagger in his tail and a whore on his arm. I demanded she take me so I may see for myself. There were snippets from Shakespeare, jokes from Johnston and mimics of Marlowe but only the bawdy dances and lovely tits won favour with the mob. Girl children too young for a hair on the giblet, suckled babies to their breasts, cocky brats stopping to drink a suck of milk themselves, all a-scream for legs and knickers; it was wonderful, it was terrible, an unleashed ferocity run riot. "Bloodstained Jewels" and "The Ghastly Murders of Cutler's Row" served well to instruct the rascals as a school of crime.

So vivid, so clear, so *fond* were Sally's memories that I felt I needs must pose a delicate question, so coughing lightly I asked, looking nowhere near her dreamy eyes: 'My dear, forgive me, but did you ever meet such creatures, a genre of dirty boy at these gatherings of your youth? In short, were you ever frigged?'

'None of your bloody business, you bastard' she booed, 'none of your bloody businesses.'

'My dear' I came again, 'I see what you are getting at, but I must trouble you to leave out the swear words.'

A bit more of 1855
How Love Does Flow With The Help Of Negroid Fleas

Sally was keen to learn all she could from the world that had been snatched from her as a child. I instructed her from bed in the rudimentaries of French, I refreshed her reading with children's tales before the novellas of Hardy and Austen, bits of Elliot and the Russian greats.

Likewise, I begged of her to impart me schooling from her own youth. She did so:

'There was a young man of Peru
Who had nothing whatever to do;
So he whipped out his carrot
And buggered his parrot
And sent the result to the Zoo.'

For I felt as a moralist, a colonialist. I saw her muff as the dark forests of Africa, and I, the missionary, come to lift her from the gloom, to shine a Lucifer match within the deep confines of her ninny and to breathe the word of God into the knockers of her soul.

The bitch truly wanted improving. I taught her piano-forte but she was more keen to blow the French horn. I showed her to eat with dainty bites yet this proved difficult for she possessed the appetite of a seal. For make of her a lady I must; embroider cushions, paint a watercolour, show her not to flash her growler when mounting an omnibus. I demonstrated how to sup at porter yet still she ended asleep on the sofa, her legs wide open, snuffling as a Doberman Pinscher.

I spoke from the London Times whilst examining her undergarments. I shaved her cunny as she laid the table. We enjoyed the elephant shows and dancing horses at Astley's in Lambeth, we did the polka at pleasure gardens and skipped at the Alhambra in Leicester Square; we heard choral singing on a Sunday afternoon, a man laying eggs from his bottom at the Albert Saloon.

Yet still I treated her to lowlier pastimes from time to time, so as not to startle too much her brain; more basic spectacles more in keeping with her boorish ways. For example, Martin's Negro Fleas – a display of some note, with more than one thousand fleas from Louisiana, performing remarkable feats of strength.

But more valuable than any blackman's fleas was the love I felt, a feeling hitherto a stranger to my soul.

I had her, I had her, I had her I wanted to shout to all in the street, to the men upon the omnibus, I had her I wanted to say to the copy clerks laden down with the dreary ways of a faceless man in a faceless city, I had her I wanted to shout to the Irish navvies, tipsy by breakfast, her beauty and youth all mine, *mine* all mine. I had her and I wanted all to know. But I daren't, for she was a whore.

And so pass the weeks, soon then the months as spring drifts again into summer and the two young lovers can be seen, hand in hand through the city's parks, laughing as they feed the sheep in St James', our hero a dream in a rich fedora and fancy collars, a Cashmere shawl round the shoulders and a tiny scent box by his heart, Sally red-cheeked and rosy and together they take the air in Green Park and Hyde, the parasols of July shading the peppermint drinks to chill the heated limbs of lovers, kissing ginger-beer from their lips, kicking up the leaves in Kensington Gardens as the days grow shorter and the stuffiness is blown from the air as the sticky breaths of summer are bitten with freezing gusts from the north. Then too, as the first snows of winter dust the streets, the horses' manes white overnight, still can they be seen in Oyster Bars across the city, watching the fireworks and puppet shows at the pleasure gardens in Vauxhall, balloon rides at Cremorne, holding hands under the prickles of a thousand gas-lights as they sip lemonade by the river. They watch the hippopotamus and the carnivores at the zoo in Surrey Gardens, then of a sudden, cough-drops to warm the croaky throats, gooseberry cakes and hot cordial when the air grows crisp; and there they are at Newgate, chuckling in the windows at the flayed corpse twisting his final jig, sharing their love of gore and death in cuddles, there they are, red-cheeked with rat blood at the fights in Islington publics, breathless at dog fights and cock fights, giddy afternoons at The Criterion, rump-steak puddings at the Cheshire Cheese on The Strand when the wind blows strong out of doors, swirling the fallen browned leaves in dizzy circles around churchyard crypts, when the rain howls in grey sheets over Blackfriars Bridge, then hot-spiced gingerbread and peppery saveloys at the food stalls along the Thames, as the gasmen flick the flames into light by the choppy waves of Westminster, huddling together in mink, a human shield of love against the London pea-soupers that darken the river and a man's lungs and soul, until, as quick as love has struck into his heart, then is that very same flame quashed, and Sally become nothing more than the furniture of his life, the passion gone, the belly sucked in to please no longer.

Sally was mine. She was grateful and pleasured me in many ways; some hurt, one was illegal and two made me laugh. She would dress to please my tastes; milkmaid, washerwoman, policeman, the sultan's wife. For days on end we remained in bed, our lips as one, our soul sharing the same beat.

I grew to adore the thing, simple as she was both in mind and manners. She let me be for much of the time and caused little fuss yet her appetite for amour was tremendous, far more than mine. Indeed it quite alarmed.

When we returned from an outing, she would claw at my breeches, pulling them down much like the lowering of a sail in a coming storm, and regardless of the state of he below deck she would shower him in praise, often quite *painful* praise for her incisors were sharp. Once I had endeavoured to misdirect my passions and made a muck twixt her breasts and from thence on, whenever she believed my ardour fading, would gather up the bashful thing between her mummies and cause upon him some terrible friction, until I am forced to yelp in deceitful delight, afeard the fellow will catch light. For I dare not impart the true agony of her deeds.

Yet despite my love and affection, my old ways returned to haunt and torture my soul, for soon did I crave more and more trollops. I would have accepted the normal female, one who did not earn her crust with her legs apart and cunty a-gaping. But those things were hard to come by and needed wooing. Some required feeding too. Eff that. I did not have it in me for such flattery. I rathered hand over the dosh and demand a nosh. Thus we rarely passed the night as one, for I must pursue other bawdy-houses, claiming appointments which tore me from her.

Because for all her lovely ways, still was I wont not to want her and would want to visit other wonton ladies like her. A wondrous one worked in the village of Wandsworth. And sometimes I would have a wonton soup. Hmm. Tasty.

But why not stay with Sally, who, it must be said I sort of loved? Why not make a home for us? A family of children and happiness with the love of my life?

Let me endeavour an explanation. I *adore* a poached egg. I once ate seven at a single sitting. And some toast. And a cup of tea. But were I to take such a dish each day, I fear I would become highly strung for they would no longer be the treat they were. I liked different foodstuffs for breakfast and too for other repasts. Surely to sate myself with the most treasured nibbles would destroy my tummy's few pleasures? In short, I had to sample each and every whore in town.

The winter fogs of London are truly hideous, thick and whispering, smarmy from the Thames, deep and choking, a bank of mist that brings candles to the table at luncheon, and gas lights to windows by day, a phantom of mud and ooze blown forth from the chilling marshes of Essex, nauseous and gaseous, burnt carbon from a city of chimneys, a miasma of disease and a clammy grip on the bones. He who never has breathed the air of a London fog can not begin to imagine its true ugliness, not even were he to inhale the very guts of a dead beast. For when drifts in the fog, the city streets are as those to a blind-man, struggling through the chocolate thickness, a bull's-eye lantern on the belt and a hallucination in the mind, strange shapes familiar and familiar shapes strange, the cabman becomes Lucifer and his horse Hannibal's elephant, love becomes hate, revulsion devotion and who knows what.

Lessons In Love And Literature.
And The Peep Of Stockings

Other dealings pressed me about Sally. She was prone to spitting while dining and once I caught her attempting to tuck into a dog. And although I liked her to dress spicy, I was concerned about her choice of garb, for I feared her globular boobies would snare some other sort. Because, while I effed myself silly, I am cursed with hypocrisy and would not have her look at another fellow.

As to her indoor outfits, they could not have been finer; busty dresses with just the faintest whiff of shoulder and neck, as soft and white as a baby chicken, a fine beast with mauve gloves and leg-o'-mutton sleeves, Balmoral boots and corsets. On hot summer days when the air was thick, she carried a fan and a yellow parasol so sweet. She would glide to me at my command until I would order her raise the gates of her cheery frock and demand the lessening of her drawers. I favoured a lacy one. I would peer, not unlike an intellectual man with spectacles, upwards, panting for a peep at the silken locks of her mound. I then too, would command a lowering of the top for an ample view of the thing's bust. Indeed, much against the creature's pleasure, I would propel her nannies under her chin with the aid of a corset. Indeed so fond of the gadget's tricks was I that I purchased for her a Dropsical Compressing Belt. I thrilled at tightening the girl ever tauter.

Her breathless gasps as the constrictions constricted came only from pleasure for I was damned sure she enjoyed it. Oftentimes she coughed and gasped of sorts.

Alas my lessons in English – she spoke poorly - proved miserly, for one day Sally came across a publication demeaning the item that so shelved her teats. Before I knew it, it seemed she had mastered the art of the printed page.

I located her one after-lunch, suffering her limited wits through the Ladies' Pocket Magazine in which there came William Coulson's review: *Deformities of the Chest and Spine*. The tearful thing had drastically caught the general sway of the words that spoke of folly.

'Frig your folly you fucking bastard' I sort of shouted out loud, making Sally squeal like a mole.

'What does this man know of breasts? What is he, a blooming tit doctor?'

'Don't let me wear veese fings again' she replied with a sob.

'Please don't. Vey are bound to do me in. I can't hardly breeve no more wiv 'em stranglin' me titties and I'm afeared I'm going to become crooked and die in the circus.'

Shocked as ever by her grammar (when in spirits high or low she would return to her previous ways), I was more than doubly aroused to see her uncorked ploppies, damp with upset and hoisting with passion. The girl had shredded the garment almost to death in her haste to rid herself of the thing, leaving two fabulous breasts ripe for the taking, like a pair of snoozing but hairless ducks a-waiting the hunter.

'But you see my dear,' I falteringly began, lapping at the gentle bowl of her milk-shops, 'your, ahem, hhhmmm, umm, your these, may well turn into those of an African negress, whose similar things hang to an inordinate length.'

I paused more for health than gravitas, then resumed my frantic licking. 'Hang downwards, you know, to their knees' I wheezed, 'to their knees and what will become of you then? Please? Knees. Squeeze. Squeeze. *Bumble* bees.'

January 6, 1856
The Sorry Ways Of The Foreigner

I needed to trifle with a stranger to rid myself of the after effects of such an emotional dispute. I knew a venue not far off. The Madame was a delightful thing and was known to many as Grey-Tooth Gerty. I never did learn the reason behind the name. For a shilling she once permitted me handle her snatch. It was covered in hair. The house was stuffed with loose-mannered women aplenty and an astonishing selection of snacks while a-waiting; sandwiches, slices of ham, red grapes, cheese and onion Pringles, whatever they may have been. The prices were competitive but the walls were thin. Indeed I do recall one man from the north, who came to the south with a loud voice and much passion. As I prepared to *ejaculer* could I hear from next door his habits. I believe he was a merchant come to purchase produce or perhaps produce purchase. He was quite simple.

'I am NOT paying for that' howled the shopper.

'Come on dear, 'ee's not going t'suck 'isself.'

I feared he was not romantic but I had other things on my mind. I was in a temper and needed a seeing-to.

But first an important visit to Holborn – an apothecary by the name of Fluff. Mr Fluff.

'Sir?'
'Mr Fluff?'

'Allow me to prescribe a bottle of Mrs. Johnson's Soothing Syrup, one of Fanny Kemble and Pandora Tulips, Stirling's Stomach Pills and some heroin.'

'Super.'

'Sir?'

'Mr Fluff?'

'Your crotchless lacy knickers?'

'Yes?'

'A week on Monday.'

'Super. For Aunty Mo.'

'Of course.'

'Good day.'

'Good day.'

'Madame' I spake when I eventually gained the home of Grey-Tooth Gerty, 'I have come for some sauce, preferably with a female. Have you got any creatures with vast tits? I would like to spunk in a room with decent walls. If you have none, some button mushrooms could I insert in my ears to block the din. Please can we hurry, for I feel as sauced up as a nipper.'

I was led up the threadbare steps which were most unhealthy. I was shown into a parlour, complete with red velvet hangings, chintzes and a chamber pot and informed thus: 'Today we have a lovely girl working for us. She is nineteen, from Sweden, has lovely blonde hairs – head and cunty wunty - and has teats the size of gooseberries.'

'*Gooseberries?*' I roared. 'I love 'em big.'

'Gooseberries? Did I say gooseberries? I meant gooses.'

'Geese.'

'Yes. Relax your clothing and wait. Would you like a sandwich?'

'Ooh yes please. Ham and cress if you would. Steady on the mustard woman – it's got quite a bite.'

I was itching for trouble. I chomped on my sandwich and relished the near future. The creature entered in a neat silk gown and monstrous breasts. Each could have had a chair of their own for afternoon chatter. She bent forward to me, pouting her painted lips, affording me a staggering view of the wobblies, and onto her nip-nops drew forward the very crumbs from my lap, like pure magnetism.

'How are you, have you been performing this employment for long, would you to taste my sandwich? Oh also, where are you from?'

'Very good, good, good. I am Sveeden.'

'Sweden you say. Really?'

'Da. Na. Ya. I am Sveeden.'

The lady lied for she came not from Sweden. She had the sniffings of a Cossack whisker, a fur hat and slurped vodka while we conversed. She was a damned Ruskie and was taking me for a fool. Which she would not. God no.

'Remind me, how is the King of Sweden? Ooooh, what was his name again, King, King erm?'

'Very good. No name.'

'Really. I am a politician and depart tomorrow for Russia where I shall attend a conference. I am very important. Remind me, what is the capital city of Russia ?'

'Saint Petersburg. Nyet. Moscow. Nyet, no. Do not know. Vot is a Russia?'

'Do you like bears?'

'Da. I loves zem. I have vun live in my house in Moscow. I mean nyet, nyet, no. Vot is bear?'

'Where are you from?'

'I am Sveeden.'

'Are you Russian?'

'Vot is a Russia?' Her breathing had accelerated and her cheeks had flushed. The sandwich had cooled my tempers and I was winning. Effing Ruskie.

'Where is Russia?'

'I do not knows. Lick my tots.' She unsheathed the titties and kneaded them with her paws as a plum-dough maker would his pastries. More pertinently her eyeballs darted around her eyes and she gulped quickly and often, like a farmer.

'Russia.'

'Sveeden.'

'Russia.'

'Sveeden.'

'Russia.'

'Sveeden.'

'Russia.'

'Sveeden.'

'Where are you from?'

'I am Sveeden. Bite my finny' she sobbed, wiping her tears on the beast of a moustache and taking a fresh snap of vodka. She jigged a Ural dance, a sure sign of dishonesty if ever there was one.

'I am from Russia' I tried, trying to coax security from the toffer.

'Da? Den take me home. I hates it here.' A prolonged pause. 'Oh. Really? Vot is a Russia?'

'Om du säger det igen så kommernjag dra av fötterna på dig. Now. Where are you from?'

'I am Sveeden.'

'Right dear' and before my final hand could be dealt I unclasped the teats from their cotton homes and played a tremendous licking game upon them. My Lord, they tasted lovely. I feared I had to lick quick for fear of expulsion. I instantly lathered them and squeezed them together with all my might. The view was exceptional, much like a Highland glen but less mossy. I was erect but would not last long. 'Dear. I have only this to say and in Russian will I say it. Russia is a second rate nation and the temperature plummets in winter.'

Her reactions were miraculous. Before my tongue could circumnavigate the naple, she had smashed the vodka glass on my back, pulled off her field boots and spat thus in violent Russian: 'How dare you. You come into my room, treat my boobs as pets, lick them until they wince, rub yourself against my bedstead, quiz me on the names of cities and then call me a shitty. I have had enough. Out' and with that she tossed a boot at my head which shattered the mirror behind me.

'Madame, kindly. You are a horrible liar and I adore you only for your baboons' and off I went.

The disagreement had alarmed the Madame. And Mister Madame. Perhaps I had been too hasty.

'Madame and Mister Madame. And that large stick in your right hand. Please forgive me. Perhaps I have been too hasty. We have had a language moot. Olga voiced some words she never should have and I fell over and damaged my skull. Good-day.'

The weather is terrible, the stink of illness too, for the city lies beneath a cold, cold cloud, as cold really as that which sits over the man seen muttering to himself close by Wardour Street. For those that see him would deem the fellow as happy as a child yet deep within lurks a terrible sadness, a pitiful loneliness that no number of assignations may yet conceal.

In London, at the close of day, doors and windows are shut firm to keep the houses from the night fumes of death, to seal the living from the sighs of typhus, yet still the very walls suck in the deadly fumes leaked from cesspools, sulphur explosions and ammonia death, seeping into the shallow wells of sustenance that the city's people call upon.

January 28, 1856
A Man Must Swing

It was a glorious morning, nicey and icy and after a prompt peep at my whiskers, I took a few rounds of toast, a pot of tea and embarked upon a plan.

Some fellow by the name of Chester Arrowsmith had poisoned his wife and killed a daughter. Mrs Ann Arrowsmith had been discovered slumped in the front parlour after breakfast. Arsenic – the poisoner's favourite, soaked out of fly-papers from the druggist – had drooled upon his wife's bacon and within moments she was breathing, somewhat raspingly if the newspapers are to be trusted, her very last. Now, Mr Arrowsmith, a once-respected alderman in Wandsworth, will hang from his neck. It was to be a hoot.

I stopped off for a glass and no more of sweet porter, the colour of bit lips and returned to the streets where I came across a pigeon on the dried branch of a plane tree. He was a sweet fellow with a cheery song and a naughty glint in his eye, which no doubt he would use in female company. I sang the gentle refrain of a little fisherman's ditty I once knew, at which point he appeared to liven up somewhat. I do fancy he smiled at me. I was tempted to proffer a tickle but he soared off and took to the sky. Who could have foreseen that ere long I would be eating his relatives all raw and chewy?

Soon, past the hullabaloo of Fleet Street and the fetid stench of the over-flowing Fleet Ditch, came Ludgate Circus and the figure of Justice atop Newgate Prison in Old Bailey, her gold sheen winking in the morning light. As I rounded the corner, passing the wretched slums of Blackfriars where snivelling street Arabs snivelled and wept their tricks, the fervent braying of the crowds, the drunken bellows emanating as from so many beasts, struck a terrible excitement into my very heart. And a slight bulge in my pantaloons.

A man is to die, hung for the pleasure of a yelling mass. Soon the noise is unbearable, seven in the morning still, hawkers peddling food for the stomachs of the hundreds, the thousands teeming through the city's narrow lanes, hungry for a glimpse of the condemned man.

'Look at veese plump 'uns' cry the whelkmen from Billingsate. Ruddy-faced and dirty, they pound the steaming little fellows with broomsticks.

'They never kicks when you boils 'em, not like 'em crabs and lobbers.'

Peppermint water and sheeps' trotters, a glutinous horror for the death watchers, for with 40,000 come to gloat there is much eating and drinking. There is beer and brandy for breakfast, a long breakfast that started late and cold last night, for many have camped outside. And as the sun comes up, it lights the faces of thousands cast in the very image of the Devil himself.

Many fancy they can hear soaring over the hubbub of the mob, a desperate plea from Mr Arrowsmith at half-past seven, as the wardens stomp to his condemned cell for the final time, as the creaking gate of his vault swings open, the clank of heavy keys on their belts and an empty feeling inside the wronged man.

He will be pushed through the sullen alleyways of the prison, wretched men and women reaching scrawny limbs through the rusty bars, imploring one last touch. Others though will shrink from his stench of death for to see once a man condemned to die does many people no good at all.

William Calcroft, the country's premier executioner, will be lacing his breeches by now, pressing his locks, thirty-five minutes past, smoothing his Italian hemp, stretched last night with a sandbag of the prisoner's weight and bound with Chamois leather, for though the body will swing in death, bloodied from bursted veins and dirty from emptied bowels, the neck will remain a picture of serenity, unblemished by the drop. Soon it is forty-minutes past.

The bells of Sepulchre sit still in the biting chill, heavy in wait for the deathly toll that will have Mr Arrowsmith dancing the Newgate jig, his limbs bouncing a spastic trot.

Children sit atop fathers' shoulders as excitement thickens the air, then a mighty cheer goes up, for rattling through the crowd are the Sheriff's carriages, come for the gore, for who can miss the scene of death on a frosty morning?

The dreaded cross-beams sit on the blackened stage as shrieks echo on the cobbles of Old Bailey.

Some fancy they hear too the shaking Mr Arrowsmith resisting death. 'Confess your sins, confess and tell all to God Almighty' chants the chaplain inside.

'I beg of you, I have done nothing wrong. I have not sinned my Lord; Please spare me' weeps Arrowsmith empty to the chaplain's ears.

The execution broadsides have been printed already, hot off the press, Mr Arrowsmith's last words concocted in Fleet Street pubs.

The Association Room is next on the condemned man's journey, clutching at brandy to ease his grip on life. There his shackles are hammered off and he staggers, wailing, bowels leaking down his shirt.

Low prostitutes busty with rouge and ripped corsets from a night in the slums, patrol the streets, one eye on the troops, the other on the punters. And many there are, sozzled and glorious in the icy nip afore the gallows creak with death.

'Calcraft, Calcraft, he's the man' sing them all. Few hope his death will be quick, rather that he will 'die hard'- more fun for the crowd with a gruesome final struggle.

Not yet eight but the streets are paved with drunks, vomiting, shitting. What a wonderful day. Perhaps I overdid the toast. Some more brandy? Ooooh.

Blackened urchins rifle the old and drunk, the infirm circus come to town. Handkerchiefs flee, watches are unclasped, soon to be sold in the cheap shops nearby.

Tie pins too as ruffians swarm round the City folk until St Sepulchre rings for death, as the Bellman breathes his humdrum chant:

All you that in the condemned hole do lie,
Prepare you for you shall die;
Watch all and pray: the hour is drawing near
That you before the Almighty must appear;
Examine well yourselves in time repent,
That you may not to eternal flames be sent.
And when St. Sepulchre's Bell in the morning tolls
The Lord above have mercy on your soul.

Beer porters scuttle to and fro the Magpie and Stump, where thirty guinea seats command the best views of death.

The landlord sights two brats scaling his drainpipe for the roof-top vantage.

'You bleeders. Come 'er fore I swipe you one. If I catches you again you'll be swingin' too, I tells yer. Now piss off.'

Drinks are brought, pies and bread. The windows let out the must of last night and welcome in the smut from the street.

Close to the barriers, the mob becomes so dense that it is with difficulty a man can keep his feet. An officer tries to break the crowd with a spray of water, for the rabble is thick with bloodlust which makes one wonder: is the Englishman really more civilised than the savage of Africa?

And down in the street, still venture the whores.

'Come on mister. Just you and me a'ter the dance. I knows ya'll love it.'

And still the death-hungry mob:

'Make him swing. Hurry up, hurry up' and these roars serve only to encourage the savage in their flippery for death.

The Debtors' Door swings open of a sudden, and the wretched Arrowsmith is yanked shaking and half blind, legs rattling with a terror he knew not existed and the weeping man, insensate with horror is pushed to the gallows steps.

A cheer goes up as the show's star turn takes to the stage but the knees give way and the man collapses. The sight is pitiful, worse than a bull suffering the matador's blade in Spain but he is soon hauled to his feet. Mr Calcraft soothes him, rubbing his brow and whipping out the white nightcap.

'Arrowsmith you vicious bastard' I yelled, half potty on booze and a quick frollic with a trollop, too drunk to ask for cash.

The beams' shadow falls from the sky onto the man, s a

farewell gesture from this world to the next. He has ceased to struggle and drowsily lets his scrawny arms be pillioned in front of him, then his shivering ankles tied, the faint screech of rope a harbinger of what soon is to come. Calcraft then pulls tight over the patient's head the cap. The hood resembles, surely, a pillow case, yet this sleep will prove more eternal than any other.

Then the cap is tied to the rope which is attached to a hook which links to a chain which hangs from the crossbeam. Imploringly, though he can not see, Arrowsmith looks to the heavens as he hears the chaplain intone over the mob: 'I am the resurrection and the life. The Lord giveth and the Lord taketh.'

'Hats off, hats off' bellow the thugs out front, not through respect but for a desire to see death as close as can be.

Then Calcraft marks in chalk a 'T' upon the trap so Arrowsmith's feet will hang correctly – if not, the consequences could be bad, yet surely no worse than death.

Still they roar, the crowd silly with drink and violence and while the prisoner is held fast, Calcraft sinks below the trap to withdraw the iron bolt to release the doors. He returns to yank the lever for the 18-inch drop to hell.

More howls for blood shake the beams as the door swings open and the body kicks and twists, the white cap getting tighter and tighter, tighter still, the head swelling and blackening, the throbbing veins in the neck, blood red, then blue, crimson, royal and black, burst, the brain, the eyes, the ears and the heart near starvation too, popping one by one.

Grabbing our hero's hand, one girl reaches with doggy eyes: 'Come on sir. We can 'ave ourselfs a lovely time. I can do all sorts of fings. You name it I'll do it. Come on sir.'

Aghast at the horror, he shoes the child away, glad when she extends herself to others.

Damn the bitch for I was intent on concentrating upon death and bid her return when the man was gone. She may have been a child, but her face was pure meant for pecking and her cooing had got me all a topsy-turvy.

Meanwhile up on the hangman's stage, the show goes on.

Oh what a day, what weather, what breasts, what pleasure to be alive.

It put me in mind of a childhood outing to a Tyburn hanging with papa and a Chinese boy brought from the East. He did reside in the family home and performed many tasks – cushion plumping, newspaper warming and pomade preparing – the very essentials of life.

The particulars of the conviction escape me now but I believe it involved a sausage dog and there were lessons to be learnt.

'These people are born into a life of crime, an existence such as theirs is inherent' said Papa with a grave smirk of sorts.

'From the moment they arrive into the world, they are destined to leave on the gallows. Agree please.'

'Yes Papa.'

'Look around you boy. That man was born to kill. As clear as King William was to take the throne, so this runt would swing into hell. Yet were it not for Scotland Yard, this crook would likely still be at large slitting the throats of innocents as they go about their business. Agree please.'

'Yes Papa.'

'Look boy at those harlots. Born into vice unto the end.

As for that coloured fellow, you see him lad, the negro with the fuzzy hair? He too will suffer the same fate as his forefathers. A life of savagery and pickpocketing. Mark my words boy, he will hang before he is grown out of his breeches. What hope is there for this city if they continue to breed thus?'

'I do not know Papa.'

'No, boy, you do not. Nor I fear does the Lord God Almighty.'

And in a thrice he bowed his head and sighed. For he was very solemn was my father.

But watching Mr Arrowsmith struggle to his fate, he wonders deep down if his father, for all his knowledge, could perhaps have been mistaken. Did he not see beyond the limits of his own conceptions? How had such a man, so powerful in business, so mighty in his office, neglected to see anything other than what sat before his eyes? Yet he soon buries the thoughts for they, surely, are wrong.

By now, the limbs have come to rest. Yet barely have the bones ceased than a tumult of desperate hands stretch up to touch the corpse and he is pulled down for the macabre afters.

But not before the lame and the wretched have their chance to grope the cadaver, kiss his jewel-less fingers in the hope he will bring salvation in death to their incurables. The drunk, the leprous, the crazed and the greedy all reach out, setting it off once more as a deathly pendulum. Up they come to maul the corpse, yanking out tufts of snowy hair to be kissed as lockets. The dead man's legs are ripped, his arms too, little tears of blood dropping to the ground. Ulcerated hands strain for a caress of this most unfortunate man, more loved in death than in life. No-one cares what he has done; they lust for the spectacle alone and now their last faith dangles afore them on the end of a rope. They wail and howl and in the crowd, a pretty girl with red hair weeps alone, her eyes forgiving the body swinging over her head, forgiving her father his crimes for he knew not what he did.

Soon his body is a bleeding hulk, jerking spastically once more as the crowd fight each other to touch the figure, diseases swapped as the drunks and the harlots meet in smoky alleys to celebrate their life amongst today's death.

For some, this is a pleasure, a succulent end to a fine morning; some men are robbed by the girls' bullies under the shadow of stairs. A blow to the head with a cosh and all is gone in an instant, his silver lost to lust. It matters not his name nor his profession: magistrate, a costermonger or toff, they all resurface the same.

And at nine o'clock, comes Calcraft again, a pot-belly and chalky beard. Cradling his handiwork, he hugs the corpse and hacks the ropes with breathless swipes until the dead man thuds to his chest; as he unhooks Arrowsmith's discoloured head he sneers: "Ooo wants a bit of this then?' slicing at the hemp.

'Ten shillins an inch 's all I ask. Ten? Seven, alright I'll even take five out of the goodness of Calcraft's 'eart' and he hee-haws for all and sundry. And despite the cold, despite the stench of death and the early hour, the same sad hands worm their way up, like a bizarre flowering giant, grabbing at the rope, smutty with death, yet as though it were the very elixir

of life itself and the corpse is thrown down and the Debtors'
Door closes once more, the crowd near sated on life and
death and gin, the frenzied relief that but for the grace of
God, death has not come for them. Until the next time then.

Mr Arrowsmith is gone, his body soon to be buried in lime,
unmarked beneath the footsteps of a thousand more
condemned men in the vaults of Newgate. His clothes gone
too, soon to adorn a waxen statue at Madame Tussaud's
ghoulish emporium.

Meanwhile, St Sepulchre sings the happy ten and the
dignitaries scoff devilled kidneys, mindless a man has just
died.

Oh But There's More

I followed a child. He intrigued me true for I was concerned at how such types did live, where they did live and why they did live.

I had spotted the ruffian at the show. He was a gory wee fellow, barely four feet in height but bizarrely similar in girth. His freckles shone through a dirt like a thousand little suns, the sort of muck found on a man's bum late at night. He was almost as a homunculus, clothed in a grown-up's apparel. He wore a patchy jacket that brushed his knees, flapping breeches and a black brogue which upon closer viewing proved to be mere soil upon the toes. At the hanging, I had discerned the fellow rifle pockets, swiping chains, wallets, even one poor soul's shoelaces as if it were the surely most natural thing on earth. There he lay, all dirtied on the ground, a-frothing at the mouth, his unclean lips milky as a jizz-tub. I feared the blighter had been struck by a fever of sorts, possibly consumption or tuberculosis, a strained rib perhaps, as his features bubbled so and he battled for breath. The kind and the gullible paused to help, yet no sooner had they gone than he scraped at his mouth with the back of his sleeve and pocketed some object that looked very similar to a Palm Olive soap. I gazed mildly deranged, his hands as swift as wasps as he sped from one victim to the next. Oooh he was a rascal and how I longed to spank him.

Once the legs of Arrowsmith had come to their final halt, the lad did scarper, careering down Old Bailey, I took it upon myself to follow the boy, out of a pure fascination for the bizarre habits of such a creature. I always maintained my distance so as not to startle him.

He appeared to be in the know of other such types, for he was forever greeting them with grunts and hoots. He stopped in beer houses in Chancery Lane, looping past the nutty cigar shops of High Holborn, scuttling through the Inns of Court, 'neath the barristers' legs, rustling their cloaks, until suddenly he darted down some crooked alley. I paused, a stranger on the threshold of streets I had walked a thousand times, for naughty night wanks from the lowly ladies, yet there was I, a foreigner in my own city. For I had no inkling as to what lay beyond those walls. A stench rose to greet me. It was as if a gorilla had not washed his bum for a week. And then bared his cheeks for all to know.

The winter sun smeared a cherry red all around and I thrust myself through. The cobbles burned in the fiery rays, puddles of excrement steaming. There were rotting vegetables too. And a pair of knickerbockers. How rum.

My God, what an assault on my senses! Not even Sanitas Fragrant Disinfectant would improve matters.

Pigs chased chickens, who squawked at dogs who bit the cats who ate the mice who tickled the dead while the living squealed, swearing and laughing, spitting and crouching in the dirt, making their toilet where they sat.

I was accosted on all sides by ogres; women; fingers raw and bleeding from picking oakum in workhouses, now not fit to walk through the curse of gin; children shoeless, their deformed feet trampling the infected sludge of dung. Bodies lay sleeping, seeping, snoring where they had fallen, whether in drink or a robber's victim. Filthy tenements leaned on each other much like God almighty drunks. More dogs chased pigs who then chased sheep who pestered the chickens, all of whom had it in for one poor chap, whose ricketed legs proved no match for the poultry. In an instant he was down and gurgling for help. He was booted in the anus by a crimson thug.

'That's where 'ee belongs, kickin' around in the shite!'

Those who could, assaulted the man with bile; they pelted him with muck and my hat too went a-flying.

Stunned, I spun to see my little chap from the hanging atop a crate with a neat blade winking in the sun.

'Oi mister, you ain't one ov 'em pansies is ya?' and in an instant the mob turned their affections upon me.

'You can't 'ave me cos I hain't like that, but I knows some boys wot would let ya touch 'em. Cocks and bums, the lot guv'nor.'

Pressing in, their beery coughs a mean stink upon my senses. As they neared closer, the light was blocked out until I slumped, terrified against a wall. I think it may have been a privy. How dreadful. Incidentally, I was both peckish and unfortunately aroused by an earlier trollop, busty and bushy. I hoped none of the fiends would spot him.

'Or perhaps' said one, a gleam of something nasty in his eye, and plucking at my gloved paw, 'there is one man wot ve knows. Likes the likes of you 'ee most certainly does. Won't cost yer much. A few guineas for 'im an' just a few for me. You know, fors introducin' 'im like?'

I snatched back my hand in a flash causing the man to cackle. I glimpsed inside his mouth at what few teeth remained the devil. Yellow, were they, the hue of rancid butter and all around me slithered a wriggling nest of hands like so many vipers.

Close up, many had faces hurt by the pox, so disfigured were they, they became like lepers. Some had wounds which wept dreadful tears, others had lost fingers God knows where. Paste for the tooth was none popular, nor were the Queen's words. I squirmed back towards the wall for fear of being struck, yet squeezed forward my ear in an attempt to snag a word of their abnormal dialect. I have since learnt not to do so in future. It will only serve to worsen one's standing, for I appeared unable to control the parts of my frame.

Sally was out of sorts when I returned to her rooms later in the day, all a-snivelling as a coot.

February 1 1856
A Terrible Scene On A Bus

Over the years, I had gathered a first-rate compilation of foul books and I viewed them with some frequency. Many came with engravings. I bought from dishonest boutiques on the Charing Cross Road, photographic prints, stereoscopic slides and stiffying lithographs of fifth-rate ballet girls and second-rate actresses in undress. Often would I read them in the bath for even the titles could bring me off if the moment proved right. "The Confessions of A Chamber Maid", "The Romance of A Barman", "The True Desires of A She-Shirt", "A Nanny Goat's Ninny." Oooh. Alas they caused me much mischief for it was a bitter morning, ever so chilly, my face feeling as though blasted by an iceman's breath and Sally had come over all cholic. She wailed as a foal and despite threats to shut it, shut it she most certainly did not.

'My dear, if you stop effing harking, I will find you tablets' I told her. She paused her noise to sob. I left in poor spirits to find an apothecary.

His name was Mr Fluff and his business was, and still is no doubt at High Holborn. I believe you know of the chap.

'Sir?'

'Mr Fluff. Woman. Ill. Knockers. Pinky nip-nops. Miserable face.'

'Try Salmon's Steady Snake Sneezers.'

'Really?'

'Yes.'

'Good?'

'Oh yes.'

'Hmmm.'

'Sir?'

'Yes?'

'Nurse's uniform and sussies?'

'Yes?'

'Friday next.'

'Good day.'

'Good day.'

Once the pills had been purchased, I sought a carriage towards Bloomsbury where had I heard talk of an impossibly busty Irishwoman. Her toots were the twins of legend and she is rumoured to once have inserted her naple into the behind of a customer. He squeaked and wet his long johns. By then had fallen a monotonous rain.

Alas. I clambered aboard the vehicle, horse plops and cinders in the air and coughed up coins to the conductor. He was a rude ass of a man if I ever, for he refused to prepare my change. I squabbled and raised my voice but I should perchance have refrained, for he was far bigger than me. I called him an oaf – there were females onboard. I could not let them face such abuse. Besides one looked decidedly mucky and had a squint. A quick tickle in exchange for gallantry would surely not be frowned upon in a court of law. As our temperatures did escalate though abysmally did I spot how the elderly lady by my side possessed a gruesome cicatrice. It scaled her cheek in the manner of a pale, very pale worm. It made me feel sick.

I whispered (not easy while travelling at speed): 'Madame, may I enquire – from where did you acquire that revolting scar? You are utterly disfigured.'

'My husband sliced me with his razor cos I wouldn't suc-'(I lost the reason for the ravishing as we drove over a nasty lump, but caught the penultimate few words. They do not add to my tale and really should not be printed. I thumped her in the kidneys under cover of a mean jolt of the wheels).

Meanwhile the issue of my change.

'Listen you brute' addressed I to the conductor.

'This good woman here. Yes the grey-looking one who is struggling to breathe tells me that the last time she rode this vehicle she was subjected to a vile attack by a fishmonger and you allowed events to unfold. Look at her frigging *wound* you snake. Give me my pennies or I will go straight to the omnibus office and demand your license is revoked. Ooh, by the way do you go near to Bloomsbury? You do? Very good, keep the coins and deliver me there or deliver the monies and keep me here. I suppose.'

The day had ripened for the better and the sun worked up not a little heat. My trousers mirrored the emotions of the skies and soon my groin was clamouring for attention. The elderly woman with the dented mug had long gone. Once she had regained her puff, she left in a huff so I was free to snuff out a muff. Is one ever enough?

Indeed my tempers had been ruffled by the ruffian and my soul wanted soothing. So too did my honker for what with the rumblings of the carriage and contemplations of matters to come, he had quite suddenly stood up and was making a scruff of my trouser.

Fearing some such situation would arise, I withdrew a copy of "A Frenchwoman's Bra" artfully stuffed within the London Times and proceeded to study. The trick was excellent on the eye but fearful the protuberance would make a mischief of himself, I next covered the contraption with my hat. Whilst heftier down there than the average urchin, the whole effect was, I add with hindsight, quite unnecessary. It was rather like standing an onion in a circus tent.

To add to the subterfuge, I popped into my mouth a cheroot and proceeded to fumble in my pocket for a Lucifer match, all the while encouraging my little monkey by flicking him on the end as though prodding a cashew nut at a fair.

Heavens! I discovered with unease that I had boobooed with my clothing. I had neglected to select the correct trousers and so needed immediately to tailor them accordingly.

I have two sharp claws on my left hand - primarily for self-defence - and applied them in the manner of a buzzard. I thrust the hand deep into the pocket and with a steady paw hacked rowdily at the material. In a jiffy it was no more. I gasped as I sensed the wind rifle through my pantaloons and in a thrice the worm was basking in my hand. 'Look at the, the, the level of FINANCES in the ooooooh, the aaaaaaarrrrrrrr, the eeeeeeeeeehh, the *stock* markets' I muttered to mask my true antics. 'My God, Lord above, oooh no, God no, a man fell off a boooob, a breast, a beaker, Bruce, Bruce a bbbbbb, a BRIDGE!!! Heavens, please help me, corn prices have ejaculated, errm, escalated to four pennies per pound. 'Aaaaaaaahhhhh. I *love* this newspaper.'

'Ooooooooos been 'fiddlin' on my omnibus?'

It was the conductor. Oohh. I was in for it. He swung down from the strap tied to the back of the vehicle and other passengers peered in from where they sat on the roof. I would not care to sit up there for I have a fear of heights. And Arabians, yet that is a different story.

'Allow me to explain. We were just passing that costermonger's stall when a child, no six children, they were mighty huge, tossed a quart of milk. Did not you witness?'

'No. Stand up. Get up. Ah, it's still happenin'. Oh you filthy man. Alight from my omnibus you bounder.'

And with that he shoved me to the road where I was nearly run over by a dray horse heavy with hops.

I returned to Sally a broken man and a battered one too.

'My dear' I began 'your tablets. A roaring success. Unfortunately I am heavily wounded, for I was travelling by omnibus whence a woman beside me was set upon by a company of rakes, seemingly in liquor and they drew their swords. I struck several in the legs and breast but they proved too great in strength for me, strength of *body* not mind, and they did beat me so.'

'Sir, there is semen on your pantaloons.'

'*Semen*? My dear, they were animals, *animals!*'

March 14, 1856. The morning.
A Railway Trip To Brighton;
How The Happy Couple Make New Friendships

I quite enjoyed life back then. I had monies enough to pursue the necessity of whoring, took pleasure in men and drink and spent some eves per week fooling with Sally's chests. They were exceptional. Also, many days would I pass in bed, stroking, as one would a kitty, my silk topper for such a hat wants much care. The fur must be caressed correctly in order to restore the nap.

Alas though, just when things were tip-top, did all become as shit.

'Sally my dear thing' coughed I as I slobbered away at her furry muffin. Not quite as jolly a hot-pot, but good nonetheless, 'do you enjoy the sea?'

'What, my King, is the sea?'

I coughed out four hairs and bellowed: 'My frigging dear. I assume you are witting. How you tickle me. This is a stunt I take it.'

'Not really. No.'

'I see. I forget at times you are a nincompoop. What you do know, is all because of me, please remember. What happens if I flick the vagina. Will it please you so?'

I flicked. She barked. 'It smarts then?'

'No, it bloody well hurts. Caress it like it was a baby. Do

not flick it like a insect. I 'ave got feelins you know.'

'Yes, of course darling. Sorry. As I was mentioning earlier afore, the sea is awfully lovely. Tomorrow we shall visit.'

There followed a brief explanation. Sorely was I tempted to chin her one for gormlessness but I had as yet not taken my afters.

After pudding, minor punishment was necessary.

'Tonight, my dear' I said, 'you sleep in the kitchen.'

'But ain't it a touch cold?'

'That is not a problem. If you light the range and wear several clothes, you will barely feel a thing. Nighty night my chicken.'

We arose early, for a trip to the coast is a time consuming business for the brightest of fellows. I had a big knockered half-wit in tow.

Five in the morning is a terrible time of day. Few good things occur at such an hour. But five was the time for me to go to Brighton. I removed my pyjamas and replaced them with a shirt and trouser. Nudity no longer becomes me as it once did.

I hastened towards the kitchen with boob-peeping and bacon-eating on my mind. They needs must appear in that exact sequence. Two years ago I developed a fascination for order and precision. Any slight variation on the theme would send me into a tizz. I would take no chances and began to bellow my instructions once I had gained the pantry.

'Sally, you must not be blue. Refrain your teeth from dancing so, the noise is terrible and it cannot be good for the enamel. Wake up dear, wake up. Enough of the common colour, you are hardly a servant. Return to pink damn you, pink I think pink!'

I knelt to grope the creature for it was apparent that brekkers was not ere served and I quite gasped, for the lady was frosty. Her limbs, through seven tea towels, one oven glove, two blankets and a nightdress were horrid to the touch. The entire sensation put me in mind of a dead being.

Sally's eyes appeared to lull about, rather like two yachts in the harbour of her sockets and chase each other back into her skull. Her teeth insisted on some ludicrous jig and her very bones rattled, while all the while she mumbled softly to herself. Almost one hour passed. Many minutes were spent prodding the lady in the rib and vagina until eventually she awoke. She resumed her conventional shades and I encouraged her to apologise for her colours.

Well, what with the boob/bacon extravaganza, the thawing of an arm and the packing of a valise, the raiding of the pantry for foodstuffs suitable for transportation, once a Hackney carriage was located to carry us to London Bridge Railway Terminus, the time was late. I once read that such excursions to the coast had become the nation's chief amusement. Not if the party included a former whore.

The station was pandemonium; steam ballooned all about, whistles shrieked, women squeaked at mischievous men taking advantage of the powdery light to grope an anus. The locomotive stood proud before us; its emerald and vermillion livery, its lively porters, its crimson footplates and oil lamps. Candles were purchased from a bookseller called WH Smith – for then third class travel had no lighting – and we settled down into our carriage. Neither did we have a roof and indeed we were open to the very elements themselves.

It was only proper to make an introduction, for we all were to share the carriage.

'Gentlemen, ladies, uhhm, dog (for there was a little one in a basket). Allow me to introduce my whor, my thing, my father. No, my WIFE!'

And at that, several shocks rang out.

'Heavens' pronounced a man. He looked to be of the cloth. 'Are you truly wed? You look surly and where is your wedding ring?'

My, how rapidly relationships sour.

'Your honour, or should I say Your Vicarness. I love my wife. She suffered from a scurvy and cannot utter well. I am a good man and if it were not for my fear of sinners and vestries, I too would have joined the church. I believe wholeheartedly in communion and organs. Anyway, my beloved has not been in ample health of late. I have decided to bring her to Brighton to take the physic in the sea and besides, we choose not to travel in first class for that is the way of the ruffian.'

A woman or two wept at my sweetness before I fixed the passengers with a nasty stare and glared: 'The ring, Your Vicarness, was vended to fund the tickets. Now if you wouldn't mind, my wife's heart demands a massage' and with that I gave Sally a jolly old booby pat.

Eventually with a jolt that would stun an elephant were we off. Mutters of excitement came forth - Sally included. The train outing was my first for quite some while but I needed to retain my superiority. Indeed just as the locomotive pulled out of the platform, I endeavoured to make a pretence of the whole show by rising to my feet and re-arranging our luggage with an insouciant nonchalance that would not have shamed a chef.

'I say wifey, did we bring mama's parasol? I have heard talk that Brighton can be quite sunny yet *windy* at the same time' I quizzed as a fair old storm blew sullenly from the Thames.

Sadly my interview had fallen on impaired ears.

'Wifey' snoodled I. 'Damn wife' kicked I. 'SALLY!' then followed a boot to the petticoat much to the alarm of our fellow passengers.

'Ouch, my God, sir. Vy is you a kickin' me flanks?' and with more jolts, jerks and thumps, were we out of the station and I was face down in the lap of the vicar. He must have been transporting a toothbrush for there certainly was something slim and stiff in his pocket. Soon he began to rasp: 'Our Father, who art in Heaven, hallowed be they name. Zzzzzzooooooo. Temperance is the parent of sobriety, wealth, prosperity, industry, modesty, providence, humanity, cheerfulness, contentment and domestic happiness. What teeth you have got in your head child, what *dazzling* teeth.'

'Your Vicarness, allow me to explain' was all I could muster as I was brusquely pulled from his groin by a burly fellow behind me. From his ways I feared he was of the working-class.

'Beggin' your pardon sir, but vot is you doin' to ve wicar? I is a-goin' to knock you in ve nose' but before such a threat could be put into action, a second jerk sent me flying backwards, quite squashing the man. He wheezily suggested I remove my bulk.

I fixed him in the eye and warned: 'Sir I know not who you are but I do not relish such language before my wife. As for your friend with the toothbrush, I think you will find tis was *he* whom drew me to his womb.' And with a wide-eyed perplexed shocked disgusted look to his face, he sank back to his chair. I decided to remain seated too for the remainder of the journey.

Indeed it was only when we passed the unenviable terraces of workers' cottages in the village of Battersea that conversation rather *hesitantly*, resumed. We all gazed through the open sides at the plumes of smoke forever rising from the chimneys, smudging the sky an unhealthy grey, past the gypsy horses, then the glinting splendours of the Crystal Palace. I began to shiver for the air was cold and nasty and then came a rain, English and chilled and piercing too and soon we all were soaked to the bone. Perhaps if we all learnt our reasons for visiting the coast, it would alleviate the discomfiture.

The vicar, an Evangelicist, an Anglicist, an atheist or a somnambulist, was to visit the church of St Peter's. He informed me of the exact purpose but I dozed off near Streatham. His neighbour was Magnus Volk. Foreign as the hills he was. He intended to invent a transport as upon which we were travelling but by using something called electricity. He spoke all this in a bizarre accent muffled by a hideous moustache. It put me in mind of a lady's noggin. What a peculiar fellow. Another chap had taken the day off work – he was an accountant in Gray's Inn Road – to visit the Marine Pavilion, the oriental caprice constructed by King George IV. Indeed, said this other chap – he did confer a name, but the locomotive hooted a fart and I was too upset to request a repetition – the King's aunt, Queen Victoria, once remarked of the building: 'A strange odd Chinese looking thing.' Extraordinarily, a harlot once said the same of my willy. I told her the little fellow had become yellow due to ill health. The sex seller secreted away her bush and ks and barked at me to clear the eff off out of her gaff. Bastard. I did a wee-wee in her Bath Cabinet on the way out.

Also aboard was a rough-looking youth of about sixteen. He had a batch of light whiskers, wore a cloth hat and ponged of pies. He only spoke when the ticket inspector found him to be travelling on a half-fare. The inspector, an awful man with feet like antelopes raised both fists and demanded a fine but when the young chap confessed he had not even a shilling, he was duly cuffed around the ear, kneed in the cock-sack and expelled at the next station, Wivelsfield.

'I vere only fuckin' tvelve ven ve journey started' screamed the culprit, no doubt a reminder to the employees of London Brighton and South Coast Railway Company that their locomotives were not quite as punctual as were meant.

Facing us were two young men. They were quite vulgar, for I noted, in the layers of the elder's coat, was a copy of 'The Hot Passions of A Dirty Maidservant.' His chum, a surly looking fellow had teeth the colour of mustard sandwiches and hair like that found on the rear end of a mule. Or a dog in decline. The younger's library boasted 'A Frenchman's Fanny,' 'The Dingles And the Dangles of a She-Dwarf' and 'Into The Bumhole of A Cowboy Snatcher.'

Lucky beast. I hoped that a sudden wind would blow the muck in my direction so with not a thing to do, I listened in to their chatter. They had heard talk of loose women in Brighton. Oooh goody. They wanted, they whispered, a 'quickie on the beach.'

Sally sadly, her ears now in repair, swooned back: 'I'll 'ave both of yers in ve lavy for a farvin' a piece. One in ve muff, uvver in ve harse.'

The two chaps quite sprang to their feet but I soon put an end to their chuff.

'Gentlemen, put away your portmanteaux. My wife is not what she seems. She is suffering from dropsy and speaks in tongues, so if you wouldn't mind, perhaps, go away.'

I turned sullenly to Sally: 'Dear, this is the 1850s, there are no lavies aboard for starters. I for one will be toileting out of the window. You for another will do it in your knickers.'

Thankfully the entire conversation had been conducted in a whisper so not a single passenger had availed of what had just occurred. Likewise I continued: 'Chaps, if you do locate a sand tart, inform me please. We plan to take rooms at the Bellevue Hotel - ample board and lodging at competitive prices - just off Marine Parade.'

Another man was a scientist who was travelling to research the matings of the seagull.

'Probably wiv a cock' guffawed the ruder of the rude men.

'Yes,' said the scientist, a tiny man of limited hairs and horn-rimmed spectacles. His sideburns were white and dazzling. They reached from the ear to the ear, joining hands under the chin like two schoolchildren at luncheon.

'It is quite common in the world of ornithology for the cock to reproduce with the hen.'

And with that he quite blushed, a man of science indeed, and his whiskers shook as he looked at Sally and, shyly coughed and smiled. Then coughed again.

The lady with the canine was a seamstress it seemed and her friend was the wife of a friend. I entertained the dog quickly by tickling it under the chin.

Lastly was a wisp of a man, the colour of pottery and

with as much strength to boot. I quite fancied taking him in an arm-wrestle, so boisterous was I feeling with the coming flux of sea-air. But I did not.

He too had heard talk of the restorative powers of the briny sea atmosphere.

The man though had an unfortunate stammer, a terrible stutter, a silly lisp and was unable also to pronounce the letter 'r'.

'Ssss,ttthhe, sss thththththth Thir. Iiiiiiiii am gg, gg-g-g-g-g going to the sssssssssssssssssssssssss tttththheeeeeeeeeeee for weathonth of hh-h-h-h-h-h-health. For m-m-m-m-m-many yearth now I have th-th-th-th-th-th-th-thuffer, th-th-th-th-th-th-uff, had thum howwwid illnetheth.'

'Pause thir, I mean sir if you will,' halted I, 'for I have of late studied several books of medicine. They are to do with the art of phrenology. I have also studied homeopathy, naturopathy, antipathy, hydroelectrics, centre parks and galvanism. Permit me to fondle your knob' and with that I prepared to make a lunge for the man's skull, but sadly the train clambered into a tunnel. It plunged the carriage into total darkness for the bare window had whooshed out our tallows. Undeterred by the blackness, I felt his gnarled head with a considerable collection of bumps, some of which felt like feathers, and others still like small potatoes and one, a meat casserole.

'Ooh sir, I fear you are melancholic, you are a regular colic and an alcoholic' surmised me as I kneaded the knots of his head. 'Indeed some of these lumps are absolutely *unique*. Never have I came across such a bizarre choice. This one here' and thus I grabbed a greater purchase, 'feels exactly as though it were made from velvet. While this one here is perfectly seven inches in height. My God you should be dead. This one, ahherm, even rotates' squawked me in shock as I spun around the man's protuberance. 'Do you wet the bed? Your head sir, is absolutely *gruesome* and I hope I have not caught bumps from you, you beast.'

I soon realised that my fears of contagion were unfounded for, as we came hurtling from the tunnel into the baffling sunlight of Surrey, I did learn that my hands had been molesting the top hat of the man who had earlier berated me for my vicar bother. He seemed not a little concerned and his cheeks did puff in and out like a Frenchman's accordion.

'Maybe you are unwell sir for your face has become nauseous. I would recommend you lower your fist – ooh and that one there – for any sudden movement could result in a plexy.'

'A jet ski?'

'Sort of. Now DOWN!!'

'Thankyou doctor.'

'Not at all. Now where is the patient?'

In seconds I had off his hat and began a rummage in his flimsy hairs.

'Sir, I assume you have suffered terribly from a pox, awfully from a cataract and have no hot water in your home. I recommend, Brighton-By-The-Sea.'

'N-n-n-n-n-n-n-n-o. I am c-c-c-c-c-c, I am c-c-c-c-consti,c-c-c-constippppppp, I am constippppppp. I can-n-n-n-n-not dooooooo, I cannot dddddooooooo. I cannot go to the toi-toi-toi.

'I cannot dooooooo a toi-toi-toiI I HAVE NOT DONE A PLOPPER FOR THREE WEEKS. I AM GOING TO DIP MY ARSE IN THE SEA!!'

Heavens above! Not a sound could be heard above the rhythmic clack of the wheels, save a gasp from the vicar.

A woman whimpered. Indeed, silence reigned. Then came a breeze, ever so sulphurous with coal smoke.

'What say we take a game of cards?' roused I for I felt it my task to restore decency.

I was moderately successful until Hayward's Heath, wiping out the vicar's funds. I lost a round to the accountant then fell foul to Sally for a penny. Damned bitch, she would pay later. The blocked-up lisper was too ashamed of his bowels to utter and let sleep rescue him from the mishaps of consciousness.

Soon the workers' cottages of Brighton, with their funnelling chimneys became a more regular sight than the farms. Afore long loomed the wrought-iron welcome of Brighton Railway Terminus. Beautiful panels of finely cut glass played colourful games with the steam from our engine and with a final few shudders the great hulking beast of a train came to a stop.

Meanwhile in London, copy clerks in black snake over Southwark Bridge, the postman and his scarlet tunic, dandies in crimson braces and sky-blue-pink gloves, a Manchester scarf and sixteen shilling trousers, bright buttons on the jacket, a rose in the hole and cigar at the mouth, a nosegay clamped to the face, eye-glasses and chin-tufts, round collars and sticks, crinoline ladies and lap dogs, footmen in jerkins, the poor workers in billycock hats, milkmaids and soap boilers, little flower girls, poisoned already by the arsenic put into the pretty green leaves, costerwomen in straw bonnets, pure-collectors trailing the carriages, the wretched men doomed to scour the streets for dog dirt – 8d a bucket from the Bermondsey tanners to take the lime from the hides. Then still come the cattle to Smithfield, hawkers and butchers, country-men and city-men, oxen, bullocks, sheep and horses, flocks of ducks a-bleating, manure making all of them as they waddle to the cowsheds; crossing sweepers and sugar bakers, bread-makers sly and cunning on the way to cheapen their loaves with chalk dust, then The Strand, umbrellas and ledgers and fat horses all, financers come in from Acton Town for a day at the Royal Exchange, then swarm ants of clerks from Putney and Richmond, Chelsea and Chiswick, off the river barges at Old Shades Pier, heaving past the fish women and dock porters and sharpers and thieves, the Jewish old-clothes men, blackguards and bit-fakers until sucked into the money houses of the City and then the noise, the incessant, villainous noise, the maddened beasts, the roofless barouches and cabriolets, all rolling battered iron wheels over ancient flags and broken cobbles, the roar of men and women and simpletons and the call of the street people and the food vendors, the yell of the dust-men shouting 'dust oy-eh' through the narrow streets in their carts, the scream of geese and the abattoir squeals, the crack of flames from a torched warehouse by the river, tomcats and murder most foul. Just another day in the city.

March 14, 1856. The post-meridian.

Having Arrived By Locomotive At Brighton-By-Sea, Events Unfold. Naturally, They Are Quite Unnatural And A Warning To Temper One's Drinking

I thanked my friends for their company, took a calling card from the vicar and bade farewell to the rude men with a telling wink and a jiggle of the foot; language known the world over for: 'Remember the beach bitches. We will be a-kipping on the first floor of the guest house. Pray leave a detailed but encrypted message if we are abroad.'

Parting from the worker was not as sweet.

'You've 'ad all me spendin' money at cards. I am a destitute' wailed he as he struggled to be heard over the screech of gulls. They quite circled us and took mighty pecks at our heads.

'So was my wife and she survived. Good luck and tête de chevre' wished I as he dismounted from the carriage with a bizarre look upon his face.

'Fuck off beaky' I screamed at a gull with my clenched fists raised truly to the skies as it sought to bite to death my hat. 'Fuck off, fuck off, fuck OFF! Ooh sorry Madame, it must be the salt. Yes, you and your friend, have a lovely stay as well. Best of luck with the dog. What? A *child*, a deformed child, a hairy baby daughter? Well I absolutely never. So sorry again. Please I must hurry, for supper is soon.'

The hotel proved less delightful ere thought. Our parlour was musty and tart all at once and sported a tiny bed which fair sagged with age. It looked like a coster's stomach. A mirror, tainted the colour of tea, threw back some grisly shapes and a fractured dressing table sat for us. The ceiling bulged with damp and I immediately sneezed. I have a sensitive chest, to be frank. The carpets owned many awful stains, certain of which were much like cartographic engravings of beasts. Yet from the balcony, most all was made up. For with a crooked neck could a guest make out the Chain Pier beneath which bathers huddled in clusters like insects on the shingles. Fishing boats nodded as ducks on the chop and a pleasure vessel span sweet circles. Wooden bathing-machines were hauled up the sands by tired horses. Open-shirted thugs roamed the pebbles striped in calico while horrid children struck one another with spades.

'Darling, look upon the vista do' offered I.

'Ooh yes sir, it is nice. The man from the train 'as got 'is bumhole in ve water.'

'Darling, I do wish you would not look at mens' bums. It is repellent. You need not call me sir whilst at the coast. Look away please Miss, for I am erect.'

Supper was super. The landlady, a huge woman with hands as preposterous as goats, cooked for us some lamb, a few potatoes and a cabbage. I loved every minute of it yet it made me emotional. Twice. I did not perform at the table for there ate other guests so I made a pretence to visit Mrs McCabe's vegetable garden. I quacked and returned.

'Mrs McCabe, I love your figs. I would so like to eat and lick them after one's meal an-'

Never in my life have I been attacked at a dining table. I refused pudding and took Sally to the town. Arse-cocks.

'Let us frigging visit a public house' I put to Sally.

'Excuse my bastard language but my chest still smarts from that bitch punch. Sorry.'

And so did we soon find ourselves in a lovely little public where I sank with some speed three quick pots of beer, without once visiting the toilet. Thus did I soon find myself in need of a voyage.

'Darling, please excuse me, I must task.' Before long, was I piddling to my heart's content when who should walk in but a rude man. He was not disgusting, nor was he venomous but he was from the locomotive.

'I say' I said, 'you are widdling too. Do you recall me?' and I offered him a hand.

'Sir, germs is often aspread via the piddle paw. I have seen vorse mannered foreigners. I got a good mind to punch you' and he quite readied to cuff me when his eyes did a little dance in his head and he refrained his hand. 'Perhaps ve does know each uvver. Are you my papa?'

'No.'

'My mama?'

'No.'

'My brother?'

My God.

'No.'

'Have we fought or baved?'

'No. Never. I shall give you a hint.'

'Please do' he sighed, 'but allow me good sir to conclude me tinkie.'

'Oh, praise the Lord above, I hope you will. Squeeze, squeeze, please, squeeze, no don't tease, please just squeeze. Ready? You appear dry. I *am*' and I coughed once, 'from the *locomotive*.'

'Locomotive?' questioned the simpleton.

'Yes. We sat together and shared a carriage. I wore a hat while my wife offered to intercourse you. In the lavatoire' I whispered.

'Carriage? Wife? Intercourse? Mmmmmm. Mmmmmmm. Do you sell chitterlings?'

'No.'

'Do you eff children?'

'I do not think so.'

'Have you recently woyaged inside a locomotive?'

'Yes.'

'From London?'

'Yes.'

'To East Anglia?'

'God no. Perhaps to Brighton.'

'Brighton? Never heard of it.'

'Sir, good sir, good *God*, good *sir*. We are currently within the town of Brighton. It is beside the seaside. I do like to be beside it. You are still widdling.'

'Brighton? I love the place. Widdle tiddle piddle fiddle. Of course I am. I know you, you vun me at cards and veedled out of the vinda near Pease Pottage. I have found a superb public house. It is called the King's Arms.'

'Yes, I know. I am in it.'

'You lucky shit.'

'So are you.'

'Yes.'

'Look, please sir. I cannot be too long, for my wife is a-waiting. In fact she is not my wife, but a common whore. But I like her. Not as much as cold venison with capers but I like her. Yet I really hanker after another woman, preferably loose. It is a perennial and possibly eternal problem of mine, how although partly snared in love by one woman I always want another an-never mind. I want too to become drunk. I would love to be as tiddly as a snake.'

'So would I. Have you seen me mate?'

'Yes I have. He sat right next to you upon the locomotive. He has black hairs, a twisted moustache and atrocious footwear.'

'Yes, but vare is he noooo?'

'In the bar.'

We arranged to meet later, but, like most such plans, that was to be my downfall. If I had never seen the man in the toilet, then I would not be where I am now, toileting in front of villains true and proper.

Sally and I supped like chickens, sharing pleasantries in the saloon. I spied the rude men perched at the bar and winked and blinked at them but made certain they did not approach me in front of Sally. An arrangement had been made. While simple to the passerby, its mechanism was extraordinary. At a given signal a black boy would tear into the snug all-a-fluster, beaming with news. A rude man had already booked him for the performance. He found him licking men's cocks under the Chain Pier for cockles yet this assignment was far more wholesome, for the lad ran less risk of illness or violence. I would be billed for use of the African, mind. A white messenger was cheaper but less effective I was told. The given sign was the ringing of the five o'clock bells plus an extra 12 minutes so as not to appear too likely.

The bells pealed and Sally squealed: 'Ooh, I so love ve bells. Vey make me all naughty. Vould you care to bite-a-boob?'

'Boob?' oohed me. Oh I loved them. 'But when?' I stammered, 'now?'

'No, no, no. Not just yet. Let me finish vis porter vich vill take abooot four minutes, ven I must go to ve gentleman's lady's room vich vill be two minutes, ven I must polish each knocker viv "Justin's Kettle Cleaner" – two minutes per boob - and ve can be outside in exactly two. Ooh!'

I performed some necessary calculations. I scrambled in my pocket for parchment and pulled out a card which read: 'Tobias Guppy. Vicar. Weddings, Funerals, Circumcisions, Tragedies and Meals. 147 Montague Road, Croydon, Surrey. Best Bloody Prices South Of The Thames.'

Rather like the whore what I hoped soon to be fondling, I spun it round on its face so its gloriously white behind beamed up at me in unsullied innocence. I used upon it a fountain pen to determine my situation as regards the time. The computations were crude but succinct.

'Four minutes for booze, plus a two-minute dirty, two a-knock-a-polish, plus another two for removal from premises. Heavens shit!' I estimated that at 12, but my mind was warm and I needed confirmation.

'Landlord!' sweated I. 'I need your help. This till of yours, I take it it functions adequately?'

'I say sir. Like a cravat.'

'Hmm. I too am considering becoming a licensed publican. I love the smell of stout, port, nuts and urine, but my mathematical skills are out of form, what, what. Myself and my wife have just postulated a likely scenario, one which I would like to confirm with you. Let us say a customer has ordered FOUR glasses of Reid's Oatmeal Stout, TWO of Dunville's Old Irish Whisky, TWO yards of ale, TWICE and TWO onions, how many things is that?'

'Hhm, let me see, have you any parchment and a feather?'

'Yes I have. I even have a J.Kearney & Co Celebrated Rapid Write Pen. Frig my teeth. Use your machine.'

'Oh yes.'

As he began the task, Sally promenaded to greet us. She curtsied before the landlord and hummed something tricky into his ear.

'Dear' I barked at dear. 'Myself and-?' and how I looked to the landlord for assistance.

'Rupert' he replied.

'Rupert. Myself and *Rupert* are conducting an experiment. Perhaps you could leave us for a moment.'

'Of course,' she obliged and obligingly effed off.

Several moments of intense labour passed until the landlord, Rupert Fiddler, brought to my attention the following: 'Oh sir, your wife asked me whether or not you still call for 'bite-a-boob. I reckon it comes to twelve.'

But before I could breathe, a grubby little black tore into the public house at a startling speed, knocking customers from their stools. He had a curious sheen

'Me say, oo-oo. Where is de man-a-bizzeeeeness from London? I do 'ave in me 'ands' he rumbled in a terribly deep voice, yet one shot through with silk, 'some real important documents for him.'

'Little boy' I yelped far more like a little boy than the little boy. 'I think I am him. I am *real* important' gushed I in tasteful homage to the child.

'You must go and see man bout sometin', me tinks' said the herald.

'One moment please' I beckoned as he made for the door, not forgetting to tip his hat to the rude men, 'are you really a black boy from the jungles?'

'No' peeped the courier.

'I am from Rottingdean. I cover my face with seaweed for added exoticism and I wrap my hairs in hot coals. I now earn three times my normal rate. Goodbye, ta, ya.'

'Oh goodbye to you too' I waved.

'Sally' nerved I.

'I bring wicked information. That boy?'

'Yes, the wogger?'

'Well, sort of. You see, he had run all the way from London. And you know my business concerns with business people?'

'No. You never tell me nuffin'. I am sick of your secrecy. You won't even tell me how many spoons of sugar you eat in your tea.'

'Yes darling' soothed I as I attempted to grope her under the table with mediocre success. 'All that is soon to change I promise. Well that little dark fellow informs me that I needs must meet a man concerning business concerns. It involves lengthy paperwork and tedious litigation. I am bored to death yet and I hate him so. If he so much as squeaks at me, I will not be able to justify my response. Never have you seen such a temper as is boiling in my breeches – ooh, I mean my kidneys and other vital organs. I shan't be long. Darling, take these coins, buy yourself a potato and perhaps some eel, consume the lot, prepare to the hotel where I would ask of you to soap your vagina inside and out and I will see you ere long. You know dear, I do quite like you' and with that I cast a kiss 'pon her brow and shoved her out of the pub.

'Chaps' wheezed I in ferment, 'the female has accepted the fib. What say you as to booze and whores? Whose round is it?'

And so that night did we drink like beasts. We all three micturated from a great height from the end of the pier onto voyagers upon a sea steamer.

We shouted obscenities at red-cheeked bands blowing brass. One man stole Punch, I stole Judy and the second punched the owner in the nose. We wonked off as we gazed at maids denuding in stereoscope visions and we were banned by the famous silhouettist, a Mr A.E.Lloyd, for striking rough positions whilst he immortalised us in black. My profile was regal, that of rude man two stumpy and lumpy. The other's demeanour was perfectly reproduced but the true horror of the pose was not revealed until the conclusion.

'One silhouette sir. Three shillings please if you could' said Mr A.E.Lloyd. 'If you look at the face, I have attempted a true resemblance of your visage. *Regard*' and here he seized the man's chin, 'the *chin* – look at the soft contours that frame it so. See how it is depicted on paper. *Regard*' and here he snatched the man's nose, 'the *nose*. Some may deem it ugly. Hideous would not be too strong a word to express the sadness of the organ, *grotesque* and monstrous too, but I find its squashed fibres, its pugilistic buoyancy a relief from the unflinching aristocratic noses that I am so oft forced to explain. The *eye*lashes,' and here he plucked at the hairs, 'ooh sorry sir. A colleague would term them feminine, my neighbour perhaps would use the word offensive. I would not. I find them utterly *rugged*. The Adam's, if you will excuse me one moment,' and here he lunged for the man's so-called apple, '*Apple* is almost hidden in the lovely contours of your jowls. And if we are to look a little further down, somewhat to the south, so to speak, we will see the ample shoulders of a working man, the magnificence of a barrel chest, the prominence of a waist fuelled no doubt by onions and-'

Poor Mr A.E.Lloyd. He most fainted with perspiration, so upset was he at the unfolding of the event.

'Quite low down, towards the breech, there has been an artistic breech of sorts. At the helm of the trousers there peeps forth something akin to a *parsnip*.

'Perhaps a twig of sorts, fairly deformed, from a tree damaged by frosts. Maybe an oak. But' and here the artiste's voice raised a notch or two above sea-level and he began to bellow rather like a manual worker, 'THIS ENCUMBRANCE IS A *COCK*. *YOUR* COCK. AND IT IS VISIBLE FOR ALL TO SEE. I have had sit for me skivvies, sailors, oilmen, gasmen, flowermen, orphans and even a *French*man. He created a mishap no doubt but that was mere folly. The crossing of the channel was boisterous and there were too many bubbles in the wine. Plus my world-renowned reputation for first-class craft had feared him somewhat.'

Back to the loud stevedore's voice. 'YOUR *COCK* ON THE OTHER HAND IS NOT A MISTAKE IN THE SLIGHTEST. MY REPUTATION IS IN SHATTERS. *EAT IT!!!*' And with that, he encouraged the fiend to dine upon the silhouette.

Alas, the rude man who had begun the havoc had hold of the artist and bellowed: 'If you try again to make me luncheon your work, you'll end up eatin' roast chicken without any teeth' and dropped him to his shaking feet.

'Chicken, roast or fried I do not eat. Indeed, I am a vegetarian' smugged the silhouettist, slashing the work into minute pieces of black and white like so many crows and gulls and let them flutter in the wind. We needed to go inland, for a drink certainly beckoned.

I was told of a pest-house as I slobbered over a landlord's table in a wild fit of drink.

That night we became truly the best of all possible friends yet to this day I have not the slightest idea of their names, if indeed had they any. At times since that evening during which my fate was sealed, oft have I wondered if the two men did even *exist*. Perhaps they were nothing more than the imaginings of a diseased mind. I fear I shall never know the truth, for there exists no record save in my memories. And they, my friend, can be mighty feeble.

In the King's Arms we played a game of darts, but were evicted after throwing them at the bottoms of customers.

Our penii were exposed and one of the rude men attempted to ram a pickled onion through the urinary opening. In medical terms I believe the organ is termed the Jap's Eye. We drank and burped winkles on the beach. We found a woman of dubious drawers and took turns to fondle her teats. A police constable bade us on and then arrested me for outraging public decency when my breeches tumbled to the sand. The misdemeanour was overlooked for a squeeze of the lady's bum by the copper. We ate candy floss spun on a stick and one of my cohorts added seven or eight of hairs to it. They were plucked from his groin and carefully inserted into the sugary snack. Growling, he announced to the vendor: 'Vere is cock hairs in me floss. Give us anuvver vun.'

'Piss off' came the riposte, 'I saw your 'and down your breaches. Daytrippers 'ave done that trick for years.'

Eventually we gathered ourselves into a Hansom Patent Safety Cab and after the driver had whipped his horse into action, we were deposited at a dirty-house.

A lady of sorts greeted us with an enormous boob. It looked like a mottled baby and I fear it squawked. That however, did not deter rude man one from taking a sup to it. The lady was elderly, perhaps five and sixty but her age appeared not detrimental to her naughtiness.

'Boys' she coughed, for she was smoking a clay pipe the while, 'I got just vot ya vont. A lovely gal. She don't stink and she gives great noshin.' If you vont a drinkee, just tug on vis bell' and as she demonstrated how best to pull on the servant's rope, she sniggered: 'Vell, I am sure you gentlemen don't need much practice at yankin' on bells.' *Dirty,* dirty.

But we did as instructed and rang and drank and tugged and pulled. The potboy was indeed a boy with an enormous pot for a belly. The situation worsened when the rude men tied my foot to a rope and yanked for all their might. The potboy giggled when he did see me dangling as a spider from the ceiling, wailing my heart out, the contents of my pockets and my hat too plummeting to the floor like apples in season. I think I did wee-wee myself at which point the potboy shrieked as he learnt he could be next. Fortunately I had tumbled to the floor by the time the Madame had returned.

'Vis avay please' and she tossed us into a great dusty chamber. Lacy cobwebs swooned from the cornices and a stuffed owl eyed us all. I gave him a quick punch when no-one was about and suddenly vomited.

'Madame I am come all poorly and have yakked in me hat. Please help' and with the pace of a woman at least two years her junior the brothel keeper zoomed to my aid. The combination of varied drink and ceiling droops had quite been my undoing. With a duster and a glass of vermouth the whole incident was but a memory.

'I am sorry, so so sorry' I apologised. 'I am not normally taken with quease within a toffer shop.'

'Don't vurry yourself. And sir? Please call me Eliza' she positively purred like a rhinoceros.

'I fear it was the whelks....Madame, do you uhhm know the Chain Pier? It is a fascinating contraption built entirely from chains, and uhhm was named for a fellow called Piers' quoth I as I peered from the corner of my eye while she attempted to unpeel, like an ageing banana, a breast from its holder, slip down her homely drawers and gallop the hand towards my quaking member.

'It is a superb building and people walk all along the, uuuuh, the pier an...Madame. Eliza, you appear to have put my widdling stick into your mouth.'

She nodded once with passion and whilst still suckling the youth, scrawled hastily a note. It read: "*Deer sir. Eye ave admyred yor Coc ever sinse you arrrrrrived and I vont to give im a little kissy wissy. Me opes u duss not mynde. Do ceep stiyl.*"

Je suis arrivé in her mouth, as they say overseas and before I could unclasp the dentures from the pole of my dingler, I was once more thrust into the chamber of whores and told to 'give 'er vun for me mister.'

My heavens, if I live to be four score years and twelve or even ten, I hope never again to see such awfulness. There, atop the bed and the mound of puffy pillows lay a gushing tart full of venom and opium. She lay on her back, spread-eagled, her blotchy legs opened as the hands of a pocket watch. She muttered a mixture of pleasantries, lies and obscenities. One hand scratched an ear, while the other smoothed an antimacassar. On top of her perched a rude man, not a man prone to outbursts nor with the eating habits of a hog but one of my two new friends. He appeared to be writhing merrily aboard the whore, rolling from side to side occasionally as though the pasty trollop was an ocean liner during a rough sea. The man's left hand squeezed the woman's right breast with quite a temper. Indeed it put me in mind of a strongman tensing his fist before a fairground brawl with a gypsy. Mind you, his right hand, which curiously was utterly hairless, described strange shapes in the air.

Sadly, atop him was a child which first I took for a growth.

'Ahem!' coughed I hoping to alert the performers without having to touch. 'Ahem. There is a being on your bum.'

I thought the small person was asleep, for it was nude and wheezing, but just as I leant forward to nudge it from the small of my pal's back I realised that it too, whilst laying face down, was swaying in a likewise motion. I felt so *nauseous* for it appeared that my friend was being bum-bummed by a youngster. 'Sir, your arse is being frigged. Stop it or I will whistle for a constable' I threatened in a timorous tone.

Surely a good man would punch the child to a pulp and

then ask questions but after my incident with the sick, I had weakened greatly. Of a sudden did a voice peep from the shadows, one which I knew so well: 'Come on ven, 'ave a go on me harse if you vonts, like.' The tone was that of the other rude man but where could he be? Surely there was just *one* of the men, a loose bitch and a naked child. Ah. Oh. No. *God* no. Did I not mention that one of the rude men was a perfectly formed midget? No? Well, one of the rude men was a perfectly formed midget and as he turned his neck some one hundred and eighty degrees did I realise with a mounting loathing that the small rude man was bumming the tall rude man while the tall rude man was intercoursing the strumpet. Indeed, the bummer wanted me to be the bummer of the bummer who was bumming the bummee who in fact was effing the main protagonist. I made my feelings known.

'How *could* you? This is *obscene*. I thought we all were friends. This' and here I paused to take in the full extent of the indignity 'is an inhuman travesty. I have seen birds of prey comport themselves with greater decorum – buzzards and hawks even.'

I think one of the gang dropped off during my sermon for I could hear a droning of snores, but upon seeing the minx's paw curl her fingers quite delicately around a candle-holder and stroke its veiny trunk, my mind was quite overcome with emotion.

'You are *gentlemen*. Ahem. You should not have bum contact' but my voice began to quaver as I watched the woman fool with her breasts while searching for God knows what on the candle. Her whore lips fell open and she allowed her tongue to crawl around her swollen mouth. 'You are gentlemen, very gentle, oooh, gentle, I like it gentle' I gushed and due to a sudden burst of sea air and motion sickness I was soon as topless as a bear kneading the girl's chests and begging for a crank. *'Gentlemen, if I become undone'* I implored, 'please refrain from touching. You may not even look. Well, if you must, do so only briefly' and within seconds, my passions were spent left, right and centre and I had fallen into a truly deep and rewarding sleep.

When I awoke the night was dark. My two chums were both 'at it' to use the language of the day and were engaged in something of a dispute. The harlot spoke first, something along the lines of: 'You've jizzed in me peepers and now I can't see. 'Ow the flip am I to go awhorin'?'

'Veren't me – vos 'im' said one man. He was definitely the taller of the two.

'Veren't me – vos 'im' said the other. He was definitely the smaller of the two and so on and so forth. The conversation was tiresome to say the least and I quite fancied a spot of complete sauce.

'Gentleman, your conversation is tiresome to say the least and I quite fancy a spot of complete sauce' I announced.

They agreed, vowing to gather later. As I clambered onboard the lady, rather like a soldier mounting a cross-breed mule, I thought it wise to ask after my friends' schedule.

'I'm goin' for booze' said the manikin.

'I'm goin' to 'ave your vife' said the other.

I thought it wise to humour the man, for he was somewhat in drink and as I gained momentum on the bitch ('Wake, up, wake up!' I screamed) I offered again my hand and shaking said: 'The best of luck. I think you are lovely.'

Oh, how we effed. We essayed several variations and I

encouraged her to whistle. I found the sound quite stimulating and it prompted a minor ejaculé.

'Madame' I sighed, 'I have passions. I concede that it is not dignified to honk in a woman's eye but you should not have flinched for I know my aim.'

'T'ain't me peeper' she spat. (We had earlier restored her sight by soaking the orbit in a warm solution of water and brandy.) 'Tis me wallpaper. You've spoffed all over it and it's probably a-goin' to peel.'

'Ah, yes, I am sorry. If your papers peel free feel free to contact me for reimbursement' and with that I offered her a card.

'You're a fuckin' wicar!' she exclaimed in some fair shock, 'a man of ve cloth? My God. Oops sorry. What nomination are you? Do you believe in eternal reincarnation? Is God all powerful? Does he shape our lives – as in are they predestined – or does mankind have a free choice and is it that which dictates how we are to live and die?'

'Wicar, vicar, eternal re-in, ree-incar? Something? God no. I have never wicared in my life. I am a perpetual bounder whose life benefits no one and whose existence would not in the remotest be pined were I to snuff it tomorrow yet who is only just now beginning to realise the abject futility of everything and that his wayward life very likely brings him no spiritual sustenance and have erroneously handed you the wrong card. I think my splodge has improved the look of your papers somewhat, do you not think? I reckon the stain looks much like a lamb. Can I finish off please Madame?'

Finish I did and not without some style. I was truly excellent at the art of coitus. I have oft considered writing of my technique, but fear a publisher would frown. When lady awoke from her nap, I shook her hand and thanked her for her efforts. I promised to write and send a sewing machine.

I felt a little unsteady on my feet so immediately visited an ale house. There I did drink several porters and made friends with a bathchair man. He had such big muscles I was rather nervous, so I bought him several porters too. I promised to write.

The rest of the evening was, alas, somewhat obscure. I did return to the lodging house though where I climbed into bed with Sally and begged for a kiss.

'Dear' warbled I, akin to a pelican, 'you have come over all hairy. You chin scratches my lips and your vagina is quite firm under your nightdress. It reminds me *bizarrely* of a penis. Are you unwell my calf? Is that the Lord's Prayer?'

I reached for a tinder box, and with a Lucifer match, attempted to scrape a spark. Eventually it came and I took it to the tape, then to the wick of our lamp. The orange glow brought life to the room which swam in strange shadows. In fact the smouldering blush of the flare gave Sally a strange aspect. She had become a man shivering with fear and grasping a Bible to her chest with her knees tucked neath her white-haired chin. I was concerned, so, with inquisitive fingers, lifted the tail of the blanket to reveal two feet and numerous toes. I counted ten. The figure was surely an impostor for Sally had but nine - one had been lost to a horse. I pinched the extra in case it proved a seaside trick and found that the thing was real with matching nail and a farthing of hairs.

'Get the eff out of my bed!' I crooned, 'and get the eff out of my room. By the way, who are you and how did you gain access?'

The person replied.

'This is *my* room, I paid an excellent tariff and the price includes a breakfast. I entered into the room with a key for it is a security measure to keep undesirables at bay. My name is Tobias Guppy and I think we have met yet.'

'Tobias Guppy, Tobias Guppy, Tobias Guppy.'

Yes, yes, yes?' replied Tobias Guppy.

'Hmmm?' I enquired.

'You called my name?' answered Tobias Guppy.

'No, Mr Tobias Guppy, I was not summoning you, merely repeating over and over your name in a bid to jog – I know the word may appear unusual – my memory. Hmmm' and then in a flash came the name; it was one and the same. It was the vicar from the locomotive. Quite what he was doing in my bed, I did not know.

'Mr Tobias Guppy. You are the vicar from the locomotive. For starters allow me confess that I bit your penis in error. This is the Bellevue Hotel - ample board and lodging at competitive prices - just off Marine Parade, is it not?'

'Heavens no. This is the Bellavista Lodging House. Bed and Board provided for capital prices. No perambulators permitted. The address you mentioned though is correct.'

'But surely it cannot be. Perhaps we should settle this out of court. What colour is the building and is this the room at the top of the stairs turn first left?'

'White and yes. Sir, perhaps the error is a simple one' and he furnished me with such a ludicrous scenario that I felt certain his brain was afuzzy.

'Wrong hotel my arse!' I blew at the vicar and grabbed

him from the bed. Sadly his squeaks of distrust and genuine pain had alerted both the landlord of the hotel – a fearsome creature, dressed in nothing but tattoos and a sailor's hat – and a police constable.

I was hauled from the room like a pig in a piggery and weeping thus: 'Please, this is *my* room. This is *my* hotel. The Bellevue Hotel – ample board and lodging at competitive prices – just off Marine Parade.

'That man is an utter impostor. He is a charlatan. He does not believe in God, nor Christianity. In fact it should be him you are hauling from the room like a pig in a piggery for I sighted him practising the black arts of devilry. He has mislaid my wife. The man is a Satanist and needs killing. Kill, kill, kill.'

'Sir' said the police constable and the nude landlord simultaneously, 'this hotel is not as you think. This is the Bellavista Lodging House. Bed and Board provided for capital prices. No perambulators permitted. It neighbours your own lodging house. You were and still are quite clearly pickled and obviously made an error in that you mistook the buildings – one for the other if you will – and joined the vicar in bed.'

'Nonsense. I am highly educated' I spluttered splattering the nude landlord's nethers with a spot of spittle. He covered the groin with his hat revealing a revolting bald pate on top. I looked away for I did not enjoy the view. I continued: 'The man is no good. He sins by day and shits in a cassock.'

The landlord spoke then with some reverence: 'How dare you malign the man. He is a vicar and always has been. He has been attending the Bellavista Lodging House. Bed and Board provided for capital prices. No perambulators permitted, for several years. You, sir, are objectionable and unmentionable. Go next door.'

Feeling deflated I chose defeat. Plus it was by now light.

Sally did not wake me after my return. I slept like a duke until moments before noon.

When I woke up my head pounded as though sat upon by a huge wog and the sun streamed through the window clothed in the curtains' haze. Outside shouted costers and a donkey brayed. My hairs were sticking up, looking rather startled when I peeked in the looking glass. As I began my toilet I opened a conversation with Sally.

'Dear, about last evening. Following a pivotal meeting with the businessman, one Rodney Kidney, I returned with haste. You were so asleep that I felt enforced to join you. But I dared not fiddle for fear of your waking. Instead I hoisted your nightdress a little, garnished a quick gander at your vagina and gave myself *optimum* pleasure. I did it on the floor, so will pay Mrs McCabe for the cleaning. Still you slept as a child and so happy was I that I cried a little. I gazed at you fondly for many hours and then I heard a robbery in the street and rushed outside to see a frail lady surrounded by footpads. They were nothing short of criminal in their language. I punched one of them in the small of the back and he fell immediately to the ground. The other, clearly terrified, fled, and I, naturally, gave chase. I punched the bones out of him. I then returned here but so exhausted was I that I fell asleep in a whorehouse and *that* my darling' and here I swooped like a swan to kiss, 'was *that*. What did you do?'

'Baved and shaved. Bought a pickle, ate it and went to bed. You said whorehouse.'

'*Whore*house, you say I say? I say. I meant *chop*house. Yes, there I did have a plate of *chops* and kidneys. Kidneys, what eh?' chortled I in an attempt to cover my folly.

'*Kidneys*, what eh? You would think I had had enough of kidneys, no? *Rodney* Kidney? The businessman? Plate of kidneys. Rodney Kidney. Plate of kidneys. Rodney Kidney. Plate of kidneys.'

I could have continued the conversation so so, but found it tiresome so suggested a visit to the sea.

'There' I said, 'you can take the waters. I hear it does wonders for a woman's bum and perhaps we may see our friends from the locomotive, but first' and there I employed a theatrical air and in mock horror I clutched my chest and wept, pretending to be negligently undressed: 'Sally, I must dash. You recall Rodney Kidney? During our meeting we both sipped coffee. At one moment, I made a suggestion so devilishly accurate that he did spill his cup upon my shirt, thus making life hard for me. He apologised and the remainder of the discussion proceeded with me bare-chested. Was I not fearful of indecent attack and other such *horrors*? No, heavens *no* for Mr Kidney is not that way inclined. While taking an active interest in my chest hairs, he left well alone. He is a true gent.'

'But you is varing your shirt' pointed out Sally rather correctly.

'Shirt, shit, shirt, shit' stammered I rather incoherently and took a surreptitious peek beneath my jacket. 'Oh *that* shirt. You see Mr Kidney kindly loaned me the part-time use of a substitute shirt. Fortunately, we are both of identical statures. Plus he has immaculate taste and thus both shirts are frigging similar. I will return in a flash.'

Once in the street I boarded a portable chair and demanded I go to the Sea Air Hotel – Families Welcome. Best Rooms In Town – in Bristol Terrace. I needed to make certain my story with my new friends. As I was carried across the roads of neat white houses with the sun in my eye and the tang of salt and donkeys in my nose, the ghostly aura of a pickle played tricks in my brain. Something did not sit correct and I was not happy.

There was a mystery at foot which deepened by the minute, rather like the deep blue water by my side, I thought, rather pleased with the analogy. I put the pickle problem to one side for that could wait. I wanted to hear of the adventures of the rude men and I came across the pair in a breakfast. On the mantelpiece above the grate sat a stuffed robin. Very smug too. I did not like the look he gave me and I fixed him with a menacing glare. Both men appeared in ill health, for they had about them the colour of a Chinaman. Two Chinamans. *Men.* They were a sickly yellow and I feared for them. Great rashers of bacon were untouched, along with barely dented tomatoes, a part sausage and some half-boned kippers. I watched them shuffle around despondently the foodstuffs on the plates, all the while cursing *sotto voce*. I did hear one of the men describe some finances to his companion. It would appear that he had left the lodging house with a purse full of money but had misplaced it during the night.

'Let me see' I overheard him burble, 'I have spent two pounds and half-a-d. I reckons vat vos one pound each for two prossies and half-a-d for a pie, for I found some crumbs in me ear vis mornin'.'

'Or' reckoned the other, 'you could have spent a-quarter-of-a-d on each whore and two pounds on the pie.'

'Morning chaps' I said only to hear a disgruntled, 'Well pull up a fuckin' chair then' in reply. I was disheartened at such a lowly response so attempted to include some relish.

'Last night I went to bed with a vicar, was arrested, and lied about a kidney. And you?' I queried.

'Uhh?'

'Do, you last night too, you?'

'Vell, I vent for a boozy-voozy, got bit by an 'orse and fell in ve sea' said the manikin to the hatred of other breakfasters for he revealed the site of the bite – his sweet, petite seat. I never knew dwarves holidayed without underclothes.

'You sir, how unfolded the night?' asked I of the other.

'I effed your vife. Right dirty troll, eh? Manners like a negro and fanny like a boat. She do give a good blower, like. From ve base of vinky to ve Jap's eye. Superb. Vaiter – salt!!'

I love a good jape yet like to keep a respectful volume on things. I desisted from scolding the fellow for he had indeed some wit about him.

'Oh I say' I joshed, waving an egg in the air, 'effed my *wife*? Jolly good eh. Didn't mind did she?' I ribbed as I quite roared with laughter.

'Put ve egg down, you is a-scarin' me mate' he barked.

'Sorry. But did you really eff me vife? I mean did you really sexualise my wife? It is just that I have already seen her and she said she bathed, shaved and ate a pickle. She is awfully truthful so perhaps you have been mistook?'

'Mistook? No. I vent to your gaff. The Bellev-'

'Yes, I know only too well the name and address' I interrupted with the temper of a boatman.

'Sorry' he continued, not very contritely. 'I found her washing her muff. I asked if she minded me votchin'. She said no, no, no, no, no and asked if I vould care to sit on her hedge. Vy not? Ve effed for vun hour and tventy five minutes. Ve did it seven times and she said she much preferred a vinky viv a good bit of girth. I don't know vot is a girth but I shook 'er 'and then gave 'er a pickle. Vat vos vat.'

Looking down at my nails, still dirty from the night before, I remained certain that the rude man was untruthful still, but there came an unnerving unease.

'Eff her you say you did eh?'

'Eh?'

'Eff. My wife. Eff. You.'

'Not again ta mate, I ain't 'ad me brekkers yet. Besides she fair vore me out last night vot viv 'er ryvin' and a-buckin' ven ve vos a–. '

We three were ushered to the dayroom where a woman with a long neck sat at the piano. Thus we resumed the conversation in rather hushed tones: 'All right, you say you made love with my wife. I have reason to disbelieve you. Firstly she is as loyal as a dog, secondly *girth*, as you phrased the word, is a term hopelessly unknown to such a woman and thirdly there is a problem with pickles. I cannot for the life of me recall the exact consequences but it will return in due course. Plus, she has a birthmark about her being. Perhaps you would be so kind to furnish me with such a description, a location, location, location and' I paused for added dramatis and playing the chord of G-minor upon the keys (sorry Madame, I saw not your fingers) ventured, "girth."

'I vos a little bit tiddly by ven, but let me have a finky.' He meandered around the room, mumbling riddles and examining the stuffed hummingbird atop the mantelpiece. I think I spotted him rubbing its speckled belly as he murmured further under his breath. The miniature man had fallen asleep beneath the piano and indeed his snorings could instantly be mistaken for the rumblings of bass notes. I occupied my time gazing at a bowl of waxed fruits and a false blancmange.

'On her arse!' screamed the man. 'Just east of ve bum'ole' he yelped. The female pianist missed a note and dropped an octave. 'I remember like it vos yesterday. She, your wife, did 'ave a enormous mark in ve shape of a chicken. Or vere it a 'orse?'

Praise the Lord Almighty, the man had a point! For in fact she did have the impression of a fowl rather near the entrance and exit to the bum. Yet perhaps there was a hole in the man's story so to speak, for the fowl in question was no chicken nor a horse, but a grouse.

'Eff my arse' I bellowed albeit quite loudly, 'Sally hates pickles. They bring her out in a rash and make her arms go all pimply. Like a turtle.'

Turning to the man in question I raised an eyebrow: 'Pickle? She did eat of it? Why?'

'I found it in me pocket and give it 'er. She ate it in vun fair go and made a noise.'

'My God,' returned I, rather concerned, 'I must depart.'

Yet unfortunately, ere I could abscond, the piano player upped and left too: 'I am so disgusted at your language. Never have I been so sickened in all my life. I intend to sample that blancmange and retire to my room where I will join my husband, a famous strongman.'

But as she approached the sham cake, I became

consumed with gallantry and indeed needed to make amends for the foulness of the morning. I rushed to the table which hosted the bogus bakeries and striking frantically a flame upon a tinder box, sought to set light to the confection, screaming all the while: 'Madame it is wax, it is *wax*. Eat not of it, it is wax and will damage teeth and intestines.'

A minor squabble ensued but ere long, I had gathered a flame and brought it down in one. 'Regard' I yelled at the ashen-faced lady, 'how the cake will burn' but before the wick could take, a great shade of blue sent sugary sparks about. Single cream whisked and an egg-white popped but the death throes of the dish were drowned out by the keening of the female.

'How could you?' she hollered, prompting my hat to the floor. 'Three days have I toiled to prepare that cake. I was to be a finalist in this evening's South Coast Cake and Pudding Bonanza. There exists nothing in my life but cakes. My daughter, lost to consumption, my son, dead on the battlefield, my husband, too brutal for words. Bridge I cannot like nor for it is dull as cobblers. I hate you' she yelped before yelping louder still for hubby.

In short, I vacated that hotel a much different man. I was battered for several minutes. The husband accused me of sabotaging the pudding to gain first prize and truly did he live up to his name. He even picked up the manikin man who had awoken to pronounce: 'I just looked up vat voman's knick-knocks.' He ended up head first in an aspidistra pot. I vowed to spend the next two weeks eating softer foods and using cushions when available.

I returned to my hotel as near a ruined man as could be via a pickle-seller where it took much time to make my request understood for he was hard of hearing and not a little slow, but eventually did I leave the premises with a pickle. And a tickle, a sickle, a cockle and a nickel.

I found Sally with a most dreamy look upon her face.

I coughed to rouse the woman and explained my bruises thus: 'It was windy. I was blown off my tootsies' and then cocking my head to one side to add an air of scrutiny, clucked: 'Darling, have you kissed a man?'

To her credit, she replied truthfully, at first saying: 'Yes sir. In 1842 vere vos a man wiv small teeth, in October, anuvver man wiv big teeth and difficulty breaving; pon Christmas Day I had anal intercourse wiv seven men in a tavern. On January 1 184-.'

'All right, all right, all right' I bawled, 'all *right*. I get the picture.'

Re-cocking my head to its natural posture I proffered forth a snack. 'Do have a pickle' I said, smiling like a child.

Sally looked at me, eyes searching the room like a lion at lunchtime, full of wariness, cunning and adultery, only to answer: 'No bloody way. 'Ate vem. Make me bum look like a turtle shell.'

'I know you "ate" them"' I said, twisting her poor English into an altogether more sinister sense. 'Yes you did "ate" one. Last night. With a rude man. We met him on the locomotive, I have never seen him before, since, after or during and you sexed him *here*!' and I thumped the linen to hammer home my point, '*here* in our marital bed. I had been gone *minutes* to lay down the finances for our future and then I went to a whorehouse, no' I bit myself twice and bleeding continued, 'CHOP, CHOP, CHOPHOUSE. And all the while you were cavorting with a rude man, a nude rude man, a rude nude lewd man. How could you? You let him see your, *our* grouse.' I began to weep and what I said thereafter was pretty much incomprehensible.

'Stop veepin'' said Sally. When in spirits high or low, Sally would often return to the lowly vernacular from whence I had dragged her. I once found it endearing. 'I know full vell vere you vas last night. Vat man come into our room and tries to kiss me, tries to wiolate me wiv a seashell, tries to seduce me wiv a cuttlefish and I tells him no, no, no. I says to 'im how much I loves you' and she too began to cry.

'Don't weep' I ordered. Note how I maintained the correct pronunciation of the verb despite the high emotion. I stroked her head and harried towards her furry dandelion but Sally forbade me. Whether she was right or wrong is a question only the Almighty may answer, but still she blubbered: 'I told him I loved you.'

'We have already covered that ground' I interceded, curt admittedly, but also quite desperately for I so required the lavatory.

'I told him vat I had changed me vays and vile I once vos a loose old strumpet I vos now a vun man voman and shoved his grubby hands off of me. "Go an play wiv your own cock" I tells him. Ven just afore he takes 'is leave 'ee asks if I knew vere you vos. I tells 'im: "Course I do. 'Ee's wiv a man, discussin' businessessess.'

'Ven he turns to me viv a most 'orrid look on 'is chops, almost like 'ee vos the devil 'isself and smiles and says: "I spose vis businessman is about one and twenty, 'as got long, curly, black 'air, dumplings like a copper's hat and talks about business naked ven?'

"'I don't know vot you're talkin' about" I says to him and tries to shove 'im out ve door but 'ee wouldn't and ven says: "Your 'usband, and he ain't your 'usband eever cos 'ee telled us you're just a tart, is wiv' anuvver 'oar.'

"'Course he ain't' says I, 'he loves me and would never go near anovver woman."

'And ven 'ee just laughed, a real evil laugh and he told me just vot you vos doin' and here poor Sally looked away in disgust and wiping a tear with the laced hem of her shawl went on: 'And vere you vere, ve man I vonted more van anyfink to call me 'usband, lyin' on top of a cheap 'oare, slappin' 'is own arse to make it go faster. Yes I *did* go to bed wiv vat man after he told me vere you vos. 'Ee were 'orrid and I never vont to see anyvune as disgustin' as vat ever again. 'Ee were laughin' and sayin' 'orrid nasty fings to me and vat 'ee vood never give me a penny even if I vos ve last prossie in ve country. But more van 'im, I 'ate *you* and I never vont to see you again.'

I am not at my best when under great pressures. For as Sally lay wretched on the bed I pulled forth from the pocket in my moleskin waistcoat three items. I rammed the pickle into her mouth and stuffed a pair of cockles up her bum, squeaking from the doorframe: 'Let's hope the grouse is fucking hungry.'

I slammed shut the door and spent the rest of the day in intoxication.

And so, as our hero battles with the hurt and the hatred and guilt and fights to drown them still with yet more stout and gin as he veers towards the lowliest of the town's low-houses, as he toys with the ropes that keep his sanity in check, as he smothers the question of his conscience under the murky ripples of drink, another someone lies in her rooms in Piccadilly, lies weeping on her bed, crying and cursing for the loss of life and the loss of love and so she wanders the streets in a haze of pity and doom, touched by men and women alike; sniffling on the crimson sleeves of troops under Waterloo Bridge, as low and dejected as the rats that trail the mudded lace of her dress, yet impervious to all, her clinches as much rape as commerce and she wanders too the city streets at the bad end of town when the roads are lit by the hiss of gas and the eternal trust of life that sees through so many unharmed, that same trust that will send men to their death and she lies at day or at night, her hair shorn and bloodied to the skull, anything to get loose that mind, crying herself to sleep, her heart wanting the eternal sleep of the doomed in the black arms of the River Thames.

March 16, 1856

The Return To London And The Hunt For Sally. Revenge And Love Battles In His Mind. And Comes Out Of His Ears

I returned to London two days later, my mind livid with Sally. How could she have betrayed me so? Exchange me for another man? Adulterate the moment I was out of sight? The duplicity of the worm. I vowed violence as the locomotive pulled back into London Bridge Terminus. My luggage was light so I shunted aside porters and hurried towards St James's to avail myself of mindless intercourse for I daren't face the reality of what I had become. Some monies remained me and I sought to locate a woman as much like Sally as possible and eventually one was found outside a coffee shop in the Burlington Arcade. I was ever so angry.

'Are you good-natured dear?' sang the child.

'*Good-natured* you ask? God no, I am taken by the darkest spirits known. You are loose, I take it, so what say we cut the chit-chat and I eff your arse?' I screamed. She was a true copy of Sally in all but teeth, for this little minx had but one. It was a curious fellow, sat all alone in the bottom of the mouth, rather like a traveller in a waiting room who had dropped off to sleep and missed his wagon. It appeared lonely so I shoved it out with the tip of her parasol. 'Bitch, I will pay extra for the fang, so if you don't mind, drawers off.'

The sobbing did little to quash my desires, indeed, and if

this makes me a bad man, then so be it; some of her weepings did even encourage my pantaloons.

In her living quarters – a dusty room with an old dresser and a cracked glass, off Soho Square with the squeal of chickens hard by – I threw up her dress and down her crinolines, stiff with horsehair were they so. Then I tugged off her bloomers to take the animal from the rear. But I fear I left the girl maybe bruised and maladjusted, for while I rocked back and forth, thrusting in and out, in and out, in and out, I began to strike a tattoo on her bottom. Such drumming soon developed in tempo and strength and ere long I was plain punching each buttock and most cursing: 'Sally, ooh!', 'How dare you, ooh!', 'This will teach you to be taken to the seaside by me and then run off with a nasty man and do it in our bed and you made it worse because I paid for that bastard room and supper and a few glasses of stout in the public house, ooh!' That last left me quite breathless. Then I began again the procedure until the lass turned her teary face to me and implored: 'Please no more sir, I 'ave 'ad enough. No more, please I beg of you sir.'

But such begging fell on deaf ears and the beating subsided only when my dreadfulness waned. But wane it did and along with my pecker I left the premises far from jolly.

And so it was that I did begin to terrorise the fallen women of London, those with red hairs especially, until I lay one night sobbing atop my bed, the hoot of owls and the clatter of night buckets my only friends. I began to long for Sally as though seeing her again could restore all to the wonders of lore. Well I knew that she was a simpleton and came of a seedy past but as oft have I said I thought, *really*, I had grown to love her. Also I recalled that indeed I was engaged in another woman's vagina during her indiscretion so there was a chance not all the blame were hers. Perhaps all was not lost.

So I did, that night, be it three or four in the morning, set out to her quarters.

April 9, 1856

The streets of London are nefarious at such a time and more so even when the man about them is sober. Mean footpads, tall hats pulled down to the eyes, stare at their prey, willing them to make the first move, like beasts on the prowl. Flickering gas-light throws fearful shadows on the piss-soaked stones. Flashes of blades and the clink of canes sound in the alleys. Open sewers run deep as rats as do the curses of the possessed, yet there does he arrive at Sally's lodgings and looks out for her candle-light. None is forthcoming, so he sits against the stoop, awaiting life for the hour is too early for business of any other sort than the flesh. As the day grows, cart-horses rattle slowly to life and the sinking moon slinks behind the chimneys, the trees like grim reapers in the moody light of dawn. Soon though, doors begin to open and from nearby comes the weary step of servants, brushing the sleep from themselves, as they venture out for the first tasks of the day. Bread is to be had, pots emptied, the butcher boys calling for the breakfast orders, later returning with a tray of meat for the day's menu, the coalman dropping his black wares through the iron holes in the pavement. The night's last drunks stagger too, passing the first drunks of the new day. I knocked on the door and was made to stand whilst an ugly face, pock-marked and pitted like a stone, eyed me with some fair suspicion only to tell: 'Mister, she hain't 'ere' and to slam the door in my face. I came back with a tremendous kick which sent the door knocker a-rattling. I followed with bad language that had several neighbours peering from garrets. I said something like this: 'You bleeding pock-marked bitch face, I'll frig your arse, you hairy woman. Look at my cock. And you!' I finished to a butcher perched in the doorway to his meat shop.

I returned the next day and the next and was met with terms ever more vulgar. They did little for my self-worth nor my tummy. I bought a can of condensed milk and some tinned mackerel and threw them at the bitch's lodging.

Ooooh. Oooh. Eeeeeh. How I howled the nights away.

Mornings became nights and nights became mornings as I was removed often with brute force from gin palaces, resplendent and loud with gas lights, stucco rosettes and gilt burners, brilliant glares and bottles. Oft times was I punched by the potboy when my natty snuffer was caught upon the mahogany. There I spent my times with Irish labourers and drunken railway builders. We all drank to forget, to drown the true nature of our souls in the meaninglessness of the bottle.

When sober I visited a stationary shop in Regent Street from where I ordered some Crystal Ivory visiting cards. My struggles were taking me only to hell. They read: "*I am looking for my wife. She is two and twenty or thereabouts, has lovely red hairs, two first-rate teats and a bearskin vagina. Please beg of her to visit to my lodgings and perhaps ask her to bring some victuals. Regards. Salmon always goes down a treat.*"

The second card was used primarily in the evening times and was more often found by constables and carriage-men. It was worded thus: "*I am not drunk, merely lively for I have a dreadful reaction to prawns. Please take me home and withdraw a farthing from my purse. Thank you and good night.*"

And so he goes back to look, those same streets where they met but he knows within that all will be doomed.

For weeks he hunts the Haymarket and Piccadilly, Covent Garden and the Strand, a haunted man, ravenous to claim back his love.

As the days grow longer and the nights hotter still, his forays into this strange new world become more frantic still. He becomes a man possessed.

'Tell me, have you seen Sally?' he cries, tearful and half-crazed.

'She has burgundy hair. You must help me, help me please' he shrieks, alone or in company, he often knows not which.

'Please help' he screams. 'Please help' he cries to the streets and the drunks. Time is lost. He sobs and shakes, unfed then bloated with bile for he hates her, dreams of tearing her to shreds, her clothes, her hair, her soul as she has his. Yet still he loves her, wants her back in his arms, because perhaps love really makes his soul.

Many times he walks close by the Thames, the sludgy snake of death that flows a miasma dredge through the city, along the mossy wharves and piers, past broken-down sail-makers and dingy pubs, rat-running streets wet with blood, painted dollies with pencilled brows, cut-throats and sailors, Lascars and Chinamen, Mulattos and Bengalees in turbans, for the alleys of Shadwell are no longer England, the language the broken tongue of Europe, the rash bite from the Orient, along the river and into another London, the London *of the doomed, baking beneath an unforgiving sun, the smoky refuge of Lethe, the shivering forgetfulness of the Chinaman's pipe in the opium den, gone to join the shrunken ghosts fallen on a fancy for the smoking-house, gone to slink with the pig-tailed Chinaman, a four penny smoke, heavy-lidded and retching, because only in sleep does he no longer mourn, only in the warm dreamless sleep can he live, weeping for Peking, sleep, sleep, sleep.*

This is where the handsome Malay becomes the broken man with the broken face, the empty body lost of soul; this is where the miserable come to suck on the devil's pipe for a respite from life; the abandoned Goans drinking Arrack in the Royal Sovereign, the Shanghai shippers off the tea clippers, this is where people come to have the very life plucked from their hearts; the final ship that is sailing nowhere, the passage the hardest one in the world.

He steels himself for hopeless searches with gin and wine and any liquor he may find at the break of dawn, pitiful, stumbling with torn clothes, a cursing drunk, stuttering his prayer. Naked children laugh as he steps, a phantom on his arm, a ghost in his soul. His downfall is set. Desperate hopes are buoyed by the goodly girls and the not so good. For by now, they share the same paths, longing for salvation on every corner. He is strung along with lies, truths and all else in between. He knows not now, but the girls see through those tears.

'Come with me, for I swears she'll be in my room. Was only yesterday what I sees her and she says to me, if I finds you to bring you back with.' Feeble oaths lead him across the city where further he parts with more coins, more dignity and heartache. And sometimes little bits of jozz.

July 1856
The Ways Of A Working Girl

Some digs were glamorous, paid by wealthy visitors to keep the madames in comfort. Such rooms were bright and cheery, green with plants and the heady scent of passion, golden mirrors and velvet curtains, deep as the sea. The harlots had maids and dressers too; Assam tea and coffee from the Americas. Other women joined us from time to time, and I would sit and watch as the ashen beauties happily pawed each other and slid their bodices, down, all the way down.

I was bid take part and they gave me the softest of jewelled hands to bring me forth. At times the pleasure was greater than eating many biscuits, yet still I moaned for the loss of Sally and prayed through a mouth of flesh to procure her soon for me. They soothed me with doting fingers and shushes that she would soon be with me and again we could lie together.

But other places were right old hovels; cheap motts in Shadwell with pendant bosoms and fanny hairs to their knees. Cock-chafers, bobtails, troopers and bunters. Others drunker than I. Many were saggy, with teats like an old dog's jowls and oftentimes was I party to the darker workings of the mind. Women tied me up and spanked me with objects, angered at my acceptance for my mind was otherwise occupied. One lady with a large mole akin to a coal on her chin begged me to slice her posterior. She reared it towards me, like a chicken drumstick and with a dainty wiggle, beckoned me forth with a knife. I obliged and cut the wench. One girl, ever so Jewish with a heavy nose performed her toilet for me. I found the affair drawn out and distressing. She crouched upon a pot, opened her legs and sprinkled. She charged more than I expected for I took no pleasure from the spectacle. I was offered dwarves, blacks, boys, a pumpkin and a blind man. From the corner of one eye did I spot a goat.

My mind sank lower, lucidity coming yet less and less and in one moment of clear compassion I dragged an urchin to her feet and gave the hairy mot a halfpenny.

'Dear, treat yourself for the streets of London are cold at night. Pieces of eel and a cup of liquor are as good as a great-coat. Night night my sweet rhubarb.' Yet I was back in ten to give her a hiding and to take to the bottle.

After a three day stint on booze I had it off with an addict, her eyes heavy with laudanum and the pipe.

One frow, mostly naughty and partly hairy preferred me to take a stick to her dumplings and would not have me leave till blood winked from her titties. Another demanded I spend a penny in her eye while her sister beseeched me to crumpet her botty, if you excuse my language.

So whether a Covent Garden tenement or an East End pit, the story is the same. Squalid rooms, airless and foul. Cologne masked not the misery, the smell of opium and cheap gin. The beds are frequently filthy, crawling in lice, lapping at their juices. Yet howls from elsewhere in these anguished quarters do not hinder the ladies' hammed writhing.

Dust sleeps on the mirrors where cracks run like whiskers and when he glimpses his fate in those murky glasses, he flies from the room, back to the streets for more, the reality of what he has become too much for the frail state of his mind, too much to consider, too hurtful and sad by far and the deeper he falls, the more does he become repulsed by his very being, the unconscious mind a constant desire.

He puts away all thoughts of Sally, veils them in the recess of a battered mind, makes believe all is well. Yet still does he want to know all shall be good upon her return, though slowly madness is calling, then he shall come back to his life as once it was. But before long he will find himself back in Haymarket, a familiar figure of the night, rain or sun begging the same sad mutter, a damsel's hand entwined, a beat in his heart and a step in his pace. Tonight, this will be the one, for they share the same hopes.

August 1856
The True Goings On Of A City At Night

My times in the dock at Bow Street did me no good; criminal damage, harassment, drunk and disorderly, resisting arrest; violations of my own humanity all. My previous good nature was soiled and I was arrested for plopping in a urinal. The invention was awkward and I was not to know.

My finances were drooping, unlike my randy doodle which still caused mischief and I could no longer trust my actions when in drink. As each attempt to recover my love took me further from my goal, I convinced myself that should be the last. Yet no sooner had I sworn the claim than I would be drunk on cheap gin, flailing the streets, naked in some pest house, lying with an Oriental, yellow and stupid on opium fumes.

Oftentimes was I taken to some finish house in a Blackfriars gin-palace under the roaring viaducts, or a tavern in Seven Dials.

Those haunts were peopled by ladies of terrible class, keen to snare a theatre-goer at the close of curtain, all nasty teeth and full of the pox. I rarely watched a play, but there were no rules for the lonely.

Saucy sluts paraded their wares as the magicians' glare of a hundred gas lamps flung dreams on the walls, as the

Parliament men from Westminster slipped out of their waistcoats and then out popped their nifty rascals.

The generous man pays well for the service yet he does not always know the price, for nimble hands are nimble hands, and it is a short journey from the front of a breech to the back of the pantaloon where the portmanteau chuckles its golden laugh.

Many dolly mongers make pretend they swallow the wine too, but most remain alert. Some though flood their gullets for what a pastime it is to see a lady plied with drink until she can no longer differ between the sofa and the floor. Soon the poor dear is dead drunk and her snoring creaks in song with her rasping neighbours. The rise and fall of her bosom climbs and sinks in the true sleep of the drunk.

Those still astir will eventually drop their drawers by dawn and find some copulation until, as the sun comes up, servants and cabmen rally around to gather their masters. The wrong trousers fasten, the wrong shirts are buttoned, a hat on another man's head and a beery wave until the next time. Those without staff are put to bed in the cellar until they head home in shame for such are the ways of lust.

3 September 1856
Time To Leave London Behind;
Perhaps Some Fresh Air Sir?

So, as summer flapped its coquettish derriere like a nipsy with the droop, flying south and leaving us in mists, I set to leave the city. I was lost. I had nowhere to go. I had brought disgrace upon my father's name and my own and my dining companions had turned their backs on me.

My hands had been crafted as nippy knife and forkers and dainty little muff-friggers. Never were they intended for the rails of courtroom docks.

But where was I to go? I was born in that cursed town, schooled and suckled there and London was all that I knew. It was my home. My mind though, was not straight. I knew not what to do and so, one morning as the sun hauled itself before the chimneys and stenches that sat above us all, I simply put one foot in front of the other and walked. And walked. And walked and walked and walked and walked and walked.

I marched at first, relishing the uncertainty, the adventure of the unknown. I sauntered between the carriages and Broughams that fouled the streets; I rambled and ambled. There was Strand and its hectic chaos, one crowd of people scurrying to earn a living, another fleecing them of that very same. Broadside sellers cried hoarse over last night's murder.

Young boys, too young really for depravity, cried: 'Man slashed to pieces wiv a sword. 'Ad out his 'eart.' Perhaps not too young after all, for the world grows speedy today. And one wore a bra. How rum.

I left them behind with the costermongers and the potato men, the dog meat criers and muck finders, stopping to buy myself a little something from a flower girl. Not much, but a fresh bud to lighten my step.

I was headed west, it seemed, my eyes bleary with questions and tears, and I took in the river for who knew when I next would be alongside Old Father Thames who had ebbed and flowed with my years since my first sight of the world? Perhaps he held answers for me. Perhaps not.

I cast a look from the Hungerford Steps. The tide had long gone, leaving the slimy banks silver in the sun with a bit of a pong. I espied several bodies delving into the mud, prodding the ground for who knows what booty lay sunk in the mire of life's stream?

Each nugget, whether a penny or a prince's jewel, gave them more than I could ever have had, I who had craved for nothing in his life, who thought that his empty soul proved a blessing not a needing. Yet for these boys did that penny bring a full belly for the night, another layer for when the sun did not appear, a respite from the bully boys who crouch under the bridge.

I looked at Parliament, then Millbank, passing Vauxhall and the dens that lay that way, the sun sudden in the sky, a child's pink gone to orange then yellow. Soon came the stuccoed grandeur of Belgravia where the fortunate lived and where I once knew another life. I saw the Royal Hospital in Chelsea and the happy pensioners living out their last in grace; Kings Road and the wandering artists, Cheyne Walk's mansions. I savoured the grand streets of Brompton, the nice maids of Kensington for one last time, peering through the windows, stopping at pubs and swiping drinks. The Anglesea Arms, past a grocery shop in Knightsbridge run by Charles Harrod; next the market gardens of South Kensington where labourers were hard at work building the museums of Albertopolis, Prince Albert's vision to educate the public with dinosaur bones; then the way soon more peaceful at Hammersmith and its pretty riverbank houses. Shepherds Bush and its green, through the suburban streets of Acton and on and on, westward and beyond until London was just a bad dream, Sally just a name.

Soon I was traipsing the country lanes of Constable, stooping to sniff the flowers; honeysuckle, sweet peas, kingfisher daisies and their sky blue whorls. Village houses of Chiswick were draped all in quiet lilac wisteria. Spanish broom flaunted its yellows as I walked. Oooh it was saucy. Cotton lavender, cherry bushes, the perfect circles of passion flowers and their orange fruits, the verdant spikes of summer sweets and the mingling of their perfumes fluttered all about as I walked past hay barns and coach houses.

The sun was waning, its strength sapped by the length of the day, tossing shadows over the fields, pricking the flies with evening kisses. Still I walked, Ealing, Osterley, Southall and beyond, my legs weak, my stomach roaring, my throat scratched and dry.

On and on I toddled, my head light and fluffy, a chunk of

bread and some pickles pinched from a saloon snug was all for I had not a penny. I was headed straight into the angry red sun. I sat by the side of the lane, the village of Heathrow an hour back, the next I knew not where. Not a soul had passed since, nor had I heard a sound save for the creatures of the countryside. Flies and bees buzzed, crickets cracked and over the fields came the woof of a dog. My legs wobbled and down I went.

I did not wake until after sunrise, the morning next whence I continued in my journey, pausing to examine some berries that grew beside the path and dampen my mouth with a puddle.

And so I lived and walked, my body wracked with hunger, my mind consumed with the desire to live, the need to eat, the vacant whole in my heart subdued for once. My existence was crude and I lived as a vagabond, a distraction from life, a need more pressing than the inner voice that longed to be heard.

I traipsed the lanes and hedgerows of southern England, bloodied by nettles and thorns. I became, in short, a vagrant, tramping the countryside often in tears, howling and thrashing at myself. How could my life turn so? A man of privilege and looks, never have I felt a pang of want. But that benefited my self-pity more than can be imagined. Hunger. It was what I needed. And a jolly good effing.

I trudged through village after village, Henley, Maidenhead, Reading, leaving behind me oast houses and labourers sunburnt in nice soft hats. I supped on the left-overs of summer. Some nights I slept where I fell, a stage for any beetle that took a fancy to me. They tickled me to sleep and I would stir at sunrise soaked in dew. If the day was good and the sun at play, then he would warm my clothes. If not, then my shivers proved another diversion to counter my loss. Eventually would I thaw when pinching farmer's eggs. And farms proved an awfully good bed for a nest of straw was a treat. As the horrors of this new life slowly lost their terror, I began to make do with the unimaginable. A night of horse dung proves a fine blanket. The warmth, if freshly made, is a joy, despite the flies that lodged therein. My beard grew and so did my strength in deprivation. At times was I sated with grapes and apples, yet more often than not, hunger proved a formidable tormentor. I would poke at devil-coloured elder berries, I looked for sloes and damsons and sucked the juicy life from wild cherries. I searched the ground for lunch and a more bounteous paradise I could not have begged. Yet only once did I misjudge my pickings and chomp a nefarious treat. A bitter blow it dealt my buds but as the juices rained upon my tongue, they tricked me into sleep. I awoke awful with cramps.

Cranberries were a favourite as were pears and wild strawberries too. When I spotted their colours through the shrubbery I would make a dive for them, stuffing my mouth and pockets until the branches were soon laid bare. Other times I nibbled on blades of grass, a chewy morsel. It was tasteless too. Naturally my diet led to abominations in my toilet. At first I sought some lea, secluded spots behind large bushes far from the eye of wayfarers. But as those needs became more pressing, stricken with not a moment's notice, I would lower my breeches wherever I must. I fear I must have startled many creatures with some hideous blasts. Which end caused the most grief I can only but suppose, for my eating arrangements often left me with the most tremendous pain.

I fear I cut a frightful figure, crouched upon some field shaking with spasms.

After such agonies my garments would be left speckled with blood and I feared the next soreness but as each day wove by and such a visit had not been summonsed my dread worsened. Constipation proved the curse of the cursed.

Unburdened by civility and driven by famine, I sought nature's creatures to feed my stomach. The days shortened; the sun traipsed his wearied face ever lower in the sky. The lush greens that once buoyed my walks, faded day by day into tired browns and deadened greys and what few berries that stayed were ugly and wizened. The fruit had long since gone and before the first frosts did I come across some wood pigeon, not long dead, in the grass. Hazy with peckishness, I stuffed him into my pocket. What I had planned for him I did not know. Soon I was upon Oxley, a cheery place of smoking chimneys and rustic types about their business. I came across a potato and some carrots and as dusk painted the sky a doomed indigo, the flick of orange spots led me to a forge. Truly had I become as a caveman in the modern world.

Time was not on my side, for I did not wish to be discovered thus, so in a flash, out came the pigeon and off with his feathers. I tossed him into the fire – it was for the best. I hopped from one foot to the other cheering on the baking, the occasional pop – his beak and toes – startling me. But soon came the smell of cooking flesh, a merry roasting and for a moment all was well again as I sat lonely in the dark, once more back in the Beef Steak Club, sirloin on the way.

But a hoot from outside brought me back to my roasting

friend and I dived in, chucking the blackened bird from the embers. He was not a pretty sight and I set about the chap with some savagery. I wrenched off the fellow's head before pulling off his wings and although I mistimed my cooking by an hour or two – indeed his pink flesh proved soggy and his innards none too sizzling – I tucked in as though he were a venison at the Garrick.

I gnawed the tiny bones once I had shredded them of all flesh but I did not spit out his head because I had been brought up well.

I left nothing of that wee fellow, the gristle a side dish, his toes and claws a tasty afters. I slept that night as a king.

More Wandering About The Countryside

'Leaves of three, let it be; berries white, poisonous sight' told me a man. His name was Obediah and he was a very ogre. Once or twice I may have made an error with his mantra and done some plops by mistake. More than twice no doubt.

But there was more to life than berries. I scavenged for corpses, laid traps for finches, strangled robins, pilfered a chicken and once crushed a hare's head with a rock. Mostly my suppers were cold and bloody for fires were not easy, but I was not alone on my travels. A whole population of vagabonds too wandered the country lanes, looking for work, looking for love, hiding from demons, hiding from life.

Many were difficult to know for they spoke with burrs. Several hailed from Ireland and told me dreadful tales of famine. Apparently the potato crop had failed and the people were dying in their thousands.

Many fled for America while others sailed to Newport and ventured to London to lay the roads and rails of the Empire's greatest city. Many came for the spring hay-harvest and often remained till it was time for corn to be gathered, the crops brightening and smelling sweet then dying. Hundreds of pedlars roamed the country lanes on the tramp. One man had an affliction with his testicles and believed the walk would do him good. Some were city scribes and factory men, come to pick hops on their break, for there was no such thing as a paid holiday back then, but before they knew it, the seasons had turned full circle, home was a more distant land and hay had grown once more.

They were truly a ragged bunch, but for every ten cut-throats came a kind-hearted crew. They ridiculed me not, nor even did they pity me and how could they for mine were indeed but nothing. But they shared with me the secrets of the road; how to catch and skin a fish, how to make the most of a dormouse and the common shrew. They schooled me twixt the death cap mushroom and its look-a-like, the parasol. They introduced me to the Beefsteak Fungus, found on the bark of oak trunks, an ironic remnant from my past life. Unfortunately, the fellow did not live up to his name. He tasted like old man's cack.

Isaac Johnson made me hot nettle soup and mugwort tea. I took notes. He was scarred from the birch and wore a smock and cloth spatter-dashes around his boots.

Johnson had begun a-thieving as a child in Middlesbrough. He moved to London where he set about stealing handkerchiefs. He recommended not touching nettle leaves after June when they become bitter and have a loosening effect on the bowels.

He went 'bug-hunting,' robbing late-night drunks to pay for bread because Johnson had a younger sister and he was not going to become her pimp whatever the cost.

Johnson lived among 'dippers' and 'cracksmen', lowly people who lived through other people's pockets. His pals 'propped' men in the road after country fairs, the victim often flush with money. I soon learnt the lingo.

The nettle leaves should be washed then boiled for a few minutes in a pan - butter, onion, salt and pepper if could be.

Johnson was caught passing bad notes. The judge gave him a flogging and four years in Wandsworth.

If I came across any milk, it should be boiled and added to the crushed nettles. The soup was utterly foul.

Johnson was a kind man, wronged in life. He appeared more aged than his fifty years and little salvation could be seen for his future. I never did know what happened to his sister Flo, but I fear she sold her body to men like me.

Summer was soon faded once and for all and the way grew pungent with ceps and fungus.

Others in the troupe showed me how to put the willies up farm dogs and beg for pennies. Danny Caffrey, a vicious red-head with a fearful history, taught me a man need not be judged on his past. A wild thug with a deft punch, he patrolled the lanes in his corduroy rags. At times his rough manhood poked out like a tortoise at the fair.

Yet with his napkins and scissors was he truly adored, as the self-taught barber roamed from village to village, making farmers and labourers ever so happy. The pennies fed us all for the fortnight I spent in their band, our evenings spent together, my face warmed by their fire, my soul by their presence.

As winter came closer, the Irish took their leave. They gave me Lucifer matches and a spoon.

I wandered endlessly, chased by farmers, bitten by horses, loved for once by the wife of a baker. She startled me digging her garden, but for the next three weeks, I feasted on hot bread brought straight to my hideout. Sweet milk came too and one night we shared some gin. She unbuttoned me as we shivered under the stars and pleasured me in her hand. She allowed me warm my chin beneath her frock and she gave forth the smell of home and all I had thrown away, everything I had rejected for all of my life. Sally sang to me that night.

Christmas came and went. I spied it from a Cotswold hill, the glowing families of Guiting Power waddling to church, eager for the vicar to wrap up his sermon so they could rush home for goose dripping and pie. I was ever so lonely. I slept that night cuddled against a foal neath the black tree skeletons and off went I in the morning, one muddied field to another, losing myself in the furrows. The sky was ashen and I was ravenous and spotted with snowflakes that had fallen that night. I had stolen again, out a-thieving not long before, climbed through a crooked window in an Oxfordshire hamlet and helped myself to some clothes drying next a crackling fire. I raided the larder and stocked on pickles and jams, hams and cured beef and a wedge of great cheese. Over the range was an iron backstore with baked oatcakes, so in they went too. A plate of tongue and suet dumplings. I had the lot and a slice of cold fowl and a glass of custard. A calf's foot soon to become jelly. I made off too with the boned paw for who knew from whence would come the next meal? Some days later a farmhouse supplied me with a new suit and undershirts too but I did not discard the tatty rags, rather used them as a pillow.

1857

New Year's Eve passed I recall not how but not, I fear, different from the past months; the hunt for food, a drink of water from a horse's trough, a bed of sorts perhaps.

Came spring and a happier earth. Soon the birds were filling the sodden skies with song, wittering the afternoons away. And then came the verges cluttered with snowdrops - virgin-white bells curled atop drowsy greens; the lilac sweetness of the crocus, the blazing cheer of the daffodil's trumpets and the marigold too. Day by day they grew and became more bright. Fresh fields of mustard rape came and went, a bright yellow sea, like a giant German pubis. A chill burst of rain drenched my night but fed the flowers.

Thus did my life pass for I lost track of the days, the weeks, keeping a scant eye 'pon the change of season. I did spot from time to time the form of the moon; some nights he would be bold, lighting forth my path when I could not rest, looking out for me as an old friend, yet others, seemingly from one night to the next, I would glimpse a sick relative of that brash globe. He no longer smiled and eventually the bashful soul would hide. Sally did not once leave my mind.

Still my beard and whiskers grew. For on a trip a-thieving I hastened a peek in a looking-glass. I fair jumped out of my skin, so dreadful was the transmutation. I was once praised for my looks, dishy as a sailor said some, but there I stood, a shorn figure in another's clothes, bearded and filthy, shrunken and old. I shed a sad tear for myself that afternoon, stopping to grab from the larder: curry powder, plovers' eggs, a jar of nutmeg, a sleeve of goose dripping and a bowl of beef liquor. Mind you, the Nestle's milk food went over a hedge, for the Bull's Head tin opener had yet to be invented.

The weather warmed slowly, the sun bringing blossoms to life, toasting my cheeks. I wanted to be fat again, I wanted to feel my breasts thump against the cloth of my shirt when I ran, I wanted to hold that hang of tum that once nestled, like a negro's lip, over the waist of my trousers. I wanted to live, I wanted my emptiness gone, I wanted Sally back and I wanted to love truly, I wanted the courage to embrace all that was good in life and I wanted so to be good; good to others, good to me.

Some days I wandered the dales alone, bedding down in a barn where I could; other times I walked through the night while the vagabonds of the country came, a secret tribe, as alien to me as the natives of the Amazon. Indeed, some of these persons were coloured as dark after years in the open. William Jefferson was a packman, who once mooched the streets of the capital hawking linens, yards of sheets, shirts, twirls of silk and shawls. But soon the Scottish tallymen hounded him from the city with their superior tartans. They had learnt their trade roaming the Highlands flogging needles and muslin, news and chitter-chatter to lonely farmers. But word soon spread that greater riches could be had in London and so down they ventured.

Jefferson took offence at the newcomers and packed his bags for the heather of Scotland. He would exact revenge but a terrible accident with a carriage put an end to his dreams. Jefferson was left with a limp and a bag of sheets that were gathering moulder. So did he traipse the fields, a bad-tempered man for eternity, eaten almost alive by bitterness. Several teeth were missing. His cough troubled all and sores spotted his limbs. Surely was it his wish to reach the Highlands that kept him alive. For despite the mischief he meant, he lived for something and that hope took him from one day to the next. He lived. I existed.

How I longed for a reason to live. For what is it that marks us as God's own creatures? Was I no more than a gorilla? What difference is there between myself and those beasts I trapped to eat? Did they have no stronger desires than warmth, food, drink and the need to reproduce? They did not and I shared their baseness, the beast that I had become.

A bit later in 1857. Quite chilly with a nip in the air

Walking Back To London To Real Life And The Realisation That While Money Does Not Necessary Maketh The Man, A Man Without Money Is As Good As A Cat. Sorry, A Rat

And thus, much as I had left the capital behind, did I wander back, slowly then quickly, a pitiable figure, stopping only for the necessities of being, and I did so without great hours of sleep.

I had then, a goal, the ambition to make me rise each day and live a life more true. I would yet again lay with Sally and the hope sped my journey east. Sadly though, I had left to me no livelihood, not a ha'penny for a potato, not a sausage for a sausage for my monies had been frittered all away, dwindled to nothing. My pounds had all but gone, spent feeding my habit, spent on too many suppers, spent on Sally for all the worth it did. All I inherited had gone, as if it never had been. I was educated well, knew a little Latin but was trained in nothing; I had ignored my father to think hard of investments, knowing I would fall one day on my wits, that something always would remain. Yet the truth was I had nothing, nowhere to go and knew not where I would sleep. The family house was long gone, sold to finance legal battles and taxes, a nasty remnant from the Opium Wars and matters neglected and I prayed my landlady would forgive my speedy departure and lend a little pity on one who had paid so promptly in the past.

June 12, 1857
Going Home To Mrs Gough; If Ever A Man Returned With A Tail Betwixt His Legs, It Was He

Once again in the Metropolis of London, I washed in the back room of a public house and begged a man for a trim before taking the first steps to my old home. I shook quite as a mammoth.

I knew not how long I had been gone, several months at least, years or more perhaps, and my passions were astir. Gradually did I become accustomed to the incessant din and smells of the city, the reckless bustle of too many people, the street souls' cry and the buzz of horse flies – a home of sorts but I missed the donkeys in the fields, missed the flowers and the birds.

I reached the house, and sweating like an octopus in an oven, my heart murmuring and my clenched hands dripping with nerves, I pressed the bell's bronze nipple. I was not outside for long, for Mrs Gough was at the door, plump and anxious in minutes. The following was not without incident.

'Yes?' she croaked. 'Can I help you sir?' she begged until she beheld my tropical tones. 'My God!! A Frenchman. You're a bludger. Please don't use on me your neddy. Fake away off you devil.'

I could but goggle back much like a pastor faced before a negro.

'Oooh' she muttered to herself, 'he probably don't understand Hinglish. Please, *monsieur, s'il vous plait*, effez offez. *Je vais* callez le coppers. Au croquette.'

'Mrs Gough' I retorted not without some haste, 'I am not a Frenchman. *Utterly* not. I am absolutely English. My forefathers were Benjamin, the, uhhm, Eighth Duke of England. And Essex, and Wessex and Grimsby. I've never been to foreign. I don't even like onions.'

I *do* though, I adore onions. Especially the red. Oooh, how I lie.

Resorting to memories past and a history true, I tried as so: 'You have known me, Mrs Gough, for several years. More in fact. What's more, I have even had my moooooth atop these' (I jestingly prodded her bosom with my forefinger.) She took the exercise badly and squeezed my testes with some tongs.

I cheeped, though it was unlike any birdsong I have heard. My eyes watered and the world before me appeared crimson in colour, then it faded and I witnessed astronomy. I performed a little jig and rubbed myself with both hands between the legs. I hoped she rinsed the tool if she were to touch a lunch for that is how cholera does spread. Go to any hospital if you doubt me.

Minutes later, that very same door of over-boiled cauliflower was once more opened. Mrs Gough, her face a shade more rosy than before peered around the jamb (I hope that is the correct word. If not, there is nothing I can do, for you will soon learn of my punishment) and with the faintest murmurings of a smile, one that crept from her few yellowy teeth to the very corners of her chops crawled into view and in a thrice had me into her arms.

'Mrs Gough' I began, the first truly coherent words spoken by me for some time. 'It is me. Your old chum and tenant. I am so sorry about leaving as I did, but I had a problem or two and I was taken ill. I have been in hospital. I sought to contact you but the doctors would not. I am so sorry.' She shrieked with laughter and, after hearing the following 'I fought you was a wog' with a furtive squint at wiry, browny me and a bosomy, homely hug, I was drooling asleep atop my very old bed.

I slept through tea, drowned as I was in the most lovely of slumbers. I slept for possibly days, as immune to the world about me as ever I had been in the most drunken of nights and awoke utterly invigorated.

What a joy it was to spend the night indoors, without fear from the heavens, nary a nibble from the vole, the mole, the fox or even the duck. I kissed the sheets and wept upon my pillow. I was home.

Mid-June, 1857
The Perils Of Bathing

A few days later, I took the staircase to find Mrs Gough rosy and charming.

'Mrs Gough' quoted I. 'It would appear from the bubbles at your elbows that you are doing the wash of my knickers with 'Harper Twelvetrees' Glycerine Soap-Powder'. Would I be correct?'

'Of course sir.'

'Capital. I am told it makes the clothes white.'

'Yes sir, it looks like you had an incident in your bockers.'

'Not me Mrs Gough, I assure you. A *Hindoo* man, not me.'

She asked if I had slept well and indeed I had and thanked her for the bed before probing: 'Are you verminous?'

'No' replied I, 'but I am certainly *rav*enous' and with that she squeaked like a goose and trotted on the spot with a most contagious joy, for what a dear woman was she. And what a selfish ogre was I.

Why did she look upon me so kindly, you may quiz yourselves? Well, once did she suckle me. As barely more than a child herself did she find service in my family home. Whilst my mother performed the duties she musted, Mrs Gough would hold me to her teats. From wet nurse, so she grew dry and eventually became our housemaid. She stayed for several years, until my papa booted her from the house. He punched her about the face for eating his personal broccoli but I never forgot her and she never me. Once the family home had gone she came about some lodgings and for four years had that place been my home.

The question of rent though, remained a moot topic yet I vowed she would be paid, more than before and as soon as I could.

Mrs Gough drew for me a bath. It was piping and inspiring and I required feeding. She brought for me, as I lapped in the waters like a submerged sir, foodstuffs of a premium type. Bacon plopped into the tub, a sardine was reacquainted with the deep, a scone evaporated in the steam, I scalded my testicular sac with tea and yelped like a rat as blood flooded the waters, overflowing to the floor and matting my boob hairs together. I stood wailing and pitted, my hands a-tremor, fearful I had committed some wicked crime upon my corpse. Perhaps the beverage had caused my genitals untold harm.

'Mrs Gough' wailed the whale, 'I think I shall bleed to death. Goodbye Mrs Gough, I love you like my own mama. Find some notepaper for my last words. Tell the neighbours I feel faint, I would like some cheese, have we some grapes amongst us? I feel faint, do hurry, do, I am not long left, take me to church.'

'It's a tomato. It come out of your sangvidge and fell into the tub' she said.

'I need God, Jesus died for our sins and now it is my turn, I have done bad. I have wet the bed, I have put bum hairs in Lucian's trumpet and he swallowed them, I have buggered- a *tomato*? Who speaks here? Oh God, oh God, no, no, please no, take someone else, take a Chinky, a woman, no please I beg not me. I will never do bad henceforth, I will curse no more, I will dedicate my life to goodness. It is too late. I have passed away' I sobbed, splashing in the lukewarm waves.

'Am I to converse only with spirits? This is shit, I am lonely. There is soap in my eye. Mrs Gough, have *you* too died? I am sorry. You were a nice lady but your passing will not be mourned as mine. Your cooking is mediocre but you are older than I, your cheeks haggard, your looks doomed to eternity. Mrs Gough, you appear before me no different. Oh the mystery of death and the afterlife too. Mrs Gough!!!'

I collapsed into a fitful nap until the waters became cold.

I did wake later that day. 'Don't be goin' worryin' yourself' she said.

'Remember I seen your what-not plenty a times when you was a little fella and he hain't grown much since. It was probably my own fault cos I drew the baaarf too 'ot for ya and you dropped them grilled tomartas in the war'er. I'm sorry.'

She handed me a towel and I admitted her apologies. What a horrid being am I.

A bit later in mid-June, 1857

The Day He Reaquaints Himself With Some Old Friends; They Go By The Name Of The Chinese Solicitors

I made a call to the apothecary for to enquire as to a riddle. His name was Mr Fluff and his business was, and still is no doubt, at High Holborn.

'You sir, yes you in the white gown. I wind at noon and quack at dusk, have bile of the spirit and nervousness after food.'

'Perhaps you should take Indian Pills.'

'Indian Pills? How dare you. Blast your Indian Pills you wag. Or should I say wog? They are made, I take it, of *Indians*?'

'No sir. They are purely vegetable and may be taken at any time.'

'Price please Mr Fluff.'

'1/1 ½ and 2/9 each.'

'Reasonable what? Four boxes please.'

'Sir?'

'Mr Fluff?'

'Your corset?'

'Yes?'

'It will arrive by Tuesday next. Good day.'

'Good day.'

Next stop Limehouse Basin. Wing, Wang, Ding, Wong, Chin

and Dong were my Chinese solicitors. My father had helped establish the firm. I believe he knew them from his days in the East for he employed Orientals when he assisted the running of the East India Company and during the Opium War in 1839 secured himself a nice plot of land in Hong Kong. The Treaty of Nanning gave that land to Queen Victoria and my father has his name to many of the roads there today. The fellows had been saved a life of misery and had been brought to England as lascars aboard the tea clippers.

Since my papa's death they had overseen the business, shipping tea and spices and opium too, the makings of which came to me, less their cut. There was a slim hope that some money remained.

Was it me, or was the stench of the heated river become more intolerable?

I puffed on the brass plate, checking my hairs in the honey mirror and tweaked the bell. A child bade me enter, and at a loss for cards, I begged him let me climb the stairs. As I neared the offices, the rattle of mah-jong pieces chimed across the banister. I knocked the requisite three times and entered, for subterfuge is essential when dealing with the Chinean.

'Hindoo, Hindoo, Hindoo' came a mighty roar and the solicitors darted for cover. Ding and Wing huddled beneath a French bureau, a colleague - I had no time to decipher who - erected himself upon a chair. Queen Anne, by the looks of things - business must be prosperous. The rest jumped upon me. I would have to act quickly, for the men had a ferocious reputation. They could skin a man in less than an hour and certainly took no nonsense. Already I could feel Chin's paw towards my spleen and a flat-as-a-top-of-a-pie nose, delve into my eye. Then appeared a molar on my rump and an incisor near the leg. If I could keep my mouth foreign free I had a chance. A thumb nail, a long one, perhaps as long as a toe, scooped into my calf. I understood rudimentary Mandarin and basic Cantonese and in fact my grasp of the Chinaman's tongue was once well-documented. Sadly though, I could never articulate the Eastern sounds and I was effectively, mute. I recognised several words in their language yet many though were muffled by the inhuman press of bodies. A chin (anatomy not solicitor) featured in my ear.

'Tasty, tasty, money, trousers,'

'Go on, go on,'

'Where's my teeth?'

'Didn't know they were false,'

'They aren't,'

'Oow,'

'Remove the child for he is young,'

'Mummy,'

'Saucepan, boiling water…' ad nauseum.

I breathed in and breathed out several times, gathered my energies and bellowed: 'Get off!!!! You are damaging my physique. Don't bite, oooh that tickles. I am not a Hindoo, I never have been, nor do I ever plan to be. I am an *Englishman* and am not normally this tawny. I am regularly as white as a cod. You all know me. I am the son of my papa, once the surrogate father to Wong and indeed used I to share a hot tub with Wong until he accidented himself in the waters and he was thrown out of my family home, except it wasn't really him that did the wee, because it was sort of indeed, actually, I'm afraid to say, *me*, because heated water plays monkeys with my pippin. Also did I cause more troubles with him by mistake. Opium, mama etc. So sorry. I forgive him and I forgive you all. Please no more biting.'

The silence was ominous. Wing and Dong (I knew it was not Ding because he was bald and had no teeth) sat befuddled in a fog of smoke, their cigarettes held effetely in the way of the Chinaman, the ash a miniature grey monolith, the finger nail an ivory cock.

'Gentleman, where is Wong?' (he was my favourite and spoke the most manageable English of the lot.)

I had to deal with Ding, for Wong, somewhat ironically, was in bed with Yellow Fever. I spotted a pair of ladies' underdrawers upon the desk. They seemed almost familiar.

'Ding' I begin, 'I need money. I have left Mrs Gough in arrears, my knees hurt and I wish to spend the day in a whorehouse. Oh yes. Sorry I have not been in for a while, but I had some business to attend to. And say sorry to Wong for piddle time. I hope he found a new home. Did I say whorehouse? I mean bath-house.'

'Herro master. We no see you one year, maybe more, what you say, where your, your, your, oooh?' and here he puffed out his cheeks like two loaves and wobbled his manicured hands around his midriff, like a man in drink playing the accordion. He accordingly raised his eyebrow. He lost the other in a boating accident. He could never remember the English for belly.

'Ah yes Ding. I have lost some weight. I stopped eating, uuhhm, oohh, baked taters.'

'And you blown as a ploppy, why, why, why?'

'That, gentlemen, is the doings of the sun.'

They were never a warm bunch, at least not with me, but

they held papa in much esteem. The men all growled phlegm from their throats, spat it upon the floor (I am told they do that in the East) and individually hugged me before Wing barked 'Take, preese, one seat of us.' Their written English was superb.

'Daddy your money you wan'?'

'Yes please and lots of it.'

'Uuuhhm, ooohhm, there is been a plobrem with manager.'

Manager, or Harold Finnish, was in charge of the company's shipping arrangements and the workers – essentially the day-to-day running of the business since the death of father.

Wing, Wang, Ding, Wong, Chin and Dong were chiefly in control of the cash.

'Manager, when you aweeeey, he take all money, shutted flirm and lun aweeeey. Solly, no lolly.'

I was in a bit of bother.

It seemed Mr Finnish had sacked the workers, declared us bankrupt and done a runner. Quite a long way. There was not a bean left.

Wing, Wang, Ding, Wong, Chin and Dong had spent my savings trying to find Finnish and seek justice on my behalf. They would do their best for me, they bleated, because they always loved father and will never forget what he did for them (I never knew what it was *exactly* he did for them. He said he wrote it all down somewhere, so one day maybe). A teary-eyed Chin bent his curious buttocks down towards the safe, generating a not so dainty whiff and handed to me a bundle of notes. They were not many, but would keep me in jam and eggs for a while. We hugged again and I went home. I did not feel well.

Mid-late June, 1857

Going To Buy A Pie, Which Proves A Hazardous Event. In Hindsight He Should Have Asked Wing, Wang, Ding, Wong, Chin and Dong For Some Vegetable Fried Noodles. With Prawns. Or Chicken.

I spared Mrs Gough the worst details of my new knowledge, kissed her cheek, made a tea, and gave her some quids. I bought also a pot of Jewsbury and Brown Tooth Paste. I tried it pon the fangs and the results were excellent. I went to bed because I had a tummy-ache and pondered my options. They were distressing all of them. I say all of them – there were in fact none.

Not all of my belongings had been sold, but the few that remained were meagre. Some shoes prevailed; my favourite, though, a pair of Wellington riding boots had gone. Mrs Gough was convinced one of the Chinese had collected them during my absence, claiming they were in fact his, a wrongdoing I found hard to accept. Gone too were my oyster forks, their handles carved from Scottish stag horn.

There remained, though, some spectacles – they were clearly not mine, for I had some of the best eyesight in London - breeches, brooches, leeches, lychees, handkerchiefs, books (clean and dirty both), shirts, skirts, shorts, shits and a letter from an old chum called Waterstones. I read the missive. It did not take long. Its contents were short and followed a scuffle we had shared many years previously. He accused me of vacating his eggs with the use of a knitting needle. Knit, I not for I had other tasks to perform that day, for with a skewer and a neckerchief, I had drilled a perfect hole in the charwoman's wall. I had so nimbly engineered the escapade that I was about to witness an unclad tit when young Waterstones chanced upon me, and in a temper over the eggs launched many blows at me. He was a successful barrister at the time.

Thinking him perhaps tiddly I joshed at him, but he proceeded with a puffy duffing which I rebuffed with a cuffing. The afternoon ended abruptly. I twisted his fingers and left.

The following morning he sent me a card which read:

Dear Sir.

You have frigged my digit. Never to call again. I hate you.

Regards.
Waterstones

I disapproved of his language but accepted his sentiments.

My tummy was raving for nourishment and I was not too cruel to deprive him so.

I had little money, but a touch more dignity and after my recent tomato tomfoolery, I would go elsewhere for feeding.

'Mrs Gough' I greeted, still a shade frosty.

'Mrs Gough' I have a tendency to repeat myself when in serious tempers 'you are a good woman but not a rich one.' (I may have lost my dignity, my money, home, livelihood, self-respect, trousers, riding boots and three toenails, but still I had my charm)

'Perhaps you could tell me of a cheap food. I am famished, I am starving, my belly, I think is hors d'oeuvring itself before my very eyes. I could eat an entire animal. With his feet on. What shall I do? Also my room wants lighting, so perhaps some tallow?'

She was in the kitchen where she prepared the laundry. A huge block of soap, possibly as large as a very small child was about to meet with my undershirts which sat bubbling in a pot to Mrs Gough's behind. She stirred the belongings once with a big stick and then turned to me.

'I am sorry, but I hain't been to the market today, butterman gone all poorly, butcher's in the clink and the fishman's a madman. I've only got some toma, uhhm, some tom, uhhm, red, uhhm, the kitchen is as bare as you vos in the tub.'

'Mrs Gough, that is of no consequence. I do not wish to trouble you further, but if you could just point me towards some cheap nosh, that will more than make up for our recent winky winky hoo-haa.'

What a feast of food was I to learn. Chop-house, pickled whelks, cook-shop, boiled puddings, pea soup, hot eels, sheeps' frigging feet. Eff that. I went to a pieman instead.

I believe I am not long left for this world and have left little to mankind, but I would like to impart to whosoever may fall upon this note, the following: if a pieman strikes you in the nose, be sure to pull your hat down low, for piping gravy can disfigure a man's looks so.

I was not to know the meat that filled his pastry was not venison nor pheasant, neither turtle nor lobster.

'But what sort of meat is what I need to know before I purchase to chomp' I persisted.

'*Meat*, you wanking bastard, *meat*.'

'I did not catch the middle, but if it contained a reference to the breed, feel free to repeat.'

'Meat, meat, fuckin', bloody, chuffin' *meat*. Blood and bloody guts and meat. *Meat*.'

Quite a crowd had developed, some no doubt frustrated by the man's patter.

'Come on you fruit, I want me brekkers,' snarled one half-wit.

'Get on wiv it, I'm almost collapsin'. Gonna eat meself if you don't get a shifty on' said another.

'Please, please, please, just buy the blazin' morsel' opined a third.

'I'm gonna meet out some justice to you.' (That last was met – ooh, even I'm at it now – with some laughter).

I gathered little other than they were likely sub-normal. They would have to make time for a pie novice.

'Sir, I may go elsewhere' I ruptured, furious as ever I have been.

'Right that's it you pansy. You've upset me, me customers, insulted me meaties. 'Ave a portion of vis you dog.' And with that he fair knocked me in the nose. As I lay stunned in the dirt he poured several measures of the delicious gravy over my face, inside my shirt and a cupful down the breeches, re-burning the unfortunate knackers. My screams went unnoticed as my mouth was snowed up with a light, crumby pastry.

Mrs Gough Is Alarmed

'Mrs Gough, do not shriek, I am not damaged, I have merely suffered sunburn.'

'It's been rainin' all the day.'

'Yes, you say raining, here maybe, but not in Clapham. The ground there was baked as hard as a bone. I was discussing a business with my niece over a venison.'

'Clap'am ain't far and you hain't got no relatives. What's that on your 'ooter? It looks like bacon.'

'Bacon, what? Oh *that* bacon, yes it is. It is excellent at keeping away the flies. I must take my leave....Hmm, what? Sorry? Yes, *exactly* what I thought, what a *bizarre* smell of food. It must be those new people at number twenty-seven. Forever roasting meat. What? *Gravy*? Can't stand the stuff. Goodnight.'

Cholera is no laughing matter, a killer disease that strikes all without mercy, with no heed to caste or class, yet the germs first were spread by the poor drinking from the same stretch of Thames where flowed the effluent of human waste, water pumped straight to the courtyards of slums, clogged with corpses and rotting matter and pigs and horses and mules, a feast for the rats and crazed dogs of the Metropolis, the most civilised on God's earth. Cesspits beneath every home send a stink to permeate even the most elegant of parlours and breed foul germs which, with coal smoke and sulphur, give London the most almighty smell, treacherous to the breath.

Thousands more will need die before Doctor John Snow stumbles upon the link between drinking water and disease, years will pass before the chief engineer of the new Metropolitan Board of Works, Sir Joseph Bazalgette will find a better way to dispose of the waste of London's millions, before Edwin Chadwick from the Poor Law Board will make Parliament order all such muck be sent away and covered with soil to keep down disease, years before the Ministers will even consider the predicament of the poor. London is a sickened place, growing worse by the hour and in his mind, the man at Mrs Gough's quietly wishes to be taken too by the disease.

June 28, 1857
And A Pigeon Is Cooked

'Mr Fluff' huffed I, for what with the smog, the miasma, the cholera, pollen, fear of rabies and general hullabaloo, I struggled for breath. I took a cab to High Holborn, despite my injuries.

'Sir?'

'Mr Fluff?'

'You should try Dr. Locock's Pulmonic Wafers. A rapid cure of asthma, consumption, influenza and coughs.'

'Mr Fluff I am hardly a wealthy man you know. Price please?'

'1s 1½d and 2s 9d per book.'

'Nine books please Mr Fluff.'

'Sir?'

'Mr Fluff?'

'The brassiere?'

'Yes?'

'Thursday next.'

'For the wife.'

'Yes. Of course.'

'Good day.'

'Good day.'

Hoping my deformities would subside with time I took to

my parlour with two quarts of whelks and vinegar, snippets of eel, seven meat puddings, a clan of flans and a piglet. I had earlier bribed a youth to buy a pie from the pieman. Thereby did I dig a hole in the crust, emptying the contents to the footpath. I next scraped a dogs' muck from the carriageway, inserted the pesty into the pasty, resealed it and returned it to display. A man once said, 'To err is human, to forgive is divine.' What a load of trotters.

Did I say that also I snared a pigeon? No? Well I did. Since returning from the countryside, I cannot pass a street bird without feeling remorse and guilt and more pertinently, a wild pang of peckishness for raw flesh. But a man is not to eat uncooked meat in London. I, however, was angry and hungry.

I begged of Mrs G a cooking pot, a Lucifer match, a salt and a water. I told her I was deep-cleansing a handkerchief and not an eyebrow was raised because she knew that, even as a boy, my nose would I blow only upon a clean material. I returned to my rooms laden with goods. While the waters bubbled, I strangled the poor creature, swearing eagerly and chomping my teeth for practice until a knock at the door bothered the boiling.

'Ah, Mrs G. I am just doing some reading. An excellent novel by a superb author. *Admirable* writing. Good night.'

Yet before the door could close, a podgy foot peeped around the frame and spake thus: 'Is you alright? I heard some skvawkin' and a-thumpin', a-cryin' and a-fryin.'

'Fryin, cryin, fryin, cryin? I have been entertaining, no more. You are correct. One of the guests, a gruesome fellow with an earthy tongue had been doing pigeon impressions.

Quite marvellous, yet his presence was unnecessary and I have since bid him leave.'

'I hain't 'ad anyone enter the house all day. You forget that I sits by the front door. Anyways, it sounded more like a crow. You know.'

'They came in the window and left accordingly' I clarified.

'You hain't got no vinder. I 'ad to block it up cos you kept on doing a toilet out of it ven you 'ad been drinkin'. Vy you got blood on your teef?'

'Window blood, blood window? I haven't, it is from the flesh of a raspberry. I love fruit.

'Vy you got fevvers all over you?'

'Mrs Gough. You have known me since I was a child. Has it never once occurred to you that I use a moustache?'

'I arranged your first moustache, I knew him vell. I meant the fevvers in your ear. And one on your head.'

'My dear, you cook too much. It is unhealthy to spend so many hours at the range. It is well-known that much cooking can harm the eyes. Please rest. Goodnight.'

I shut the door and returned to my commission. He tasted lovely.

June 29, 1857
The First Steps Into A Painful World
Of Hitherto Unknown Vulgarity

A penny remained to me which allowed three options: a boat trip from Woolwich to London Bridge, a bread and butter breakfast, a sparrow from a street seller or a lavatory at Smithfield Wash House. That was four.

My parlour stank like a foreigner and I moped for a long time. There was much to do: find Sally, more pigeon meat, earn money, buy sperm oil to light my rooms. And kill pigeons.

Kill. Alas was I beaten viciously as I searched for the lighting. When under duress, my mind is prone to weakness and it was as I wandered, that a dreadful rumpus did come about. I muttered and uttered to myself, keen to locate the oils, yet for the life of me could I not recall the correct name.

'Sir' I begged him for a pardon as I traipsed gaily into a haberdasher's. 'I have of late been to the countryside. Very pretty. I am now returned to London but one's rooms are dark like a Kenyan. All my monies are invested in great wealth – ships, bullion, horse fur and the like – and I require lighting for my apartment. I believe, so I am told, that what I require is sperm and lots of it. Sir, cover me in spunk.'

I really was in a pickle, it would seem. My monies had dried up and I was at a loss. In short, I was alone and truly terrified for the first time in my life and I could not think of what to do. However fond I was of my fellows at the Beef Steak Club, it really was unthinkable to beg from them a loan, for in truth, none of us were friends. Indeed, I had even let it be known through a messenger boy some days previously that I had been taken awful ill with the gout and was at my wits end and could one of them perhaps see to it to loan me some pounds to pay for my medication but the answer came back no. Never had I ventured to think of such a situation but now that my mind was put to the test, really did it come as no surprise. For while London be the most chattery of cities, really it is as a prison when your life takes a downturn.

So I stayed indoors, locked away from temptation and life. Also was I hidden from foodstuffs and drink for really I had not the means to pay.

Over and over in my mind did I play the actions of my life hitherto now and truly did it make for sorry viewing.

Mrs Gough I kept from my quarters for she needn't see me in such low tempers but it was while thumbing through my old Man About Town handbook, recuperating from some villainous wounds caused by the spunk/sperm misunderstanding, that I could see through the darkness a speck of light, a sign perhaps of hope, of salvation.

While indispensable to the gentleman in search of tomfoolery, the sweetest place to procure a drink or how best to rid oneself of the pox, there came a chapter dealing in pedication and uranism, the ways of a margerie. Or in the language of the commoner, whoopsiness.

And, so in jiffy, was the awful idea upon me. I would sell my backside to passing gays for a few shillings a pop. How the very thought shook me with fear and disgust, my stomach rolled at the thought, my morals thus far fallen, how could this be? Yet there was nothing else that could be done. I needed to eat and needed to live and had lost my last penny during the scuffle in the haberdasher's. I too needed to tickle the fannies of strumpets and with the scars from the pieman a gross disfigurement, such pleasures would not come free.

Thus it was one evening that I found myself a-powdering my tremulous posterior for an initial outing. It quivered as an angel's wing beholding heaven for the first time.

I rubbed it freshly, fearful not to repel my clients by bringing the cheeks to rawness, and freckled it with sweet smelling talc, puffed it down with my shaving brush and, tightly breeched and steeled with a hint of whisky, walked the short distance to The Strand. Indeed little time had passed when I discovered the sign which read: "Beware of Sods." I knew this as a warning to right-thinking patrons, and taking the caution to heart I prepared to enter. I was petrified, truly I was. I knew from the handbook such types were on the look for similar men and at a given sign would place their fingers in a peculiar manner underneath the tails of their coats, and wag them about.

Thus instructed in the ways of a pixie, I, sadder than one could ever know, set off to the task of procuring a man to corrupt my bum.

My mind could not take in the enormity of what lay ahead, the acts I knew lay in store for me, but I was desperate. I was needy for the first time in my life, *truly* needy and I wanted to atone myself for my dreadful ways, to seek penance, to beg forgiveness from all. And the handbook spoke of a new floozy from Bruges who sold her knockers for tuppence a nibble.

The act was dangerous and in truth, I knew not into what I entered. Too I ran the risk of upsetting a police constable were I caught in the act of bum action.

I re-examined the warning on the door, and with the shake of a ninny and a lump in my throat, entered the threshold of a new life and the Queen and Garter.

I was ready to perform a contrasexual act.

July 3, 1857
In Which He Chances His Arm At Unanism And The Beginnings Of A New Life

My actions that night were poor. Uncertain as to the finger wagging, I chose invention and performed many turns, yet each did fail as I paraded across the carpet, glancing to see which gentleman had followed.

Unimpressed, but determined, I altered the gamut of my show, switching from the stoop of an aged lady with a mild apoplexy to the haughtiness of an owl with only one taker. A large man took a swipe at me when I winked at him. The beast hurt my chin and could have loosened a fang had I not swooped aside at the final moment.

I chose to locate alternative venues and study the ways of the genuine bummer. So it was that for many a night did I observe and note the techniques to best find a gent. I stood at the bar with paper and a drink. Time was pressing. My writing desk, an ancient wooden thing given to me by father had fetched a few shillings, as had a pocket watch, a flotilla of handkerchiefs and a clink of tie pins to an indecent man behind St Paul's. My unwitting bum tutors would soon begin to cost me dearly for hardly could I stay in this beer house or that, viewing without supping and the beverages were sucking dry my pocket. With time did I learn how best to emulate the queer characters, how to, God forbid and bless and forgive me, *mimic* their walk, the awful flutter of their pansy digits, their unnatural demeanour and the unwholesome ways of a man so inclined. Please God, let this not be long. Just a few pounds to begin again, and then with your blessing, no more.

July 8, 1857

In Which He Meets The First Of Many Customers. How Horrid

My first taker had a gentleman's accent but the manners of a boar. We met as I rehearsed my steps outside the Drury Lane Theatre. He did not give his name, nor shake my hand; instead he led me through a river lane full of excreta and half a mouse. He declined my lodgings, preferring instead some dismal cellar for which he had the key. The room was absolutely unlit and perfumed with brine and cat's tiddle and it was there, upon the damp floor, that I lay down to accept my penance. Terrified at what was to come – violence, pain, murder even – I wobbled down my breeches, feeling the mild sighs of pleasure which stank of pork streaming from my client's mouth, like evil thoughts drifting in on evil winds. I wanted to die as I felt the warm thumpish hands offer me a reach-around as he described upon my hateful soul an act of indecency, known in later years as femoral homosexuality, emptying himself between my testicles and my thigh. Please God let me forget this.

Once the vomiting had passed, I ate well in the morning.

I waited several evenings before any brute would again use my bottom as a makeshift vagina, and when it occurred I wept. He bade me continue my whine insisting it stiffened him more readily. He thrusted into me like a dog and I lay forward clutching the sheets, biting my lip and wailing and bleeding, sobbing and praying for oblivion and an end to this nasty business, an end too, to what remained of my life. He bit into my shoulder and rammed and rammed and sweated and then emptied himself. He tossed some coins on the bed then barked at me to dress and take my leave.

I was never the same again and have not been since. I am soiled now for all time and may God disown me as a man.

In Which The True Horror And Repugnance Of His Life Comes Home To Roost.

Returning to my lodgings, I passed a drink shop and stocked up on cheap gin. I did not leave my rooms and was fluffy for a week.

I left my rent for Mrs Gough in an envelope, placed under her doorframe as she whistled an innocent sleep. I could not face her, nor anyone else, and steered full clear of the looking glass that once beamed so gleefully in the mornings.

There was left for me on the hallway table a note. I did not want to read it. Why face the paper when there can surely be nothing good in such news?

I barely ate. I vomited still more and writhed in agony, fearing my insides had been ruptured by that man's noo-noo. I cursed my life and truly did I loathe what I had become. How the comforts of my circumstances had changed. I once enjoyed the choice of the city's women, but had turned them aside for a more *dignified* life I thought, favouring the city's dispossessed, but for what? So I could be fucked in the arse worse than the cheapest Whitechapel whore?

I abused the heavens and denounced God and then I begged the Almighty for forgiveness and cried for help and bizarrely desired a plate of whitebait. Hmmm, how odd can be the human mind. I wanted no more of this. I wanted to do away with myself, take my life but I had no money for the pharmacist to ease my journey and I was too fearful to attempt an alternative. The sound of pistols startled me and gas ovens had yet to be invented so I drank another bottle. In the morning I was still there but my money was not for it had dwindled once more to nothing. Whilst pickled on stout, I burnt the unread note with a fallen cheroot and never did I learn its content.

I delayed my suicide for breakfast. Mrs Gough had, I have mentioned, a kind heart and a kind face. And on that day, she had the kindest eggs in London Town.

July 15 1857

The body proves a most gruesome spectacle for the high heat does not help. No, not at all.

The streets blow with a fetid gust, dust swirling through the hazy days while gin-soaked whores whoop the close nights.

The day presses from the bleached sky, bringing pain in its sapping wantonness. Few have known heat like it.

Men about the streets wear a powdery soot on their face as they stomp their teeth on ices to soothe the heat. The Thames reeks still and bubbles in the broiling sun and noxious waste from the city's millions and again there is talk of the return of the hideous death that came in its waves before. Those who must walk by the Thames carry handkerchiefs to block out the germs.

But old death makes no room for new and deep in the broken bowels of Black Horse Yard in St Giles lies the body, the skin now a marbled patchwork, the burst vessels that once carried his life's liquid now defunct, serving solely to add to the palette of his face.

His limbs stiffened days ago and now look ready to snap and the unmade bed lies caked with a crimson painting of blood.

His gums have near died and become a phantom yellow, and can keep a grip no longer on the teeth that have most rotted inside his head and now they sit side by side under the rictus snarl, marched upon by the midsummer maggots. A very Hades on earth.

July 20, 1857

Slowly, Slowly, Ever So Slowly, Does He Learn To Live With His New Ways

'Everythin' been alright dear 'as it? Just that I ain't seen a lot of yer this last week' asked Mrs G as she drew my bath.

'I am worried. I been 'earin' some funny noises from your room. I do hope you're not poorly or… You would tell me if there was anyfink troublin' wouldn't yer?' and she held my arm as she said this last. The soft touch of her fingers, fingers I have known since a child, took me back to a place I thought I never would see again, a world whose clouds rained drops of love. I felt tears meeting in my eyes as she patted my hand, my soiled, foul hand and I choked as I raced to answer.

Could I tell her all? How I had wasted my father's money? Could I really sit her down and tell piece by piece, how I had drunk it away, how I had smoked it in dusty dens with half-asleep chinky-chonks? And the *rest*? she would ask, innocence and love in her eyes. The *rest*, my dear Mrs Gough who adored papa and doted on me, who played my games, took me to bed, wiped my tears when I came home from school sorrowful and snivelling. The *rest*, I would tell her with my head held high, the *rest* was blown on whores of all colours. Really? Yes, really. Not all were cheap mind you. There was one though, I met her in Piccadilly. She was lovely, *really* lovely this one, and I gave her vast sums of money and paid for her meals and her rent and my rent and lots of chicken. *Good* then, she would say, good for you, well done, for she kept you from the worst of the city's ladies. Of course not, dear Mrs Gough, who nursed papa on his death bed even after she had been thrown from our house by the heartless, rancid old bastard. Of *course* not, if anything, she *increased* my appetite. *Really*, how so? Well, because I was paying her expenditure and there were certain things she would not allow me to do. Like what she may have asked? Like what, well like fucking her up the arse, something I know quite a bit about to tell you the truth dear Mrs Gough, pissing in her mouth, oh, you know, things like that. So you see, I felt I had earned the right to whore and whore more and more. That's lovely to hear she may have said. Anything else? Well just the occasional court fine, considerable losses at cards and a sorry spate of robberies. So you see papa's money was certainly not wasted because much went back into the community.

And what do you do now my dear?

Now? I am a whore myself. To men. Quite apt don't you think?

What could I *really* tell poor Mrs Gough, who barely subsided as it was, with late rents and tenants like me?

'Well you see Mrs Gough, it's all about, it's all to do with, it's' I stuttered and faltered and tried, *really* tried.

'Ssshhhh now. Your papa isn't it? You know I misses him too. *Terribly*. I knows he was a sour old goat sometimes' and she chuckled as she wiped away an angel tear 'and he couldn't 'alf complain, but 'ee 'ad a lovely 'art. I swears that' and with that she held me close to her heaving bosom which smelt of

Palm Olive soap and happiness and childhood and childhood and rocked me as we both spluttered on our tears.

'You know, I 'ave always loved you like me own. And really if there's *hanyfink* I can do for you, if you're strugglin' likes, with the rent at all, cos, remember I know what a bully can be like, then please, just come and tells me. Promise?'

'I promise' I said and went to bed.

August 2 1857
How Not To Police The Metropolis Of London

Sergeant Franklyn Bates slammed his truncheon on the desk at Bow Street Station House and yanked off his hat.

He was tired and not a little furious.

'Where the fucking heavens have you been?' he bellowed at the quivering PC.

'Well sir,' offered PC Arthur Widdle, 'I told you, I'm pursuing that funny murderer chap. You know, the one what, um, you know, he kills those,' he paused to cough.

'Come on you – fucking out with it. I've not got all day by Jove. You do realise I run a very fucking busy station house?' boomed the sergeant.

'Well sir. As what I says the other day. He's that *odd* fella that um, um well, he kills them other *odd* fellas.'

'Widdle, you toad' raised the sergeant's cumbersome eyebrows, like two blackmen on a hillock. 'You are *aware*, I assume, of the equipment we use to maintain a level of decency on the streets of this rotten metropolis?'

'Of course sir.'

'If you do not actually fucking inform me precisely what fucking manner of nonsense you're spouting, your *truncheon*, will pay a one-way visit somewhere most abominable.'

'Sir?'

'Your backside.'

'Ooh sir that would pain a bit.'

'Oh I daresay it would. Now what the fucking devils are you on about?'

'Well sir,' he proffered timidly, 'that funny man what's been slicing up them 'omosexuals.'

'Get out.'

And that, in a word was that.

It Gets Worse

Another man, another night, another tearful sleep on the dropsy of life.

I will get through this sordid interlude of life, a life soon to be lived again I hoped and told myself yet, if not for me, who deserved nothing more than this, then for the greying lady upstairs who dreamt so much that I would make all good one day. I could not bear to see any more loss in her eyes.

The Newspapers Tell Of Death And
The Coroner Dreams Of Oysters. How Peculiar

The Times of London. August 7, 1857.

ANOTHER GRUESOME FIND, THIS TIME IN A
PICCADILLY LODGING HOUSE ROOM.

*A fourth body has been discovered horribly dismembered
with a carving knife. A charwoman, Mrs Eileen Brewster
came across the corpse early yesterday morning which police
detectives think may have been dead since at least the night
previously. Only a small amount of cash has been found
missing; too a pocket watch, a miniature Datshchund
ornament and several of the gentleman's handkerchiefs.
Detectives found at the scene some bootprints of a decent
size and some footprints of a tiny size. Also did they find tiny
wood-shavings, cigarette ash, a slice of prawn toast and some
lady's knickers. How rum.*

'All rise for Her Majesty's Coroner.'

The coroner, Dr Herbert Mansfield, sighed in the smutty
gloom that had become his home from home.

He sat on his wooden bench, peering over the dusted half-
moons of his latest spectacles, for although his living was
gained at the waxen hands of the city's dead, he was most

definitely a very keen follower of the fashion of the living.

He peered tiredly over the lenses at the crumpled parchment, like a burnt boy's foreskin.

The officer of the court, a macabre stick of a man, eyebrowed his lordship, indicating a vulgar little man with a pad nearby. Neither man could abide the resident journalist.

If that penny-a-liner weren't 'ere wiv 'is friggin' quill, I could be out a 'ere in a jiffy and snaffle meself a table at that new oyster bar near the Adelphi, thought Dr Mansfield, agreeing in spirit with the officer of the court who was thinking exactly the same but in far less sophisticated tones.

And banged one out in the morgue - ooh so much cooler in the summer.

Because it was well known that Rule's on Maiden Lane provide a generous Lynnhaven Oyster and the occasional Colchester chap. *Hhhm. Pepper, lemon juice. Ooh frig these corpses.*

The clatter of hooves struck the steamy cobbles outside. The heat was horrific, no rain for weeks, and the dreadful river reek worsened each day. *S'only a matter of days afore the bleedin' corpses gets up off vem slabs and start doin' a bleedin' paddy's jig, it's so bleedin' 'ot out,* grinned the coroner to himself until he was snapped out of it by the newspaperboy, walloping on about a murder most horrid or thereabouts.

Heavens, mused the coroner, *the sooner he pops 'is clogs and ends up on the marble, the better for us all cos I might get a bit of peace and bleedin' quiet. 'Ow the cack am I supposed to do me inquests wiv vat bleedin' racket?'*

Dr Mansfield brought an end to his oysters and pondered

reluctantly the matters of the day, yet still could he afford a smirk, for, since becoming Westminster's top purveyor of the dead, hardships such as fingering dead bums were a thing of the past. Rotten cadavers were, for the coroner at least, mere paperwork.

Let the pathologists mucky their hands.

Friggin' drunks squashed by carts and tots squished by 'orses and bleedin' carbolic of soda and cholera and please Lord above somethin' good for once thought Dr Mansfield *and* the officer of the court *and* Jeremiah Bindy the penny-a-liner, all desperate for novelty in death, so bored to death by death were they.

The accidents were bolted through; the crushed bodies, smothered by drink and the wheels of a cab; fallen ladies pecked by slum diseases; the consumptions of the old and lonely, cholera's latest, fresh from the stinking water of the poor; unloved corpses piling up on the marble. No relatives to grieve, just a sozzled peeler to recount the discovery of death if they're lucky.

The lazy, dreadful heat lolled outside, fluttering the curtains with its steamy caress, bringing sleepiness, prompting, again, Dr Mansfield to develop rather his thoughts of the briny bite of chilled oysters he could see laying like a willing trollop in the restaurant. Across the court sat Mr Bindy, so hungry for death in a novel guise. His last story of any worth was that of Edmund Prostrate who ate a jar of false eyes thinking them pickled onions.

Because this writer, like the rest, has no income of his

own for he is a coal-heaver of words, a desperate man, frantic for a story to pay his 15 guinea lodging, traipsing his pen and ink-stand across the city's courts, the bowels of the coroners, the depths of gaol cells.

Dead bodies were his breakfast, murders his lunch, the drowning of infants in Thames mud his supper, the brutal knifing of a seamstress by a crazed Chink half potty on plum sauce and opium his pudding, for who does not relish the misery of another, and the sorrier and gorier the better by far. And so he writes and listens and chews his nails to the very quick, needy for something awful, a death above the ordinary, a demise uncommon for the common lives or the better world of attractive beauties found dead in the height of fashion in the Regent's Canal.

He knows death inside out, a gin drinker not far from the marble slab of his stories himself, a more unenviable existence of sore feet and empty stomachs hard to imagine, living on the precipice between dinner and starvation. Yet does anyone really care who plunged the deadly blade?

As the first witness took the Bible and swore her oath and shifted rather uncomfortably in the witness box and started again for the oath was upside down and when said likewise was actually a very crude Flemish riddle, Dr Mansfield slipped guiltlessly into a revered slumber of grub, a horsey smile on his rum old face, dreaming of slap-ups in Sweeting's and dreaming up too, titles for his memoirs, ready for the booksellers the day he returns his final verdict.

'I Have Come Out Of My Shell. (Ooh Tickle Me Do!): The Life And Times Of A Coroner And Oysterman – In Two Halves (Ooh Tickle Me Do!).

'Well your honour,' muttered Mrs Eileen Brewster, 'it vos a few hours after eleven and I vos just finishin' me shoppin'. I vos preparin' a stew, so bought two carrots, no *three* carrots, no it were two, a bag of peas, some oysters, even tatties and a shin of beef. And a candle vax and half a snuff, a bit of suet pudding, an ox-gall for to clean the knives wiv, a big horse's cock an-......'

'That's quite all right Mrs Brewster, while I appreciate your housekeeping skills are not in any way wanting, I am sure the court does not wish to hear fully the details of your provisions,' interrupted Dr Mansfield in his posh-voice-for-the-court and then back to thinking *cor, oysters and suet puddin'* he mused, partially erect at the very thought, *she may be an old boiler wiv a face like a butcher 'avin' a plop and ain't got no teef and the charisma of a black wiv no legs but she might be worf gettin' to know wot wiv cookin' like that,* 'but before we continue, pray allow me just two more questions.

'Mrs Brewster, did you kill this man?'

'No.'

'Super. How do you serve your oysters?'

'Lemon juice. Cayenne pepper.'

'Beautiful. And would you ever find a coroner attractive?'

Oh bleedin' Nora, they don't 'alf go on these lower class nipsies, oooh pea-soup vis, coalman vat, ooooh, oooooh and in he slipped, further, deep down into the dreams of a world free of corpses and the cholic hands of Satan, a world free of misery yet one full of oysters and those lovely little nancies that wear tight breeches and, *ah but I do love 'em oysters, oooh tickle me do, bring the gloves cos you can't relish the sweet flesh without a fight and remember, protection of the hands is a must cos you can't go pokin' around at Coroner's Courts with mangled old claws. I'd be fucked. I angle me oyster knife between the two shells like a muff, then cut the bleedin' muscle what holds the shells togevver. Wiggle it if you must, but don't force, heavens no, don't ever, ever, never, ever pry open the oyster. If it don't cut the muscle, jiggle the knife along the side of the oyster and bring the blade toward you and here it comes, you juicy, beastly, salty bugger of a bitch. Pull on the top shell and scrape the oyster off the bottom and eat that bleedin' bastard! Ooh tickle me do I've sploffed.*

'And ven, your honour, after ve market I stopped for a tipple of gin. Ven I saw ve body covered in blood and dogs vos all eatin' it. Vun had a kidney in 'is mouff. Another had 'is cock in 'is paws.......'

Cor, I remember lunch at Sweeting's like it were yesterday. Hold on, it was *bleedin' yesterday. Ooh tickle me do! 'Ad to put on a posh bleedin' coroner's voice, case anyone spied me.*

'Waiter. A table by the piano-forte, an extra-large napkin and twelve of your finest oysters.'

'Sir, we....'

'Shut it Lawrence. Two dozen Blue Points or Bleue Points as the frogs call them and two dozen Marennes, or Marennes as the frogs call 'em.'

'Begging your pardon sir, I have tragic news.'

'Oh what now? Cholera, whooping cough, tuberculosis? You bastard. No more friggin' death. My own life may as well be over too.'

Evidence was called and witnesses swooned; a cabman recalled driving a rapid figure with gorgeous boots. PC Widdle was called to the stand, PC Widdle and his grapish bruise, come from knocking his head on the pavement when he saw the killer's work. He found tiny wood splinters in the wounds, a strange biscuit with riddles written within and a stick of sugar rock too.

Then came the pathologist whose temper proved adequately intemperate. A jet black hair, as dark as the night itself had lodged in the man's duodenum.

'Does that hurt you sir?'

'Your honour, not my duodenum, the victim's. I doubt it pains him in the least now' replied the pathologist. Oooh. What a temper.

And the poor man's wife who called for layman definitions of 'traces of male semen' which meant nothing to her thirty-year marriage but bizarrely did it seem that Dr Mansfield was smiling the dreamer's smile as she once did at a time when her husband's step could be heard by their lane.

'Sir,' said the waiter at Sweeting's, 'I have worked in restaurants since the age of three and never, never have I witnessed a man take his own life by lying under a chair. Now let me help you up.'

'Oh thank you. If ever you die, I will give you the nicest inquest imaginable. What would you like upon your death certificate?'

'Uhhm, I do not know. Sir. As I tried to inform you, we have no oysters.'

'I think I have passed water. How would one know?'

'Sir, it is custom to place your hand betwixt the legs and test for moisture.'

'Ooh tickle me do! One moment. My legs?'

'Yes.'

'Ooh. Yes. Utterly damp.'

'Piddle. Simple really.'

'No oysters?'

'Yes. Please do not weep. We expect a new batch tomorrow from Billingsgate.'

'Fuck Billingsgate. Do you manage?'

'Yes, thank you sir, I cope handsomely, especially on the quieter days.'

'No you oaf, I meant, are you the manager of Sweeting's?'

'Yes I am.'

'Do you employ foreign staffs?'

'Foreign?'

'Sir, your voice has risen an octave and you display the hallmarks of a liar.'

'Yes sir. Two Swahilis, seven Frenchmen, one Hungarian and a half a Jew.'

'Half a Jew? Is he absolutely tiny?'

'No, he has Jesuit blood from his mother and Anglo-Saxon from his father.'

'And are they all permitted to labour within Great Britain?'

'Sort of.'

'Sort of?'

'No, not at all in fact. None of them is entitled to be in the country. They are all wanted crooks and bathe together.'

'Knew it. I have thought long and hard. And HARD. Ahem. HARD Ahem. If you feed me in a, ahem, another manner, then your staff will be free to remain criminals, but unknown ones at that. If however you mock my advances, I look forward to seeing you, the two Swahilis, the seven Frenchmen, the one Hungarian and the half-a-Jew in the dock at Newgate. And then upon the slab at my coroner's court. Now, remove your waiting costume, bend forward and let us make believe your bottom is an oyster. Ooh tickle me do! KEEP STILL. Allow me to prise open these hairy shells with my knife.'

'Sir, are you sure the knife is big enough? It do feel rather flimsy. Aargh, that is not a knife, it is a genital.'

Lovely.

A tremendous coughing, a barrage of rasping and tittle of hacking brought Dr Mansfield back. The coroner's officer mouthed in a dubious whisper: 'The verdict, the *verdict*, your honour' and crooked his neck in the direction of the morgue.

'Verdict? Ah yes. Well, that has been the inquest into the death of Roland Shoe. He was a man of fifty-seven years, had no sign of congenital heart defects and enjoyed boating. Verdict: Natural death.'

There were screams for resignation, howls of disbelief, whelps and yelps of disgust as the verdict was returned. A miniature riot ensued as books flew, tomes tumbled and the coroner's officer took complete advantage of the melee to undo his breeches and tinkle into the reporter's inkpot.

'Coroner are you *mad*? Mr Shoe has had his trachea shattered, his tummy taken and a sharp piece of wood put in his mooooth.'

'Yes, he has been dismembered and a fella has spunked up his pooper. And you say death by natural causes? I am never to come here again as long as I live.'

'Please members of the coroners court, I uhhm, I eerm, I wore the incorrect spectacles. I meant to say. Verdict: Unlawful Killing. MURDER!!!'

Bath Time For Gays

I soon learnt many new tricks – the most important of all to distance my soul from what I did. Once my quarters had been left, so my body could hunt the alleys and public houses, take up position outside the barracks, undress for money at the Hyde Park swimming lagoon, my mind frozen numb. I tried to sever all sensations for if I did not, surely could I not go on, either in this behaviour or this life. While my bottom frolicked like a baby dear and I became ever more deft at pleasing my clients, inside I froze, only to thaw once the hideous exploit was at an end and I knew I could be alone once more.

I was once approached by a meaty fellow in St James' as I loitered near a hat shop with my bum sticking out. I felt then that I had quite mastered baring the derriere to passing gents for the angle was superb and one could have rested a pot of drink upon my seat if one were so inclined. I am not these days for I once attempted to balance some tea upon a lady's bottom. My angle was tremendous but I neglected the breeze. An unpredictable gust ensured her behind carries a momento of the event to this very day.

I picked up gays in Faulkners Turkish Baths, 9d for a plunge, nancies in the Jermyn Street tubs, an umbrella-maker in Green Park, a milk-skimmer by Battersea-fields who yelped: 'Half-penny half-pint' as he poodled my noodle in his frock.

And there were more, more, many, *many* more.

August 21, 1857
The Policing Of A Metropolis. Again

The station house at Bow Street was particularly warm. There was talk in the newspapers of some miasma of sorts, a foetid cloud that drenched the Thames in stink. Apparently it had struck before and killed hundreds. No, thousands.

But death of another kind had struck last night and the London Times reported it thus:

FIFTH CORPSE DISCOVERED HALF-NIBBLED. SOMEONE FOUND IT AND NEARLY DIED OF FRIGHT

"Yesterday evening, just after teatime, was a cadaver found, draped over a staircase like a scarf. A labourer called Barnaby Bernard Bertrand, aged 51, stumbled, quite literally across the corpse as he slid down the banisters. 'There is nothing unusual about my method of going to work' said Mr Bertrand.

'I have done this every day for 40 years and I am in better living conditions than when I was eight. No, nothing wrong with my sanitation, but there was a God-almighty lot wrong with that body. It was like a side of beef in that it was full of tooth-marks as though it had been eated for breakfast or an early supper. I think there was horseradish a-peeping from his bottom but I could not be sure for before I could sample, I did

knock the body to the ground by error. I think I broke some of its bones but it probably did not feel a ting. A ting? Tis what dey say in Cork. For oi am an Oirishman.'

Scotland Yard are as yet not releasing the name of the deceased, though if any wives are missing a husband they are urgently required not to panic, said a Chief Inspector from the Yard, for they often turn up when it is dark. Detectives are releasing very few details as to what was seen at the obscene scene save this: a neighbour did hear a light clicking sound before there came a scream and the corpse did have a faint coating of tobacco ash. Scotland Yard are now urging all heavy smokers and light murderers and all light smokers and heavy murderers to either stop and hand yourselves in or stop and promise to do no more of either. Or just stop murdering and resume fuming, but preferably in a well-ventilated room with little straw, hay, wood or parchment. Or naked flame, gas or chickens."

My God, my fucking God, thought Sgt Bates then quickly apologised to the Lord Almighty. For though the Yard had him as a bad-tempered, bad-mouthed, bad-breathed, badly-behaved police sergeant, he was *still*, he believed, a fucking good man who lived with his fucking parents and believed in fucking, NO, NO, NO, NO, God and temperance and sobriety and alms. Mind you, his moderations did not last long at all.

'Fucking hell. I need Widdle and need Widdle now!'

'Sergeant, if you exit the station and describe a right you will soon face a privy. The conditions are primitive but realistic. While there you can widdle all you like. You may even prepare a shit.'

'Sir, may I ask what rank you possess in the Metropolitan Police Force?'

'You may sir. I am a Police Constable. I joined on Thursday. I love policing and kicking people.'

'You fucking bastard. I know full well where the fucking toilet is. It was paid for by a fucking elephant. An Indian elephant. When I said Widdle, I was referring to PC Widdle, PC Arthur *fucking* Widdle.'

'PC Arthur Fucking Widdle? Is he related to PC Arthur Widdle?'

'Fucking related? He is one and the fucking same.'

'Oh.'

'Widdle! NOW!'

Sgt Bates was a large man of middle age with bright colouring. At the best of times he was pinkish, at the worst, absolutely bright red purple garish blood-clottable crimson mauve. Today he fell into the latter.

'Sir?' It was PC Widdle.

'Yes?'

'You called.'

'Not particularly. The day is quite warm. Indeed fucking warm would not be an understatement. I can barely fucking breathe an-'

'No sir. Not cold. You *called*.'

'I fucking certainly did.'

'How can I help sir?'

'*Help?* Fuck? Corpse? Oh yes. A man has been fucking murdered again. Why did I not know about it before the newspapers?'

'Sir, well, you see, things, hhhm, oh God, oh God. Please sir, ask someone else.'

'I want to know why I did not know. I am an extraordinary policeman. Fucking tell me for I can sense a temper.'

'Well sir, it had not happened.'

'When?'

'When I saw you last.'

'No, fucking no. Why did not you inform me once it had occurred?'

'The body was only found, uhhm, quite, you know.'

'No.'

'Well you see, the cadaver was still inhaling and exhaling, breathing is the new word, when it was early.'

'And when did it stop inhaling and exhaling, or fucking *breathing* as you say?'

'Late.'

'Widdle?'

'Sir?'

'You speak in a *riddle*. Please hasten. I am need of a tiddle.'

'Sir, you were not to be found. Night was upon you. You were in bed. Asleep. And the last time I awoke you, you beat me in the balls with an almanac. You said, sorry for the language: "If you dare fucking harm my kipping ever, ever, *ever* again, I will ensure that you will never reproduce. Now get out. Fucking out."'

'How dare you instruct a superior to get out. *You* get out. *Fucking* out.'

'No sir.'

'Are you disobeying me?'

'No sir. I meant when I said, "Now get out. Fucking ou"

'You've done it again.'

'No sir. I meant when I said, "Now get out. Fucking out",

I was quoting you from the evening upon which I roused you. That was your reaction.'

'Ooh yes' chortled the copper. 'I remember that, you was terrible fucking scared. I remember you did a wind.'

'I did?'

'Yes. It put me in mind of a donkey.'

'Sorry. That is why we did not tell you about the murder.'

'I see. Have you found him?'

'Sir, I do not know.'

'You do not *know*?'

'Yes.'

'You do *not* know?'

'No.'

'Which is it?'

'What?'

'Which?'

'Have you found him?'

'Who sir?'

'The murderer, the beast, the killer, the butcher, the slayer.'

'No. None of them.'

'Why did you fucking say you don't know.'

'I don't know.'

'You don't know?'

'Yes.'

'You *do* not know?'

'No.'

'Which is it?'

'What?'

'Which? You said you don't know.'

'Oh yes sir. You asked if you should phrase your phrase,

again excuse the language but I am quoting. "Or should I say, have you *fucking* found him?"

'Found who Widdle?'

'The murderer.'

'How can I have found him? I only fucking discovered the death seconds ago.'

'No sir that is what you asked me before you asked me if I had found him and when I said I don't know I was referring to your question to me about how you should say your question.'

'Widdle.'

'Sir?'

'You are absolutely fucking baffling me. What say we curb this nonsense and do some policing.'

'Excellent sir.'

'Now listen' instructed Sgt Bates, 'we have got a problem here.'

'Yes' rumoured Widdle, rather out of sorts by the way.

'The fucking problem is as fucking follows. Two men anus each other. One man ends up dead as a door with his body parts severed and somewhat eaten. We must find him. If we don't, we get in trouble. Any suggestions?'

'What we could do' commenced the novice 'is this. Firstly, whenever we arrest a suspect we could record some distinguishing mark, for example the prints of a finger. If you look briefly Sergeant at the tip of your finger' and here he demonstrated his plan. 'No sir, the other way round. As you see, if you compare yours to mine' and again facilitating proceedings, the PC brought the two digits together emphasising the following: 'They are both of them, while of a similar length-'

'Mine is longer than yours' interrupted Mr Bates.

'Yes, of course' immediately agreed the dejected PC 'but they are absolutely different. It is widely believed that every single human being has unique finger markings and they remain pretty much constant throughout one's life. Therefore if we keep a record of everyone's finger details when such a crime occurs, we can check the body or items nearby – ie banisters, barristers, bastards – for these marks and align them with what we have amassed in the Yard to pinpoint a known suspect.'

'Uhhm' uhhmed Sgt Bates.

'And further it is widely believed that each individual's blood and spunk are different thus making it possible to do a similar check with a person's juices. Once someone is arrested we finger them and then distil some of their blood and jism which we also keep o-'

'*Jism*? And where would you expect to fucking put a pot of spunk? In the fucking larder? Perhaps next to the bread sauce? Or maybe by the onions?'

'No sir, I really meant keep a written record somehow of its makeup and, again, once the dead body is found, we have a look-see for tell-tale cuts or spots of jizz, make a test and see if our villain is not already recorded and then we arrest him, read him his rights, interview him, make a note of what is said, charge him if we think there is enough evidence to eventually secure a conviction in a court of criminal law, remand him in custody if there are fears he may otherwise abscond, take him to a Crown Court, arraign him and let twelve good men and women of the British jury system – ie the defendant's peers - try him by hearing evidence from both the Crown and the defence, and if convicted accept what sentence is passed by the judge.' And an exhausted Widdle exhaled and sat back with an expectant look on his chops.

'Widdle?' bellowed Sgt Bates.'

'Yes sir' replied rather quite eagerly the PC.

'You are positively medieval. You talk fucking nonsense. Any other suggestions?'

'Well I suppose we can ask the neighbours if they are the murderer.'

'Excellent. Far more fucking sensible.'

August 25, 1857

A Chapter Which Truly Is Quite Horrid In Which We Learn That Members From All Extremes Of Society Like A Bit Of Bumming. And An Expensive Chair Gets Ruined

'Ooh tickle me do! You look new, you'll have to do. Have you got a name? Mine is Mansfield. Herbert Mansfield. Herbert Joshua Mansfield. Herbert Joshua Jacob Mansfield. Herbert Joshua Jacob's Crackers Mansfield. *Dr* Herbert Joshua Jacob's Crackers Mansfield' said the man before me.

'Pleased to meet you' I fibbed. I would earn my supper and a quick pump off a whore but I did not enjoy the muck.

'Ooh tickle me do!' toodled the queer old goat. 'Fancy one back at my gaff? Brilliant lodgings, what? Do you like ham?'

'Well yes. I suppose I do' I supposed. 'Wiltshire?'

'No, Bloomsbury.'

'Bloomsbury ham?'

'No you mad gay. It's where I lives.'

'Oh, I see. I meant the ham. Damn.'

'Ooh tickle me do you wheezer, yes.'

And barely had he susurrated the serpentine syllables that fondled the end of his 'yes' than we were in his quarters. They were dusty and full of books – the general topics were medicine, cadavers and oysters. What a strange man was he.

'Tell me' he whispered as he unbuttoned my breeches and bit off my hat. 'How do you earn your living young Sandy?'

'*Me*? I eff men. Please excuse me. I was not Christened Sandy nor do I expect to either. If you must, I would prefer a simple Andy. Like Sandy but without the 'ssss' hissed I.

'Ooh tickle me do! Look at my fiddle, it is all stately. *I*, my young boy' and he reached under my legs, 'corone at courts.'

'You erm, *corone*? Pray what is that?'

'If you have heard of the craze known as an inquest, well then I rule on matters of death. I make important announcements and several people like me. Most popular fella in court. Yes. Hiss, hiss, hiss.'

'Sssssss, ssssss, sssssss, ssssssss.'

'Ooh tickle me do! I have soiled myself. And my dad's Louise XIV chair. Please sir, could you pass me that tub of "Jizz Rinse. Manufactured in Yorkshire, For The Removal Of All Terrible Errors. For the Man Of The House. Anoint Twice A Day. Do Not Eat. Do Not Feed To Children. Do Not Alight Nor Inhale. Your Spunk Is Our Bunk."

'Just a little dab and he'll never know the difference. As good as new. Now, if you would, your anus.'

'Straight away or in portions, Dr Mansfield?'

'Ooh tickle me do. *Immediatemente s'il vous plait*. Call me Herbie.'

'Yes, Dr erm Herbie' and I unrolled my French knickers to announce my bum chops. They had recently been polished and packed quite a shine. 'Have you coroned well of late doctor, erm Herbie?' small-talked I as he careered like a lobster towards my troubled end.

'Yes' groaned the Herbie. 'Only recently did I corone into the death of Roland Shoe.

'He was a man of fifty-seven years, had no sign of congenital heart defects and enjoyed boating. Verdict: Natural death.'

'Fascinating. Any distinguishing marks to distinguish his extinguish?' I quizzed as he jizzed.

'Let me think. Possibly a slight rash on his chin. Or was it an ingrown toenail? Ooh I like it when a fellow does that. Hiss, hiss, hiss.'

'Ssssss, ssssss, sssss.'

'MY CHRIST!!!'

I bit the man in shock, somewhere only his mother would know but he seemed not molested.

'MY CHRIST!! I recall,' recalled he, 'Mr Shoe had been cruelly mutilated, savagely beaten, his limbs severed, several of his organs had been removed like so many peas from a pod, his stomach had been pulled over his head like a hat and his fingers slashed off and rammed into his ear like so many violets in a vase. I remember too he had been wildly bummed.'

'*Bummed*?' I uhhmed.

'Yes bummed......by a man' and as he spake did crash a heavenly crack of thunder which very shook my bones.

'Ooh.'

'Yes, I love you. How disgusting it is for a man to sex another man. In the bottom. The Lord never wanted this to flippin' 'appen. How 'orrid. Please sir, raise yourself in the air, yes, yes, that's it, like a donkey, for I cannot get a purchase on your hips and my cock keeps falling out of your arse. Ah, that is lovely. Do you mind if I sing?'

'No Herbie, feel free' and free he was to pound out a verse or two. In some respects I found the affair soothing.

'Drink up boys, and have a glass with me,
For it isn't every day I am out upon the spree,
I'm all right for I've got the £ s. d.,
And I mean to keep it up for I'm as happy as can be.'

High summer, 1857
What A Way To Earn A Crust

And so as was this new chapter developing, I recall with horror now, how, as night fell with its doomy gloved hands throttling the light from life, I would pick up horny bachelors and seedy husbands, spoiled by drink along the back lanes of Piccadilly; Magistrates and Constables, playful guardsmen outside the army quarters. I was once assaulted with an un-oiled rifle. It made my bum sing a sad tune and I was unable to dance for weeks. I frequented the Hundred Guinea club where I flounced with strangers and used a girl's name. I thought Ada rather suited. I wore a dress and Parisian drawers, for some gentlemen would pay double when I dressed so. Too, I appeared as a porter boy to oblige gentlemen travelers for a shilling. Thus attired, I oft tried my hand on the country's locomotives, steaming and whistling around the Metropolis. When the weather proved foul and the beer houses muggy I took an advertisement in The Times. It read: *lovely young fellow, stunning bum. Fancy a bit? Not half! Only a few farthings.*

Sally, it appeared was long gone, but still her very name haunted me to the quick. When I closed my eyes to take the accursed genital of carriage drivers and soldiers, I made believe it was my love in some hellish disguise. But once my eyes opened once more, I soon knew all was doomed still. I prayed for an end.

I soon became accomplished at my affairs of the anus, yet keep abreast of modern life I must. I read newspaper reports of mungo bummers in Cheapside and Shadwell, fancy fruits from Le Havre come to these shores with a tang and a song and if I was to remain a top-class sort, I would need to learn new tricks; I would speak in French to encourage the men and use the cash for a lady or two. Some customers begged of me only to read and so with the nightclothes up and my dayclothes down would I recite; the Bible, recipes for suet pudding, pigeon with bread sauce, scientific journals into the work of Dr John Snow and his water-pumps, the battles of Crimea. I once met a client who shared the exact same desires as me. He begged of me to take brandy with him while peering down my trouser flap.

Yet as my name grew in stature, so did shrink my soul, for the bumming of a man does a fellow no good in the end.

Hearing About Some Bad Incidents In A Family House

The Magistrates Court at Bow Street in the summer is a stifling hell of urine and old mans' plops.

I shuffled in, a bleary wretch, to take my place in the dock. I nodded to the clerk of the court for I knew his face and he, my name.

He was a grey-haired sop and he bade me stand while he put the charge; drunk and disorderly, guilty; outraging public decency, guilty; fear or provocation of violence, guilty; criminal damage, guilty; common assault, guilty.

I sat as the prosecutor, as boozy as a man could be, aligned his papers. Gustave McWinkle (German and Scottish parents I am told) coughed a tickle of gin before addressing the judge, Mr Justice Norbert Faulks.

'May it please your honour' tottered McWinkle, 'I appear for the prosecution, and my learned friend, Mr, Mr, Mr *Wong* appears for the defence. Your honour, allow me to open the facts.

'In the early hours of the eighteenth of August just past, the defendant, heavily in drink, arrived at 23 Air Street in Piccadilly. Slurring his words, he banged regularly upon the door, yelping, "By God, you must let me enter. I have had a couple, no more and demand some how's your father. This is a pest house is it not, now let me in please."

'The residents of the dwelling, a Mr and Mrs Fridge were naturally alarmed at the disturbance and bid the defendant goodnight, by which point he was already asleep upon the doorstep.

'The Fridges sent down to investigate the footman, a Mr Terrence Bush, instructing him to remove the menace, your honour. But upon opening the door, the defendant was awoken, possibly by the noise, possibly by something far more deep within his soul and burst forthwith, herewith as follows: "Bum my arse."

'Mr Bush was moved to tears and fell to his knees, only for the defendant, who by now, presented his breeches not quite at full length, to clamber, like a monkey, up the stairs and into the drawing room, where Mr Fridge had taken refuge.

'He then shouted: "Where's Sally? I know she to be here. Hand her over or I will" and then, please your honour, he fell asleep. But only briefly, for by the time Mr Fridge had ordered his biggest shoes to be brought him and laced up, the defendant was once more awake and had entered the marital parlour, where he, uhhm, I am sorry to say this my lord, but the defendant removed his what-not from its you-know-where and…'

I fancied myself a titter as the bashful McWinkle, for I have seen him with his arse on show in a Southwark brothel, stumbled along.

'The defendant removed his what from his where?' hooted the judge.

'He exposed his thing to the lady, your honour.'

'Counsel, please. This is a court of law, there is nothing that will shock me. I have seen much, *much* sin. Now please

Mr McWinkle, for the last time, in *English*, tell the court what happened.'

'Your honour, he got out his cock, span it in an anti-clockwise fashion, like a windmill from the Low Countries, stretched it as a *haricot vert*, directed the business end in the lady's face, piddled in the cupboard, and climbed in bed with the valet.'

Quite ashen-faced his honour whispered to me in a wheeze, 'What have you to say, you, you, you *monster*?'

'Sorry!'

'Oh, please your honour, just one more thing, if I could' went the brief.

'Yes?' squeezed his honour.

'Perhaps' puffed McWinkle, 'the court should hear the victim impact statement in Chambers. It is tender in places and not necessarily good for the public.'

In short, many of us were banished while McWinkle let Judge Faulks into a little secret.

Much after noon, we were ushered once more into court. The judge was laying down as my Mr Wong prepared to save me from gaol.

The Chinaman hauled his great bulk before the judge, his oriental frame creaking the splintered benches of the court, echoing to the ancient sounds of shipwrecks: 'Prease, youw honaw. I impwore you to fink of my crient who is inhelentry a good man. He has fooren on hard times, youw honaw and committed this clime out of sheew despelation. He has effectivery rost his good chalacter and his leputation has been inteleminabry smeared. He has had to rive with the consequences of his actions, and in admitting his guirt, he has crealry learised his behaviour was wlong. In crosing my mitigation, I would say in arr honesty that this is a man of otherwise good, if not excerrent chalacter. He does not melit plison.'

I walked from that court a free man. I was bound over to keep the peace and if I so much as dropped my farting crackers in public, I would be going down. I later learned that Mrs Fridge (I must write to her) has since developed a tic when faced with her husband's penis. It is somewhat of a predicament. When they are to share relations, he must disguise his cuckoo as a swede or the good lady will go into seizure. Unfortunately cook mistook the swede for a parsnip and something terrible happened with very hot water. Oh yes. Judge Faulks no longer sits at court. He remains at home and talks to himself.

November 19, 1857
Winter Comes To London

The day was hot, awfully hot. It felt as though a devilish fire
was breathing its spicy flames in my face. It was. I had fallen
asleep in the grate of Mrs Gough's hearth, for by now it was
November and I had been drinking.

'Mrs Gough, I am so truly, terribly, truthfully sorry about
my antics in the fireplace. I can explain. I went out last night,
and I, I, uuhhm, returned last night and what with the clouds
of late, the cumulus and a nimbus and a minibus, the
awfulness of lamplights and fear of snakes, it was far too
dark to tackle the staircase. I did not want to bother you for
the hour was heavy so I resolved upon settling down here. It
was so warm and sweet and I was all a-snuggle. Please do not
fine me.'

'Boy, my lovely young boy, how could I? I have milked you
as a baby and I will milk you as a man but next time you
snooze in the hearth, please do not wear my bleedin'
nightdress. Our hips is different shaped and it takes many
days for the contour to come back good and well.'

'Nightdress?' addressed I, partly ashamed of my ways for
my father once told me: 'Son, if you ever don a female's garb,
always beg of permission beforehand, for it saves a lot of
bother in the long run.'

'*Night*dress? Are you certain Mrs G tis yours?' voiced a

sorry me, for I feared I was in the soup without a spoon. 'I do have one which is similar.'

'Well, yes you did, except that was a mournin' suit all in black. Mine is pink as a knee and is all of one piece.'

'Hmmm. One piece. I hazard mine eyes are not exact of late. I will ask a man look at them. Would you like a snoot Mrs G?' and I unveiled my eye, rather like the peeling of an egg, and pointed it towards my lady landlord's own ball.

'Please sir. Your retina revolts me. Go to bed.'

Really. Bed could wait, for after such an attack on my character I needs musted find a haircut. I loved barbers.

December 3, 1857

He Goes For Some Fish And A Haircut
But All Goes Wrong

Omnibus, big and dirty, heavy and noisy. It belonged to Thomas Tilling Ltd and I scaled the exterior staircase which wound its way along the back of the vehicle like a snail. I sat down for a moment. It was cold and the metallic bite of the seat did sting my bottom so. The floor was matted with straw, I paid a few ds, was advised to use Oakey's Wellington Knife Polish by an advertisement, and lowered myself at Gladstone and Son's Barbers, Shampooers and Shavers. My neck tingled with the excitement of a good strop and my nose tickled with the eagerness of Wilson's Shaving Cream. Any longer and an erection would be upon me so I bounded towards the door. It was locked. "No murderers velcom. Ve don't lyke you'r tipe. Eff off. And dont take our towels. Back in a veek."

What a day. Could events develop any for the worse? Surely not.

I turned to face Jermyn Street; vagrants, thieves, smoking women, a barrel organist, a whistling monkey, an Indian with white ribbons on his head, a fried fish man and a child with a basket of baskets perched upon *his* head.

Indeed, I stopped by him for the man was all out of herrings. Instead I bought some hot peas. They are quite tasty and as green as a pea. The vegetable is boiled in the pod which in turn is dipped in melted butter with a little pepper, salt, and vinegar. I normally pay a halfpenny for a quart pint of the monkeys.

I was, by then, a pea expert, having made a boo-boo initially by attempting to snaffle the peas, pod and all at once.

These days, like other members of the lower classes, I draw the creatures through the teeth, sounding much like a Chinean in soup. I have become quite good chums with the peaman although I forget his name now.

As I ate, a horse made a mess and a crossing-sweeper rushed to gather the article which he placed into his pocket. A shoeblack scurried rat-like between the legs, hungry for dirty shoes. A hound, drunk on port, gnawed at his leg until squashed by a mule, while a fight arose between a woman and a man. She kicked him in the downstairs. He kicked her in the upstairs. They began to fornicate, shredding each other's outfits and whooping until the man shook with snores. A stranger, surely as evil as Lucifer himself, tossed a child at me. I ducked and darted into McMustard and Cress Hair Removers.

The setting was soothing. An enormous chair, as large as a man's mother, sat waiting for me, its leather limbs winking rather, as though a four-legged whore, while above it sat a looking glass, grainy with dust and talc. A brass machine of pumping water was upon the wall and the man was lovely.

'Vot vill it be mine gut Herr?' put probably McMustard.

'What is this with the vots?'

'Vot is zis viz ze whats?' was the reaction.

'No, I said, "what is this with the vots?" Are you German by any chance?'

'German? Gott no. Munchen, lederhosen, Hoffmeister, Gott no. Do you believe me now? Please are you satisfied?'

'Bloody yes. I should not have suggested it, but it was merely that you were voicing the letter 'w' much like the letter 'v' and consequently pronouncing the letter 'v' akin to the letter 'w'. And you have got a feather in your leather hat, constantly use sausages and are dipping your shaving brushes in a beer stein. Also the clock is set for the time in Düsseldorf.'

'Mine gut Herr. Düsseldorf? Shaving? Vee and Wee? You must excuse me, I was still munching on my breakfast when you visited and there was some, oh, you know, what is that substance you, I mean, *we* Englishmans eat for a morning meal? Intense, soft, but inflexible. Wildly tasteless? It comes in one or two colours?'

'Porridge?'

'Porridge, yes of course. Well some of that porridge was stuck between my front teeth making my pronunciations quite absurd. Would you care for some porridge?'

'No thank you. I have just egged.'

'Would you care to look at my teeth?'

'Thank you Mr McMustard, but no. I have my own.'

'Hmmm. Well?'

'I usually frequent Gladstone and Son's Barbers, Shampooers and Shavers. They do an ample cut, shampoo, shave and singe all for 3d but appear closed. Do you have anything similar?' requested I and then unbuttoned myself and waited.

'Hhhhhhhhhhhm' mumbled Mr McMustard in tones a

little bit lengthy for my liking, 'let me just have a look-see' and with that he fumbled and tumbled in the hairdressing cabinet.

'We are out of 3d cut, shampoo, shave and singeings alas, but we can offer a comparable service. I can cut, shampoo, shave and singe you for 2d. Do you love it?'

'In theory yes, but be so good as to allow me time to think. Can you recommend food?'

'Yes. I eat it most days, it increases my bulk, provides me with energy and makes my tum-tum all warm.'

'I see. But would you recommend some *local* food? I especially relish radish.'

'Oh I see what you mean. You can always attempt Rudolph Richard Raymond and Son, We Provide Radish In A Bun. Exit my premises, describe a right-turn, and you will be there.'

The radish was a crime. I threw it back in Rudolph Richard Raymond and Sons' faces, striking them with the bulbous bastard and returned to McMustard.

I flung open the door, removed my hat and bellowed: 'Bugger me McMustard, cut, scrub and raze me. Singe my tips if you please, I am all yours. Ooh before the onset, let me sip your refreshment and crunch a wafer. Crawford's Biscuits I assume. Ouch.'

I was thrust out in a sordid manner. I had wandered inappropriately into a church. I never knew vicars had such tempers.

'Herr, you have a radish on your cheek. Oh no, oh no, oh no, it is a bruise. Were you beaten?' asked the benevolent barber when eventually back in his premises.

'Only once and I did not mind it. Now if you would be so kind as to do my hairs.'

What a touch that man did have. Light and feathery as a girl but at times as brusque as a soldier. Stunning service. We spoke of this and then we spoke of that, all the while my hairs were strummed, stretched, loosened and twiddled. 2d he said. A more ample businessman would augment the fees but I was not to suggest such a suggestion. I dozed off momentarily as he lathered my chin in a froth, rustling my whiskers like a bum and preparing his blade. According to McMustard, Gladstone and Son had deserted their premises that morning after learning of another murder. The details were outrageous, but sadly, predictable. A man's clothes were sliced, his penis was missing and his offal left upon the pavement.

He dipped a cup into a bowl of hot shaving-water, kept beastly and bubbling over a glowing charcoal brazier.

First he fought among my whiskers, flinging and stinging and occasionally singing, the brute, the thug, smooth and nice no more, towels and combs and reeking of scent. I feared utterly then for my life, for after supping late at porter, I oft entertain dark thoughts the following day; a stifling pounding within my brain that half afears me to death, that clobbers and hammers so my heart, until I fear that he will very burst. And upon me then came such a moment as I looked up to see the evil eyes and grinning glints of blades and all of McMustard's menace towards me and my throat. I care for my throat. And the razor is a deadly weapon in the wrong paws.

The wax tape was lit and the glowing orange moon pressed onto the ends of the hairs as McMustard asked the following question.

'Sir. Are you funny?'

'Funny? Well I like to think I can quip a jape or two. I once made a man swallow a rhubarb in glee when I impersonated Prime Minister Peel. I can also achieve convincing likenesses of certain animals. Namely the pig, the goose, the eel and the house fly. Many years ago, I performed a passable imitation of a buzzard but I fear that was more due to chance than ability. Would you care to hear one?'

'Erm, no thank you.'

'Why not? They are bloody good.'

'Uhhm, my premises does not have a licence. Sorry.'

'Well, perhaps we could go outside. Let us play name that noise.'

'Bloody hell no' fumed the man, his visage almost red with rage.

'Sorry' sulked rightly I 'I will never ask you again.'

'Versplatz. I have forgotten about it already. I did not mean funny as in humour, I meant are you a gaylord, a fruit, a what-not, a nancy pansy? Do you love men? If you do, be careful for this murderer chooses funny victims.'

'That brand of funny? God no. How dare you' cried the aggrieved. 'Why did you think that, before I storm out of here by the way?'

'For starters, the mode of your walk, your fragrance, the length of your whiskers. Oh yes, you are wearing a basque beneath your clothing.'

'It is not a basque. It is a nightdress. Have you never seen a tailor you bounder?' and with that last hanging in the air like a raven, I wiped my chin upon McMustard's apron, kicked the hairs that lay on the floor like so many eyebrows into a cloud of strands and with hat on head hurried from the accursed shop.

'Sir sir, sorry sir, sir. Your hat' oohed the proprietor, but I was in no mood for idle chatter.

'I know it is my hat.'

'Sir, sir, your hat is....'

'Lovely, high and expensive. Name this noise' roared a more aggressive me and socked the man in the Adam's Apple.

He replied: 'Ooooooh.'

'No. Incorrect. It is: "Barber bleeting because someone hoofed him in the neck"' and before I left I showed him how funny I could be and arranged a Shakespearean riddle for him. '2d or not 2d, that is the question.'

I was arrested moments later for being in possession of a flammable hat. I was called an 'incendiary hazard' by a Police Constable, my head was doused with a sherbert and water costing ½d and I was further charged with making off without payment. My hair was absolutely on fire and I was becoming partially bald. Frigging hell.

December 15, 1857
Dining With The Beef Steakers When A New Topic Is Brought Up; And Mention Of A Lady's Breasts. Again

'But you do prossies, don't you, William?' squeaked a scarlet Timothy Jacobs, his commodious backside squeaking back and forth in his chair much like a dove with heartburn.

'You told me. They stick their thumbs up your bottom for a guinea' piped he.

This brought forth a sudden whoosh of the tablecloth, and leaning forward into the flesh of his salmon, the poor lad burped out pain. Pure pain.

It appeared the violence was borne from the other side of the table. William's side. He wore large riding boots. We were fond, perhaps unnaturally so, of William's deeds and misdeeds with the common ladies of London, for it livened many a dull supper.

Yet William was, to all intents and purposes, married. To a pretty little woman who knew nothing of his operations, which she in fact funded. He convinced the wiff that he invested her papa's monies overseas, in the Indies or somewhere, in the trade business, spices, that sort of thing.

As lonely as I was before I met Sally, I was more lonely still; my only company the cock and bum of loathsome strangers. I had decided recently to re-acquaint myself with the Steakers. How many months or years had passed since my last supper with the fellows I do not know, but they appeared nonplussed by my appearance. Waterstones had vanished, they knew not where. Hastings mentioned that he hadn't seen me for a week and had heard I contracted the dropsy. I agreed, for when a man is truly alone, what is the point in displaying his solitude for all to see?

Jacobs cleared his throat and began again: 'Are you not happy with your wife? Do you not regard each day as Christmas when you awake beside her, happy with the gift of marriage, the sacrosanct pleasure God-given to the chosen few? Do you not...' for he was a funny little romantic was Jacobs, but his analogies, were cut short. Cut *very* short. Executed, snipped, snapped, beheaded if you will.

'No I do not, you arse. *Christmas*, you say. Well if, in your queer little world, Christmas is gloomy as can be, it rains without end and we eat just a bread and dripping, well then yes. I do indeed reckon my mornings to be as fine as the Yule.'

He was a sarcastic man was William, but he made clear his point.

'But what is it that makes you thus, do you not share any affection for the woman, are you odd?' piped up another chap, a bachelor by all accounts.

'Yes of course I do. I love the woman. But I also love my mother and my aunt and my brother. And my dog. She is awful tiresome, snores like a pig and has horrible teeth. That does not stop me from loving her though. The human heart is capable of many loves, diverse each of them. My heart has many portals, each separate from the rest, you see, for a man can love two score and ten and hurt no one but himself. But you see' and here he looked to the younger around the table with a view to instruct. 'I *love* her. Indeed were she to die or leave the country I would probably be upset but I have needs. *Base, rotten* needs and no decent man should pester his wife for satisfaction.'

'Really?'

'Yes really.'

'*Really?*'

'Yes really.'

'But you pay for these sexings, do you not?'

'Yes. For that is how such things proceed. They are a transaction, much in the same way as a baker would sell you, or I for that matter, yes especially I, a loaf of bread perhaps or pudding. Or a butcher would sell you some pork. In fact, why keep a slice of bacon when all you want is a pig?'

Silence.

'Mmmm. Let me see. Perhaps it is the other way round. Pigs, whores, something like that.'

'Right. Well, what such actions do you like to do with loose types?' asked another young fellow. 'I have always believed a married man would have his needs catered for. My cousin is married and he never stops fornicating. Last week he performed more than five times. Once up the ar-'

'Well, let me stop you, young Bumshaw. Allow me this. How many years has your cousin?'

'No more than three and twenty I believe.'

'Well, therein lies my gripe. At least some of it. I am twice that age. No, I am not. I am three times that age,' a pause to drink 'and when I was a younger man, before I became grey, before my chim-chim began to wilt, I too had passions for Melanie, my wife. We shared the same bed and once she even licked my testes. But there comes a time in a man's life when certain sensations can no longer be sensated. New stimuli are required for the same end.

'Her breasts were once fabulous. They swung violently from side to side when uncorked, but now, my wants can no longer be quenched by the duo. They had become too friendly, too well-known, too predictable, too familiar by far. I knew them as well as my own. They were my family and may God strike down that man who so soils his own kin. For I need to be *aroused*, my God, I do.'

'But *what*' came next for the perspiring and wheezing William, 'what if your wife were to offer a *relief* for your desires in the privacy of your own parlour? And for free to boot?'

Wiping a crumb from his eye, (a mystery indeed) he endeavoured to put the young fox in the know.

'You smutty little man, I would not dare basen my wife so forth. Have her dress and talk like a Frenchwoman? For the life of me no. I love this woman. I respect her at times, but have her behave in an outlandish manner, in the way of a slut? God no. The very thought of it.'

'But what could be more reasonable? Your urgencies dealt with in your home by someone you trust and who is unlikely to rob your breeches?'

And with a sigh, one that rattled the very forks on the plates, one that rippled the bloodied lakes in our glasses, he wearily drew the conversation to a close.

'No' he said. 'Such would be wrong for I love my wife. I tolerate her noises and ignore her mind. But I crave novel ninnies. I want the tingle of an unknown nymph. I love to finger a fresh corset, I want a woman's bubblies to surprise me so and I want to surprise them alike. I know my wife, I love her and I would never hurt or rotten her. I am tired. Goodnight men.'

How I felt for the poor man for it seemed I was not alone. I still whored yet still did I love my Sally. My lust was oft insatiable, incurable, immoral and ill-timed. Some days, at the bolt of breakfast, I would dart towards the river, Limehouse or Southwark, peckish for muck, and on I dizzied, while the tea sloshed inside my belly still. Other times would I squint from my lodgings, my bottom aching from the last client, his coins still warm in my pocket, tainted by the unnatural love he had fostered on me.

Yet my anal economy did soothe me for I felt it was the only way for justice to act.

January 26, 1858

After The Discovery Of One Murder Too Many, He Takes His Leave From Mrs Gough's Household, Ending Up In A Place Worse By Far. Much Much Worse, For In Reality Mrs Gough's Was Quite Lovely

In a flash was I gone. Mrs Gough had been surprised by some police officers whilst I was abroad searching for clients. I hear the fuzz were quite horrible.

One copper had sketched an unlikeness of me and armed with a nightstick and a deplorable vocabulary, demanded answers to his questions, none of which were pleasant for poor Mrs G. Did I entertain members of my sex in my rooms, had I seemed excessive with hygiene of late, had I, in short, assassinated anyone and disposed of their dismembered bodies in a side street? Poor Mrs G was taken peculiar and accused the officers of disparaging her home and her tenants. She was right furious.

My situation became worse I learnt upon my return home. Worse even than a man who has the company of a female in his quarters yet upon unsheathing the bedclothes did forget that within the darkness of the night before had done a terrible plop under his pillow. Ooh, worse, far worse.

I had to abandon my rooms for I was by now a wanted man, the prime suspect for the homo murders.

In the time it took to pack a valise and kiss her pon the

cheek, I was gone – as speedily as I had let her down the last time.

Things really had taken a turn for the worse; my finances had dwindled further still and my employment as such necessitated a hiatus. It was no longer safe to continue the arse trade as before. And quite frankly, I had had more than enough.

So let me tell you how I came to be resident of the most godforsaken place on this earth. A living hell, a foetid, putrid seething mass of what pains me to call humanity. A more indecorous, pitiable site can not be imagined, not even with the most fervent nor pickled of minds. The Rookeries of St Giles. A place, whose boundaries I had traversed on many happy occasions but of whose existence I had never the slightest inkling. Bizarre how yards from its tortuous confines, as the hansom cabs and carriages rattle past in the street, the wretched howls from those near-dead, the frantic pleading wails of life's lost, the screams of death and the wildest of passions, the incoherent whoops of the terminally insane are muted, kept from the ears of the good.

The hell of St Giles, a very inferno of warrens, a nether world, another life of cut-throats, the very despised who walk God's fine earth. A more despicable nest surely there must not be and I pray none of you ever land there.

Recall you that cursed brat from the hanging?

January 26, 1858. About tea-time

The First Night In His New Home, His First Calling In A New Profession And The Pong Of Nasty People

I walked the streets that night, as nervous as a monkey.

It was mighty cold and at the entrance of The Rookery I spotted a berk.

The lad, he cannot have been more than eight, was, by the looks of things, ill. As ill as a horse with no hair and pots of arse scurvy.

I was in a damned hurry – to where, I knew not, yet from where I certainly knew, for still was I wracked with worry; frustration, fear and fury at the monstrous ignominy, this edifying disgrace, this awful opprobrium that had cursed me so. I was, once again alone, *truly* alone, sickened by my new ways and afeard of what might be to come. I was in a screaming flutter, my mind torn apart without coherence, when I stumbled upon the thing.

He was as grubby as a dog and wore a remarkable odour. With him was a howling woman, her face as grimy as an African, smeared with soot and tears; her breathing most rash. She thought me a doctor and in truth, did I have no option. I musted to help the lad, who I knew at once to be that very same mongrel who had caused me so much mischief after the hanging. It was as a lifetime ago but he had barely grown.

His little legs, no longer than a baguette, twitched ahoy and his brow was feverish as he lay on the ground. Oh the sound.

Having not long ago read Buchan's Domestic Medicine (I had serviced a paediatrician and when he fell asleep, I rifled his bag. It held tummy pills and reading matter), I recalled the root causes of many illnesses; diseased parents, night air, bad air, sedentary habits, wet feet and cucumbers. A change of air was out of the question and a leech at this hour – to cleanse his tiny body from impurities – too. Its mother was tearful and beating her breast. I felt obligated to perform and I resolved to execute a purgatory.

In a flash I had down the blighters's breeches, grimacing at the scent emanating from his nasty little behind. The poor fellow knew not what happened. While an enema would do the infant much good, I did not feel apt to the task. Instead I swooned the mama with Latin and coughed on his buttocks. For good measure I prodded his anus with my cane and bade him stay clear of spices. He barely cried. The fevered cheeks, earlier aburst with flame, had soothed into a pallor altogether more natural.

The mother, I begged to hear no more of and I was set to take my leave when there came squeaks from the impoverished old bat.

She begged to repay my goodliness and leant her ninnies towards mine eyes. They were fearsome and quavered with flies. I wanted away from her but on a whim, now she mentioned it: 'There is just one thing' said I, thinking perhaps of two. Hhhhm. Not bad.

How odd is life. I moved that night into a common boarding house and became a doctor.

In short, if any place would accept such a man as I, it was here.

His first night in the Rookery is hell, for sleep stays shy and comes not. He lies awake beneath the bulging, black ceiling, thinking of Sally, Mrs Gough, the hansom cabs to the supper clubs and the Lyceum, hearing the roaring wind howling through the broken casement, spinning a sorry dance in the fireless grate, thinking of himself, calling for death that very night through the puffed tears of a lost man, hoping that his life will soon end. In the tiny room where he lays, half a dozen bodies wrestle with their consciences on that very floor. Their snores and groans, grunts and wheezes prove dreadful. Many shake awake in a run of tears. Yet is he thankful still, for their tortured barks mask the worse sounds of torment from outside. As the night slips into dawn and the sounds of drinking fade, and murderous screams abate, and pious orgasms shake the very foundations of life, then come the hullabaloo of sobs. The silver clank of knives and the wretched howl of dogs and men, course through the grimy air. Harlots ply their wares until the coming of the sun. Footsteps rush through the night chased by the piercing blow of a bobby's whistle. Yet there he lies in fear of his life, watchful of any hands that may care to do him harm or to rifle his meagre effects. He fancies he does hear the tiny scraping of tiny feet, the plashing of rats' claws scurrying from the cesspools of the warrens, paddling through the puddles that run through the streaming cellars of the tenements. Vermin, he knows, are scrambling over his body, giving him frightful shivers. He fears the daybreak will never come.

January 27, 1858
A Chapter In Which We Learn The True Ways Of A Man Of Medicine.

This was certainly no hotel.

I normally breakfast no earlier than 10am, sometimes post-meridian and in short, I was as hungry as a Turk.

'Where to I ring for feeding?' I enquired of a bearded thing, 'and while you are about, is there attendance within? Boot-cleaning, soap, fresh linen, cooking tools with fire and steady ventilation too?'

He growled as though poorly. I continued.

'I am unfamiliar with the procedures and hence shall prepare a list of requirements anon. They shall include a bolster for the bed, some chintz hangings, a palliasse – I am not sure what this is but it sounds tasty – a counterpane, a stuffed bird, scenes of duck-shooting in the Scottish Highlands, some pink briar roses for the trellis around the bed edged in gold which will reflect both the morning sunlight and evening by candle, some forget-me-nots, a brace of chiffoniers, several whatnots and some French mahogany with marble top for the water closet.

'Besides, could one perhaps *clean*? This floor is terribly dirty. Here is *muck*.'

I pointed to a site not far away.

'There is *sperm*.' I pointed to a site quite close by before continuing anew with my breakfast musts.

'Sweet cream with my oatmeal,' I hastened again, 'and I prefer my sardines mustard-less. Beef tongue I do *not* care for and marmalade makes me burp' I almost finished. 'Oh, and you' I beckoned to a youngster, 'I take a glass of brandy, Spanish if you would, after my tea. And my *cushions*? Plumped? Where?'

My waiter made me weep for he had a powerful thump and a rotten boot.

Breakfast was not brung. It would needs must be eaten with the other guests at the grate. Bread and tea was I given but butter was extra.

By bingo it was low, lower than a viper's chin.

Most fellow guests were filthy and many were in drink.

The worst swine was a child of nine. His eyes permanently were bloody, his breathing shocking and his language no better. I feared he was to go for me, like an overgrown stoat, but as he leapt in my direction, he was overcome by tiredness and mid-bound turned to sleep.

'Ooooh. 'Ere's that fairy 'gain. I telled yas 'eed be back one day' said a man.

'Don't you go talkin' baht 'im like that' said another. 'This man is a doctor, a physician, a scholar, an expert in the art of medicine. He can cure gout at a glance. He can heal a hernia, rectify a rectum, look at a lady's bubblies and demand a fee. He has just saved a boy's life.'

I soon knew with horror anew that my new neighbours were those same beasts that bullied me, all that time ago, the day of Arrowsmith's hanging. How I rue the day the nitwit poisoned his wife. The prime vocalist, a pig of indecipherable years, had rounded upon me again, and fearing for a painful snout, I backed into his friend. I was fingered by many, but following explanations, they left me alone and went about their way.

If I was going to stay there (while safe from constables for the now, I feared the tenants), change was required because from day one my pampered tones, my delicious moustache (more of him later) and my burnt nose were singled out for ridicule. How little know the lowly.

March 1858

Medicine

Changes did come though and in a peculiar fashion. Seeking my medical knowledge, many residents found ailments in need of healing. I learnt to think on my feet. Some were truly too ill and thus could I grant them no cure; others suffered from boredom and hypochondria. One man, he bore a striking resemblance to a fox with his red brows and cunning gizzards appeared to gain pleasure from revealing himself to me. He claimed his sex organ could mutter in a strident baritone and so vociferous was the chap that it kept his owner awake at nights. He loosened his pantaloons, unfurled the creature (it put me in mind of a Continental snack. I believe the Spanish call it a *chorizo*) and bade him chat.

'Hello, vot is your name?' spoke the man kindly. 'Come now , don't be shy, doctor vonts to say 'ello.'

'Sir' ventured the patient as he gripped his patient in a fiery grasp, near throttling the thing, 'Maybe he vill talk if you asks him a kvestion. Go on, say 'ello.'

Not wishing to appear rude or indeed afeard, I inhaled deeply and, rolling up my shirtsleeves, stepped up to greet the thing. I leant forward and stooped as I would were I to meet a Member of Parliament. Upon my arrival, it began to twitch. Indeed he was full of whiskers and could have passed for an Indian. 'Hello,' began I 'have you a name? Uhhm. Did you sleep well yesterday? Errrm. Do you enjoy angling?'

Nonsense. I was once the dishiest chap in town, owned almost a dozen suits and knew many horses, yet here was I engaging a penis in conversation. 'I am sorry my man, but he seems to have lost the art of talk. I really have not the time for this. There are children with the whoooooping cough.'

'No, you must stay a little bit longer' he really pleaded.

'He's bashful. I fink he likes you, please stay, *please*, I beg of you. Oh please.' And with that he increased his purchase on the tiddler, which had grown in length and girth. It really was a frightful gadget and the man had begun to sweat. I was concerned he may use violence.

'Uhhm, tell me, for how long has your, well, you know what. *Sorry? Alan?* Yes, a delightful name for it. Not it, *him*, of course. I could not think of a better name myself. Yes, for how long have you been speaking to Alan? Why do you think he talks too much at night?'

'You're the fucking doctor, you tell me.'

'Yes, I *am* the doctor, aren't I? How foolish. I suggest you sleep earlier. And perhaps loosen the grasp on your co-, on Alan because he appears poorly. He has become red and bloated. Look, he is even crying. I think you do not know your strength. Let me know if your sleep betters.'

The matters worsened. One man was unable to bend the right leg. I begged him lower his slacks for access to the limbs. He rolled forward onto his front like a lizard at the seaside and exposed the source of the mystery. He had tied a large spoon to the back of the leg, thus restricting movement. He was as surprised by the discovery as was I and indeed he was at a loss to explain its arrival. I advised him not to use the tool for eating.

One patient suffered from catarrh, another a cold, three had spots, a fourth a wooden leg that caught fire when close by the range. More had missing teeth and begged of me to make them anew. I told them, with some temper, I was not a dentist. One child had swallowed a matchstick, another had a desperate rash. I recommended dabbing milk upon it.

Two men and one woman, a vulgar specimen with a fine breast, displayed tuberculosis. I told them they had the sniffles and suggested they move out. The work made me terribly tired.

I found one patient particularly distressing for he was a villainous-looking fellow and not of good cheer. The matter was most delicate and I bade him raise his night-shirt. My heavens, a more infernal backside surely cannot exist in this metropolis of millions. His bottom was as bare as a newt, bald and fairly shocking. The whole thing was almost perished. I learnt that he had attempted an omelette upon a Defrie's Magic Heater when the contraption exploded and burnt off his bum hair. Poor, *poor* man.

My next diagnosis was frightful too yet utterly different from the last. The patient did lower his drawers to bare before me something most evil. His bottom, for that is what I shall call it, was likely the most hairy commodity I *ever* have viewed. I once saw a lithograph of a brown bear far less bristly. It was wild, unkempt and abysmal. So matted was it that I yet do not know if beneath the fur lurked two buttocks or a quiet Jewish man. I fear I will never know. I was tempted to proffer a gammon to see if the Jesuit would balk at the meat but I did not for three reasons. Firstly, if there did prowl a Shonk neath the behind-whiskers, then surely would he be so hidden from daylight that he would not distinguish the meat. Secondly, the dish, once volunteered, may go missing for several days and I would have little cognisance whether it had been refused by the Ikey or eaten by him under the cover of bum darkness. Thirdly? Oh yes, thirdly, I possessed no pork and shellfish were very seedy. If I had ventured forth with an oyster I did not wish the burden of gastric harm.

Yet this strange man, a happy man too, plucked from the forest of his bottom some almighty grape-looking things. Haemorrhoids indeed.

'Yes, I see' I saw, 'truly terrible.'

'Ooooh noooo. Nooooo nooooo nooooo.'

My God was he an imbecile as well as anal? I wanted him up-trousered and away anon.

'Nooooo, look at them, they is vunderful' he beamed and, with his legs describing fifteen minutes before three post-meridian, he gyrated his hips in a smooth bearing while his contraptions built up speed and flared remarkably in an anti-clockwise direction. I felt quite dizzy.

'My God. We will have to do something about them.'

Quite what I did not know. I was uncertain about amputation and besides I possessed but a moustache spoon and a walnut fork as instruments. Perhaps with much force and a vinegar, could a procedure take place.

'My God' repeated I as they gathered momentum. I feared if one should escape from the dangle, it could take an eye with it. Mine, his, a fellow resident's. In short, a catastrophe.

'My God. My God. Do they cause discomfort, perhaps mischief? My God. My God.'

I wanted dearly to look away, yet they were remarkable,

truly remarkable. They mesmerised. I felt vertiginous and not a little crazy and I believe I may have said some things never normally voiced without porter. At least one bottle's worth. And some veal. The room became a twirl as his dervish dance developed. A whooshing sound, not unlike the sea, shushed too and a faint breeze caressed my face. All colours merged as one gaudy purple. All noises bled dry. I knew not what I did for I caught myself leaning towards the bum and beckoning forth the deformities with a kiss. But no sooner had the spell been spun, than the wizardry of the marbles was broken.

'My God. My God. We will have to do something about those things of yours. They are truly wilder than the beasts of Africa.'

'Noooooo. Nooooooo. I love 'em. I get special tickets on the omnibus, I got a special seat at the chop-'ouse and they once stopped me going to jail.'

'How? My God. My God.'

'Well, I was caught foisting a fella's purse and told the judge I was desperate for dosh for to pay for some bum cream. And do you know, Judge Fockle only gone and wept when I showed him them. He wiped away a tear and said: "Billingsgate. Billingsgate. You keep out of trouble, look after your things and we will hear no more of it. How much costs the ointment?" and the gent, for he truly is, gave me a 6d for to go and get me cream.'

'And did you procure the poodle potion?' I prompted post-haste.

'Did I eff. I got a gin and a floosie.'

He Learns The Nasty Tricks Of His New Company And Makes The Acquaintance Of The Landlord. He's Certainly No Mrs Gough

The place was riddled with children who saw no future. Indeed, all was bleak, a life of hope gone with the first flame of life, extinguished on their mammies' bosom, suckled dry by age and drink. Perhaps life for them would be better in the Colonies, for there is nothing here for them save wretchedness and the hangman's noose. And maybe some child bumming under a bridge.

And what's more, their habits were peculiar. Children of all shapes and ages, some with barely a stitch to cover their what-nots, slept all together, where they fumbled beneath the rags, giggling, and groaning, while their little paws performed a topsy-turvy dance. What little shame they had, fornicating so young in this breeding ground for pure devilry. Those who were bed-less nested betwixt their fellows on straw, like horrid little bastard frigging hens.

Elsewhere, an overweight monster played chopsticks with himself, one eye shut in concentration, the other keeping a firm eye on the dome of his jolly nugget.

'Sir,' began I, not as confident since my recent duffing. 'Sir, if you would be so kind as to point your stick, your sausage, your lolly, sir perhaps elsewhere, I would be eternally grateful.'

He snarled his teeth.

'Sir, it is a dazzling contraption, a fine string, a magnificent hermit, but, you see, in its condition, it is a hazard. I fear-'

And with that the hulk popped off on my head. I went to bed in a huff.

My sole companion proved to be Bernard, the little chap I had saved from death. I still maintain that the shock of cold air on his rump invigorated the boy to health all that time ago. It emerged though, that he had eaten a foul pie recently, claiming it tasted of dog do. The poor beast, he must have been made ill by the cursed meal. Ungrateful indeed – he called me a baboon when I trod on his face – yet he was my only hope of survival in that devil's nest of adders. His mother had gone, doing the naughty with soldiers in the park. Bernard was an odd-job boy who turned his hand to anything to earn a penny – horse-holder, parcel carrier, matchbox seller, skewer hawker, birdnest flogger. Alas Bernard told me that I needed 8s a week if I was to keep my bed. Another 7s and all would be covered.

I learnt to keep my distance from these brutes until I had conceived of a plan, so to occupy my time, I watched a troupe of ants climb over my shoe and under the bed, then crawling across, in single-file, the gentleman who had recently fouled my pate. I began also to enumerate them and time their passage. Indeed I named some of them, but soon the soldiers ran out and I dropped off. I was terribly tired.

Women, bare-headed and drunk on gin at nine, suckle babies on their teets; fell-mongers and tripe-dressers, glue-makers and scum-boilers, bone-grubbers and rag-gatherers prove a hellish reek for all; they live here, also too the growing thousands displaced by the coming of the railways, their homes run through by the new tracks, nowhere to go, desperate and destitute, ragged children old before their years dragging themselves to the soup kitchen in Farringdon, trepanners prowling the back streets looking to snatch pretty youngsters for the West End brothels, others on the hunt for lapdogs and then hoping to snare the reward. For all, this is their home.

May 1858. Or it may have been later. Sorry

The Ins And Outs Of The House. And A Most Hideous Goings-On One Night. Oooh.

Slowly I and little Bernard became better friends. He still eyed me terribly when it was his wont, but I felt less at risk from him and his crazy fangs – I once saw him take a chunk of a man's leg for a minor crime. How the man did weep.

Whilst I bemoaned my life and made greater pretence to learn the ways of medicine, Bernard would bring things to the lodging which he and his friends had snaffled from the city.

Bernard's crew were Ethel (her nose was drippy); Cuthbert (prone to erections); Martha (a girl of eight yet in the know of many sex acts); hairy Fanny; Eleanor (she had a sweet bottom and was older than the rest); Hester (not a tooth in his head); squinting Ambrose (he squinted); and the unpleasantly named Pleasant.

They starred the glaze, broke the drum, pinched the bob – in short helped themselves to which they had no right. Candles, buttons, ladies' drawers, cigars, cats, bacon from Leadenhall, plums, snuff-boxes, fish wheedled from Billingsgate, pint pots, bones, string and offal.

Slowly was I learning new rules, new classes, new castes. Much as once ran butlers and plumpers, valets and cooks in my family home, so too did these monsters share the duties in this underworld of theirs for it was from their own role that each gained his purpose in life.

So with his ripped shirt, marked by rats teeth and his breeches stained with big jobs, was Pleasant our kitten-nipper. His job was to plunder public houses for pewter pots. When not about pot pilfering, he was a pudding snammer; filling his pockets with as much grub as any cook shop could stock. Fanny was a fine moll-buzzer. Barely one woman in twenty had the slightest ken that their purse had been lightened as she trotted sweetly behind. She was too hairy for other roles.

Ethel's post was to pinch coats from houses and inns. Eleanor had outsized teets like a Scotsman's chin and was a garreteer; she scaled London walls and earnt a fortune through the attics of the City.

Ambrose made a superb snakes-man by wriggling into lovely homes via the drain.

Martha's manners were so torrid, she had no option other than to lay in wait for little girls on their way home and pounce with scissors. Snipped off hair was worth a lot.

Presiding over all was Norris Moorcock, the Deputy of the house and a useless pig of a man, his face pitted by the pox. He claimed to be related to a leading academic – Lawrence Moorcock – for they used the same name. Indeed the money-snatcher would impress upon us all that he had studied the classics at Oxford and he believed me a kindred spirit in academia, thus wanting of me a friend. In fact he was nothing more than a crook. He oversaw the passing of nabbed booty and placed his orders, especially in the line of snatched foodstuff to distribute amongst us all. At a price of course.

Not a soul thought more of the man than they would a fly, a flea or a bee for he governed the place on a mean budget, was thoroughly untrustworthy and immoral. He had the teeth of a duck and the smile of a toad, but owned the building alas. It had been in the family for years and he was hopefully the last in a long line of scoundrels with similar features. Few liked the man, but he had thugs - brutal ruffians with sticks and tempers and he could call upon them in a flash.

His habits were extortionate and viler than those of a Greek. Indeed soon after my arrival did I catch the man perched atop a pail of soil in which lurked carrots and one cauliflower. Alas his breeches were as low as a snake and how he heaved and grunted.

'Sir!' I did shout. 'Are you trapped, in pain, hurt, in discomfort?'

'No. Ploppin'.'

'Plopping?'

'Yes. According to J.C. Loudon in his 1842 book The Suburban Horticulturist, *"The most valuable animal manure is that of man....as abounding with ammonia and nitrogen...in every suburban villa, arrangement should be made for collecting all the liq-"*

'In short sir' I interrupted, 'may I enquire as to what you are proposing?'

'You may. From this day on, we shall all cack on me veg. Come round for tea sir? Carrot cake. Ooh.'

A more filthy man I had not ere known.

And Cuthbert, he was amply developed. Barely twelve, he sported a terrific beard, spoke in deep, deep tones and had a honker like a hat-stand. Yet, poor fellow, his contraption was unappreciated within doors and brought him no awe, but embarrassment alone. At a time when boys were bum-dancing or bonking with trollops, Cuthbert was struggling with the bean which oft poked up with nary a warning and would only nod ta-ta once dealt with firmly. The boy's fiddle-tiddle, his Father Abraham, would arise, much like an auntie in curlers and nod his head in time with the rough beat of his master's heart. He hoped all along none had witnessed his belly-ruffian's habit. So would poor Cuthbert take to the streets, much hunched over like a Jew, to deal with the matter in hand. Dawn or dusk, noon or night, rain or shine.

How tragic, but back then they were all I had. Some say we are put on this earth to make the most of life's sadness. Others say other things.

I lay a-bed regularly rigid with fear for the Deputy was often so in drink that he knew not who entered the house. Indeed, mobs of footpads were known to strike, robbing and looting, beating, whipping and frigging. The racket from fellow residents helped keep me awake during the long hours of darkness, the drunken stumblings, the awful grunting sounds, the cries and sobs and the wild farting from the bog shop. Plus it was too unsafe for the streets during the day what with the slayings and the coppers, so would I nap throughout the afternoon and thus implore insomnia when darkness came.

Yet this cursed sleeplessness did prove good with time, for one night did I witness Cuthbert and his wandering bob commit a truly awful sin. Fully turgid, his member bold like a barber's pole with hairs on, its tip prodding the moonlight neath his rotten trousers, he began to aggravate it, beating the cursed hog whilst gazing in awe at Pleasant's buttocks. They sat open in the heat of a warm evening. Knelt over Pleasant, Cuthbert yanked himself violently with the venom of a cabman running late for supper, while staring fixedly on his neighbour's chuff. It was uncivilised. I would have a new friend by tea time.

An Interlude Of Letter-Writing

The following morning, I composed a letter:

"*Dear Mrs Gough*" it read.

There was more: "*Please forgive me again for the ache I have caused you. One day I hope I will be in a position to repay you for everything, everything you have done for me and equally I trust I will have the answers you and I both seek as to these extraordinary events of late. I will not impart to you my whereabouts, other than to tell you that I am not a hundred miles from you, where I should be, and I am as well as can be. I do this purely for reasons of security. There would be the potential of mishap to us both from other parties should you know too much of me as yet. Believe not everything you may hear in future.*

"*Please give this boy before you my eyeglass, cuff links, lexicon, portmanteau, night-shirt and whatever else I may have left behind. I cannot begin to express how much I miss my rooms and your company and soon will I be back once more, but in the meantime, perhaps some pickles from the larder and maybe a slice of meat. Also please some bath salts. Oh, I have no bath, but include them nonetheless, for they may prove useful. Thank you so much. Oh, and be sure not to tell our little friend with what you entrust him for fear of theft. Thank you.*

For ever, your very good, true friend

XXXXXXXX

My words were simple to Cuthbert.

'Go to this house, ask no questions, answer no questions, pass this note, accept what you are given, do not look at it, sell it, sniff it, steal it or lose it. Return in haste. Any failings and your friends will learn all about your moonlight botty cocky tricks. *Got* it runty?'

I could have kissed the boy, so speedy was his return. In fact I *did* peck him a little, but once I realised my error, I held firmly his gaze and administered the same ere threat. It worked. All was intact; nightshirt, a vast hat to fend off vermin and a box of goodies that would see me through hardship. I could not grumble. Oh yes. And another grisly murder said the Times.

June 15, 1858

A Chapter Of Which All Those Who Have A Full Head Of Hair Should Take Heed

'This sir, is the sitting room. It is south-facing and enjoys sunlight until the early afternoon.' The man seemed impressed. I led him elsewhere, pointed out for him other rooms for such was my role of late. I rather hoped he would take the lodgings for he seemed a generous man.

'This I call the lavatory. Indeed, it is a little small and, yes it is most unusual to see three upon the pot at once, but this is an *ever* so friendly environment. Hmm. Downstairs there are plans to convert the drawing room into a library. And here, the range. One may cook a supper: quail in caper sauce, partridge pie, perhaps even a side of beef. Do you like a beef sir?'

'*Beef?* Indeed. Especially when cooked. And have you dined well today?'

'Me? Well? Most lovely. A potato.'

'A potato?'

'Yes. And a pig.'

'An entire *pig*?'

'Not exactly. Part of his nose. I diet you see.'

'You needn't. Your physique, sir, is magnificent. Like a Greek sailor. On a boat.'

'Thankyou. Your name?'

'Washington. With a 'w.''

So, as yet another life began to unfold, so too did events slowly improve and I was no longer beaten for my manners. Some told me of their lives, their troubles, their dreams, for I was not alone in my loneliness. Take away my fondness for asparagus and tight trousers, many years of prime education and a deep knowledge of West End musicals such as Miss Saigon and we were all lonely together, all lost souls floundering to survive. How the truth can better a man.

One day Washington, though he reeked like a rat with the splats, whispered in a voice once reminiscent of my own, when asked why he moved in to such a frightful new home: 'When a man has lost caste in society, he may as well go the whole hog, bristles and all, and a low lodging house is the entire pig.'

I would have a friend in Washington. We talked of life, of love and other matters too. He was well-versed and well-bred, but a curious hunting accident had brought an end to his ways. Yet he did not complain. He accepted the traumas of life and blamed no-one for having to share a bed with three youths who piddled throughout the night.

'Tell me' croaked I one morning. My coverings had been whipped away by a thief whilst I napped and I awoke with a frightful chill. 'Tell me' (have I ever mentioned I have a tendency to repeat myself?), 'your life.'

Washington's replies were heartening: 'I like you, not as much as mama or my horse or as much as I enjoy the potty during the evening, so I shall be frank and candid.

'I grasp you are no physician, but understand one must do

all one can to survive in this inferno. Life is hard enough for man, be he rich as a lord or poor as a bee, for everything, sir, is relative.

'When I was a rich fellow, I knew several wealthy men. Probably much like a younger you or I. Nourished on turtles and sole, a bottom cleaner, a tooth scrubber, one man more to shave the beard and another still to comb the hairs and iron the news, but yet, still did they suffer woes for money maketh not joy, money bringeth not light nor love.'

I agreed with the man quite marginally.

He continued: 'One dear friend enjoyed all life could offer. His biceps were outstanding. He was once suckled by twelve women during a single supper. But where is he now? Dead. Took his life at twenty-seven. Why? Had he lost his health, his family, his love, his mind, his standing, his dignity, his French maid lithographs? No. He lost his hairs. Every last one of them. Overnight, almost, did he lose his entire hair - black and bushy, much like an African's but damn straight, it was frankly the talk of many a tavern. Thick and boisterous was it at cards on the Tuesday. By Saturday his pate gleamed and shone like a minor planet. Rather like Uranus.'

'How dare you' I growled from the throat like a goat, 'my behind is beautiful and as cunning as a fowl.'

'The planet I meant, which twinkles so at night.'

'Ah.'

'Oh.'

'Well. The hair. There sat yet a thatch about the ears, but the top of the skull was sparse. In fact with the surrounding tussles bordering the nudity, the whole contraption put me in mind of a gorilla's arse. With his money, the finest wigs in the world could be stitched. He could have favoured the most glamorous hats of Piccadilly, or even left the *tête* as bare as a babe and remained none the poorer of life, yet on the Sunday morning was he found dead as a dog. He had shorn off his downstairs hairs and fixed them to his dome with paste and left behind a scrawled notice. "I cannot bear life" it read.

"'I love my hair. Goodbye. There may be a better place awaiting me around the corner. Washington, you may keep my dressing robe and my cat.'"

Washington wept the tears of a battered man.

June 29, 1858

The Makings Of A True And Beautiful Friendship; The Problems Of Women, Horses And Pepper. And Peeling Italians

He was kind was Washington, decent and hairy as all men should be and I looked much forward to our debates and biscuits after tea. His knowledge was a tonic, a welcome lozenge indeed and I looked up to him (really I did for he towered above me in his naked feet. This was not frequent, for I would not converse with the man in an unclod hoof) and felt for him as I should a pappy.

He filled me with wise words. 'Always look a man in the eye and grip firm his hand in conversation.'

'Do unto others as you would others unto you.'

'Never touch a priest.'

I grew fond of Washington and indeed, had it not been for his terrible demise soon to befall the unfortunate chap, a fine companionship may have blossomed.

And as our friendship developed, I felt I needs must to tell him of my circumstances. After tea – no milk, no sugar – I approached.

He was not in bed, yet in the privy.

'Washington. Are you fine?'

'Yes my friend, top shape now you ask.'

'Washington?'

'Yes?'

'What are you doing, if I may be so bold?'

'Having a shat.'

'Why?'

'It is excellent. Everyone does so these days. You really should attempt to- eeeurrghh. Ooow. I say.'

'I mean why? You performed the act not ten minutes ago.'

'I did? Did I? Well. What can I say?'

'Hhm. I must talk.'

'I am just adjourning my trouser. Ooow. Never put your penis in the buttonhole. *Never* I tell you, for the outcome smarts.'

'Never. Thank you. Ha. There you are. You are still undone. *Ready?* I was wealthy, exceedingly healthy, I loved a whore and sold my bum for more.'

Slowly I began to unburden my woes; I unravelled the crossings of my life, told how I lost all and not once did he scold. He did not mind I had appeared before Magistrates and never was he churlish and he told me too of his life for he had been in showbusiness. He managed performers and toured many countries with them; Zorba, The Laughing Fish; Signore Montepulciano, The Incredible Peeling Italian; Bruce, The Singing Waiter; Simpson The Racist Duck. He had a happy life, money, food and a woman he loved.

But one day, out riding with Solomon, Washington's best chum, an abominable accident befell him.

For both men shared affection for the same female, yet Washington knew nothing of Solomon's yearnings and indeed was a stranger to his friend's scheming ways. In short, nothing good can come from the fairer sex.

For earlier that fateful morning, Solomon had prepared

for Washington's horse a breakfast. A very special breakfast. A very, *very* special breakfast.

He added pepper and brandy to the horse's usual oats and ere long, so drunk was the foal, his eyes could barely focus. Once a model horse of positive manners, he was soon farting like a soldier and larking terribly. Indeed he was given a sharp dressing-down when he tried to nuzzle Washington's privates. The scene was reportedly awful. But Solomon was a crook. He told Washington the nag was merely in season and looking to reproduce. He made no mention of the animal's boozing. The horse though, sobered throughout the day and with an apologetic look about his face led Washington into a trot. But the breakfast pepper had collected around the beast's nostrils and as his trot became a canter and the canter became a gallop, the wind propelled the spice into his nose, thus inviting a God almighty sneeze, throwing my friend from his saddle. He broke both legs, part of an arm, half a baker's dozen vertebrae and bashed his head.

Washington lay a-bed for several months and was unable to keep his performers to himself but they needed to work, and, much as they adored their manager, they soon looked elsewhere. Zorba, The Laughing Fish and the others would not survive without the stage. In short, the man was ruined. Solomon *did* marry the lady in question.

A vicious end for Solomon the villain and the missus was all that Washington could think of and for several years was he consumed with the blackest of passions and dreamt of death.

'But, my dear, revenge is a young man's pudding' said

Washington and do you know, maybe he was right. All thoughts of vengeance passed as suddenly as they arrived. It came to him on a spring day four years past, that with his life he was content. A blissful lull had settled upon him. He was happy to go about the parks and watch the flowers and listen to the sweet trill of bird song. And what's more, the woman snored like a beast and had tiny knockers.

How He Puts His Brain To The Fore And Pays His Way.
With His Breeches Up

Money, that two-tongued beast, with a golden coin for a heart, bit again as the malevolent deputy pounced once more, pinching my balls as I dozed.

I gave him a cuff-link so he left me alone, but before he had returned to curse that he had no shirt with which to sport his link, I had vowed that I would use my education to educate and thus pay my way. Coupled with my doctoring, I reckoned I could get by, for it was hard to whoopsie myself out of doors what with the fuzz on my tail.

When Cuthbert unfolded the newspappy I had bid him swipe (it had not been ironed, but the damp had poodled off with the breaths of summer) it was immediate that I was living with half-wits. Those that knew what it was were left cold by the words. An exam of their literacy left me in no doubt as to their skill. Starting with Bernard, I tutored him in the ways of the word. It was an arduous process and by the first puffs of autumn he could spell his name seven times out of ten.

Soon, other nincompoops were clamouring to be 'learned the vords' as they called my lessons. As they grasped how to make basic signs and differentiate betwixt noise, so too did I learn that it was not mere idleness that had plonked them in such ignorance. Most all of them had received no schooling. Cuthbert had spent a day at a Ragged School. Of Queen Victoria, he knew this: 'She's a big fat buzzard vot sits her arse on a yoooouge chair. I reckons she's got millions of quids and sleeps in her own room.'

This marked him out as a scholar.

The ignorance was heart-breaking for their lives would be always lowly. I had failed utterly with my giving of knowledge to Sally, for it was inevitable that the wanton lust that slept in her belly would come ultimately to curse me. But here, cheerful as I was with a second grab at goodness, I made it my duty to school the uneducated. I would receive payment too, for among the scoundrels, the thieves, the coiners, the dolly-mongers, jilts, doxies, wagtails and blowzes, night-soil men and rag-finders who called this place home, were those who had a living of sorts. There were costermongers and labourers, cab-men and street-sellers, who all brought back a wage and smiled at me for the schooling of their young.

And so, as the days pass and the evenings grow colder, dead bodies lie still unanswered, Police Constables search for a killer and our friend knows a new life, ticking and marking, enunciating and pronouncing, sharing for once, giving pleasure to others, and wanting little in return. At nights he sits crouched on a bench, his back arched and crooked, half a face lit by the orange glow of the range, a candle snuff warming his smile, pen, tallow, scrawl, while Bessy is home now with a riot of flowers; roses, buttercups, carnations, to gather them together in sweet bunches so she can set off after tea to offer the blooms to City gents at Ludgate bleating 'sweet violets,' a fresh reminder of life outside the Metropolis, the sweet fragrance a chastise to the wicked sins of man.

July 1858
Life With The Lice; And A Treatise On Sports, Gambling And Someone Called God.

Brutal as they were and unlettered in books, the brightest among them possessed a bestial intelligence that could not be gleaned from study, that no school could give; a cunning shrewdness to outwit one another. They had some aptness, an expertise in shillings and bobs, tanners and coppers. They were ruthless even in their games.

Often during bad weather, when the rains ran muck into our streets, when the gaseous stench of shit sneaked in at night and the vermin would swim, bloated past our beds, cards were brought out to play. But for many inhabitants was there more at stake; name, honour, blood and many a brawl has erupted over Roly-Poly, or Hazard, dicey dice or coins.

In fact were it not for the blood-stains at game's end, the chipped teeth that lay, like sea shells upon the floor, the drunken knifings, such was the excitement that many a viewer could mistake themselves at the Royal Saloon in Piccadilly. Many players developed superstitions. Some turned their coats inside out for luck, one man would not visit the bog on the day of a game, claiming a greater concentration if forced to squeeze his legs together. Another played with one eye open and the other closed while an old man would not have a woman in the room. Some still wore a mask to hide their emotions and many were armed. Well do I recall my first attendance. Whitebread and Whitfield, notorious sharps both, had amassed a pregnant pot upon the floor; the coins would be won or lost with the turn of the next card. Whitebread required a seven or more. He drew a queen, but lost an eye.

Violence was intrinsic. Some days later, two huge women, squat and furry, both fatty, tattooed and forever with little clay pipes rammed to their faces took to the table for whist. Much porter and gin had been on the menus. Anus Anna was the first to draw blood as she poked a stick into the other's behind. Seconds later, few clothings remained on them as they wrestled, as unlike a team of Romans as any beastly-fat drunken bitches could be. The scene was tremendous. 'Get 'er, let 'er 'av it, give it 'er in the arse.

'Make 'er bleed, do 'er bones, fuck' er eye off, kick 'er in the muff.'

The language was dreadful, the sight worse but out came the coins; bets were made, cash changed hands at speed, and some took pot-shots at the enormous bums. I made four shillings and could not wait for the next.

As noted, many of the herberts had super brains when it came to the basics of living. They could perform tricky calculus and it had not been for their lack of teeth and tearful manners, a calling in accounting or the law could have come. But alas, such urchins had not been granted such fortune and with sadness did I observe how they coped with that which they had been dealt from the card table in the sky.

Soon though, was I to be making far graver gambles. My

novelty still abounded and so questions were forever put. Some were simple. Why did I use a knife and fork to eat? I thought them cleaner than a spoon and a hand. Why did I defecate in private? God wishes me to. Who is God? A man. Why do you not you bring him round to watch the wrestling? He's very busy. Eventually they asked me why I never left the house. They were people who had been to prison, they had killed and raped, probably in the bumhole, they stole newspapers and biscuits and held up coaches so I could hardly hoodwink them with weak excuses. I was no murderer but the papers and the fuzz would soon think otherwise. I could not be dishonest, nor patronise their intelligence, but yet I sought to be not entirely truthful for fear I would be trapped. 'I am scared of trees.' It seemed to work.

July 19 1858
The Shock Arrival Of A Coloured Man. Those Of A Nervous Disposition Should Pause Before Reading Further. A Cup Of Tea Or A Nip Of Something Stronger May Assist

I saw a black fellow from without the window. I was taking the stairs desperate for the maid to change my linen for a small error had occurred during the night.

He was a very small yet cheery negro with the darkest of skins, as black as night, as black as coal and other such things. I gave him a wave which he returned. I wondered what he was about. Likely an errand for a wealthy man. If only I had one too, a personal black man, a negro man-servant. Oh what glee. He would save much time but could I trust him? Some say that these fellows from the forests of Africa can be light-fingered and fiery, they have a feeble intellect I am told and thus are prone to evil.

Two days later, I saw the very same negro again, this time *in* the house, drifting up the stairs like a phantom. I noticed how he mumbled to himself, probably some African chants, dark rituals from the jungles of that mysterious continent. I was curious as to what he was saying, but fearful I would break his concentration, I left the fellow in peace. I returned to bed for the rest of the morning, until the thought suddenly occurred that this man was likely not just a black, but a housebreaker too. I decided to apprehend the wog before he could loot too much. Also I recalled an advertisement for a missing slave. The reward was fine were he he. He he.

I bounded up the stairs and found the man seated upon the floor, chorusing his carol, this time more tearfully. I stepped closer to hear the bizarre words: 'me doaan like laydeez, me doaan like laydeez, me doaan like laydeez.'

I cautiously approached the brute.

'Sir' began I, thinking it wise to grant him the respect due a stranger. I have mentioned that his height was not great, but his colouring was alarming. It was plain that a man of such darkness was capable of immense violence. 'Sir' rebegan I 'are you perhaps *lost* or are you searching for some person? A calling card would not hurt? This is a *private* residence and you are a, uhhm, erm, a well, you really are a *black* man.'

'Well you done got meee dair' retorted he. 'May be dis 'ere gaff is a private, but it ain't half not a sheet 'ole. Been in more nicer smelling lavees, know what I mean? Oh yeah, me doaan like laydeez.'

I could barely decipher the darky's curious lingo but learnt that he was still not fond of women.

Quite what the dickens the rest of his talk meant was beyond me, but from his tone I mustered that he was not altogether happy.

'Have you come here to rob or rape or pilfer mister? Perhaps you are escaped from a ship?'

'What the 'ell is dair wort me 'avin'? I doaan like laydeez.'

'Dear man, I accept that English be not your chosen tongue, but barely can I make out a word. If you have come here to plunder, then you will have to fight me' and with that the ruffian thumped me on the nose.

The Coloured Man Becomes A Fine Companion And Hopes Well To Serve His Purpose

The black man shared my bed that night. After attempting to wipe clean his face, I knew he was no made-up minstrel. I daren't ask his name for I feared I would not comprehend the response and so, did name him Nelson, for a childhood dog, a lovely little creature with hair on his tail like my Sal's fanny.

There was no hanky-panky – I am not that way inclined and he snored like a horse. He was a kind man who meant well, but whose mind had been scarred by love. He had fled the service of an awful household and, upon meeting a female black, began living with her in rooms near the Cathedral at Southwark. To earn a living he was loaned to wealthy families for novelty functions. He would don an outfit cut from hemp and grass, as though he were in the forests of Africa. Then would he chase the guests and try to eat them. The job was humiliating but well-paid. Unfortunately, upon returning from a party in Great Titchfield Street, he discovered that his black wife was effing his white neighbour so Nelson got upset and left. He had heard speak of lodgings on the cheap in the Rookery of St Giles. He had lost his heart, poor man. And his shoes, for he was utterly barefoot. I apologised for thinking him a thief and we became quite close.

After supper, I begged of Nelson a request. I inhaled deeply and leant forward, for all intents and purposes much like a fireman.

'Nelson, it seems we are more alike than I had ere imagined. I know your hair is far curlier than mine and we have different hues, but I too have had my heart broken by a woman. A *white* woman. A *very* white woman, with the most *creamy* skin imaginable, adventurous breasts and a lovely nest at her thighs which-

'Nelson, are you unwell? Loosen your shirt if you are too warm man. Mind, you types should be used to a bit of heat eh? What, what? As I mentioned, the crook in this matter goes by the name of Sally. I will provide you with a resemblance and I would love you to find her whereabouts. I cannot go outside.'

'Right den. So you wants me to find dis wooomaaan and den what? Kill her?'

'Nelson, no. That shall not be necessary. If you can *locate* her, perhaps by asking questions in public houses and gin palaces, I will assure you are in soup for the rest of your time. Good-day' and with that I made my toilet.

True to my word, I furnished Nelson with a likeness of Sally and waited for the Gods to grant him success.

August 1858
The Search For Sally Continues, Both In The Real World And That Of The Darkened World Of The Sleeping Brain.
Something Nasty Happens Soon

Not all those in the house were truly bad. Many were scoundrels true, but more yet endeavoured to better the lot they had been granted. How they did it though, was up to each man, up to each woman, up to each child.

Nelson for one, was a dark man, so dark that barely could I make him out when night was upon us. Indeed, often he scared me, popping out from corners, under beds, inside cupboards and I would shriek with fear. He would shriek with laughter. Quite why he chose to hide around the house, I cannot say – maybe a humour of his type and if so, it is base compared to the more sedate pleasantry I enjoy; wafers, the opera, a trip to the mental house, a balloon ride over the Thames.

But, despite his pigment, I believe he meant well, and true to his word, he did go a-looking for Sally.

Bastard strumpet.

At first I shared his enthusiasm in his progress as I stirred the broth over the fire. It would make him happy for he was a simple man with simple wants – a warm cover and nutrition for the tum, so like a gorilla.

Sometimes though, his information may have been, I fear, like a Hindoo's supper, over-cooked.

'Her is becomed an 'oooorse, mister.'

'Really Nelson, a horse?'

'Yes sirree, dat is what dey telled me.'

'I see.'

In time, Nelson began to enjoy our meetings far more than me and although he may have been wrongly informed, I remained true to my word and I accommodated him with *pottage*. Mind you, our contract mooted nought about the size of the soupity, hoopity. Drink my thimble you wog.

You may think my times were a hoot, merrily chatting with blacks, gazing at the dinging breasts of young and old, cleansed by children.

I watched youngsters develop; some grew too vast for the chimney pots and sneaky windows of London, grew too tall for the drain-work and thus passed down their skills to the younger types. Some blasphemed in Latin and I was proud. But life was not so joyous for, in truth, was I a *prisoner*, I feared to touch the streets, for I was a wanted man. The heat grew once more. I wanted cheering. From the thieves I ordered a houseplant in exchange for a dirty French limerick. My African Violet proved lovely, its leaves green as grass, as furry as a fanny, with faint whispers of mauve blushed on its virgin flowers. I did as bade; kept him out of direct sunlight, watered the chap once a week and gazed fondly at him, reminding me as he did of the world beyond those musty walls. It died before the close of the month. A rascal weed on him, flooding the blossom with piddle.

I ordered a new one and some chicken wire in exchange for the English translation of the poem.

There still lurked craftiness within me.

August 9 1858
How The Night Dreams Of A Sleeping Man Can Rouse The Passions So Of A Dim-Wit Crowd

Relations with residents had improved of late. It appeared I had harvested in them some seed of respect. If not respect, whose roots were still perhaps unbudded, then at least acceptance. Probably tolerance would be better. I had a friend in Nelson and another in Washington. Also, some of the children were growing fond of me. I was doctor of medicine, professor of English and house guide.

But not long after, there came a morning when I awoke to a terrible to-do. Of a sudden, much of the toil I had invested in convincing the residents to refrain from beating me threatened to be lost, for see, in my little world of napping dreams, I was once more a well man. My finances were excellent, my bottom intact and my clothes wonderful, I had never set eyes on these perverts and I dined top-notch.

But that night, it was not my brain, nor my soul that was amiss. No. It was my naughty little humbert. And Sally. *Two* Sallys. And another one who looked like her but was weightier. They all three of them took it in turns to pleasure my weeping gentleman, coaxing him with feathers and they sat on him even, but it did not hurt. Indeed it provoked. They whistled velvety airs down his eye and over his hairs. I berated the twins, though, for yanking the fellow like a broomstick. It was not nice. They apologised and placed all four teats on him but he proved a sturdy youth for he did not wilt. Sally Two kissed him goodnight. She wore a see-through gown. Sally One dappled the apparel in water.

'Would you care to bite me Sally?' swooned Sally One.

'Touch my giblets, rub me on the knockers and punch me in the bush' barked one of the Sallys. Sally One perhaps. Or even Sally Two. Could have been Three. Forgive me. My dreams often take place in the dark. Another took me in hand and used me as a conductor's baton and as we were to crescendo in the orchestra pit of muck, I was awoken.

'You beast!' was the alarm and alarming it was. 'You beast' and I was struck with an instrument.

'A *beast* you say?' I said. '*Twice*? I have been published. I may count in Latin, I am gifted in Greek, know the French for serviette and I am a promising gymnast. Missus, a beast is a donkey or a wolf, or a sheep. You make me sick. How can I help?' I understood from the looks of folk that an object adhered to my face. A flash of a hand removed the offending article without even blinking. The bitch of a female had socked me in the jawbone with a pair of drawers. I may have ere mentioned, that my looks were not what they once were, what with sleeping in ditches and eating raw animals, drinking heavily, caressing the Chinaman's pipe, oodles of mighty strong heroin for my sore throat and having piping hot meat gravy tossed on my snout, but still I treasured them so.

I hoped the garments came not from the lady, for they were unclean and forested with hairs; tight black ones, much like those on Nelson's head but of an altogether different nature. I certainly would not eat my dinner off them. Nor my lunch. A sandwich if pressed, but not a cooked supper so I tossed them onto the floor.

She squealed once more: 'You're a beast, you're a beast, you're a beast, you're a be-.'

'I have gathered that, lady. Continue. And please put away your teeth. What it is alleged that I have dooed?'

I looked around me, left and right as my question met with horror. The silence overbore.

'*Done?*' I spoke out loud. The clamour returned like a locomotive on the way to Farringdon. From Paddington. I fear the ignorance was contagious like the pox.

'You're a be-.'

'I am warning you' I snarled and put my head to one side, fingers unfurling in the air.

'Little Enoch vos only lyin' on ya' said woman. 'He vos lookin' for ya heart and you gone and poked 'im in the ear'ole wiv ya sausage. It stood up like a soldier and went straight in.' And then the mother, she was in her teens, but smelt older, began to screech like a hen. She turned to the appalling little bastard to keen the following: 'Enoch my baby, is you gorn deaf?'

If *he* was not, then *I* certainly could be if the rumpus progressed.

'Ya mama. I can't 'ear nuffink. What what what? Ooooo me ears, oooooh me ears, ooooooh me ears. Where is I?'

'Madame' began I with much more dignity, 'I have not the slightest inkling of what you babble. Perhaps you would allow me to ask your, uhhm, boy just *exactly* it was he was doing on my lap whilst I was a-snoozing.'

I turned to the toddler with a quiz on my face and asked: 'Young man. Maybe you would care to tell me the basis of your actions and what in fact took you down, down, down *there*. Well?'

'Vell mister, I vos just vontin' to be like you. A duck tower. I love you. You is so tasty.'

Hhhhm. The reply was unenlightening. I had had my dreams, quite *literally*, dashed by the brat and wanted explanations. I also appeared to be leaking - an ejaculation by Jove! I placed a tortoise over the stain and whistled meekly. An ominous crowd had advanced.

'Please, what the gibbons is a (I realigned my fingers, lowering two from the left hand and raising next door another duo to create an 'apostrophe') 'duck tower?'

'Mister, it is vot is you is. You look at people's botties and make 'em better. Vey cough in your face and you gives 'em sugar. Vey does veeedles in your 'at and you gives 'em soap. Vey lift up vair arms and you bash 'em in 'a abdomen. Somevink's stickin' ooot of ya trusssers. It don't look very nice.'

In a flash, I garnished his nonsense. 'I think you mean *doctor*' I told the twit.

'Yes I do cure people but it is not easy. *I* listen to their chests. You, you *mouse*, you had your head on my....my...my co....my...(the mood of the mob had grown evil) my kno.....my peeee.....my don...my old bo....my private area.

A handful of grown-ups had understood my erection and they walked away going like this: 'Tutt, tttut, ttuuut, tttututt, tuuttt, ttuttt' and other such noises. Mama Enoch took leave of me too, but not before flinging a final insult.

''Eeere, take your knickers back you beast.' If I learnt

anything from the episode, it is that nasty little hairs give rise to a terrible tickle in the throat when ingested. I also estimated Ms Enoch to have given birth to the mongrel aged eleven. The hypocrisy of the place.

August 12, 1858
Farewell To A Bushy Baby And Welcome To The Outside World, A Very Hades To Behold

I would have to venture outside ere long and the sooner the better, for those filthy beasts had begun to grate and I feared my health was becoming worse. Plus, I hated Norris with an increasing hatred. He awoke me the night previous to warn of a rent increase. Things would have to alter.

But before the world was to be re-meed, a disguise was in need just in case a bobby may spot me, so off with the moustache. Cuthbert, when flaccid, proved an admirable barber, even with a knife and fork for the operation. First though, did I bid him rub bright the blades with emery powder. Ooh the sadness. How I mourned his loss. And then I had a sandwich. Tasty.

I kept the deceased whiskers in a little hiding hole. I feared at first to impart its resting place, but with regard to where I now write this account and its inevitable outcome I can safely tell that my feathery friend still lies within a cavity at the top of the staircase. The hole was never far from my head where it lay at night and thus the remnants of my once adored creature could be salvaged in an instant along with my buttons, rings and pins. Sadly, I fear I have no time to grow a new such chap.

Also my Chesterfield, a lovely overcoat with its velvet tickly bits and a fur-trim, was ditched for a stained rag; the braids which the gents had once so liked, came off, the felt hat discarded. In its place, a damned lowly cap. I kept the shirt for I could not abide the touch of a common chest upon my male knockeroos. God no. I learnt to spit, to growl, to beg for pennies and thus was I become a commoner over night.

I was ready to go, so go I did.

He emerges, blinking in shock after such a time in the rotten bowels of this awful twilight world. The streets are rife with cholera, women bloated with famine and gin, their dirty clay pipes rammed to their mouths, often bare-breasted and without shoes. Men sleep and fight like half-dead ghouls, wrapped in rags and moaning. Piles of garbage reach up from the stagnant gloom that is the roof over the broken lanes. He looks inwards to the broken windows from whence he has come to the gloom and the many families living dreadful lives in tiny rooms; cobblers and charwomen, leather-dressers and undressers all among the slops, blackened coal-porters soaked to the bone from the wind and rain gushing in from the rotten ceilings, hungry children and men from the Empire; Aden and Yemen, Oman and Omagh, come to this graveyard of misery; starving babies, infants tiny and grown men big, weeping in the mould and rats, wretched life in its worst, scared men and scarred women, the stink of drains flooding the rotting courtyards, childbirth in the straw, women with cracked bones and missing faces, a place where very phantoms beg alms and fall into stagnant ditches; wooden galleries crack and watch the sad fall of good men with bad families in a hell's kitchen; the abominable vice of a place with no morals; here snort pigs who fatten on the stench of death and the guts of offal in the cinder-heaps, the filthy splashes of privies for all to see, night-soil in the washing pail, yet no one dare moan to the landlord for there are far worse families. London may be the richest city in the world, *her opera houses and theatres golden and bright, but scratch the surface and there awaits Hell itself, the cruel tenements of Hades where birth and death go hand in hand, the sooner the better for most, yet no shroud for the dead when that time does come. And all about this reels a strange man with strange ways, yet left alone, unmolested, free to go about his business a small way beyond the confines of the Rookery, the lilts of Ireland drowsy in the heat of ordure.*

August 12 1858 – A bit later
He Meets An Awful Shit

I quickened my pace, which by now was of no great speed, for my legs were unused to exercise and searched for the London I once knew.

'Good man, my man' I posed to a good man in a great coat.

'I have lost my way, could you please direct me t-' said I as the gentleman dashed in the contrary direction. Strange sausage. Another one yes, but he too made off in a great hurry. But the third stood his ground and, hoping for a direction, I took off my hat, cap, and bid him commence.

'You awful shit. It is types such as you who cause typhus. I have nothing save this' and with that he levelled two fingers at me, formed the shape of a capital V for vagina and vamoosed.

I returned to the house an angry man. My face ran with tears, for the crook who cursed me was my old chum Bumshaw, my old friend from the Steakers. Have I *changed* so much? *Really*, have I so?

August 19, 1858
A Second Outing Into The Streets Proves A Grissly Affair With Some Really Bad News

Another murder had occurred. Although afeared that this beast would lay his hands upon me and enact some hideous deed, my body most shook with relief. Relief at bloodshed may strike you as odd, but believe me please kind reader, it put away the terror I had long feared, that the hands of the killer were indeed mine. Certainly I cannot recall dismembering any gentlemen, but my mind, when tiddly is a tricky fellow and my memoir dizzy. When in drink, my behaviour is foul indeed, my tempers unpredictable. Yet until that day's news, I never knew for certain, but surely as the man's throat was being sucked clean of his juices, as he screamed his last breath, I was in my low, low lodging-house weeping there for myself.

By all accounts, the motions of the ghoul sounded gruesome. It was in a public house that I became learned of such details for I rather fancied a booze.

While the two men who spoke before me were clearly shaken by events, I feared their information was riddled with riddles. It would seem that the victim, a man in his early 20s or late 50s was a tiny squeak of a titan whose bald pate was possibly covered with many hairs but what I did garnish was this:

'Where was he stabbed?'

'I told you, near Piccadilly.'

'No; the anatomy.'

'Ah. Twice in the abdomen, once in the neck, thrice in the thigh and seven in the back. Also his windpipe was shattered as though he were hit in the throat by a large lump of wood. Or a fake leg. Plus he was buggered to buggery. By a cock.'

'You reckons the fella what done it were a nancy?'

'That I do.'

'What would lead you to that assumption?'

'Because he left behind a pink nightgown and a corset. In short, this bears all the marks of a gangland bumming.'

I also learnt he had been left to bleed to death like a Muslim foodstuff. His abdomen had been slit asunder, his organs, i.e. heart, stomach, St Pancras were ripped out and more worryingly still, others, for example kidney, islets of Langerhan and gall bladder, had been disfigured by teeth. Surely an abomination of God's truth. I looked at the man in his snug. He was dressed in the blue cloth coat and oilskin cape of a peeler. He wore too the tall leather hat of his type and carried with him a truncheon, a rattle and a lamp. His number was embroidered on his collar and he wore neat white gloves. The copper had been the first on the scene so it had to be right.

The news soon spreads and the city's emotions are broken with fear. Many see the crimes as a righteous evil, the repayment of a vengeful God keen to show man the error of his ways, the murders a visitation for man's erroneous life of music halls and gin palaces, flash houses, flophouses and netherskens. These slayings are the true way of the Lord say the nervous and holy and many men stay within doors after the fall of night, as comes the darkness, comes the fear, a huge rush of London's blackened millions rushing for home, cramming the streets, flooding the omnibuses and carriages with panic, yet really only he who rides the streets to look for fleeting love in the arms of another man need fear his life.

A bit later in the day, August 19, 1858
Bad News Is Quick To Spread, Like A Floozy's Knees

I returned a-feared of the news, for before long, word had spread and supper proved new questions.

'Vot if vis beast comes in 'ere?'

''Ow does ve keeps 'im out?'

'Vot 'appens if 'ee chances upon me at night, when I'm a-piddlin'?'

'Dya fink he snores vorse than 'Arold?'

'Dya fink 'ee's really the devil?'

They were bandied around, back and forth, back and forth, back and forth for days on end until, inevitably, as sure as my die was cast the day I met Sally, did the beasted tongue of fate come licking at my crotch.

That night though, I had Nelson for company.

'Nelson?'

'Sir?'

'Where have you been?'

'Bin lookin' for Sally.'

'You have not. I can see it in your eye. Pray tell the truth.'

'You sure sir?'

'Never more. Sure. Before.'

'Well, now you ask, I have been to the Holy Trinity Church in Clapham with William Wilberforce to assist in ending the cruelty of the slave trade in the colonies of the

Americas, for a man is only a man when he has his dignity and freedom; without those necessities of life he is no more than a beast. The voice of God must be spread to those who keep man in chains. Slavery must be no more.'

Hhhm. What a strange egg.

It was the following afternoon, as I abluted non-stop, that I knew my life was in danger for a violent man came upon me at great speed.

'Is you ze killer of zem dead chappies?'

I replied to the man, rumoured to be part a Frenchie, very much in the negative and struck back with a question of my own. It was less wordy than Jean-Paul's and went as follows: 'Why?'

'Oh, no reason. Just zat me and Clement 'ad a bet on it. Oh bastard cocks, I now owes him a threepenny.'

Has The Killer Been Caught? An Inside View Of The Workings Of The Country's Most Important Police Station House. And A Well-Earned Breather From The Rookery

'I assume, fucking, you have not fucking caught the fucking murderer yet.'

'Well, sort of sir.'

'*Sort* of? Fucking *sort* of? Is that good news Widdle?'

'I reckon it is sir.'

'Is that how you received that severe bruise on your face?'

'I suppose so sir.'

'Ooooh, I may have to kiss you - on the cheek, not on the fucking mouth for that is not fucking hygienic. Are you saying, this man, this *monster*, the *butcher* who has slaughtered so many innocent men and has turned the 'omosexual members of London into gibbering incontinent wrecks, are you saying his reign of terror which has brought violence, the appearance of gaylords and terror into our lives, has come to an end and that no more blood shall be shed and no more organs shall be left lying in public thoroughfares and whoopsies can continue fucking bumming each other?'

'Well, sort of sir.'

'Ooh I can't wait. Fucking explain. Oh yes, his name please also and where currently he is detained.'

'Well sir, I did as you said and started walking funny. I

bought a handkerchief, visited molly houses and patted the back of every man's hand I saw.'

'Fucking superb. I assume you caught the eye of the killer with your boyish looks and disreputable perfume and accompanied him, either to his lodgings, a cheap hotel or your scantily furnished apartments, so sad with the pong of cold cuts and despair?'

'Sir, I live with you.'

'Oh yes. *Not*, of course as man and wife. Anyway, at the venue, you would have slowly begun to kiss each other whilst whispering endearing names. For example: "Ducky," "Little Miss Saucy," or "Big Chap." Maybe you would have shared a glass of wine and a cheroot as he caressed your rump. Maybe not. I don't fucking know, I was not there.'

PC Widdle began to display physical signs of unease. Sgt Bates did not.

'By this stage, I imagine you both lying wrapped in each other's arms upon the floor when one of you would suggest retiring to the bed where your kisses increased in ferocity and amour, peck, peck, peck. Perhaps one of the party, sporting an erection, removed some clothing and kissed the other on the penis. And then when he attempted, as was his natural wont, to disembowel you, clearly you pinned him to the ground, read him his civil rights and placed him under arrest. Not forgetting of course to reveal to him your tipstaff, made of brass and engraved thus: 'Metropolitan Police Force Constable employed in plain clothes.'

'Sir' implored Widdle, a touch grey around the face.

'Please' wheezed the sergeant, a touch rouge around the face, 'I have not yet finished my theory of criminology. And besides, only one of you has got his fucking cock out. Who was it, you or him, *you* or *him?*' screamed the sergeant, 'tell me please, I cannot go on much further.'

'Sir, it was not like that. I had no luck in attracting the chaps, not even when I adopted a girl's name as recommended.'

'What the fucking hell? You tell me that the lads did not relish to ravish Annabel Horatio Emental Bates?'

'Yes they did not.'

'*Bastards*, that is my mother's name. Anyway, how did you proceed?'

'*Frankly* sir, I d-'

'Widdle, do not use my Christian name.'

'Sorry sir. Besides, I cut away the seat of my trousers so my bottom was displayed and wrote a little note upon it.'

'Pray, what did it say?'

'It was supposed to read: "I Love Chaps." An enticer if you will.'

'However?'

'However my words was never good at school. I wrote instead: "I Love Chops."'

'So do I. Not *too* well done and with a few potatoes alongside. Parsley, the sauce from Holland, lots of salt. Oh I *see*. Fucking terrible. And the criminal?'

'Well I was picked up by a man, a big man.'

'Oh good, *very* good.'

'Yes. He claimed to be the proprietor of a chophouse in Cheapside. He asked to see my bum and wore a monocle for the purpose.'

'Yes, good, good. Carry on.'

'I asked if he wanted a kiss and should we return to his gaff for a spot of how's your father and then he punched me in the rump with his tipstaff, made of brass and engraved thus: 'Metropolitan Police Force Constable employed in plain clothes.' He arrested me for outraging public decency, soliciting for bum sauce and touting for hire without a licence, then thumped me in the face – which is how I came about the bruise. He was a *copper* sir. A *copper*.'

'You stupid fucking *idiot*. Did you not even grope his balls?'

'Heavens no sir. I hate a man's genitalia.'

'Oh yes, so do I. I hate yours and I hate mine so much too. Terrible fucking things. Not even a kiss?'

'No.'

'Right, that will be it' Sgt Bates spouted. He appeared in a wild temper and would surely have frightened even men with nerves of steel or metal. God, he was a demon in such spirits.

'Stay there Widdle. No do not fiddle. I will return' and off ran Bates through the narrow corridors of the Bow Street Station House, careering off the gloomy yellow walls, the colour of an old man's knees. He reached a closed room, unlocked the door and with a peek over his shoulder entered within. There was no time for candles and thus all remained in darkness. Ooooh it was ever so black. Like a Hindoo's chuff. He grabbed a box and was back with Widdle before the poor PC had even breathed. Well almost.

Opening the box, the sergeant delved with his hairy hand and emerged bearing a rustling, shuffling bundle of papers, thrust like a groin into the PC's face.

'Read this Widdle, *read*' barked Sgt Bates frankly sending spittle all about.

'I cannot sir, it is utterly difficult.'

'*Cannot* sir? Are you *illiterate* as well impotent?'

'The print is right before my eyes. All is a blur, all is a mess.'

'Oh I see' sympathised the police man of several years' experience. 'I see that you cannot see. Allow me to realign the thing so it is in suitable viewing conditions. Read!'

And he read, rather slowly, for PC Widdle was not blessed with a breakneck mind, but read he did.

A Story From A Newspaper. It Really Is Quite Interesting. And Involves An Elephant. Really, It Does.

The Pall Mall Gazette 27 July 1851

Terror At The Great Exhibition As An Indian Elephant Escapes From The Crystal Palace And Displays An Alarming Appetite For Things. Several People Are Dead. Because Of The Elephant.

Yesterday, at a few minutes past three in the afternoon, in Room 57 of the Great

Exhibition, celebrating Queen Victoria's civilising Imperial Empire stretching far across the Globe, a terrible thing did happen when an Indian elephant from the Jungles of Karnataka did escape. For a Farthing, visitors could sit upon her back. For less, a peanut could be fed to her trunk and for less, one could hang off her ears. The Animal was dressed in finery as would befit Victoria, with tassels, tiaras and jewellery. In short she looked magnificent. But at the time, a bee did enter the Tent, and cause havoc as it flew under the tail of the great beast. A child was hurled into the air from the saddle, suffering severe brain damage and with a shriek reportedly heard as far away as Penge in Surrey, the elephant did rupture her chains and trumpet off. Seven people were trampled to death in the ensuing chaos and are still absolutely squashed, a child lost its shoes up the elephant's snout and a Baker from Knightsbridge mislaid his gingerbread-nuts likewise. The famous tightrope walker Blondin gave chase but the animal proved too much of a match for the Frenchman. The beast is currently at large within the City. All Omnibus drivers are instructed not to allow the beast board their vehicle. Publicans are warned not to serve the monster booze for fear the drink may addle its mind and warp it into a killer. The only members of society allowed to attempt an arrest are Police Officers. Standard citizens are encouraged to not look her even in the eye, lest such an act sends the creature loopy, say chiefs from Scotland Yard's Escaped Mammal Special Enquiry Team. Oh, I have just now been informed that the large elephant which is still at large has just sat on a man. He too is squashed.

'Recall that?' barked Bates. 'Do you remember the terrors of the elephant that cursed the city so? Do you feel still the *shivers* coursing down your backbone at the mere *mention* of the beast? Do you *shake* still when you hear the sound of a *trumpet*? When was the last time you did not soil yourself at the call of a brass band? Do you shudder still when a *shadow*, a *great booming* shadow falls upon you without warning, when the sun leaves the earth and the air turns cold? Well? Eh, eh, fucking eh?'

'No sir. I was but a child when the elephant reigned its rule of horror. I have never heard speak of it until this day and besides I lived in a village near Derby. What is an elephant please sir?'

'Ooooh you make me angry. But enough, enough. This *animal*, this *ogre* that so horrified Queen Victoria's city, that ate more than 120 gardens, that drank dry ponds, swallowing ducks and gooses, this ogre that inhaled a woman whole, how was she stopped? I *beg* to fucking ask you how?'

'I really do not know, for I was but a child and I lived in a vil-'

'It was a man whom you know rather well. One you have seen even in the bath. Excellent whiskers mind you. *Well?*'

'My papa?'

'No.'

'My uncle?'

'No.'

'My grandpapa?'

'No.'

'That man I met in the Blue Anchor Public House while dressed in my sissie's tights?'

'Heavens no. Was that *really* a man? I thought he was a wooooooman. She wore French knickers.'

'I do not know who trapped the animal and saved London from more death and horror.'

'Me. It was *me, me,* me. Do you know how I ambushed the beast?'

'No sir. I was but a child. I took little interest in current affairs or wild beasts and lived in a vil-'

'I employed cunning. I prepared myself as bait and thought, "Now Franklyn, what do elephants like?" I did not know, so I recalled the penny gaff performances – great plays like Bloodstained Jewels and Mrs Oswald's Great Big Hairy Knockers, how those actors put themselves in the *mind* of the characters, how they very lived and breathed their beings and that is what I needs musted do. I would *live* as an *elephant*. Method acting, I think the art should be called. I thought of grey, *grey* and only grey. I set to trumpet myself to sleep thinking only as an elephant. I walked on all fours and did shits in my bedroom. I scanned the booksellers of Charing Cross and learnt of the diet of the beasts and thus the scheme was born. I would disguise myself in the skin of several fruits, a bamboo, some tamarind. And a fig leaf.

'I employed numerous bananas, apples and a pear. Then I added some cakes – recall her love of confectionery – lay back and waited. My God. Three days on my back in St James' Park, tormented by hungers, teased like a god by the treasures that sat upon my chest yet too dedicated was I to lick even a cake.

'How I wept, *praying* for an elephant, hoping for a creature. And then one very early morning, before the milk girls in their straw bonnets had yet cried 'Milk, ho, milk ho!' as the feathers of mist sat still upon the grass, did I feel the ground commence to fucking shake. Between the trees could I make out the lumbering shape of the elephant, her tiara and earrings glinting all lovely in the first rays of the sun. Her trunk quivered much like a grown man's penis as she plodded towards me, sniffing the air for fruit and cakes.

'Next time I shall save myself a fucking fortune by using a fruitcake. I tremored momentarily but remained composed as she began to feed from me. And then, quick as a flash, I fastened a pair of hand-cuffs to the animal's trunk and began to punch the fucking elephant.

'I produced my tipstaff and read out the engraving. No court could contain her bulk so she was sold to a butcher for steaks and with the cash a privy was constructed for Bow Street Station House.'

How An Elephant Foot Ends All In Tears

'My heavens sir, do not you think that a little *cruel*?'

'*Cruel? Cruel?* Do you not think a constable or sergeant is entitled to lavatoire whilst fighting crime? Or should he do it in his hat and toss it from the window and maybe hit a man in the face?'

'Sir, I meant in relation to the elephant.'

'Are you aware of the current situation in India?'

'Not entirely.'

'Well let me tell you a succinct fucking summary Widdle and then may you make an assumption. *India.* Brown people. Tea, curry, spice, no cow, no cow, Ganges, temple, no cow, ooh, oooh. Later. *England*, road, government, good, good, English words, building, civilised, ooh yes, *civilised*, cricket, golf, hats. Now Indian angry. 1857. Mutiny. Kill England men, women, children. Put in curry and eat. Therefore elephant symbol of Indian uprising ungrateful evil. I punch it in face. Butcher chops to death. People of Queen Victoria eat for supper. Who is cruel, I or the elephant, *I* or the fucking *elephant*?'

'But you duffed up the elephant six years before the Mutiny Of India. Hence there lives in you an awful cruelty barely known to man, what, what?'

'I am a man suckled on politics and I knew then how the Indians would later treat the good men, women and children and animals of England. Treat the situation as a *prophesy* Widdle.'

'Sir you are correct. The elephant was evil and you should have punched her in the eye.'

'Oooh, don't you fucking worry, I *did*, I fucking *did*.'

'And the neck?'

'Yes, twice.'

'Oooh good. One quick question sergeant if you do not mind.'

'Yes?' breathed Bates in apparent zeal.

'Did she taste nice?'

'*Taste?* Utterly *foul* when raw but braised with a pair of onions and a glass of port, *delicious*. Slam the meat between two rounds of bread, add a following of pickles and fuck me, what a snack.'

'Any left your honour?'

'Mealwise none. This was six years ago. You know I am a keen watercolourist and oilist?'

'Yes, I have seen your series, Cadavers and Corpses, 1836-1858. They hang in our conservatory. My particular favourite is of a lascar stabbed to death by a lascar. You can actually see his kidney, how it gleams in the gaslight so.'

'Widdle?'

'Yes sir.'

'It was not the kidney, but his pancreas. An excellent organ. Named after a huge railway station. Well, those oeuvres were in fact painted on a canvas of elephant skin. And Widdle?'

'Oh yes.'

'Where we keep our umbrellas, parasols, blackmen sticks and canes?'

'Yes?'

'The beast's foreleg. That is how to catch a suspect. Remind me again, once more, just for old time's sake. Why did you join the police force?'

'To rid the streets of unenviable people.

'To make the streets safe to walk upon. To ensure the next generation – our children's' children, and our children's children's children and our children's children's children's children are born into a better world. One in which goodness will prosper and benevolence will flourish. Where compassion between men – not bumfoolery mind – but *true* compassion will prosper.

'I want my children to run *naked* in the streets with their arses out and remain safe from criminals. I wish to own valuable paintings and leave them on my front doorstep for all to enjoy.

'I have a dream that my children will one day live in a nation where they will not be judged by the colour of their skin but by the content of their character. I have a dream today. I have a dream that one day little black boys and black girls will be able to join hands with little white boys and white girls and walk together as sisters and brothers. I have a dream today.

'The whirlwinds of revolt will continue to shake the foundations of our nation until the bright day of justice emerges. But there is something that I must say to my people who stand on the warm threshold which leads into the palace of justice. In the process of gaining our rightful place we must not be guilty of wrongful deeds. Let us not seek to satisfy our thirst for freedom by drinking from the cup of bitterness and hatred.

'When we let freedom ring, when we let it ring from every village and every hamlet, from every state and every city, we will be able to speed up that day when all of God's children, black men and white men, Jews and Gentiles, Protestants and Catholics, will be able to join hands and sing in the words of the old Negro spiritual, "Free at last! free at last! thank God Almighty, we are free at last!"

'It will matter not if you are white, yellow, brown, black. No one will care that Africans do not wash and that the Dutch fiddle themselves. I want to clear the town of vagrants, drunks, thieves, wogs, murderers, rapists – anus and vagina – cardsharps, juveniles, flashers, prostitutes, mothers, chippers, dentists, bystanders, pickpockets, philanderers and philanthropists, sightseers, Romans, nanny-nickers, vagabonds, polluters and bubonic plaguers. Oh and she-shirts, ninnies, savages and elephants' and sat down Widdle, slumped and exhausted.

'Is that *true*?' questioned the ever doubtful Bates.

'Uhhmmm, oooooh, oh no' squeaked Widdle.

'Now the *truth!*'

Poor Mr PC Arthur Widdle squirmed like a worm. There was nothing for it but the truth indeed, so with an exhalation heavy with omens, he glumly revealed: 'Because I like the hats. And the whistle.'

'*Right*, Widdle, you are fucking expelled from coppering. Strip naked from your uniform, write an apology to the head of Scotland Yard, prepare a valise and fuck off out of my house.'

'*Really?*' gasped Widdle as the tears swelled in his eyes, gathering in size like marbles until they burst forth and streaked down his face, coursing black marks upon his quivering cheeks. It was a terrible sight to behold as a young man's dreams were dashed pon the rocks of fate. The awful rocks that, now like Widdle's life, were smeared in seagull droppings.

'Please Sergeant Bates. Do not do this. I beg you. I will copper *without* the hat, without the *whistle*. I will copper in the nude, I will do it for free. PLEASE! What about my naked children with their arses hanging out in a better world?'

'You made it up Widdle, now fuck off.'

'Oh yes, so I did. Goodbye.' And with a wipe of the eyes and a quick striptease, he was no more.

August 25, 1858
The Story Of The Duck With The Ring

The day was drenched in rain, the sort of rain that foreigners adore, when I discovered a little nugget from my past. The children had gathered an impromptu marketing; a coat was spread over the floor while the goods were laid out. Eye-glasses, pencils, a pair of sausages, a budgerigar, some teeth, a shoe, a straw helmet and a ring; a nice gold ring emblazoned with a single letter, the sussurant serpentine letter 'S' prompting the young to bandy around, with their new news of the English language some corresponding words.

'Shit.'

'Shat.'

'Short arse hairs.'

'Suck my fanny.'

'Swindle my bum.'

'Spinach.'

'Spanish.'

'Cider.'

'Salmon.'

'Seasoning.'

'Shaving rash' and so on. The ring had come to me but I did not join in the hullabaloo, content merely to utter an expletive of my choosing: 'Arse knackers!'

For this ring was once intended for Sally's finger. I had bought the jewel from a puddingly man in Hatton Garden and it had cost a small fortune. She had looked lovely with it on her hand, its corn field gold a perfect shade for her onion skin. I recall the day I presented it to her.

'Sally, my pretty little thing. With this on your finger you are even *more* delectable than ever and I am really quite proud of your looks. And your mounds.'

She held my hand: 'Thank you, thank you *so* much. You may not be 'andsome but you are good and you are kind.'

The mutton of her! I am lovely. Although not as spicy as once, my face is still well-bred, if a touch too long, stretched as though I were forever in a pleasure palace mirror.

My nose still retains some haughtiness, bent in the correct places and as smooth as a child's below, but where I once looked down it, I now glance around its corner, knowing what life does bring to a man.

Mine eyes do still bewitch. I have seen washerwomen swoon, milkmaids squeak and I once made a tripe-cutter pop.

I was tempted to strike the animal, but we were over-looked by a parson and thus I decided to over-look her mishap.

She promised me always she would wear the ring.

'Vot you reckon it's vorth?' voiced a brat in the gaff.

'Ooooooo, I'd say about half-a-quid, at least.'

'You dirty bummer, it's at least lots more than about double that, look, it's metal.'

'Let me 'ave a look.'

'No, frig off, I'm next.'

'Come on, it was me vot found it you Welshman.'

Eff the insults for I had questions and I wanted answers. Namely:

How had this ring come into their hands? What fate had befallen my beloved? Had she been harmed? Had these idiots done her mischief? Did I brush my teeth this morning? I had to make enquiries.

'From whence did this jewellery come? Who is the source of its find? Was any matter of foul play involved in its recovery?'

A muffled mutter was all that came, an uncomprehending cannon of grunts.

They carried on jabbering and farting and I was without answer. I moderated my language and began again.

'You bastards, where you fucking find it?'

'Your harse mister' jollied one twit. I did not find the remark amusing, but the group thought differently because they tittered and snivelled. This, unfortunately, aroused a more contemporaneous nonsense.

'Put your finger up vere and see vot else you procure.'

'Go on, show us your botty.'

'Drop your drawers you nancy.'

'Horace told me you've got a big 'airy spider what lives up there.'

'And vare's a silly little worm vot is 'is neighbour' which last comment did Pleasant no favour.

'Right you *trollop*' cited I, admittedly in a manner too hasty and I kicked over the girl at my feet, whose tweaky breasts gave the appearance of more than her seven years, then I bounded to the cheeky boy.

I rarely become physical, but I was damn well fuming so I grabbed the blighter by his ears.

'You little *effer*, you've got ten seconds, no, no way José, *eight* seconds to spill the beans or I'll pull your bum off and make it into pâté and make you eat it – COLD (he shivered with fear) and then, *then*....'(I could think of no postscript to his predicted punishment) and dropped him menacingly.

There was no laughing then, because they knew I meant business. In the absence of my dear moustache (if ever I sire a daughter, I will name her Natasha, for the thing), I looked bloody tough.

Speaking at a remarkable rate, he informed me of events. The boys had harmed no one. The ring, it would seem, came from the leg of a duck.

August 28, 1858
How He Becomes Like A Loaf And Develops A Bad Mood

Pleasant and his cronies knew another group of nincompoops. They did not reside at our low, low house, but at a shack more base in Shadwell. Once a month my little boys would meet with this grisly gang to mudlark. I demanded they take me to see for myself the duck with the ring.

I rose early to prepare my wardrobe. My appearance was once enviable and indeed my look attracted many comments; some were errors, others aimed at nearby pedestrians, but many a favourable aside was meant just for me. I was particularly pleased to be mistaken for a dignitary as I gambolled down Coventry Street.

'I am not *actually* knighted' I returned, 'but may be soon. I am quite well known and I eat good food.'

'No, you're a *gay*lord.'

'Why thank you, I am *extremely* happy today. I have just bought a coat and used an eye-catching breakfast. I like not the coffee bean because it repeats on one. *Eh*? Good day.'

Having few decent items remaining me, they either having been stolen, exchanged, damaged, eaten or stained, I fashioned, in the gloom, a cravat. Also I whitened my shirt, pressed my pantaloons under the sleeping body of the biggest man in the house and polished my pins and shoes. I bounded downstairs as frilly as a lamb in parsley.

'Mister vot 'as 'appened to you? You beeeen fightin' wiv feeves?' asked one.

'Tell us 'oo done it and ve vill get 'em.'

'Vot's vat queer fing round your neck. It looks like a grotty old 'hankychef.'

'Boys you are partly right. I have not been clashing. It is not in my nature, but yes, I did prepare this 'cravat' myself. From some handkerchiefs. And some socks. Oh and a pant. *Striking,* what?'

'Ave you toileted yourself Doctor?'

The flour I had adopted to lighten the shirt was self-raising. The house is warm and damp – in short, ideal for baking. I had several breads about my being and I feared a youth would attempt to breakfast me.

So, more yeasty than anyone could *ever* have dreamt of, we trooped towards the river. There had I been promised a viewing of the duck with the 'S' ring and perchance learn more details about my missing beloved.

The plan had been an early departure to catch the tide. I am not a morning person. I like to breakfast at similar hours to a working man's luncheon.

Mind you, I once stayed awake until four in the morning drinking brandy with a well-known child. I was baffled when I went to bed.

Steamboats and barges loaded with grain and building stone for the new hotels in Charing Cross and the mansions for the wealthy in Camberwell, police hulks and great lighters laden with ashes; oyster boats at Billingsgate, wharves and factories, tumbledown waterside pubs; breweries and warehouses; tea clippers from China, masts all a-flapping, huge junks at Blackwall; spices from the Orient, ice from Norway, fruit and musk and ivory, Italian marble, frozen lamb from Australia, coconut oil from Ceylon and at Westminster, Charles Barry's dream nearly finished, a new palace for the Commons and the Lords. Life on London's river.

August 28, 1858. A little bit later than last time

He Becomes Involved With A Lady Of Awful Ways

The sun was making shrewd work of the clouds, sending them off with extraordinary ease. The streets still reeked of badness and gumbo and many people called the footways their home. Some bedded as horses on straw, sunning themselves on their backs like dreamy alligators, others used cobbles as a bed. Eventually we came to the river where I ran at the speed of a rabbit, the call 'whores, whores' revitalising and whippy.

'Sir' I beckoned to a grubby man, a stevedore hat upon his brow. 'I would *love* a quick trollop please. Preferably with knockers. Larger than a mange-tout, smaller than a casserole. Farthings and pennies I have none, alas. Perhaps you would like my trousers?'

A youngster dragged me to safety for it appeared the grub was set to clobber me.

I had mistaken the ferryman's call of *'oars, oars'* to passengers wishing to cross the waters. Oh what an error.

We moved on and soon *real* harlots aplenty appeared. I became erect momentarily and wished for coins. One strumpet, sensing my affliction, favoured to pity me, so, as the little folk marched ahead, she revealed some breasts. They were of ample size and remembered me of a bread. With a carrot on top, for the woman had vast nipples. I feared they could not be true yet I could not help myself. 'Boys' I bade.

'Continue. I am shortly to sneeze. I will be with you in seconds' and with that I launched myself towards them, at quite an alarming speed. Indeed the mistress of the teets did not know what had struck her as I perched, like a parakeet in a gust, on the side of the breast. I gave the right titty a right suckling and fed heartily upon the nip. I lapped back and forth like a parched hound in a pond. It was refreshing, but I feared the proprietor of the pups thought otherly. I was to explore for some thankyou coins when, in a tic, I had accidentally imprisoned the randy button in my mouth. Have I ever mentioned I have a great gap between the two front fangs? Well I have. It is of width enough to accommodate a cheroot and alas, the lady's naple found itself embedded between the teeth rather like a pig rammed twixt two fences. The floozy became aware and berated me accordingly: 'You 'orrid li'le man. Look vot you done. You sticked me knocker nut down your rattlers.'

True, I was to bear some guilt yet was modest enough to propose an explanation. 'Mmmggaamme, aaarrwaaa mgee too egspraine....' She slapped me, did the crow, and with extended claws. I tried my damnedest to extricate, if not my fangs and the tut, then at least my soul. But to the untrained ear, my account may have borne an awful grunting sound. The bat was in a fluster and was moving her hands and feet at quite a rate. I hoped she would not take off as I have seen birds do in the park.

Mind you, the scale of the meat did not shrink. Indeed it tasted all the more succulent with its constant wriggling.

I seized the waist with one hand and the other I shoved into the mouth. I inserted one finger into my gobbler and proceeded to urge forward the nut. It was not easy and my mouth soon became dry. I gestured for drink and it did not look nice. To a pedestrian the scene may have appeared frightful. I was crouched forward at an almighty angle with my posterior protruding backwards. There must be a nautical term for the posture but it escapes me (I was once instructed in expressions of the sea but the teacher was ruthless. He wore a sailing outfit and tried to molest my trousers as he indicated Ursula Major). Where was I? Oh yes. Straddling a lively highway with my arse a-dangling, my head down like a horse-rider's for purchase on the gadget, my feet relatively firm and my hands frantic. They spun back and forth like the webs of a duck. The fluff had wit enough to employ science and we heave-hoed, she in a northerly direction, I southbound until, with an abominable pop, the two were detached. Regrettably I had neglected to calculate for momentum for I rolled backwards. The eroticism occurred at the peak of a slight incline.

We had scaled the summit during tooth sex and I had in fact nudged her to the crest in my eagerness to suckle. I concluded the ceremony at the foot of the bevel narrowly missing Pleasant with my perambulations. 'You you, you've damaged mee tatties. I villl never vork again. You owes me four sovereigns. I've got twelve children to feed wiv me knocker-knackers. Vey'll 'ave to starve.'

'Madame, I am deeply sorry about your tooty-nose but I could not resist a munch.

'Perhaps you should not have unveiled him. But if you could see fit to curb your sauce, there are kiddy-winkles at my side. Such language distresses them. Look, one has already begun to blush. Oh, how he sobs. It appears he has the wifflewoffle. Indeed it is infectious. They are *all* at it. Hear that? 'Tis your fault you pubic biddy. No more please.'

'Fuck off you fuckin' fucker.'

'*Madame.*'

'Fuck off.'

The boys found the harlot a diversion for they giggled heartily.

'Mister, you already 'ad your bwekkies. Surely you can't still be 'ungry?'

'Eat my vankle for a tanner.'

'I got me a pair of knockeroos too. You vont a go a-nibblin'?'

'GENTLEMEN. I fear you have the heat-stroke for you talk gibberish. *This* way' and we went to the mud.

We Learn What Has Happened To A Good Man
Since Going To War. War Is Bad

We arrived at a grotty abode near Wapping. It stank of wet decay and the house was fairly tumbling like an old cheese. The largest child – I forget his name, he was a trifle – rapped on the door. I thought it would canker, but it did not. He knocked again, this time with a strange rhythm that left me dazzled. He beat thrice then followed the tattoo with a rattle-a-tattle before the wood parted with an absurd creak and a phantom of a man appeared.

Without a word, he nodded and brought forth youngsters. They were much as my party but they spoke not. They were as squalid ghouls; spectres, tatty with firm hair, stiffened and filthy. Many were drippy and squelchy with cold, their outfits oozed fluid. Canvas trousers flapped, the slime seeped from the pockets that prayed for filling. Who *were* these beings? What *do* they do? What was I doing *there*? I hoped they don't bite. We trundled forwards in silence, the sodden flop of their bare feet slapping like birds on the paving, the hawk of gulls and the low swish of the tide the noises of the morning.

I fretted that the dingy spirits were to do me harm. Perhaps they were set to eat me, for I was still a dishy chap in certain lighting. Perhaps they sought advantage of my physique for a bargain. I was sure they were armed and panic set in like a toothache. I began to mutter to myself: 'Oh no, oh no, oh no, oh no, oh God, oh God, oh God, oh no, oh no, oh no. Here we go, go, go. Too late. I've had it. Dead, dead die. Shitty, shitty, shit shit. Calm. Breathe. No, don't breathe.' I felt light-headed and became a sullen red. As a drunken coalman with a burdensome load, I stumbled until a hand reached for my waist.

'Eeeuurggh. Whho, wwwhoooo, leave me for I have nothing. I am poor, oh so poor, I have eaten nought. I sold my soul for soup and I sleep standing up. I warn you I am *awfully* tough. I once fought a man. I am friends with blacks. Stay your distance, I beg. I am demented with wrath and cannot accept what I am to do. Do, do, ooooohhh, ooooohhh.'

'Is it, is it, it is, is it?' said a man.

'Sorry?'

'I know you, by heavens I do. Remember *this*?' and the man unfastened his breeches and exhibited two hideous buttocks, stained most grey. And one had the appearance of a slight macaroon yet they were as cold mutton.

'Yes, charming. Two arses.' I craved home.

'No,' he sang, 'look *closer*, look at the one of the right.'

I gazed.

'No. *My* right, not *your* right.'

How he was aware I had peeked at the incorrect flank, I will never know.

'*Yes, yes* look at the right, rub the murk and gaze.'

And do you know, I think I recognised it. For underneath the loam there appeared as I wiped, as if by sleight of hand, a shape in the form of a draughts board. A lonely surge of warmth and at the same time shock and a little loneliness swept over me. For I recognised that birthmark.

'*Eggs,* remember them? Recall the wounding to my tentacle?'

I felt sick with trauma. It was Waterstones. A man whose name once denoted the best of London society. His tastes were exquisite, his shoulders questionable, yet here was he, leading these rag-tag monkeys, in and out of the mire, in and out, in and out.

He apologised for the terse note that I had found so long ago at Mrs Gough's.

It transpired that it had been *he* who had fouled his eggs after some port-wine. He had fallen out with the eggman and meant to display the empty eggs around his neighbourhood so as to discredit the vendor, but had forgotten about the fraud due to vast drinking. How did he end up so base? Oh, simple; Waterstones' charwoman alerted the authorities that he was a pervert because she had found the hole in her bedroom wall, assumed Waterstones to be the culprit and then left. Word soon passed; he was beaten by the charwoman's brother, lost several teeth and all his clients.

He enrolled in the British Army and was posted overseas to the War in the Crimea. He fought at Balaclava, that fateful day on October 25 1854, part of the Royal Dragoon Guards.

He narrated something like this: 'It was *fabulous*. Delicious food, super broth and chicken drumsticks. Pressed uniforms, tobacco, vermouth and pickles. The weather was ideal, excellent sunshine, a pinch of cloud and an evening rain.'

'Did you witness any action?' queried someone who closely resembled me. Well, it was me. I do love a fib.

'Action??!?!' guffawed my once playmate. 'Oooh.. I was wanked by a peasant and spoofed galore. One woman allowed me to kiss her giblets for a sniff of my snuff. Filthy bitch, they were covered in hair. Quite reminded me of a pet dog. Action??!!? Ooh I might say. Oh yes, I was molested by a sergeant. Then we left Aldershot and they sent us abroad. Diarrhoea or some nonsense.'

'Perhaps you mean Crimea?'

'Do you know you bugger, you're absolutely spot on. Crimea, yes, terrible place, revolting people. Stink worse than bastards and twice as hairy to boot. Quite where they hail from, I do not know.'

'Crimea.'

'Yes.'

I sighed. 'Please continue' I yawned beneath a stifle. 'I am *fascinated*.'

'Well. Got there, hated it, lost my whiskers for scurvy, but did my job. I love Queen Victoria but I hate the Crimeans. Treacherous bunch. I detonated two, decapitated three, decimated a further and defecated.'

'My God, did you use a gun? A musket perhaps, a revolver, a sabre?'

'Not ex*actly*. I mislaid a gunpowder into the beef stew. Blew the kitchen sky-high. I was demoted to a corporal so packed it in. It was full of Turks and they use not papers to cleanse their behinds – filthy whales. Plus winter proved terribly cold. Spent a week in hospital and returned home. God bless the Queen and my country.'

'*Hospital*? My lord, were you wounded? Shrapnel, stab wounds, dysentery? Please inform me but if it is too awful do not tell me because of late I am prone to weep.'

'Hospital, shrapnel, stab wounds, dysentery? My God no. Never had it in my life. I froze my helmet to a mess-tin. The poor little blighter was jammed solid to the cooking pot. Caused me terrible pain and the helmet peeled. Several layers came off and one could view the internal workings. A fly became trapped in the webbing.'

'My word, you emaciated wisp of a man, I am so sorry' said I as I wiped away a tear of guilt, remorse, sadness, sympathy, anger, fear and mirth. All rolled into one.

'Your *helmet*, your lovely little helmet with the freckle on the right-hand fringe? Does it pain, is it hideous, how do you toilet?'

'*Toilet* you odd fish? Why I simply find a suitable area, preferably a privy or a back garden. Or a bath tub. Then I extricate my John Thomas, point him in a suitable way, squeeze him thrice (once for luck, once for custom and once because I love the emotion), whisper encouragement, close my eyes and hope for the best. Seven times out of ten I am a roaring success. Would you care to watch?'

'*Watch*? Heavens no. I hate to observe a Homo Sapiens perform his lavatory. But does not the acid of the wee harm the mangled fiddle-hat?'

'Harm, hurt, pain, tears? What are you talking about? Have you become indisposed? You appear to be obsessed, possessed with concern for my Wilmot.'

'Your *Wilmot*?'

'I meant my helmet. Perhaps we should sever anew our friendship for such talk is causing disgust with my digestion.'

'But you *told* me that your helmet was damaged in the icy temperatures and by its cohesion to your army saucepot. I am merely concerned with the welfare of your Gentleman Jim.'

'My Gintleman *Jem*?'

'No.'

'My Gentleman Jim?'

'Yes, yes, yes.'

'He enjoys the most radiant health. *Oh I see*. My *helmet*. I referred to the tin hat I wore upon my head to protect the cranium and its contents against passing bullets, masonry and birds of prey.'

'Ah. Sorry for the controversy.'

'No, not at all, in fact I am delighted that you expressed anxiety towards my dong.'

Anyway, after leaving the armed forces, Waterstones took up residence in a lowly, lowly boarding house where he led young boys to search for treasures in the muds of Father Thames.

He promised he would help find Sally.

Yet although a friend had been found, the shock proved too great and what with the early awakening, the breakfast booby, the yeast to-do and the extensive hike, I musted go home. Little Callum was enrolled to take me there. The duck could wait and so could Sally for what use is a man when he is in such need of sleep?

And so he goes to bed, exhausted with the day. For these poor lost souls, sodden down with the detritus of life are mudlarks. They scour the river at low tides, seeking to drain the shores of a single scrap that may pay for the next meal, fend off the landlord with a few coins drained from the deep. Here do they risk their lives daily, where many a child is lost to the fogs that sweep in without warning, to the frozen slush that so sucks a man to his doom. Shipwrecked barges, sunken coal boats and trawlers, they ravage them for a scrap of wood, nails, iron pieces, scrags of rope, and all could be dried and cleaned and sold and thus stay alive for another day. Some live in the sewers, truly they do. Many a rich man has lost a belonging to the drain only for it to be swept along the choking tunnels that crawl under the city and then found by the underground man, the raker, the flusher, the sewer-hunter. These poor men and children, who have sunk lower than a human ever need, are the bowels of the megalopolis. Others make the lethal cesspools their homes. They carry hoes to beat off the rats. They swim in the venomous pits that take the effluent from the rich people's homes. For beneath every house in Mayfair with maids and dressers swarm a rabble of deformed souls, raring to find some valuable taken with the night-soil. But for every ruby brooch, there come a hundred days of entrails, dung, pigsty sweepings, dead dogs and the corpses of their little friends.

Everyday the newspapers tell of a child's death. But who will miss them when their life is snuffed out by the gasses?

Who shall weep when a schoolchild who will never read a book lays down and dies where he drops with exhaustion? And when the bricks crush a poor lad's head and his bones picked dry by the rats, who shall know his name?

And does he who sees the glint of a lantern as he walks over a street grate even wish to know who scuttles underneath?

Who in St James's that hears the mysterious bangs knows that the gasses have combusted and taken another child who shall never be a man? Or a woman for that matter, for the only calling for such work is desperation.

How We Almost Lose Our Hero To A Terrible Demise And The Case Of The Mysterious Tooth Marks. How Odd

God, God. The mud. The terror. Will I ever walk again? *Never* have I known such mud.

We had progressed not far, clinging our way along the river's edge when we espied a partly-sunken ship. The vessel, it emerged, was submerged. The craft was polluted with woodworm, for great swathes of the hull were missing. Some script was scrawled along the starboard (Or was it the port? I never am sure. I learnt the two several years earlier but the man was a sailor and tried to kiss me) but it was faint. A mast stood in the middle of the ship with a beast of a sail, which flapped loosely like an old man's drawers in a breeze of some force. But, said the larks, it could be ripe for pickings and be laden with beans, ivory or coins. For they were natural scavengers – like hyeanas but less hairy. The ship had no doubt been run aground and the crew fled, for the waters of the Thames are notoriously foul-tempered and can play havoc with a man.

We left the shelter of the wall and plunged into the Thames itself. The waters had very much receded and left in their wake a baboon-brown sludge, a mess of mud and flatulence. A dead fish, silver in colour gaped, its eyes blank, its body gnawed open by gulls. A couple of birds too lay dead nearby. And a dog. There came a terrific squelch as we struck the surface, a grisly bubble of miasma set a-flying. I felt slightly excited at the prospect of unearthing untold goods, much as a pirate, and for a moment was tempted to add the deceased fowl to my person. I turned to look for him when I spied a lad shovel him into his knapsack. The blighter was certainly rapid and I hoped he had no designs on me too.

How did they amble in such a place? Barely could I move, so uncertain was my footing, yet on they skated, like insects all of them, on towards the vessel. I hastened after them but of a sudden I was gone. My legs were swallowed by the sodden ground. They had been consumed at some great speed and indeed I had little time to struggle.

'Help' of course was the saying that I used. I tried it again, at greater volume.

'Help!' came a third. Two children and Waterstones rushed to see me. I hoped they would arrive in time, for I could feel my limbs sinking ever lower into the watery earth. What began at my ankles, a gentle sucking much like a young goat would with his mother, soon became a horrifying slurp that drenched my knees in mucky kisses, then my thighs. Never had I felt so close to death and my eyes were filled with hellish visions from Beelzebub: torture, snakes, sailors, all manner of things too awful to behold, too dreadful. A weaker man may have emptied his bladder upon himself.

'Quick, I am soon to die. Call the police please, assist me you bleeders. Tell Mrs Gough not to worry for me in the after-life. Tell her I stole her honey and blamed it on the coalman. Apologise to him for losing his job. And to his wife who sold her snatch to keep them from the poor house. And their son who became a chimney-sweep. If he is still stuck, tell him I empathise. Tell him how I died, please do. Oh God, the pain, the *pain*. I am being swallowed whole. Not even a lion would do this and now my eyesight has forsaken me. Who *are* you? Wifey, wifey, come to bed. Let us do it in the bum. Help. *Help*. Invite your loved ones to my funeral. Prepare some victuals but not too much. Two sandwiches per person. And don't butter the bread. God forgive me. I took a cabbage from a blind man. I kicked a child in the spleen. Forgive me. I love church, I love the Bible and, uhhm, errm, disciples.'

I fainted but still heard I phantom voices: 'Stop wriggling, keep still, bloody stop it.'

'It's no good. The man's an idiot.

'Simmer down.'

'Ee's deleewious. 'Ee's gibberin' to 'isself.'

'I know. Apparently 'ee alvays does vis.'

'Kick 'im vun. 'Ee'll never know. Vot's vat smell of wee?'

'It's probably wee.'

'*Oui?*'

'No.'

'*Non?*'

'Yes.'

'No. Wee.'

When I awoke, it was light and I knew not if I were alive or dead. I must have slept the night thus, but my mind was too afeared for dreams. I was heartened to learn my men had not forsaken me.

'Fellows. I have been here for several days and I am shivering with the cold' I shivered. 'I have lost, as you can see, several pounds in weight and my strength fades by the second. Food, I need food. We must eat to survive. Bring me some mustard and a napkin. I need flesh, lambs, pigs, oxes' and with that I lunged a nibble at my arm, for meat is what I craved. I again swooned away ever closer to death until I was wrenched from my grave by a child.

'Oh Lord' I wept, hugging this infant to my emaciated body. I feared he would not recognise me, so haggard was I from this relentless hunger and beating. 'Tell me,' spoke I. 'For how long have I been trapped in this mud, wrestling with death? Spare me nothing. Give me the truth, the *truth* damn you, you eel.'

And with a heavy sigh, the youth wiped his hands on his cap, and with a mournful gaze that spoke of tragedy, unclasped a pocket watch from the tatters of his coat.

'Sir, three, no more than four minutes, sir.'

'Unclog my ears of mud for I heard you to say four minutes. Thank you for giving up your life for mine. You are loyal. What month be this? Dig, dig, talk as you dig.'

'September still. We met ten minutes ago. I am sorry, but you lost your trousers in the mud. We can make you a new one.'

I was, I am sorry to say, helped home quite without any trousers. None whatsoever. My behind was utterly destitute and dishonoured. My bum, in short, was humbled.

'I am fine now children, I assure you. I can find my way home from here. I beseech you, go and play, *play*. Thank you so much for all your help. You, littler one, I vow to cleanse your hat. I am truly sorry my penis became entangled in the embroidery. The larger of you two, I am confident your back will heal in time. It is called a vertebra and you have several more. Dozens. You carry a man *exceptionally* well and I will ensure you are treated accordingly. Please I am not far now. I can continue these last few steps. Indeed I can even smell my bed.'

'Oh hello Washington. How have you been? *That?* Oh it rained heavily and my trousers became washed away. My Lord, the drizzles were torrential. I saw an entire horse swept off its feet.'

'Really?' replied the smarty 'you must have been awfully far away for I have spent the day basking in the garden. Like a dog.'

'Voshington, Voshington, Voshington. 'Ee vet 'isself, ven he et 'isself.'

'God no. You are both shits. I appreciate using you as a make shift carriage but I am likely suffering an influenza. The disease KILLS. Perhaps you would be so kind as to leave? Out!'

'Have you r*eally* been trying to eat yourself?' asked Washington with genuine kindness.

'You can tell me. This is Washington you are talking to.'

'Eat, me, eat, me, my own *arms*? God no.'

'There are wounds.'

'Wounds, yes. Rat, snake, owl. The perils of the wild.'

'You *have* nibbled – I recognise the tooth prints.'

I wept upon the man until I fell asleep. He put me to bed.

September 14, 1858
The Hazards Of Smoking A Pipe Are Laid Bare For All To See.
And A Bad-Tempered Copper

Do you know, I soon developed a fondness for crawling through the grimy wastes, hunting for rope, for paper, china, bones. I looked too the part. I was good. I would roll up the trouser to the knee and the shirt to the elbow before plunging in. Ankle boots wore I, for I had seen the bare soles of many a larker slashed by broken glass and oyster shells. One child lost a toe to an eel. The poor creature. How could hunger force a being to eat a foot-finger?

The work was not pleasing but the rewards often were. I once found a cigar and I gave it to Edna. She has now developed a liking for tobacco and coughs like a goat. In the sun-baked days of summer's end, the slime was a tonic for our footsies. The miasma stank and I am sure many of our number have since died of cholera but it was certainly lovely to lie in the mire and wait for the first ripple of the tide to soothe our bodies. I once performed my larking shirt-less but was wounded. A passing bastard called me a fancy-pants and launched a rhubarb from a moving barge. The man was a crook, but had a rare aim for it struck me full in the eye. I could not wink for weeks. If his lunch had been a little sharper, for example, a whelk or a hot potato I could be blind today.

We toiled in silence till the tide came, taking away the findings in our hats, in baskets, in tin kettles. Coins were shared and if many in number, we would gorge on cheap food, lousy cuts from awful butchers, fish heads from malodorous mongers. Cigar ends for Edna, shoes for the town's cobblers, poos went to farmyards in Kent, copper nails plonked at rag-shops and a pot of coal would fetch a penny. Prussian-blue makers cherished rags and oyster shell went to the builders. Any nonsense – false teeth, toenails, watch chains, went to the shops on Ratcliffe Highway, perhaps the most desperate of all the city's stores, decrepit as the goods they sold and as the clients they sought. This is where three-legged chairs that so wanted a sitter came to die, as too the battered tables that would never again see a family roast. Here were books that would never be read, keys with no door, jackets with no chest to love, rotten handkerchiefs more disease ridden than the most afeared nose in the most afeared hospital. The stock was melancholy but keepers would pay for this litter and it kept us in chops and slops.

One day did I find, poking from the mud like a chicken leg, a pipe. It was not made from clay like those puffed on by common dogfaces in dirty courtyards where they sit intent on looking ugly surrounded by soiled sheets with holes in. No way. This was not made from clay. It was pure china. I put it in my pocket. I was not going to let those fuckers get their paws on it. I had toiled like an Arab and I had to hasten.

'I must leave afore the tide for I am not well' announced I.

'I have swallowed some *mud*. I am going to be sick.' And here I retched at my audience to add credence to the tale. To do so I merely thought of Nelson's cooking. The man is as black as the devil himself, but he has a sweet soul. Yet can he cook? Not on your nelly. He once prepared a modern dish known as cheese on toast and the ingredients are simple. But the negro had neglected the cheese and laid his hands on no toast either. I find it hard to talk about to this day and we did not speak for a week.

So with the pipe in my paws, I bounded for a tobacconists. I brought to mind the fuggy loveliness of Carlin's of Oxford Street and its cheery tobacco tubs. Dreamily I fancied I could smell the dungy essence of ruddy men smoking, swirling brandy, painting their faces the most bizarre colours with splashes of crimson drink and fluffy brown flake.

The proprietor of the tobacconists, a florid swine named Reuben, would offer me a price for the piece, no doubt. But first the pipe wanted a cleaning. But first I needed to ejaculate. I spotted an excellent tart and charmed her into joining me, arm-in-arm. We made a lovely couple.

'Dear, I love to be wanked and hope you may assist. To loan me a *hand* if you will.'

I loved the joke but I reckoned the dame did not understand. She had venerable breasts and I fancied she kept her whim-wham fine but her face could not belie her lack of intelligence. In fact with her mouth a-gaping she took on the appearance of a monkey. A gibbon I think I thought. I think. I required her presence in the tobacconist to give rise to a more respectable character for with my ragged clothes, grubby chin and exclusive pipe, I ran the risk of being mistaken for a crook. A wife by my side would dispel all such illusions. Also I was penniless and the pipe would pay for the nooky.

'You vonts vankeey? Extract cock.' I don't think she was born on these isles.

'Cock later. Money later later. Me pipe. Me shop. Sell pipe. You. Shop come with. Man give money. Cock yes. Titties please. Vinkety, vankety, vonkety. Ooh, ooh, ooh.'

'You vonts vankeey? Extract cock.'

Perhaps the attempts were unregistered. 'Are you keen on golf?'

'You vonts vankeey? Extract cock.'

'How big is the queen?'

'You vonts vankeey? Extract cock.'

I would not accept nonsense, even from one with such tats. Hopefully she would let me gander them while bringing me off but she would must accompany me to the tobacco man. So we walked and I enjoyed it much, unencumbered by the boarding house doom. I almost fancied I was a dandy once more, strolling loosely with a goose of a girl. But as we rounded a corner busy with bakers and candlestick makers, we came across a policeman. He was a burly fellow, hunched and shitty. He had a horrid glint and I did not like him.

'Hexcuse me. You may not henter into this harea' he said. 'Hit his strictly forbidden.'

'Officer, there seems to be an error. I am a doctor, I can spot tumours at four feet distance and can cure dysentery with vegetables. My you're a dishy man. *Officer?*'

'Yes. Do not henter. What his hit?'

'My wife has a little something to show you, uhm don't you, uhh, er, uhhm Enid?'

'You vonts vankeey? Extract cock.'

'My God' said the constable. 'What did you say you filthy medic?'

'*Me?* Oh I said nothing my little monkey. It was my wife, she has the whoooping cough and…'

'She made reference, at heleven forty-six hours, to heither a male chicken or my sausage. Now, now, now, hello, hello, hello.'

I sought to converse with the whore in whispers. 'Show him your titties, show him your titties. Just your nip-naps will do' I sussurated breathlessly.

'You vonts vankeey? Extract cock.'

'Did you speak sir? quizzed the fuzz.

'God no. I haven't the time for idle chatter. I would just love to go past. I have an urgent call to attend. There is a man here who is dreadfully ill.'

'Ooh yes, you are right, terribly hill' chuckled the copper. I sure liked him less and less with each tick of the clock. He was enormous as he stood in his oilskins and his black as a black man top hat. How I loathed crushers like him.

I needed some craft to please his pies and would have to act as fast as a hawk. I had the one chance and the one chance only.

'Czechoslovakia!' I barked at the floozy.

'Vere?' replied she and as I pointed eastwards and upwards and round the back of her neck, and her eyes rolled and her head described so many circles, I plucked at the droopy neckline of the female's apron exposing the merest hint of a boob. I *knew* she hailed from Czechoslovakia. I winked wildly at the policeman as I gestured at the tat.

'Hmmm' sighed the copper, albeit nonplussed at the sight. I, though, cherished the wee cherries that sat on board the boobs like two pink children on a haystack. Yet still the mammal would not have us pass. Perhaps he preferred the sight of a young boy, smooth as a dumpling, with his cheroot asunder rather than a bird with her boobs a-floating and her beard inviting. Speed again was of the essence. I chanted the following to myself: 'Give him the pipe, give him the pipe, give him the pipe, give him the pipe.'

'Ooowww. You hound, I am so wounded. You have dislocated something, and I can barely breathe' I most wailed.

In the heat of the moment it appeared that, instead of doling out the pipe to the peeler, I had unfastened my herbert and placed it in my hand, rather as an old-fashioned reptile and offered him to the police constable. The Charley smashed my Charlie over its head with his truncheon, making him blubber. Coupled with that, the thug twisted the toad. The poor fellow resembled an old man's finger, so decrepit did he become.

'Sir, be you or be you no doctor, I ham harresting you for han houtrageous hoffence. Hat heleven fifty-two you did hunravel yourself hand hoffer ha genital to me, possibly has ha bribe. The penis was dishevelled hand faced hin ha northwesterly direction. My feet har moist. His there rain? You bastard. You har going to jail.'

'I am not, for you must guard with your life this thoroughfare. What has happened? And officer?'

'Sir?'

'Drop the haitches.'

'Oh yes. Well now you ask there has been a murder. A pansy had his neck broke after bumming another fellow, in the bum. Good-day to you sir.'

'Good-day. Sorry about the footwear. I was nervous. Some carbolic soda and a week in the sun will have them better than new. Could you lend me a tanner?'

'No.'

Murder, blood, insides, the devil. But surely I was in the clear and I *did* get fiddled with. She did it behind a coffee stall and I ran away when she had finished.

But I never did sell that pipe. I fear in the fracas with the constabulary it must have vanished. Arses, I damned needed a feed. My time would come again – such is life and such is hope.

September 18, 1858
Ooh What A Temper!

I believe I had contracted a malady from the rivers. I went out, I came back in. I had been away from my quarters for minutes, a child's time no less, but still did a person do me a most terrible deed. I placed my exhausted head on my pillow only for my neck to be damped. In my absence, the pillow had been exchanged for a pot; one containing an effluence, like the very beasts of hell. I assume a neighbour had been concerned for me and for that I love him. No. I do not. I *hate* him, for he killed my only friend left me in this world.

I picked up the contraption and made a scene.

'Norris. *Norris.* Norris. How dare you. I am lovely and this is not. It is shitty. What sort of *house* is this when a man, or a woman or a child can harm another man in his own bed with a miniature lavatory the very second his back is turned? Have you no shame, no manners, no niceness in you? I refuse to pay any more rent.'

'I see. I am damned sorry but I will have your money you bee.'

He removed his spectacles and fixed me with a hideous stare.

'You will pay your rent you crab. If not I shall haul you before the beaks. My uncle is the Lord of the Chancellor. I think.'

'Norris, I have never liked you. You may not sue me, for *my* uncle *really* is the Lord Chancellor and you will end up in prison if you proceed with this façade. Halt my payments now you bastard or I shall tell every man, woman and child and anyone else what a cheating, lying pig you are.'

I had him surely.

'Fuck, fuck, fuck, fuckety, fuck, fuck. I must call you sir but I don't want to. How I wish your uncle wasn't your uncle and I was as clever as you. Ooh god I am doomed.'

He fiddled the spectacle, and what a spectacle it was to view him so, his tongue poking from the corner of his mouth, like a worm on holiday.

'Is this about your wind? If so, then I prescribe this' – and do you know he had the cheek to read from the bottle as follows: 'Pitkeathly Table Water. A Remedial Agent For a Sluggish Liver, Plethoric States Of The System, Chronic Affection Of The Organs Of Respiration And Circulation, Gastric Derangement And Biliousness.'

And the monkey stood back a pace, uncapped the bottle, served a dollop on a spoon and leant it forwards, whispering all the while: 'Sup, sup, sup.'

'I will sup nothing you vile pork' and nudging the spoon and the Pitkeathly Table Water to the floor continued: 'No. It surely is not right to share a bed with a potty.'

'How about these Indian Pills. They Are Invalu-'

'I know exactly of what they may be capable. A fortnight later and I was hooked on heroin. Now leave me alone and shove your pills up your arse.'

Gripping the pot (my arms were outstretched, like the necks of two pelicans) I proffered before him, yodelling somewhat: 'You bastard shit, you vulture, regard this muck, *look* at it, look *at* it, look at *it*,' and grabbing the tufts of his skull, thrust downwards with his head, like a man playing a timpani drum in an orchestra, towards the mulch.

How he flinched and squealed and cowered and bit, ooh, yes he bit like a bat. Once he had wriggled free, he hurried yonder, screaming as a woman half his age: 'That is an excellent pot please. It is Ming, do not fling!' but so enraged was I, that I performed just that and in a whoosh I had cast the holder up, up, up into the air and across, across, across the room. The nearly hairless deputy used some prowess, for he did bend, thus missing the spinning contents as the machine continued its arc and indeed flew out of the window until there came a tragic howling from without and a thump, preceded by Norris' attempts to shout the warning to 'gardyloo, gardyloo.'

Exhausted by the toilet trouble, I lay down once more and snoozed like a beast.

September 23, 1858
A Crab, A Murder, Some Bumming And A Lesson In What Happens To Dead People. When They're Dead

Rollocks! I meant to give the larking business a rest, for the day was not much of a lark. I found nothing and lost my handkerchief and nearly a toe for as I squelched around, a crab set about on a picnic. He had a ferocious pincer and a very short life. I howled like an ox as I raised my foot to the heavens, to find the being dangling from my appendage. Christ in a bun, it hurt so, causing me to further howl, albeit briefly: 'Ooh help, my foot-finger's been a-munched. A crustacean is upon me. I have no blood left, I am a phantom, and shall never play the piano again.'

My sufferings though, were short-lived, for a kindly youth flicked it from the toe with a deft tick, sending him spinning into the air. I am a Christian man and I believe in redemption, the inherent goodness of humanity and the omnipresence of an all-seeing God, reason and language setting us apart from the beasts. I smashed the bugger to smithereens, then trod on his abdomen and thorax, sobbing until I felt faint and was carried home.

The afternoon had fallen kindly, a cosy pink glow for autumn was nearing and the days were growing ever shorter. I needed

a cup of tea but Washington was not to be. No, for he had
been killed the day before. His death was horrid and made me
blub.

He had been struck down by a full chamber pot. How
cursed is this existence? Having spent much of his life in good
quarters, he had not known the warning 'gardy-loo' and was
knocked out by a toilet flinger. I believe we would have
become fine friends. The poor man: whacked to death by a
chamber pot, his body tossed into a hole at the pauper's
burial ground at St Bride's, the call of crows cackling over the
clergyman's indifferent mumbling.

What sort of animal could commit such a crime? Is it not
enough that a demon stalks the streets and slaughters nancies
in my wake without a man of honour to be butchered with a
basin? I wanted a cuddle.

Detectives called to the house and made a mighty scene
but the killer remained at large. I now had no one with whom
to talk and consoled myself by spending more time with
Waterstones and the sewer boys. I travelled to Wapping and
knocked for the man, desperate for some company.

I spoke thus: 'Waterstones, you are a good man, but a
better one has just died. His head was broken by a flying
toilet and I have cried. I also miss Sally. You promised you
would help find her. I have lost many clothes, almost a digit
and I have had vegetation tossed at me. Do help, *do*.'

And he did. He bared for me a terrible secret. For these
dredgermen also hunt the river for bodies, for drowned,
bloated corpses, whose faces were blown out of all
recognition.

'Mister' said one body hunter when introduced, 'there

ain't nuffink vrong viv vis practice. We don't kills 'em. No, tis God or ve vaves or a eel vot kills. If a person gone missin', if vey is rich ven vere is a revard. And ve morgues, vey love us to bring in a body or two. And ve hospitals, cos vey got to learn all ve young doctors vot is a brain, vot is a cock, vot is a cunny and vot is a arm. Ooh yes, I remember I found a 'uuge voman, must have been bigger van four coffee-stalls, it needed free of us to drag the bitch's corpse to St Thomas'. Vey vos so happy cos her fanny ain't been eaten. Paid me like a king and kept me in scran for a week. Hhmm, herrings.'

'Lovely' confirmed I, 'lovely.'

'I sees ve looks you givin' me' he most snarled.

'You finks you's better van me. You is a lovely lookin' man and if I vosn't married, I vould ask you to a horse race, but I is and I von't but you is no better van me. Ve first carcass I found vos more than vun year ago. In fact it was sixteen years ago. He vos a young man, bit of a toff; two cravats, fevver muff and monocle. And a villy ve size of a slipper. But I reckoned he had been to Lushville. Must have taken a few too many pots of beer and fallen in ve Thames. Vell, I drags him out ve mud and leaves him viv ve vife. Ve had just married. I said: "Vife dear, I loves you and you loves me and vun day our sprogs vill love us too and ve vill love 'em an' all. Hold vis corpse, if he vakes up do not be alarmed. I am going to look for a blue bottle."'

'A *fly*, but why? Oh my.' I was so confused. 'Left with a corpse and hunting for aphids? How bizarre.'

'Oh. A blue bottle is a policeman. 'Tis slang.'

'Ah. Yes.'

He continued: 'Ve vos near ve Hungerford Stairs ven I finds 'im. I dashes to Charing Cross. And do you know vot?'

'Vot? I mean what?'

'Vair voz two of the grimmest coppers I ever did see. '"Coppers" says I. "'I have found a cadaver and it looks like 'ee ain't got no 'ome. But I fink he's got a sovereign or two."

'And viv vat vey ran tovords ve vater, vistles vistling, gloves uhhm, gloving and hats, vell, hatting. Vey grab ve body from ve vife. Do you know, she looks a little bit like you. *Is* you her? Have you got knockers and do you like it in ve bum?'

'*Certainly* not. I am a well-read gentleman, know basic mechanics and I do not take kindly to such practices.'

I feared I may once have bummed with him for cash and was, naturally, keen to allay him from the scent. I could ill afford the truth.

'Please continue.'

'Vell, vey takes ve body and tells us vey vould make a little check on sumfink and promise vey would return in a coupl'a minutes. Vey run like ve devil hisself if he vos in a hurry. I can 'ear 'em shaking ve man about. Vey search 'is pockets, strip 'im of his cloves and viv a mighty splash, sploosh, splish, splosh, sp-'

'It is fine, I accept the noises. Continue please for I may turn violent.'

'Splooo-'

'*Violent.*'

'Vey chucks his naked body back into ve Thames. From vat day onwards I vowed vat every body will be mine.'

'*Everybody?*'

'Yes, everybody. No, no, no, no, no. No. I do not vont to possess everybody, but every deceased body I find in ve river I vill use for my own gains. Every. Body.'

'Oh.'

'My name is Joshua Roderick Broderick Frederick Rufus Lucius Leander Coriander Amanda Ulysses Seth Jeff Jefferson.'

'Pleased to make your acquaintance Joshua Roderick Broderick Frederick Rufus Lucius Coriander Leander Amanda Ulysses Seth Jeff Jefferson.'

My word. So this was the sorry end that awaited those who fell into Father Thames. Joshua Roderick Broderick Frederick Rufus Lucius Leander Coriander Amanda Ulysses Seth Jeff Jefferson and the ilk, would trawl the muds hunting for corpses and taking their finds to the city's surgeons.

'Joshua Roderick Broderick Frederick Rufus Lucius Leander Coriander Amanda Ulysses Seth Jeff Jefferson tell me three things. Firstly, how many cadavers have you found in your lifetime? Secondly have you ever found Sally, my love, and thirdly, can I perhaps shorten your name? Josh, Rodders or Freddie perhaps?'

Joshua Roderick Broderick Frederick Rufus Lucius Leander Coriander Amanda Ulysses Seth Jeff Jefferson responded thus: 'Ninety-three, don't call me love and who is Sally? Rodders vill do.'

'You have been busy' complimented me. 'Sally is the woman I love and I fear she has been bad done by. She vanished several months ago and a child found her ring on a duck so I fear the worst' I concluded with a ponderous sigh.

'Ohh, sorry' apologised Rodders. 'And I meant ninety-*two* bodies, vun vos a fish.'

'Perhaps' perhapsed me, 'I could make easier my desire with a portrayal of Sally. Well, gentlemen, she looks somewhat like this' and here I stood back to amply define the breast.

'She has hair more lovely even than mine. It is reddish, not

the colour of a tomato, nor a fresh meat, but a saucy
Scotsman. Her skin is white as frost with a lone freckle, just
about *here*.' I pointed to the mole's home, just above her right
shoulder blade. The notion drew gasps. 'Gentlemen, there is
more, *far* more. Her eyes are as green as an adder's, her voice
trills like a crow. No, not a crow, a *lark*. Her eyebrows would
not look common on our Queen. Her elbows are as soft as
milk, her legs silken and smooth, without a hint of fur and
when the right words are said, they open like the gates to a
manor house. Her breasts.' I paused to wipe my head with a
kerchief for the day was certainly toasty. 'Her breasts I *love*.
They are smooth as stone and soft as rabbits. They taste
exquisite, better than plover eggs. Her nip-naps are the
gentlest of beings, never do they squeal or differ. At the
merest blow from the moooooth, they will arise. Her quiff is
perfection. Like so many strands of loose tobacco, together
they make the most valuable carpet from the East look as a
dowdy rug whereby persons unknown have wiped their boots
of dog dirt. If I had a child I would vouch never to see him
again, punch him in the face and push him into the sea, if I
were never allowed to monkey again with her gong. Her
bungo, her chuff, *damn* you, her bum cheeks are angelic.
They are as warm as potatoes, yet as soft as a child.'

A mighty gurgling demolished all. I looked up to see poor
Waterstones, face-down in the mud with an elaborate
Rodders roosting a-top him, conducting the most almighty
grunts and thrusting his dirty zones in and out at my old
friend's pooper. I needed to act fast.

'Rodders' shouted I. 'What the spots do you seek to do?
That object you covet is none other than another man's
bumhole. It is *dangerous*. Perhaps you are unwell. Get *off* you

cuckoo' and with that, I pulled him off. Hmmm. I demanded an explanation. Waterstones' was brief, Rodders' was not. Waterstones said: 'I fainted with lust.'

Rodders said: 'Your description vere lovely and I vonted to cry so I vent to look for a tissue but veren't none and ven I saw Vilford fainted in ve mud so I fought I vould resuscitate him and I leaned onto him and began to blow viv my villy, cos he got more bwef van his pappa, into his mouth, only it vos not his mouth I now knows. It vent dark for a minute and I could not see properly you understand and I finked his bum vere his mouth. Please don't tell no one. I am never a whoopsie and I ain't never arsed a man before.'

'I hope you tell the truth Rodders. I have known Waterstones for a decade and the very thought of his bum being bummed by another man with his own bum makes me, uhhm, feel humdrum. It is a despicable act.'

Hypocrisy indeed, but in so tricky a predicament, I musted tell a tale to keep my derriere details private. A smokescreen if you shall.

'Look me in the eye. No not the *Japanese* eye, by heavens, nor if you do not mind, the backdoor peephole eye. Straighten up and glint at my pupils. Did you mean to anus Waterstones or were you really offering him the gift of life from your humpty?'

'I swear on my neighbour's life. I only vonted to save him. A man's bottom is not fit for anyfink uvver van expulsion of waste. I hate it, I hate it, I hate it' and here he formed a spit and sent it whizzing towards Waterstones. Poor man; fainted, bummed and spat.

'Rodders, that is unnecessary. Please no more spatting, a little less bumming and a lot more looking.'

So, as once more our man trots back to bed, these men of the underworld traipse the mortuaries of the city, looking for the dead and the jewels taken with them to limbo. They hope always somewhere, such a body as Sally's will one day arrive, putting their friend out of his misery. These desperate men trawl the river yet for swollen corpses, to pest fields where the city's poor are laid to rest. Typhoid, consumption, smallpox, dyptheria; names that bring so much death and also life in the shape of the coin. Hundreds lie where they fall. Others are tossed from the slums, out into the crooked alleys with the nightsoil. Many are murdered, their throats slit in darkened streets by footpads, half-crazed with opium. Many die from the miasma that colours the skies a hellish brown; then there is the drinking water and those who sup from the stinking pools that fester in the rookeries. There are those who die of fumes, of workshop accidents. Off to the hospitals, stealing in the rear door where the refuse lies all stinking. Keep the hospital nightmen in drink and he'll nod the wink. A penny for a cabman, a slippery copper, a trip to the opium dens at Limehouse and the smokers who never wake. Sooner or later the corpse will arrive.

In Which We See The True Might Of The Pen; An Animal Is Libelled And Peas Go Flying

Days went by, my lessons grew more popular and my medical prowess improved. I cured a man of a squint by sticking open his eye with raspberry jam. It was home made; Washington the chef. It may have been a present for me, but I will not know until I pass over into the next world, which you will soon realise is much nearer than ere thought. Then will I thank him for his preserve.

I grew frustrated though at the lack of progress with Sally, either in perfect health or in several pieces. I would, I suppose, have preferred the former, but the latter would put my questioning to rest. No it would not, it would have ravaged my mind further and a possible return to lunacy once more. But that was by the by. I began to panic, and there were another two murders

There was only one option; blackmail Waterstones. I sent Cuthbert with a note for he was a weak reader. In fact he had not been to a lesson since I asked him to sign his name in front of the class. Haunted by bad luck and worse sight, he scribbled the name 'Cuntsquirt.' I did not guffaw for I do not like the 'C' word, but several others did. One child urinated himself in humour and another ate his own cap.

The contents of the missive to Waterstones though, were dark in nature and anonymous in name. A copy of the minute sits by my knees.

'Waterstones, I know you do not know me, nor do you know that I know that you do not know me. You do not recognise me, you have no idea who I am, but I know you. You do not know now that I know you, but one day you will know that I will know you. I know all there is about you; your age, your size, your favourite inn, the teeth in your head, the hairs on your belly. And your arse. I know that you once intercoursed a lamb. Perhaps you have chosen to erase the incident, but I certainly have not. For I was nearby, seated within the boughs of the tree which you used to steady yourself. In fact I depicted a rather tasty etching of the scene (which I have before me now) as you rollicked behind the creature. How the pair of you howled like wildmen. I recall as though the incident were yesterday, how you wooed the beast by proffering him ham and then tickled him under its chin. You called him sweet names, mentioning the words 'child,' 'missus' and 'darling'. Barely could one contain one's disgust and I feared I would tumble to the ground. And after you had uncorked, you parted with a fleeting kiss on the mouth. I do not want money. I want you to assist a friend find his friend. A woman friend. Her name is Sally and she has lovely breasts. The hairs on her croft are superb and are useful for lighting fires. Please help him, or these engravings may well find their way to a most unfortunate place.

Heed this warning.'

The note was simple, its purpose acute. It could not fail to work, for Waterstones was a proud man with little acumen. He could ill afford to lose what respect remained him by exposure as an animal effer but the only cause for concern was this; none of what was written in the letter had actually happened. There were two hopeful, but remote situations were this to work. Either that such an act had indeed once occurred, or he did accept the facts and conclude that he had previously wiped clean the foul images from his cranium.

I did not need wait long. That afternoon, as storm clouds banged over the Thames, I observed a hay cart career into a hot-pea seller, sending scalding greens, salt, vinegar, pepper and a ladle soaring into the rumbling sky. The cries of the pea-man changed frantically from 'Hot peas cod, hot peas cod, hot peas cod' to 'you fucking bastard sod, you fucking bastard sod, you fucking bastard sod,' as the hayman lay in a growing pond of green, smothering himself in hay to quench the boiling legume. Quite a crowd had gathered. Even the German marching band were silenced by the wrestling.

'Oooh. Zat man has kicked ze uzzer man in ze kernackers. Meine eyeseses is vatering. Oh. And mine villy. I must make ze toilet.'

'Meine Gott, zere is a pea in mine trombone. Gott in Himmel you volf. Come here and I vill be teaching you a lesson. Now all songs mine vill sound like peas.'

'Franz, *Franz*, leave alone ze man. His fault vos not is. It vos ze horse vot did bitted him on ze vinkle.'

'It vos not ze vinkle Hans, it vos ze nasen. Ooh nein, now I fallen over I did in ze horsee dirt. Scheiße.'

'Jurgen, put down ze clarinet. A spoon tovards you is coming. Gott in Himmel!'

'Herren, herren, who has got ze horn?'

'Claus, I have got ze horn. Look at my villy, it is ze size of a bratwurst and red has gone. It must be ze vezzer.'

'Nein Adolf, I mean not *zat* horn. Up do ze hosen. I meant my *French* horn vich ze jingles does play. It is expensive and brass.'

'Sorry Claus. I zought you vos meaning ze vinky-vonky.'

They rolled over and over in the peas, the horse dung, the flooded cesspools and the dog turds. And the cause of the terrible tumble? A wild looking man with a ferocious twitch. Indeed so bad was the tic of his shoulders that as he passed a crossing sweeper he nudged the man's stick which consequently tormented the horse's backside. Needless to say it sent the beast into a fury and understandably, the animal bit the peaman on the nose. Hence vegetables, swear words, blood, vinegar, manure, Germans, tubas.

And the man, the culprit, the miscreant, the throbber whose arms nor cheek, nor eyes nor chin could remain still for a moment, who was wracked with the most dreadful squints ever seen by man? Or horse? Poor Waterstones himself. He must have taken the epistle badly.

Ere long was I summonsed to meet the man himself, or rather a paler, more windswept version, who having developed a stutter and a twitch and an alarming bald pate, took me to a gruesome zone of the capital. I had never visited the place before and I never want to again; Waterloo.

Waterstones spoke very little during our journey. The streets there were darkened and sooty and teeming with not unbeautiful streetwalkers. The knockers appeared more violent than in my part of town. An Irishwoman caught my eye as she watered her boobie with a mouth of gin and made the little fellow on top of the teet stand up like a puppet by flicking the thing with a finger. It quite aroused me and I cursed myself for not bringing my winking breeches. Physicians may doubt the procedure, but I advocate wonk-walking highly.

What Waterstones did utter though, was a rant of the highest nonsense, a fume of mutters, fit, frankly, for nutters. Barely could I make head or tail of it and I feared I had wronged him. I was wracked with remorse.

'Waterstones, my old friend. What has happened to you? You are squinting like a frog, your eyes know not where to look, you have dirtied the seat of your breeches too. And now, *now* you are squeaking. Tell me please, what *is* it?"

But all I received was a shriek.

'Letter, oh no, letter, oh no, animal, lovely, lovely animal, kiss, kissy, kissy, kiss. More too. Mistake. LAMB!!!!, lovely mouth, many brandy, death, death, death.'

The frightening rumble of trains bangs on by, the engines snoring jet-black quills of smoke into the sky. Our hero is lost under a maze of bridges, where vagabonds lie in their excrement and children scream with hunger. Not yet tea-time but already the gas lights are turning all a jaundiced parody of life. Here under these archways, the clatter of locomotive wheels hurtling past is tortuous, the railways, good for many, yet torment for the poor who live beneath its tracks. But still they wander, he pensive, Waterstones muttering, his hair all a flutter. Bodies crawl in the gloom, hands reaching for salvation, rats snickering at the forlorn fall of man. Then come the faint whispers of newsboys chanting the headlines of murder, echoing off the damp walls and bare-chested men fighting to the blood until they fall and can wait only for the body-snatchers and bird-sellers too, whistling men, 'lamb, lamb, love' the dust of colliers, 'only a kiss' the cry of the hungry, vagrants, drunks, the taste of cesspools. My God, what an inferno.

Yet still they walk and stumble, the paving stones a mess of rotting vegetables and faeces and men dressed in rags, until eventually they come across a low-roofed hovel, whose walls are drunker still than the rascals who piss through the streets. Here hens scratch in the cinder heaps. All above flaps yellow linen that never will become clean. Ditches stink of death and between the houses run rickety little bridges spanning the sewers where float distended corpses – pigs, cocks, a horse, a child. The sound of night-soil buckets being tossed into the *water which will never see the sun is a dreadful sound for a man, yet still come children, young and old, sick and well, to dip their tin cups into the foetid moat and to sup to their lips. Oh cholera, so much to answer for.*

In Which We Learn What Really Went On In The War In The Crimea. A Big Man Throws Our Hero To His Back Like A Pepper-Pot And The Truth About Waterstones. Disgusting

'Please,' hissed Waterstones as we entered the abode, 'meet Sergeant Nettle-Teeth. Seventh Brigade, Royal Battalion Brigadiers and Privates, Crimea. Lambs, lambs, tickle hair, kissy, kissy. Medals, marches, bullet in the sternum and a chestnut in the rectum. Love, love, lamb. Billet together. Baby sheep letter. He will find the body of the woman.'

And with that poor Waterstones burst into tears and we put him to bed, thus affording myself and the Sergeant the opportunity to better know each other.

He was a bear of a man, a big bear of a big man, with countless teeth and a slovenly whiff. His clothes appeared to come straight from the battle fields of the Black Sea. Several holes in his tunic gave him the appearance of a rather overgrown Swiss cheese.

But before the conversation could commence, I musted gather myself from the floor for I had meant to put out my hand to the Sergeant to shake like two gents but with a snort and a shriek, a twitch and a hop, he had quite up-ended me like a man in a restaurant hungry for pepper on his pork.

'Sorry old bean. Touch of nerves from foreign. Sneaky little buggers, what? Forever jumping out at one. Your dark good looks put the frighteners on me. Once met such a type in the privy.

'Reading the Times when I felt this almighty gnashing on my buttocks, what? Sunk his fangs all the way in. A lesser troop may have cried, but stuff the swarthy buzzard, what? I rose, kicked the Arab in the eyes and rammed him down the pot.

'Won't try that again eh, what? Imagine he felt awfully flushed, eh, what?' and here he punched me between the breasts. Gosh.

'Flushed, *flushed*, flushed, *flushed*, a jape, a jape, eh, what?'

And with a lavatory mime and a further thump to the chest did I end up the wrong way up on the floor. Once more.

'Please Sergeant Nettle-Teeth, enough joshing, please. I am not a well man, you are larger than me and this is your gaff. I know not from whence may come the next blow and besides it is impolite to strike a host.'

'Sir, forgive me, you are correct. Perhaps some tea?'

'Ooh I say. I do enjoy a beverage. If you would be so kind.'

'*Kind?* Eff off. Certainly. BLACKIE!!'

And with that, a rather dark boy, perhaps not much beyond five, with dark eyes, dark hair, dark ears and a dark bum (he sported no lower garments) dashed to the Sergeant with hands open wide.

'Blackie, tea times two, super, eh, what, NOW!'

And with that, Sergeant Nettle-Teeth rammed a footwear up the boy's bare behind and picking him up by the ears tossed him like a bread roll through the door.

'BLACKIE! You forgot the cups.'

And with the last of the with thats, Sergeant Nettle-Teeth pitched two copper cups towards Blackie. He caught them both and darted to the street.

'Excellent tea Sergeant Nettle-Teeth' complimented the guest when our mini waiter had returned with the brimming vessels. 'May I ask which leaf you choose? I use a Darjeeling. Excellent pungency and not a little bite upon it... Ahem, the *leaf*?'

'I have my own pot out of doors. You recall the ditch water you may have passed afore the gaff?'

'Yes' I ventured, doubt already raping my mind.

'Well.'

'Well?'

'Well.'

'Ill' and I sicked up on me knees.

'Sir Sergeant Nettle-Teeth. I am so sorry for regurgitating the refreshment, but of late I have suffered from an early-morning buttock what-not. I fear such draughts may enlighten it once more. I have several kerchiefs for mopping.'

'Sir, worry not. Blackie shall see to that.'

'Blackie? No, he can *not*, he is a *child*, it is my detritus and therefore perhaps, you know, well, if I were to use a glove, maybe a night-dress, well, maybe this once. BLACKIE!! Sick floor cloth NOW!!'

A fine child was Blackie. He swabbed as an expert and in less than a minute not an ounce of quease was visible. Nor did he complain as he swept sick with a dispatch second to none. My only criticism was that whilst bent forward on all fours, dabbing at the vomit, the child did show off the soot of his bottom. It was a terrible sight. The child's anus was not evil, was far from scruffy or unkempt, but I believe something lived there. Possibly a cuckoo or a mole for it did make a Godforsaken squeak. And I fancied I saw something wink at me from the bum cave for he wore no livery. I asked Sergeant Nettle-Teeth to sell me the boy. He agreed but I recalled I had no money.

'Money, wank my spit! What are pennies between fellows, eh, what what what?' said the sergeant.

'What?' was I.

'What, what, what?' was he.

'What?'

'What, what, what?'

'Uhhm, the *boy*, the *black* boy. Blackie. I would love to take him with me. He is superb and would make a fine present for, umm, erm, haaaaaa, a *cousin* but I have no means. Alas. I had just realised such when you said: "Money, wank my spit" and more.

'Wank *your* spit, what, eh? Disgusting.'

'No not my spit, *your* spit.'

'Let us have no more talk of wanking and spitting. They are the both of them foul habits. I once caught that Waterstones fellow doing both. He was preparing for a tickle in the Crimea. The man had just basted his tool with some 'cranking cream,' as I think is the term, and was encouraging growth when I chanced upon him. I entered the tent and peered at him for some minutes before he glanced up and saw me. Do you know what I said, what, what, what?'

'No, what?'

'I said: "Waterstones." Do you know what he said?'

'No, what?'

'He said: "Yes." Do you know what I said?'

'No, what?'

'No. I said: "Waterstones, I do not like a man to fondle himself. It is a dirty custom and threatens one's integrity. Plus it is dangerous, noisy and a public nuisance what with the artillery all ahoot. Plus you are rubbing it the wrong way. You would be better to attempt an 'up and down' movement with the thumb and forefinger of *one* hand. You may find it more effective than using only the little fingers of each hand. Plus the Light Brigade is about to charge. Maybe you should write a poem about it. Plus this is my tent and that is my 'cranking cream.' Replace the lid and visit your *own* tent."

'Disgusting. And the spitting?'

'Oh, that. He once spat a sputum during a spat about a hat and that was that. Oh drat.'

'Something wrong?'

'No. It is just that I have some work to do. Perhaps you would care to join me?'

A Bubbling Pot Which May Put You Off Your Tea And The Whisper In The Ear Of A Man

Sergeant Nettle-Teeth led me to a rotting staircase. We scaled it in unison, except he went first. Downstairs was dirty yet upstairs was dirtier still. As he unlocked a locked door at the top, out came a tremendous odour. It was like dead horses, with a faint tinge of sausages, a slight taste of offal, a delicate aroma of bananas and the unmistakable stench of about 70 wild arses.

'Oooh what a surprise,' snorted I through my trousers which I had stuffed into my mouth to hush the emanation.

'Is my deputy residing with you? A man called Norris Moorcock?'

'Moorcock? Heavens no. This is not a hotel.'

'Oh. Sorry for the assumption. I assume that I assumed that he was visiting, for the odour remembered me of him. A terrible man, *terrible* man. '

'Not at all, what, what, what? *This*' and he gesticulated at a large pot announcing 'is a large pot.'

'Yes. Huge. And it bubbles. I am sure you will not begrudge me the chance to put a sock or two in with your washing. And possibly these carrots for my tea.'

And in a flash I had unlaced my boots, removed my socks and popped them into the vat. And the carrots.

'The washing facilities at mine are awful. You *will* join me in the vegetables?'

'*Vegetables? Socks?* Are you a *mad*man? Are you depraved? Are you deranged? Are you deprived? Are you decongested? This is not an effing kitchen, nor is it an effing laundry. This is my effing pot. Frig your vegetables you sneak!' and with that he fished out the socks and carrots and flung them from his window. I rushed to the pane to see a man of middle years with a puzzled expression, struggle to remove a veg from his bottom. It appeared that he had momentarily paused to unclasp his trousers and attempt a toilet on the footpath and was crouching down so forth when a vegetable came from the house and landed up his bumhole. I thought it best to leave the pot and the bum alone for fear of further mischief.

'Sergeant Nettle-Teeth' gambitted the faux-paser, 'I really am *absolutely* sorry. You see I saw your pot and again wrongly assumed that you were either conducting some washing or making a *cuisine*. I fear you were doing neither.'

'Neither? You are not wrong there man, eh, what, what, what? I can appreciate your wrong-doing and I was perhaps a little harsh in the punishment of your vegetables.'

'And socks.'

'And socks, but that pot, that pot which is very hot and bubbles a lot, is *not* a traditional vessel, it is not. If word were to get out of its true doings surely would I be a dead man. You will learn why.'

'What? Pot? Not?'

'Ya. For I am the practitioner of a little known practice. I hate it but I must. I have three children, all of whom want constant feeding.'

'Three children – lovely. Boys or girls?'

'Yes. One of each. This is why I do that. Or is it that is

why I do this? I cannot recall, but the outcome is the same. Follow me.'

And so it was that I gained knowledge of one of the foulest deeds known to humanity. How such a sergeant could crawl into the darkest embers of the human brain I can not know. Maybe he had hardened to depravity during a battle overseas. Perhaps not.

The former soldier led me by the hand back towards the pot. He opened the lid and bade me look.

'Look.'

It was off-putting. There was a sorry goo and bits of white sticks.

'Rice soup? Fish haddock? Chicken parsley? I have no idea Sergeant.'

They were bones, human bones all of them. And chunks of flesh, every bit as human as the bones. And they were fast becoming dripping; these femurs, these tibias, ulnas, sternums, vertebrae and ribs, flanks, buttocks, thighs and backs. And one little cock and balls. Sergeant Nettle-Smith was an alchemist of sorts. He bought corpses from scavengers, stripped them of their skin then plucked apart their bones. The skin was cured and sold to book-binders; the organs were taken to East End butchers or sold to cat and dog meat vendors and the bones and left-over flesh boiled down in this vast vat into fat and hawked round Waterloo as dripping.

The smell was quite nauseating and I am ashamed to say I vomited, for the second time that afternoon and collapsed weeping beside the mess.

'I'm sorry Sergeant Nettle-Smith, but I feel unwell. Blackie! Sick on floor. Please, *please*.'

'I too am sorry that you have had to learn this and I am equally sorry that I have to earn my living in this ghoulish manner.'

'Your children, do they know?' I spluttered.

'*Children*, God no. They are in their forties and I know not where they live. I am past seventy years of age and what need have I for children? Besides they were mistakenly told I had passed away in the Crimea. So jubilant were they that I no longer have it in me to suggest to them otherwise. This crime, however salacious, hurts no-one mind. The dead bodies are dead already and are not mourned. My customers are delighted and besides it do taste lovely on a loaf. Perhaps you would care to stay for supper? BLACKIE!! Spoons, bread, and two bowls of special.'

'Heavens no! Thank you. I must eat at home, for, you see, what day be it, oh Tuesday, yes, and I have promised to treat a friend to a fish. Flounder. No, the other one. Yes, a trout. Without doubt a trout. Thank you again for the tea. Perhaps you could bring me news if you do come across a female corpse. Caucasian, early 20s, hair of a Highland bitch and' (I whispered into the ear, for I still become bashful) 'has a birthmark in the shape of a grouse near her bum. Waterstones knows my residence. I do not use calling cards to save on the plight of the earth's trees. Good-day.'

What a place, what a man, what a pot and what an idea. If only I had a Blackie.

It is late at night when Cuthbert runs from the Rookery, clambering through the broken door and running down Oxford Street, past the windows patched with newspaper, and the cheap rooms stinking with stewpot rabbits, the sad song of the singing birds stuffy and sooty in cages, turned up bedsteads and stinking cesspools, out into the rotten night air with its clammy claws sucking the life from city, gone midnight, yet still lurk many, drunk, a young boy, fine meat for the predators of the night, pawing him as he races past, for he runs as though his very life depends upon it, runs til his heart pounds, until his mouth aches and his tongue sticks to his palate as though set down with glue, clutching still a folded sheet of newspaper, past the knackers'-yards with the howls of slaughtered horses and stench of boiling flesh, past the carriers, hauling yards of tripe, the wretched piles of homeless, sleeping wrapped in paper and arms along Blackfriars, clinging in misery to each other tight against the biting Thames wind. Then further west he goes, to streets lit by gas and plagued by shadows until he finds the doorway he requires in Bow Street.

October 12, 1858. Nightfall

In Which Our Hero Has Time For A Little Self-Reflection. He Asks: Was It All Worth It?

I went home in a grizzled state, still missing Washington and envious of the Blackie. If only I still enjoyed the income that once I had. But was I *really* a happier man before I had embarked upon the hellish journey through the bowels of life?

When I frittered my money away in supper clubs, blew the lot on showgirls and white-bait dinners, on iced punch and fish eggs?

Before I had wrung my soul through the most almighty mangle known to man? Before I had to beg and steal to eat and to sell my arse to strange men in gutter stenches? God yes. Life was a giggle back then.

For the time being though, I wanted a newspaper and I wanted Cuthbert. He could steal them like no other but alas the young pervert was abroad. The news could wait for after such sicking and bone boiling I felt a little bit weary. My bed had rarely looked so inviting.

October 13, 1858
In Which Our Hero Is Taken By Surprise Whilst He Naps And Dreams Of Boobies

'How many fucking feet have you got?' was the first question. It was as rude as it sounded and three times more frightening, for I was experiencing a dream at the time. It involved a lady. I met her in a chophouse and asked her to step out with me. She then begged me to nibble her nipples and spray her quango with milk. I had almost completed the squirting, when, with a meaty paw on my shoulder and that oniony question in my ear I was awake.

'Darling, if we are to fornicate, please let us keep my hoofs out of the matter. Just budge off your drawers, open the vulva and let us commence. Ooh I cannot wait.'

I was dealt a thump to the chin accompanied by the words: 'You saucy bugger. I am not your darling, I am fucking a policeman, so get back into bed.' I got back into bed. 'Now get out of bed,' he shouted. I got out of bed.

'Actually I am not *fucking* a policeman, I meant to say I am a *fucking* policeman. After that all the rest is true.'

With a start I was as flaccid as a child but far hairier. A policeman towered over me. He was ever so big and seemed eager to growl and squint at once.

'Mister. How big is your feet?'

'About *this* big' I roared and with a flourish, launched both of them into the air, ensuring that at least one of them patted the underside of the PC's chin. One of *my* toes penetrated one of *his* eyes while another of *my* toes set foot in one of *his* ears.

The heel of a foot span a petite foxtrot on the man's forehead while he sought to pluck a digit from his ear.

'Get out you blighter, frig out of me ear'ole. Ooh God, out, I am writhing. Please sir take him out. I do not want to be disfigured. I am married.'

'Officer' responded the guilty party. 'I truly would love to wring the thing from the ear within, but if you would be so kind as to look' and here I contorted somewhat the object, alas ramming it still deeper into the organ. 'Ooh, I think he is stuck. Best let him sleep the night there – I am quite sure he'll be out in the morning.'

'What? Can't hear a fucking thing. Got a great big fucking toe in my ear.'

'Try the other ear.'

'What? Can't hear a fucking thing. Got a great big fucking toe in my ear.'

'TRY THE OTHER EAR!!'

'Not necessary to fucking shout. I ain't deaf. Just me other fucking ear's got a fucking toe in it. *Your* fucking toe, so get it fucking out.'

I could abuse such time to use some language, albeit quietly, for a copper in rage is like a beast in a cage.

'You are a bastard. You reek of the pox.'

'Fucking what?'

'Nothing officer, I am merely mumbling.'

'What?'

'You are a wog. You've got male knockers you dumpy cobbler.'

'What? Who's got a fucking frog?'

'Frog? You beastly effer. I hate your arse.'

'Oh, who whispers so?'

'A-hole, cunny hair, bum tits, baby wank, knocker jizz, downstairs hairs.'

'*Bears?*'

I soon tired of the sport so I repeated again, for the benefit of the other ear: 'I truly would love to wring the thing from the ear within, but if you would be so kind as to look' and here I again contorted somewhat the object, alas ramming it still deeper into the organ. 'Ooh, I think he is stuck. Best let him sleep the night there – I am quite sure he'll be out in the morning.'

'Sleep, thing, squirm, worm? Get it out. Aaaargh me fucking neck.

'Perhaps some butter?'

'*Butter*, fucking *butter*? It is unlikely I will see another sunrise and all you can fucking think about is your belly.'

'Officer, I have seen children weep at less language. Please refrain your tongue. The dairy product was proposed as a lubricant. A helping hand if you will for the toe. Perhaps you, or a colleague, could issue into the auricale a dribble and with a wriggle, maybe me toe and your ear would separate.'

'Lovely idea. Have you got any butter?'

'Officer, not an ounce. I am banned from using it. Do not ask why for I do not blinking know. Excuse my language.'

'That's all fucking-right. I have elderly parents.'

Said produce was produced. It was poured exactly into the lughole. I located some purchase on a boy's head while I wriggled, twisted and damned well swore until the digit was exempt. It came out with an unfortunate popping sound and I fear at least one child must have weed itself at the retort.

'Thank the fuck for that' was the officer's language. He had disgusting manners and the sooner he was gone the better. Many had come to watch.

Some squeaked so forth: 'Oh look, he's covered in foot-fingers.'

'Look at 'is truncheon.'

'Look at 'is whistle.'

'Look at 'is 'elmet.'

I turned aside from the throng and put my ears to better use for my life was obviously in peril.

The officer gave his ear a final rinsing from a flask, cleared his throat and began to bark orders. Rather like a dog.

'Hold him down constable, pin down the fucking shit.'

'Ooh sir, I ain't trained.'

'Not trained? I'll fucking train you, you hob. Hold him down or I'll fucking well hold *you* down.'

'Sir. I ain't never qualified.'

'God almighty' bellowed the superior as I looked from one to the other, lying on my back with two of my feet describing cycles in the air. Ooh what a breeze it made.

'You see I ain't a proper police copper. I am a bastard tramp.'

'A fucking bastard *tramp*? Is there still a toe in my fucking ear or am I fucking hearing fucking things? *Fuck*?'

'Let me lookie' said the hookie rookie and clambered aboard a chair better to procure a peek. Unfortunately he fell off the furniture and hurt himself. And the Sergeant.

'Fucking fuck fuck. You pooper, I was being fucking

rhetorical, of course there's no fucking toe in my fucking ear. Now you've damaged *my* fucking toes. Fuck!'

'Rhetorical? Sir what you mean?'

'Rhetorical? Well it means that if, when, uhhm, always as, sometimes of *course*, likely perhaps, often no, never at times, thoroughly so, erm, beastly. Look it does not fucking matter. Why the fuck are you a fucking bastard tramp?'

'Well sir, I was born in a poor house, my mama and papa died of the pox and I lived in a black man's shed for several ye-'

'I do not fucking care of your fucking origins. Why the fucking fuck are you not a fucking policeman?'

'I ain't been trained.'

'That, have I fucking realised. Why are you fucking wearing a peeler's clobber?'

'Eh?'

'Why are you dressed like me? With a fucking whistle?'

'One night a bobby was murdered and I witnessed everything. Awful vicious like. When he were dead, I returned to his cadaver and had away his clothes. I was as cold as a hen.'

'And then?'

'I pretend to arrest people for crimes and then.'

'And then?'

'I steal their clothes as well. Don't tell the police.'

'I *am* the fucking police. Now pin him down. And stop him fucking wriggling.'

'I cannot. I ain't a proper police copper.'

'Fasten him now. If not I shall fucking arrest you.'

'You cannot arrest me sir. I am a police man.'

'You just told me you are not a fucking policeman.'

The time was ripe for piping so up I piped: 'Please, I am bored to death with your tripe. I vouch I will refrain from wriggling.'

'Excellent. Officer bastard tramp. Pencil, ligature and policeman pad. FUCKING NOW!'

As the police gentlemen began to measure my feet, I was handed The London Times.

'Is this *you*?' asked the more impolite of the two coppers.

'Hhhm, perhaps you are right. Gauge my foots while I read in leisure.'

And as I said I read.

The London Times, October 12, 1858

AN INCORRIGIBLE RASCAL.

Police at Scotland Yard believe they have an accurate description of the Whoopsie Butcher (So that is what the media call me.) *After his latest slaying during which his victim had his bottom chopped off and his windpipe broken, many witnesses caught sight of the killer. He is not far off six-feet in height. He has perfect hair, black and shiny which reaches the collar of his shirt, is clean shaven save for an occasional moustache worn above the top lip and just beneath the nose. He does not use spectacles but dresses in a top hat and fine suits. His complexion is quite dark, perhaps like that of an Italian man or a Spanish. He has two very dark brown eyes that are like brown pebbles, one nose which is aquiline, a chin that spouts no hair, two ears of average length, a predictable forehead – in short the man is quite dishy. And he has size eight Wellington-style hunting boots and wears the underclothes of*

a woman. He has left such Wellington boot marks at several
scenes of crime. All of them in fact. Police urge members of the
public not to attempt an arrest of the man, for he is believed
to be dangerous and armed with a blade. Be vigilant and if he
is spotted, alert Scotland Yard.

'An exact size eight sir. To the inch. Measured every single toe. They are really quite lovely, mind' said the tramp/policeman as he raised his head from between my legs with a puzzling grin about his chops.

'Good fucking work' said the sergeant and clearing his throat, he pronounced: 'I fucking arrest you.'

'For *what*?' queried I.

'Murder.'

'*Murder?* Murder? *Murder?* Murder? *Murder?* Murder? *Murder?* Of whom?'

'Seven men, also the murder of your friend Washington, cruelty to animals, namely pigeons and ducks, child abuse, impersonating a doctor, procuring the theft of a newspaper, unlawful sexual intercourse with a man, indecent assault on a minor, sh-'

'I have never been to a mine-shaft in my life' remonstrated the accused, 'I have a fear of coal.'

'I meant a *minor*. A person under sixteen.'

'Oh I see. Anything else?'

'Shitting in a pie.'

'I have never shat in, on or even *near* a foodstuff. It was a dog mess and I put it in there with a stick.'

'What a revolting man you have turned out to be. Let's go to fucking prison.'

And that is how I ended up in Newgate Gaol.

October 14, 1858
A True Account Of Life In The Dock

I was taken with haste before the Magistrates at Bow Street – quite near the Opera House and a stone's throw from the vegetables of Covent Garden.

The cell was full of lunatics; many were chanting and rattling the bars. Some were naked, others unkempt, one man was dressed in silk pyjamas but the appearance was marred by his penis from between the gates of his drawers. It was not very dignified and put me in mind of a puppy wrapped in a handkerchief.

The following morning I was hauled into Court One, a little green room with several oak bookcases and a lovely wooden dock. It was rather like my papa's library and I felt quite at home. Mind you, I had been before that very beak in that very dock sitting at that very bench on several occasions and I knew only too well the procedures. This time however I was to be indicted with *murder*. And animal stuff. I pleaded not guilty and was remanded in custody to Newgate Gaol, the most fearful prison ever to have stood. I was loaded into a black carriage by several burly policemen, some of whom knocked me around a bit. I was in no mood for such games but they removed their high hats and took swipes at me. They hurt quite a bit and I began to blubber. I will not tell you what I said for it was undignified but I will at least say this. It is never wise to call a constable in temper a homosexualist lest he take exception and kick you in the balls. They wear ever such sturdy boots.

I did see nothing from the carriage as we rattled across the City, through Covent Garden, the Rookery no doubt, up Strand, past the new hotels that were being constructed at a fearful rate. We went past, I assume, the Royal Courts of Justice, over the stench of the River Fleet, inns, taverns, and lodging houses, past the theatres, the Inns of Temple and up, up towards the looming bulk of St Paul's Cathedral, Wren's masterpiece. I fancied I could feel the steam flowing from the Holborn Viaduct and hear the shouts of the broadsheet vendors and then a left into Old Bailey and through the doomed gates of Newgate.

Throughout the clinking halls stagger very phantoms of humans. Once people with lives of their own, they are now little more than shells of the living. Women wobble half-naked and red drunk, ghastly figures turning tricks for a swig of drink as children suckle their leathered breasts. Most prisoners though are no murderers; they are common thieves, debtors and vagabonds. Their crime is poverty. Here the lagged prisoners wait to be sent to the Colonies, wait in the squalor of the cheerless stench until a boat can be found for the oceans. Rape is common and the guards unlock the women's cells for the night's victim. Many howl through the night, others are kept shackled and scream until beaten hoarse. Self-murder is not unheard of in this Hades within London. But there are no high garetts here, no apothecary's arsenic too. A slit wrist with a broken bottle will do. Which guard has never smelt the reek of death before the iron gates of the cell are creaked open? Who has never seen the tell-tale trickle of shit and blood leaking from beneath the condemned's door? Yet if the damned of this earth do not have the means to take their own lives, then can there be found scores of their fellows to assist. Murder is a universal feature of life in the darkened bowels of the earth. Snatchers, blaggers, cracksmen, dragsmen, hoisters, jumpers, kidsmen, lurkers and macers, mobsmen and scroungers, palmers, rampers and rollers, poachers and preachers all locked up with the most deviant of God's creatures. Child murderers, rapists, anarchists, Jacobists, conspirators, smugglers and

thugs share cells with the weak. Sure they have been caught,
but who can say that their perversions have been quenched?
They have paid the price and are to die. Why not one more
dance with a blade, let blood flow again, unveil the yearnings
to have a child in his sleep, to see him wake and with a knife
to his throat have your way just one more time?

Pain is spared no one, not even the latest man, a funny
looking fellow who will soon be standing trail for murder.

October 15, 1858
A Rude Welcome For A Brave Man And A Strange Reaction From An Old Friend

Newgate Prison – a more infernal place can not exist on this earth. My first night was terrible and alas I wet my straw in fear. I was attacked by a madman with a spoon and some bread. It was ever so hard. And a mutton bone. It was ever so hard. Nor was I treated kindly by the gaol's warders. They thrust into my hands a bowl of gruel and a piss-pot. When I mentioned that it had not been emptied, the guard splashed it atop my tootsies and said: 'Piss off.'

Oh for a world without irony.

I slept not that night for I shared a cell with that same madman who had lunged at me with his dinner. He spoke largely in tongues. When not conversing to himself, he would fix me with a dog eye and froth, tearfully: 'I never meaned to killt 'im. 'Ee never should of vaked up. Besides the jury was prejudiced, cos I is a black man. Oh, I hate Bates.'

'Black man?' I queried, thinking that perhaps my ears had clogged with misery. 'You, my sir, are truly white as a bean' and I neared him for a hug with which I hoped to lighten the tension. But he appeared not to like that, for again, in a flash, he was topless and armed with the shin of a sheep; he leapt at me and inflicted some not inconsiderable pain to my forehead. He wore a filthy great-coat, a blue badge and had a whistle perched twixt his chapped lips which he blew when aroused. I bleated for a warden. 'Please, somebody, for I have been harmed by a man with a bone. He is coming for me anew. Oooh.'

'Be grateful for anyfink you can gets in 'ere' hoofed my neighbour.

'I hain't been prepositioned by a fella's bone for eight mumfs. Go awn. Getcher trousees awf. Suck it!!!' and he accompanied his burlesque with a hammering, and a clanking on his bars. This prompted others to set up too a racket and ere long, some scores of prisoners were screaming and shaking their shackles, eventually rousing the guards from their slumbers. Sadly I was given full blame for the fracas and banned for eating for two days as all night long wailed that thin, pale man from my cell, dressed all in blue and sunk to gin, who clutched a badge bearing who knows what to his chest.

When eventually I did recover my senses, immediately I called for my solicitors, a Chinese team of lawmen, known if you do not know as Wing, Wang, Ding, Wong, Chin and Dong. I sent a note to their offices only to be told that save for Wong, the remainder of the Orientals had decamped, quite smartly, from their premises.

I left briefly my eight by six foot cell of damp. There was little in the way of effects save a rug, a bible, and an iron candlestick fixed into the wall. The stool I used to climb to the bars where I dreamt of outside; the plate and mug for dining, the basin for piddling. Truly did I not like the place. In the visitors' room was a large fire with a deal table before it, round which a dozen women were seated on benches. They ate beef stew and bread - some say dog meat, others say cat - slurped from grey pewter bowls; a few suckled tots with their tits. Emaciated and waxen, many sold tricks for babies' bread to gaolers once night fell and gin flowed. Large hooks were fixed in the wall; on each hung the prisoner's sleeping mat – the rug and blanket were folded and placed on the shelf above.

The ward stank of festering meals that thickened in the feeble orange blush of a pitiful fire. Many men sat bored, some ruffians, some not, all wishing to be the next Jack Sheppard – Newgate's notorious escapee.

I glanced at the scriptures above the fireplace calling for salvation and humility before our Lord. Further I went, through the colon and duodenum of the dungeons, nodding at the schoolboys in their pinafores, the wardsmen on their bedsteads, through studded oaken gates, gratings and alleys, chamber-pots and piss and into the yard where Wong glinted at me, the winky chinky, sweet and minky through the cullis. The turnkey beckoned me forthwith. Fifteen minutes were we allowed, fifteen minutes for a man with whom I had once bathed. What a travesty is life that can reduce a man to such base a want as this?

There Wong was and with an upturned nose (difficult for the Orientals I can assure you) muttered some greetings.

'Prease, sir, all the uhhm, all the the the, oh dear, every one of all the, I forget name' and here he pointed, quite flummoxed, at his groin. He thrust at it savagely, for a Chinean with a temper is truly terrifying. I called for a pot but the guard said no. Confused all the more, I could only watch in horror, as Wong, the guardian of my erstwhile fortune and keeper of my father's name, aimed a smokey-yellow digit at my lap. Perhaps the air of evil that so pervades Newgate had got to him yet, for surely this was not the behaviour of a man of law, chinky or not.

'Please Wong, I accept your peculiarities and if you like touching fellows, it bothers me not. But please, I beg of you, do help. You may not realise, but I am detained here against my will, charged with several murders and a couple of animal husbandry misdemeanours. You *must* help clear my name. Now where are the rest of the gang?'

'Prease mister sir, cannot lemember me word for opposite of dirty bitch woman whore female.'

'*Man*, Wong, *man*.'

'Zank you, zank you, zank you. Kissy?'

'No Wong, a kiss will not be necessary. If you wish to express your gratitude, shake my hand. If you like other men, that is your choice, but I for one am virile. My body steams with sperm and I overflow with semen. Wong, you were saying?'

'All other mens goned have noo.'

He was a good man, but conversation was troublesome. Especially when one's head may be in the hangman's noose before tea.

Anyway, the rest of Wong's lot had fled in a hurry in a cab.

Bail had been refused me, unsurprisingly given the nature of the charges I was facing and I would need representation, for trial loomed ahead. If convicted, it would be the gallows. I began to weep and begged the man to help me escape. I fixed Wong in the eye, for although a touch slanted, I have read that the eyes of a Chinky Mcflinky are almost every bit as good as an Englishman's.

'I have in this paw,' announced I to the Oriental, 'a fang brush.'

'Hmmm.'

'But not just any old fang brush, for it is reinforced with my very own gnashers and four hours digging per day will have me out in seven months. Pay me one visit daily, dress in a greatcoat, and the brick dust can lay beneath it. Just like a cat. You can feign a tum-tum problem. I believe you fellows are prone to gout. What say you to that? No, yes, no, yes?

'Perhaps you could indeed smuggle me out. Like a big cat, or a dog with whiskers. I could be your sister, a nightsoil bucket, a cadaver even? Eff my arse, Wong, eff it' but I had to restrain the man from unbuttoning his tweeds and fruitioning my request for he was a literal man was he.

Wong, oh how he did pong did Wong, assured me that all was under control.

He would visit in the morning, said he. He did not and I never saw him again.

I was taken back to my room where I sat on my bucket. I also did a little plop.

Autumn 1858
In Which Reputations Mean Much

At first, I sought to convince the inmates that I had been framed and was as innocent as a chicken.

So that first day a turnkey did visit, ambling the corridor with a tallow candle, rattling his leather belt of keys and clinking his heavy boots, that first morning he opened the square Judas and asked for what I was in, I replied: 'In reality, my good screw, I have done next to nothing. I am a dishy and highly read man. I know several poems and whistle in French. I hum superb and know the clavicle. And the clavichord. I am a good man, always have been and always will be. Alas, my natty looks have been confused with those of someone else - a fiend with the false face of mine has been a little busy and thus was I collared by a fuzz thinking they had snooted the right fellow. In fact my larcenous look-a-like is even fairly sweet. He merely pilfered a bloomer and forgot to pay the milkboy. Also he tried a go of thimble-rigging and used obscene language at an oast house. Ooh what a farmer!'

'You nancy' bellowed the screw guffawing and off he rushed, rattling from cell to cell telling all my lies. My ploy was poor for ridicule came sharp.

As I strolled about, several times was I tripped and twice did I receive the contents of a bum bucket.

'Watch it' bleated the mobsmen in mock terror, 'old fruity's around, better keep yer peepers on yer kerchiefs. Lock yourselves up, tain't safe to walk the corridors of Newgate no more.'

And so would echo round the galleries such mirth that I feared it did harm my reputation. How was it that the rapists and murderers had the screws bending at the knee?

That is because the menace of violence demanded fear. One day I visited the dining room, where I did grab a child, one of the orphans doomed to hang before his balls would drop, and yanking him by the pinafore, beheld his sullied chops a-tremble. A-tremble that is, until he in beheld my softly features and sniggering, muttered: 'Ooh, tis ve voopsie vot does nick knickers. Vould you care to get your 'ands on mine?' but in a second my eyes did change, my brows met at a sharp angle and I began to growl, much like a wasp or a terrier and I watched the colour drain from his face, much as the sands sink away while cooking an egg.

'Boy' I snarled, ever so angry like, and showing to full effect my teeth, 'you believe you know my *crrrrrimes* do you?' asked I. 'But let me tell you' and here I adopted an accent from the Highlands of Scotland, 'My *crrrrrrrimes*, dear boy are sickening. I wake trembling with horror at the evils I have done. I have killed, dismembered, disembodied and discarded. I have violated, validalated and garrotted the most muscular men in town. In *essence* I am *pure* evil. I once had breakfast with the devil and let me tell you this. He does not eat eggs, nor *toast!*' and I concluded with a rather tempestuous laugh. He begged me let him go and as he scampered like a bumble bee from my clutches I charged him not to forget our meeting and perhaps if he could possibly mention my true horrors to others amongst us.

'Cry not child, for you are not to my liking. Had you been, surely would you be dead. Heed well my warning.'

Thankfully, so petrified was the urchin that he noticed not how my speech dropped to that of a Midlander during the final murmurs.

From thence on was I granted more respect and was subject to no more potty violence nor titters. Indeed was I requested to 'sort people out.'

I accepted only those demands that required me to ambush some half-wit in a passageway and whisper a little something in his ear. I was well reimbursed. But life soon became the worse for it for really I had nothing to fear, save the unease of death and the nibble of rats. Unlike life in the boarding house, to eat was not a struggle and I had my daily requirements provided. In short, I became utterly bored.

I was awoken with some news - the man who shared my cell, a Mr Arthur Widdle, had passed away in the night. He had taken his life with a shard of glass and bled to death ignored in life and ignored in the afterworld.

Rumour has it he dreamt of joining the Metropolitan Police.

I was to stand trial at Old Bailey. Surely am I innocent, surely could no jury convict me of these crimes, surely a mistake. My life may be over in weeks.

October 29, 1858
An Old Friend Comes To Visit
And Brings Some Shocking News

One morning, as I rose from my bed, did I hark the screech of a key in the lock and with it came the gloomy face of a screw, a morose sort of fellow, with a nose like the bum of a dog. But then again who would not be so, labouring day after day in such a place? Further, the poor wretch was so distasteful that his very appearance made me feel nauseous and I could barely look at the man. But having heard talk of my wildness, he waited while I fanged myself and cocked a snoot at the London Times. Cholera was becoming more fearsome.

I prepared my outfit – blue quilted dressing gown and matching bobble hat, then the morning piddle. The turnkey had seen worse than a gentleman's yellow, so I gushed brazenly. To ease any discomfort, I ventured forth: 'Screw, screw my guest, behest, be it who?' I riddled as I tiddled.

'I ain't none too sure' he replied twisting the few hairs of his whiskers. On each occassion, he would not finish until at least one had ended up in his mouth. How horrid are the traits of some I mused as I fastened away my genitals. Mild drops soiled the front of my trouser but that mattered not for this was hardly the Grafton.

'I certainly ain't seen vis one before a-wisitin'. I reckons he's eever a coal miner or a Hindoo. NO! I remember now, 'ee's a Blackie' and with that we left together, two lost souls doomed in a wretched existence until death proves our saviour.

As we ambled, I wondered what had brought Nelson. I wondered too of other topics; my escape plans, the mysterious whereabouts of the Orientals, Sally, how my life had deteriorated and who had committed these murders. Too I wondered if I would be charged for damage to the cell – incident stains, ripped up Bible - and what time was tea? But ere long, with more doors creaked open and slammed shut, more chains loosened and fastened, more keys tumbled and groaned in rusted locks, there, before me, stood Nelson. My God he was black, yet how lovely did he look in his scuffed old topper.

'Nelson' commenced I, 'I assume you are not here by pure hazard. Perhaps you too have been brought forth following the commission of some crime such as your type are fond. What is it eh? Rape – per vaginum, or per anum; little difference save the physiological obvious, murder, arson, treason? Surely you are not an Anarchist or a philanderer? Horse pilferer, thing rifler, man toucher? Pray tell me, for are we not chums? But by the looks of your chops I would say you've got something to tell me, you sly old nag.'

And do you know, the dark-skinned simpleton appeared a little less gormless as he fixed me a most unusual stare. In part it was terrible, in other parts it was conniving, convivial, convoluted and convex. He faltered in his speech, stumbling across syllables and consonants. And capital letters. Eventually he made himself clear.

'I found me wife' he mumbled.

'That is *excellent,* Nelson, excellent. I pray she is in tremendous health and that your love has been rekindled. Oh *do* stop weeping. To shed a tear at your time of life is indecorous – a terrible trait, no matter what your hue.'

Nelson sniffed once or twice – it was actually nearer three but I gave him the benefit of the doubt.

'Well, she ain't not hat all well. Her fanny is aboot to fall off – in fact it probably be already on de floor de noo.'

His speech had little improved, but I humoured the soul.

'Fanny, funny, Nelson, fannies are *ten* a penny these days.

'You mentioned your *wife's* fanny, or should I say *former* fanny, was a touch poorly if you will. I take it though that the rest of her, ie her knockeroos, chin, vital organs are in tip-top condition?'

'Not particularly. Dey is all red and is covered in spots. She in de lock hospital.'

'Hospital? How *marvellous.* Bless her for she has become a nurse? Helping all who are doomed to die a lonely, painful death, these loose no-goods who have contracted hideous diseases of the organs. She is helping those in their final days as the ravages of sexual disease eats through their very minds and souls like so many maggots in a rotting corpse. How wonderful that she is making their last hours on God's earth less insufferable. Before long, these wretched souls' brains will be so savaged that they will not even be able to recall the faces of their loved ones. How sad, yet how good that such a woman as your wife, one whose morals may once have impeded entrance into heaven has so repented an-'

'No, she ain't no nursey. She do got syphi, syphi, syphi, syphi. A disease of de muff.'

'Ah. Perhaps you mean syphilis.'

'Sir, I ain't no doctor nor no scriber, so please don't get juicy with me. She got de syphilis and about to die.'

'Nelson, that is *terrible*. It is quite possibly one of the worst things I have learnt today. Here I stand before a man who I have known since childhood itself. Well, a few months at least, and must I watch him come to terms first with the loss of his beloved wife to a white man and then to suffer years of desperation and then to find her once more only to learn she is to be lost, this time to eternity. I say eternity, for I doubt whether you believe in an after-life. What have I said ere of tears? Where was I? Misery, death, eternal loss. Oh yes, but I fear you have not ventured to this wretched gaol to tell me your wife's fuzz has gone fizzy. Eh?'

'Well den. Guess who me vife share a bed wiv.'

'*Share?* I have not the slightest of inklings. Never have I even been there, for never have I had a poorly pansy.'

'I know dat, but I just tryin' to get you tinkin'. Like a game like.'

'Game? At a time like this, when your very own wife is at death's door? I do not know, the Duke of Wellington perhaps?'

'No. He dead in 1852'

'Sir Robert Peel? Edward Cardwell, the Peelite Free Trader and military reformer?'

'No.'

'William Gladstone, likely the country's future Prime Minister? Sir Franklyn Gaulton, the founder of eugenics?'

'No. Your vifey – Sally.'

At this, or more pertinently *that*, I dropped to the floor. I hurt my knees and if you were to look today, very, *very* closely, would you espy a little cicatrice about the bone.

'Frig a pig!' I expleted and then asked Nelson for a repetition, for it sounded as though he had located my Sally sharing a bed with a diseased Negro woman in a hospital of veneral disease. He repeated it word for word.

'But for wog's sake – excuse me Nelson I don't see you as a real one – how in the name of mutton are you certain she is she?'

He explained that her looks appeared familiar from my description and begged of her her name. His interest aroused, he confirmed that he and I were indeed the best of friends at which point she began to swear.

'But how can you be sure such a violent reaction was prompted by the mention of me?'

'Mister. I been wid sailors – not in de bum but in de pub. I been to prison. I know certain tings. Plus she did 'ave a piccycha of ya and was stabbin' it wid a fork. And a spoon. Dey don't be allowed knifes in dat 'ospital, or I dares say she would ha done the piccycha good and proper. Plus she said she 'ated you and never wanted to see you nor 'ear your bastard name never again.'

The poor man wiped away a tear. Who was it who said the African does not feel as the white man?

'Was she perhaps visiting a poorly trollop perhaps, perhaps, perhaps?' I rashly asked, remembering me of a little rash I had recently developed.

'Anyway, before you answer, dear Nelson please allow me' I paused, and began rather hastily to scratch, for many insects had feasted on the region about my downstairs hairs. The procedure was light-hearted, if not intense.

'Ooh,' I oohed, 'Aah' I aahed, 'Eeeeeh,' I eeeeehed and more, much more. And why not? I adopted a good-natured technique at first, but the more I attempted to assuage the tingling, the more aggravated became the rawness and thus did my temper worsen. In short, the experience was infernal torture and I bade Nelson to look away. We had suffered much together and I had washed his hair, but to watch a grown man ruffle his cock and balls would be wicked. He reminded me there would be no need to avert his eyes for he had bathed me often. I allowed him watch. The event went on for not some little time. I have been known to become hostile when scratching. I warned Nelson not to interrupt and begged of him occupy himself. Indeed he began to whistle a ditty.

'This was *really* her you say?' I said, the itch no more.

'Yes' replied Nelson, he having brought to an end the jingle. 'She got a birt mark on 'er bum in de shape of a 'eron.'

'My God' spluttered I, 'how do you know that you ruffian?'

'Well, she was all delirious and paradin' aboot full starkers. You is right. She do got de most lovely knockeroos. I am sorry to tells ya, but she too is sufferin' from de pox and de doctor do not tink she got long left. Oh by de way, she got a bebeee.'

'A what?'

'A bebeeeee.'

'A bebeeee?'

'No. A bebeeeee.'

'That is precisely what I said.'

'No you did say a bebeeee.'

'Yes?'

'She do be 'avin' a bebeeeee.'

'My God. Have you seen it? Does it have my looks, has it

got my hair and my nose. Does it speak English? In short, is he lovely?'

'Yes. 'Ee lovely.'

Time with Nelson was soon over and I was led back through the dining room once more with its cheap stench of last week's stew, where growled the insane and slept the lonely. One man, a wisp of a fellow and no taller than a post-box was unfastened by a screw and slapped about the face for he had tried to take his life by hanging himself from the wall.

Back in my cell I lay down my head, rustled beneath my blanket and with a tear in my eye and lumps throughout, I begged for sleep. Several questions still wanted replies. All would come.

What Happens When Twelve Members Of The Public Hear The Most Harrowing Evidence A Man Could Imagine. Or Woman

He stands in dread, head shaking, his body clenched and drips of sweat making of his back a small stream. His heart raps and throws itself at the cage of his breast like a creature desperate to escape and it beats and shakes until he fears it will burst, a not altogether unhappy prospect. His knees are as a river steamer on the stormy Thames, his stomach swirls a horrid dance, each step a final move in the ballroom of life. He grips the wooden dock, catches the judge's eye, cold and rheumy and watches the twelve jurors march slowly back in. The room falls hushed, benches creaking for the jury's verdict, the public gallery whispers shushed for once, a flash of red hair bowed.

The officer of the court rises slowly.

'Would the foreman of the jury please stand.'

He stands.

'Members of the jury, on count one of the indictment, have you reached verdicts on which you all agree?'

'Yes.'

'Members of the jury, do you find the defendant guilty or not guilty of the murder of Jethro Hubbard?'

My heart sank, my blood swirled, my bowels dropped. I

caught the eye of a grubby man, pen swilling the ink of his well, his gnarled nails bitten fore to the quick. I think I recognised him from somewhere; he smiled at me, a rat's grin.

'Guilty.'

I heard not the remaining verdicts, heard not my guilt as to the murders, the robberies, the sexual assaults, for I was lost to my own grief, the deaths of my supposed victims meaningless.

I recall not the judge placing the silken black cap upon his fatty head, yet somehow do I know his words chilled my heart though I remained a mute, deaf and blind to all: 'You are sentenced to be taken hence to Newgate Prison and from there to a place of execution where you will be hanged by the neck until dead and thereafter your body buried within the precincts of Newgate Prison and may the Lord have mercy upon your soul.'

I was later told that I could appeal and plead insanity.

My sentence could prove transmuted, a ship to Van Diemen's Land or a bed in Bethlem. But no, I stayed firm, true to the word of the jury. I was guilty. If not of the murders, then of a frivolous life, a life in which I brought nothing but pain, one in which I gave nothing and took much and if seven men had died (and a few larks, pigeons and a little puppy dog) then my life should end too. If only for my son who knows not his papa for I would save his shame when it shall be his turn to play the game of life. Better a boy not know his father be he someone as me, than to have the dreaded name loom over his little head. Hang I would.

I was taken to a condemned cell where I am guarded day and night by three warders. They watch for my suicide. I spend my days in writing a record of my sorry life, thinking of Sally, that beautiful girl whose life I had ruined, whose soul I had destroyed, eaten away by my vanity and the pox as she lies with my baby son close to death. Sometimes too I read a newspaper, the news of cholera and the death it brings; plans of Joseph Bazalgette to cure the city's ancient sewers; I read news that there is a formula afoot to construct a railway beneath the earth to make better London's traffic; I read the inquests of the dead. I learn that Harold Finnish has died, battered at the hands of Orientals, too I read of my own trial; the death also some days later of Mrs Gough who took her life alone, sliced through her wrists with the bread knife and fell to the floor clutching the letters I had written to her from the lodging-house, embracing some shirts of mine left behind. She left upon the kitchen table a note. She believed that she had failed me in life. Mrs Gough's body was not found for two weeks, half-decayed. My heart breaks anew and I hope to hasten forth death. Please come, for I am more ready than ever a man can be.

I am given a brief exercise each day along Dead Man's Walk. Were I to try and take my life, I can not believe the warders would save me from my own hands. I am a hated man yet none hates my soul more than me. Only when taken for air do I see my fellow prisoners. They have their faces masked by a peaked brown cap which reaches to the chin. There are two eyeholes as a skull. Some are put to work on the treadmill, others pick oakum. I was visited by the prison chaplain seeking salvation from my soul of darkness. His name was Tobias Guppy and he claimed we had ere made one another's acquaintance. Brighton he said, a train ride and bed fellows, yet I recall neither the name nor the face. Curious fellow.

My hanging will be on a Monday. The streets of Newgate will be pressed solid with masses, come to see me swing. Calcraft will be the man again, the country's finest hangman. How I will join the cheers of the mobs as I die. At night I say farewell prayers to those I have loved, those other than myself. I say my thanks to mother and father, Mrs Gough, more a mother to me than my own; I speak too to Wong, who once lived with us as a boy and I weep as I remember how I had him thrown onto the streets, for I as a young lad was a cruel and jealous boy; how I lied behind his back, how I told father he had taken my spinning tops, how he had spied on mother in her dressing room, how he had stolen and the dreams haunt me now of how he went in silence with his little suitcase from the front door, the stare from Wong never have I forgotten. I think of the heartless ways of father, his harsh hand, the bite of his tongue. I cry tears for myself, the loss of my liberty, my looks too. How things have changed. Father would barely know me now.

I think too of Sally and our son and Nelson and Washington and the wasted years of my life and the children I taught to read and I weep again until sleep comes of a sudden and the days pass so slowly yet so quickly too and soon will come my last meal and now is the Sunday before my execution, my final Sunday on earth, a day of religion, the hope in the after-life, the desperate dream of salvation of the soul. I am taken to the Chapel for the Condemned Sermon. I am alone now, yet the Chapel is fair bursting with prisoners, eager to hear what comes in store, to count down the days to death of one of their number for not even in God's sacred house does mercy live. Here reads the chaplain the burial service for my soul.

'And may this deter further crimes from other of God's children' he sighs to the pews. They all are oblivious to me, yet thankful for time away from their cells.

'While there is time, repent, confess, turn, and flee from the wrath to come!' I look at the man at the altar and think perhaps I know him. I look at the Ten Commandments on the wall above and say a prayer for myself until outside, as dawn kisses the sky, can I hear the workmen come hammering at the scaffold.

And I fancy I can see the lights flickering round the beams at four as I try to sleep and am woken by the mob, a crowd much in liquor, heckling for my death. Each swing of the hammer rings fear in my cell, the stage almost set for the final journey of my life. This, the most truthful of all.

No cast will be made of my head for the physicians to study, for mine were passionless crimes, borne of a sickened mind; no struggle will rattle the gallows for my corpse. The dissectionists from St Thomas' are welcome to me; no relatives and mourners will weep my loss.

I know my body will be tossed in a sack and buried, covered with quicklime to hasten my decomposition, an initial on either side, the only remnant of my pointless life on this earth a scar in the flagstones of Newgate. A more infernal resting place can there not be, yet merited to the last.

November 22, 1858
Goodbye Cruel World

The kitchens of Newgate are already turned black with drapes, for soon will the kitchen be a mausoleum for the dead. Of a sudden, there is a huge swell towards the barricades, as tens of thousands shove, bawdy and dark and as low as any gathered before in London, many still drunk from last night, many drunk from the first swigs at dawn with a crew of leering policemen, hungry too for death as a man is dragged from the prison, out of the Debtor's Door, arms tied in front, wrists pinioned to his sides by a leather belt, then is he taken to the noose and Calcraft comes before the crowds and so begins the familiar process of death, the hemp and hood and the clink of metal and the tear of breath and a Blackman sobs, a Chinaman stands firm in the mob, the faintest smile on his face as the chaplain whispers: 'My son, I will be with you upon the gallows' and the men in booths selling beer and backy do a roaring trade and the black flag is hoisted and passions are all the more feverish with relief that each of the mob is not up the scaffold this day to greet death in person and at the loss of bowels from the hanging man, there comes a painful howl, a deep, deep cry of loss and a woman with once beautiful red hair pulls at her eyes and the baby at her breast thinks of nothing as she falls somewhere dark and cold and a sheet of paper flutters from her pocket, trampled underfoot, too late to reach the man now swinging dead and swollen above the crowd, too late to give forgiveness and she is swept away by the drunken mass. Some would call it rape.

My darling. I pray this missive finds you in time. I must explain how come you have ended at Newgate soon to hang. For these years past have I hated you with a passion hitherto unknown in my breast, feelings I knew not existed. Here I lie in the Lock Hospital, sick with a disease, one that eats my face and takes my hair and my teeth. Syphilis. I am as a woman of sixty, so haggard do I seem. There is no cure yet they treat me with Mercury. My life is as good as done yet from bad does come good; I am now come to read and write, just as you wished me so.

I know not from whence the sickness came, though likely from my life as a harlot. Perhaps though, even from you, for I know of your ways, I know the girls you have chosen, the girls, like me, you did pluck from the streets for pleasures. Throughout my life have I suffered the most terrible violence; men who paid for my body with one hand then beat it terrible with the other. Yet the worst one was not you. No, you were so lovely to me; I minded not your ways, I minded not that you would ravage another, because for all your cruelty did I become to love you. No, the worst of all was a man known well to me before. My father first raped me as I slept. I was but seven. I recall even now the scent of beer on his mouth, come in from the inn after his pig's fry supper. I remember the hair from his nose in his goodnight kiss. And the pain was most unbearable. These events happened for many years. I ran away to the home of the Melbournes until I could no more and began to walk the Piccadilly. You know the rest. Never again did we speak but word reached my father that his daughter had taken to the streets. So the monster took my mother, thinking she had been, in some way, the cause. He used arsenic from the fly-papers. My family name is Arrowsmith. No man could do me more hurt than he. With you I believed I had found a good man come to take me from the evil of this world and how I loved you and yearned to please you, yet in Brighton did my heart break again. You are the only man whom I have allowed embrace me when I sleep and I sought you everywhere upon my return. I roamed too the accursed streets of Brighton, hunted London, yet you were lost to the bottle and to the whores who could give more than I. After some months did I begin to feel sick until I no longer could search, nor work the streets. I learnt soon I was both with child and stricken by disease. I wrote for your help and delivered the note to your lodgings. Mrs Gough is a dear lady and she left it atop the hall table. You responded not and it was then that I knew you and I could be no more. I became possessed with revenge; revenge for your indifference, revenge on man, revenge on life. I reacquainted myself with Wong, your solicitor. He was once my client who had declared his love for me often, before I did meet you. But for all the goodness in his heart he was nothing compared to you and I could not love him. Yet was I desperate, truly was I more needy than ever have I been. I am sorry to say, we lived from your father's wealth and Wong treated me as a lady. He too enjoyed the money for he has truly loathed you since you were as children. We dreamt of your destruction, how to ruin your life as you had ours, how to bring misery to you. Soon was I in thrall to Wong and as his passions of revenge grew stronger still, so did mine. I was lost to his desires. We used that money to pay the servant girl next door to Mrs Gough to follow you across London. Truly was I shocked to learn of the depths to which you had fallen and how my heart broke to learn of the foul way by which you lived, yet still in part did I feel nothing but joy. Wong was well trained in the martial arts and thus did the killings of your customers begin. A karate chop to the windpipe, a knife to the stomach and we planted your clothing at the scene. For I recalled how you enjoyed to wear a lady's garment. Also your vile friend whom we met in Brighton - the littler of the two. We used him for he was violent and small, yet did I pity you so as I learnt of your time in St Giles. To ease my heart did I give to Moorcock the Ming vase taken from the Chineans, for I knew of its expense and hoped it would assist in your rent. I have dared not visit your cell but now have I read of your impending death, I hope to save you for in fact you are a good man. Thus do I make with haste to Newgate. Pray it be not too late. You will be saved and I hope too, above all else you can find it within your heart to forgive me my wrongs as I have forgiven yours and we, you I and little Winston can live all together as one. Until the morning. All my love. Sally.

THE END

Alternative Ending

The trial and execution of Horace Longboat, who suffered this morning at Newgate on the twenty-second day of November, in the year one thousand eight hundred and fifty-eight.

Horace Longboat, aged 49 years, was Capital Indicted in October Sessions last of several instances of tax evasion and forgery.

He had worked as a clerical Clerk in the City and was a married man, with a wife, Sally and three children, Cuthbert, Washington and Nelson.

He had not paid taxes for several years and when interrogated by the Metropolitan Police Force, it was discovered that he was in the possession of several plates to assist in the forgery of bank notes. Upon further search of his home in Acton, a small suitcase of such notes was found in the larder. Many were traced to a serious incident of forgery committed upon small shopkeepers and costermongers, especially around the Seven Dials area of London.

At the trial he attempted to justify his conduct by insisting that he had been the victim of a bizarre set of circumstances involving the planting of said notes at his home by some Chinese villains, fresh off the boat from Hong Kong.

Also he insisted that his wife had deserted him after suffering rape at the seaside and needed to retain such cash as should have been paid towards his tax to assist Sally to overcome the huge trauma of such a deed.

Also he spoke in tongues, a dead language he claimed was a tribal dialect from Southern China, more evidence of a diseased mind. In short, Longboat was a fantasist and had concocted within his lonely life another existence beyond that which was tangible in his daily routine.

Today the sheriffs arrived at the usual time.

The wretched man was conducted away from his cell to be pinioned. His legs were freed and the operation was performed in perfect resignation. But when he left the debtor's door, his great mental strength finally forsook him. He made a request to be blindfolded.

The fatal procession was formed and in a slow and solemn manner he moved forwards towards the drop, the prison bell tolling.

He walked to his doom with a firm, unfaltering step.

At last 8 o'clock struck and he emerged onto the prison roof.

Calcraft proceeded to draw over his head the white nightcap and adjust the fateful rope. Once complete the scaffold was cleared of all its occupants except the wretched beings.

In an instant Calcraft withdrew the bolt, the rope fell and the sentence of the law fulfilled.

Having been left to hang one hour he was cut down and later that evening buried in the precincts of the gaol. Very few people turned out to witness Longboat's death save a mysterious Chinaman, a lady with bright red hair and a man from Africa.

THE END